RIVER'S EDGE
RIVER'S END SERIES, BOOK NINETEEN

LEANNE DAVIS

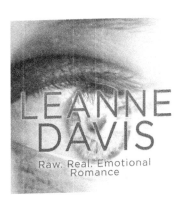

This is a work of fiction. Names, characters, places, and incidents are either the product of the author's imagination or are used fictitiously, and any resemblance to actual events, locales, or persons, living or dead, is entirely coincidental.

River's Edge

COPYRIGHT © 2023 by Leanne Davis

All rights reserved. No part of this book may be used or reproduced in any manner whatsoever without written permission of the author except in the case of brief quotations embodied in critical articles or reviews.

Contact Information: dvsleanne@aol.com

Publishing History First Edition,

ISBN: **978-1-957233-26-0**

River's End Series, Book Nineteen

Edited by Teri at The Editing Fairy (editingfairy@yahoo.com)

To Keith Stuhr
A legend to all who knew and loved him.

CHAPTER 1

~YEAR FORTY-THREE FROM THE START OF THE SERIES~

"DAD, NO. LET'S NOT do this. There has to be another way."

"Is there? Where are you finding money? Because I sure as shit don't have any and don't know where else to get it. Unless you're holding out on us?" Chance Poletti's gnarled, old lips curled up in a feeble mimic of a smile. He was seventy-one and looked it with a face map of wrinkles, harsh, cold eyes and gray hair.

"No. Of course not. But… there must be another way."

"I've yet to find it in all my many years here on earth. Your brother needs bail money now. Unless you think he should rot in jail just because he doesn't have a rich family. Real fair, huh? Go free if you can buy it. Great system we got here."

Cole Poletti shifted around in the old truck seat with obvious discomfort at his dad's heated tone. No. It wasn't fair. But Zack was the one who decided to rob a liquor store with a shotgun, and he got caught. Things did not look well for him. That was why their dad decided they needed to get him out of jail and then he'd just have to jump bail and run.

He was guilty as all sin and the evidence was piling up against him. There were many years in prison for Zack Poletti to serve.

Chance drove the old truck that shuddered and groaned along a ridiculously rural road that bisected a steep mountain. The single, dirt road was surrounded by high-reaching rocky cliffs and covered with shards of sharp, shale rock that often randomly dropped onto the road. Cole hoped none of the mountain rock suddenly collapsed and crashed into their vehicle.

Suddenly, his dad pulled the truck off at a sandy turn-out. "Where are we?"

They'd been driving for two hours. His dad kept cussing and swearing for every mile of the drive. He'd insisted Cole come with him, saying they had to work something out. When they were nearing the turnoff on this godforsaken road, Cole would finally learn the whole nitty gritty about what his dad intended to do.

Chance's plan was to rob a business to get the bail money required to release Zack from jail for the crime of robbing another business. Yeah, such a brilliant idea.

His dad didn't answer his current inquiry but got out of the truck, walking around the dented hood and towards the edge of the cliff. He sighed. Did Chance bring him up here merely for sight-seeing?

Cole got out and walked over to his dad. Standing there, he took in the awesome views.

Yeah, something pretty special. But so what? Why did they drive over a mountain pass to get here without his dad clarifying anything to him? All Chance did was continue to rant and rave about the unfair system they were always caught up in. Cole knew from years of experience not to interrupt his father when he got like this. The nasty spewing would then turn to action *against* Cole instead of just an endless loop of vitriol.

"What is this place? Why'd you stop here?"

They stood at the top of the cliff that was maybe three hundred feet high. It was a sheer vertical rise with rocks and bushes scattered here and there for ground cover. A river rumbled at the base of the cliff before it turned and flowed away. A unique, large rock formation stood directly below them with a deep, green-gold waterhole in front of it.

The entire valley seemed to spread out before them from this vantage point. The small town they'd driven through stood regal and quaint, higher up the river bank on the left side. Another sprawling ranch took up all the land for as far as Cole could see on the right side of the river. It stretched clear up to the horizon. There were a few outbuildings, barns, and sheds, with private houses tucked below them that hugged the river.

There were also endless acres of fenced land, orchards and horses. *So many horses.*

"Why are we here? What's going on?"

"That's the Rydell River Ranch."

Cole had to restrain an eyeroll and sigh at his dad's dramatic wording. So what? What the hell did the Rydell River Ranch mean to him? To them?

"Dad?" Cole groaned. "What's going on?"

A long, deep silence followed. His dad rubbed his scraggly, white goatee-beard that he'd worn for the last decade or so. "Did you know I have a sister?" Chance finally asked.

Startled, Cole turned around to face Chance, staring opened-mouthed at his father. His lying, cagy, mean, old, mother-fucker of a father.

He had a sister?

"I've never heard you mention a sister."

"Erin Poletti," he paused again with a dramatic hand wave down toward the land below them, "*Rydell.*"

Rydell? As in Rydell River Ranch? Cole's stomach instantly tightened with regret. This was the reason they were here. But why? Why here? Why now? After his entire lifetime, why was he just learning about his dad having a sister today? And why were they standing above the place where she lived?

"How could that be? Why have I never met her?"

"She betrayed me. She accused me of stealing from the Rydell family. I used to work for them." He waved his hand towards the fields. "Only Jack Rydell, that old prick of an owner, didn't like me. He accused me of things that weren't true. Guess who my sister got married to?"

"But how long has it been since you've seen her?"

"Forty-two years."

Cole's stomach fully knotted at hearing that. *Accused*, his ass. There was no doubt in Cole's mind what really happened. "So now you want to rob her?"

"Not her, *them*. I want to take what should have been mine all along. I should have been allowed to keep working there so I could succeed too, right along with her. She was fucking Jack's little brother the last time I saw her. Naturally, I never imagined she'd marry the only Rydell who really mattered. Just recently, the idea occurred to me to see what happened to her and I was shocked to learn she's still there. She married Jack. That possibility never occurred to me. I never could have guessed in a million years that would happen."

Cole just bet he couldn't. As if her marriage to the ranch owner should have guaranteed Chance Poletti a salary and a job. Cole was well aware that his father was nothing more than a user and abuser. His career was a two-bit con artist. That, and he stole things too, but usually nothing of much value. He grabbed cash when it was easy or the opportunity arose, and many a careless cashier or homeowner had been ripped off by Chance Poletti. He was a petty criminal who relied on pure chance. Just like his name, that was the way he lived his debauched life. His forte was conning people and getting what he needed or wanted out of them for himself. Just like he conned Cole's own mother.

But planning a full... what? What was this latest scheme called? A heist? Not really Cole's thing. Not for any *real* money.

"Why now?"

"I always assumed after I was kicked off their place that she left too, or soon after me. Old Jack did not like us. That included her. Figured she'd fuck the little brother awhile and then be kicked off the ranch like I was. I just never dreamed she'd end up with all of *that.* If I'd known about it sooner, well, shit. I'd have come back for what they owed me a long time ago."

Oh, sure, his dad was owed something now. Yeah, right. Chance raised his family all over the country and lived in almost every state. Only a few years ago, they arrived in Washington, following the money trail, as always. Well, at least Chance and Zack were constantly sniffing out cash.

Cole was simply following Penny. Since Chance had custody of her, he also had control of Cole.

"I'm not going to rob some aunt I never knew about on some dude ranch that has nothing to do with any of us."

"You aren't? I guess you don't want to see Penny again either then, huh?"

Cole's gut twisted painfully. Fuck Chance. Cole clenched his fists and had to breathe slowly to resist the burning urge inside him to pummel the old fucker's face as hard as he could. He'd love to ruin his dad's smug expression. And ruin him too.

Chance always used Penny as a bargaining chip against him. That's because Chance knew Cole loved Penny so that's how he kept him in line.

Penelope Poletti was only twelve years old. She was Cole's Achilles' heel. His sweet, smart, savvy, good, little sister. Penny was nothing like Zack, Chance, Everett... or even him. She was the sum of all the good things their lousy gene pool could offer. Cole honestly didn't know where she came from. But he'd made it his life's mission to continue to protect her from Chance.

Chance was legally her father and guardian. Cole was only her brother. That meant Chance had all the power and sway over Penny, as well as Cole.

"Don't. Don't bring her into this."

"She's always part of this. How do you think I'm going to support her without any money? And now without Zack?"

Support Penny? Chance never supported her. The state did. And Cole too.

Hell, Chance could have tried working for once. Cole sighed, knowing his family was allergic to the concept, as well as the word.

Money? Damn. He needed money. *They* needed money. They, being him and Penny. Not him and his father and no good brothers.

But as long as his dad had custody of Penny, his dad controlled him too.

"What... what do you have in mind?"

"They've beefed up security, it seems. Didn't expect that. Back in the day, anyone could just drive through the gate. They'd leave cash in the barn for crap's sake. I noticed as I drove past the entrance, they now have a full system, wired-up gate with video and all the extras."

Cole guessed Chance knew about the cash in the barn because he must've helped himself to it.

"What makes you think they have any cash on hand to begin with?"

"'Cause I looked into it. They started offering private horseback riding lessons. Right here. Right on their ranch. Easy way for a person to have a reason to be on their land, giving them access to their horses and what not."

"So? You get access? Then what are you going to do?"

"Rob 'em of whatever they got in their tills. They have a big arena now, with all kinds of side businesses around them."

"So… lots of people, and in this area? You gotta expect some of the land owners will have guns. You're setting yourself up to get shot. They might not be the type to call the cops, either."

His dad rubbed his face. "True that. Maybe one of you boys could pretend to need riding lessons to get the lay of land and any other inside dope. Then we sneak back and hide until we find the perfect opportunity. But there's a hitch, the truth of the matter is, *you* gotta do it."

"What? Me? Why?"

"I'm too old to move fast anymore. Fuckin' age. But you ain't. And they might recognize me."

Cole couldn't trust his dad and didn't know if he would double cross him and call the police or set the Rydells on him and collect the reward for turning him in. That was just the kind of low-level, low-paying scam his dad usually dreamt up. Chance was selfish, mean, miserly, and worst of all, stupid. He was also lazy and unimaginative. But more than anything else, Chance was a huge-assed coward. He was fully willing to set up his least favorite son just to get a few hundred bucks for it.

"This is total bullshit. I'm not robbing some old aunt I never knew about. Let's just go home. We'll figure out another way to get some money."

His dad grabbed his arm. "You *will* do this."

He shoved his dad away. "I won't do it." Storming back to the truck, Cole shut the door, ignoring his dad and all the shit he had to say.

But when he got home, he couldn't find Penny.

Calling it *home* was a stretch. A fifth wheel that they all shared was where they lived. He slept on the floor right below Penny's small bunkbed that was made from what should have been the breakfast dinette. To protect her, Cole slept right below her makeshift bed to guard her and make sure none of the scum his dad or brothers brought around ever got near her.

When he couldn't find Penny, Cole's entire world twisted with dread. Panic instantaneously ensued. He rushed out of the small enclosure, racing down the steps, past the other trailers and finally towards the beaver pond, where she sometimes went.

There she was. Relief soared through him. She was safe. Everything was okay.

For now.

How much longer could this odd dance continue? There was so much pitted against them. Penny was the reason his anxiety never left him. She was so small, so pretty and a *girl*. A girl in a world of awful, disgusting, rude, crude men. A girl who was starting to look less girlish and more like a young woman.

A girl being raised by really bad men.

Her own father being the worst of all.

Chance didn't threaten to do anything bad to her, but he exploited Penny in his calculated method of how to use her to his own advantage to get whatever he wanted or needed.

Cole had to get Penny away from him forever.

But how?

His heart twisted when he found her huddled in a little

ball. She was rubbing her face with her knees. Obviously, she'd been crying.

"What happened?" Cole asked as he carefully sat down beside her. She was stressed. Damn it. What did Chance or Everett say or do to her? He was constantly having to protect her, not only from their words and cruel taunts, but their thoughtless deeds, and ridiculous refusal to allow her any privacy... or decency. She was being further ruined each day that passed. Cole had to get her away from them. He *had* to. But he didn't know how.

He needed money to bribe Chance into relinquishing custody of her. Her mother was long dead, so Chance was her only parent and he relished his odd control over her. Mostly because he could manipulate Cole by employing it.

"Nothing."

"Well, clearly that's a lie. Now, we don't do that, do we? We don't lie to each other. Otherwise, how can we say we're not like them?"

They had a mutual understanding. Less than a decade separated them, but they were all the other one had. What little decency the Poletti name evoked resided in them and not their brothers or their dad.

She shrugged. "Some kids were making fun of me at school. It's dumb. I don't care. They're all dumb. At least, I'm not dumb."

He squeezed her against his side. At least, she believed it. How she could still, to be honest, kind of amazed him, especially considering their family DNA. Of Chance's four kids, three could either not read, or just barely. Cole knew he was dumb as a rock. He couldn't string together more than a few words at a time to read accurately. Penny however? She refused to believe they were born stupid. Even though she, too, couldn't read.

"My brain works just fine. I don't know why the stupid

letters don't work." That's how she always worded it. "I know I'm not stupid. I've met stupid, and I'm not that."

He had to give her confidence kudos; but... the proof was kind of in the family pudding, so to speak. Naturally, their common lack of reading and basic writing abilities made them all targets for ridicule in school.

"What did they say?"

"Not about reading."

"Then what?"

She hid her face, and it seemed to be one of the rare times he witnessed her being affected by the cruel words of others. She was a unicorn, in his opinion. Despite their family genes, stupidity being the primary thing they shared, she had a strong sense of self and positive self-esteem. Where did that come from? Cole wished he had it too, but he couldn't find it.

Seeing Penny shame-faced and red-eyed broke his heart. "What did they say?"

"My stupid teeth. They're just stupid anyway. It doesn't matter."

But it *did* matter. She was only twelve years old but her teeth were badly bucked, gapped, and crooked. They were unusually bad, especially for an adolescent girl.

Dental care, never mind orthodontics were not part of the vocabulary of the Poletti offspring. Cole was blessed with even, fine teeth. But Penny? Not so lucky.

Penny's awful teeth ruined her smile. Cole tried to ignore it and shore up her confidence, but she had a mirror and could see they were atrocious.

She needed braces. Now. Not later. Not after she was ridiculed, hurt and ultimately ruined by it. Cole feared it could shatter all the goodness inside her before she was sixteen years old.

He needed money.

For Penny's braces. And decent clothing for her to wear.

The other kids made fun of her for that too. He also needed to buy food. Maybe at some point, he could find a real damn bed for her.

He pushed a finger into his aching temple, then he shook his head and sighed. "Let's call that number we found. Who was it? Dr. Spindler? He's willing to help low-income kids with braces, right? The dentist the school recommended? Let's call him and set up an appointment."

Penny's entire face transformed. There was no other word for it. The grin she usually hid, or tried to hide behind her tightly closed lips fully shone and went way up to her eyes. "Are you fucking with me?"

"No." He laughed at her disbelief, even though he knew she shouldn't use that kind of language. But there were only so many battles he could fight at a time while raising her. He wasn't exactly her mother or father. But then, neither was Chance. Penny had nobody but Cole.

Cole was the only family member who truly loved her.

"I'm not fucking with you."

Her little face was streaked with excitement before the glow dimmed. "How though? How can we pay for it?"

"I got money. I hid it from Dad and everyone else. I finally have enough now. Let's go call the dentist and get it started."

She flung herself at him. After a full body hug, she squeezed her arms around his middle tightly. "Thank you. Thank you. Thank you. I love you. Thank you, Cole."

He squeezed her too. She was all he loved in the whole world. He watched her sprint off and smiled at the joy she expressed in her steps. Lately, those times were growing less and less frequent. Age was showing her the harsh realities of where she lived, whom she lived with, and what her future looked like. Age was also showing her how mean her own father was, and what losers her brothers were.

Except for Cole. Thankfully, she didn't see that in him yet.

But she would.

He sighed as he followed her. He helped her make the call and set up an orthodontic consultation. Good news, the initial consultation was free. Thousands of dollars were due after that; but no worries, they were willing to accept monthly payments and he could set it all up through their financial advisor.

Cole had no credit. And no way to even read the forms. Yeah, right as if his dad would help him. There was no one but him.

But Penny bounced like a ball through the small trailer they shared.

Cole walked down the steps to the small enclosure where a fire could be built safely. At least, he was protected from the rain and inclement weather. Cole sat down without being asked and started drinking.

"What?" Chance growled at his arrival.

"I'm in."

"Good. There's been a slight change of plans. Everett didn't like the new security system and I have to agree. Sit. I'll fill you in." Chance's smile, as usual, was smug. His eyes gleamed with the joy of knowing a secret. He also knew somehow that Cole would come to him… eventually.

After hearing the new plan, Cole nodded. *Fine*. One bad deed led to another. Then he turned and walked away, his stomach aching, his head spinning. His whole existence was damned long ago so why not finish it off? At least this time, he was doing it for a good cause.

He'd do anything for Penny. Even this.

CHAPTER 2

*J*ADE RYDELL WAS THE LAST one in the riding arena. Getting back late from guiding a string of horses on one of their easier trail rides, she was just finishing her task by putting away fifteen saddles, blankets, and bridles before releasing the horses into the pasture.

She liked working on her family's ranch and resort. Providing private lessons and guided tour rides for horseback riding was a popular hobby that Jade thoroughly enjoyed. She never tired of exploring the many trails through the mountains as well as around them. By offering both private and group rates, they ran a pretty successful business.

As always, the ride had started and ended from the large, commercial-sized arena where the many stables and gear were located for the resort operation.

Thank goodness for a plethora of horse-loving tourists who kept the ranch side of their business thriving.

Hearing some scuffles and the front door shutting, she paused. There was no horse show scheduled tonight. Or any other exhibition or club meeting. Probably more wanderers drifting from the resort grounds. Sometimes they roamed too far.

"We're closed. Sorry. You'll have to come back in the morning." She called out from the tack room she was busily organizing.

No answer. Well, they probably wouldn't come back. Jade was tired, sweaty, and dirty. More than ripe and ready for a shower, food, and the sweet comfort of a real bed. She had no desire, much less patience to coddle a clueless tourist who decided eight-thirty at night was the perfect time to book a random horseback riding lesson.

She hung the last pair of reins on the appropriate hook and wandered out, shutting the door behind her before approaching the main part of the arena.

She stopped dead in her tracks when her eyes lifted.

Holy. Damn.

Her heart skipped a beat or two and sputtered back to life with a painful jerk.

Three men were standing inside the main door. They wore cowboy hats and had bandannas across their faces and under their eyes, like movie bandits in a bad western. But the guns were trained on her, which didn't feel like any corny actors from an old movie.

"Don't freak out. Stay calm and all will be fine. But if you make any noise or a scene, we'll shoot you."

His voice was gruff and sharp. Her eyes nearly fell out of her head after growing huge as she stared at them. She immediately nodded.

"Hands up."

She obeyed the order. Instantly. Scanning the group before her, the only details she could catalogue were that two were younger than the one barking the orders and the two were huge in stature. Wide shoulders, big, strapping torsos and arms. The older one and main spokesperson was stooped, his wrinkles clearly showing around his eyes. Old and wretched. But snarling mean.

"Go to the cash register and open it."

During the popular horse shows, they had concession stands that sold food, drinks and miscellaneous merchandise. The cash register was located in the center of that area. They also collected money from all the horseback riding and lesson fees from there.

She scurried to the register, moving clumsily as her nerves overcame her. Nevertheless, she proceeded to open the cash register despite having a gun pointed at her head.

"Do it. Don't fuck around." The words exploded from behind her, making her entire body jerk upright and a small exclamation escaped from her mouth. The old man again.

"I'm n-n-not… Sorry. Just my nerves," she stuttered fearfully. After what seemed like ages, the confounded contraption finally dinged before it opened. Damn it, the cash register hadn't been closed down properly today. The workers in the arena could be pretty slack about following the nightly closing ritual. The daily cash and receipts should have been removed and locked up in the safe. But tonight, there were a significant amount of bills left in the drawer. Her heart sinking, she cringed internally. All the times she'd chided the many workers who might have been assigned to close up, she often received no more than a grin and some version or another of: "It's River's End. What ever happens here?"

Well… apparently, stuff did happen here. Things like armed robbery.

She gulped, still staring at the gun. The silent one of the three threw a bag at her. It was a cotton, nondescript bag that could've come from anywhere.

"Put the cash in there," the old guy demanded, and his

mean voice filled her with repulsion. The distasteful sensation traveled through her.

She filled the bag up with all the cash in the till. Her hands were still shaking.

"Grab your keys. Lead us to the back."

Why? She bit her lip as the grip of raw fear enveloped her. *Why did they want to take her back there?* How did they even know what "the back" was? They definitely seemed to have some kind of inner knowledge regarding the private workings of the place. They knew money was kept in the concessions area. Perhaps they guessed more was stored in the safe that was on the same level, hidden in one of the many rooms and wings off the large arena.

Her guts started to liquify. She feared she'd heave from the nausea. What did they plan to do to her?

Someone pushed her when she stood there contemplating the command with tears filling her eyes. Surprised by the sudden force of the shove, she started to step forward but stumbled and caught the display beside her. It was filled with artificial roses and stuffed animals that resembled horses and were often featured in the Rydell River Ranch horse show. That was another line of business they profited from. Jade knocked one over in her haste and went down with it. The contents flew everywhere.

"What the hell are you doing?"

The words behind her sounded panicked. She wasn't doing anything. Not on purpose anyway. It just happened. An accident. Tears of fear filled her eyes and rolled down her cheeks. Shit. Damn. What did they want from her? What more? They already had the money. They could take anything in there. But they wanted something else... Was it her?

Someone jerked her back to standing, one of the younger

guys. He pulled her arm way too hard. So naturally, she let out a scream.

"Shut the fuck up." The guy who still held her arm said, but his voice was worried. Scared. Almost panicked.

"Calm down." The second man replied. The one who hadn't spoken yet. "She fell. No one's around to hear it."

But the one holding her arm dragged her back into the supply room. She struggled but didn't dare make a sound out loud.

What? Why? Please don't let them rape me.

Her hands shook and her disbelief was choking her. This could not be happening. Not to her. Not here. Why her? Not on the very ranch where she felt safe for her entire life. No. No way. Not to her.

Someone pushed her again.

"Is there a safe back here?"

She almost wept with temporary relief. Money. All they wanted was more money. They suspected there might be a safe and they just wanted more money. Sure. Fine. She scrambled over to it. "Here. Here. It's all here." She quickly inserted the combination for the spinning padlock as her heart hammered and her hands were rendered otherwise useless. It took her two attempts before she got it open.

"Here." She stepped aside.

The quiet one came forward and started filling the bag with all the money and receipts they had in there.

She breathed easier as they finally finished their dirty crime. They'd leave now. They had their cash and so what if they wiped them clean out? Who cared? Just so long as they left. As long as they—

Then an excruciating pain came from nowhere. Jade crumpled to the ground without realizing what could have happened.

CHAPTER 3

*I*T WENT SO WRONG.

"Why the hell did you do that? We agreed to take the money from the cash register and the safe. That was it. All we planned to steal. How could you? Why'd you do that?" Cole screamed at his brother as they drove down the valley highway. He tried to keep their speed under the limit to avoid drawing unwanted attention to themselves. They stole a truck at the ranch, and now ditched it in favor of their own truck. Careening into a forgotten spot in the back country around Winthrop, Chance went south while they went north. They separated out of caution.

Once he was free from the vehicle, Cole went after his brother. He tackled him to the ground and pummeled his torso with a quick series of punches. "Why the fuck would you do that," he screamed until his voice cracked.

"Dad told me to. If we saw anyone, he told me to make them forget us. Those were *his* words."

"Dad? *Dad?* He told you to do what? Hurt an innocent woman who did nothing but obey everything you said. We were *already* in disguise, dickwad. There was no reason to hurt her. Fuck you!"

He hit his brother until the sheer exhaustion of beating him wore him out. Meanwhile, his brother fought back but wasn't nearly as strong as Cole. He shoved his brother down and fell to the side of him on his knees. Then he turned and coughed, spewing out his disgust and trying to calm his nerves.

Everett crawled away and flopped over on his ass, also coughing, and rubbing the blood off his face. "You're a psycho, Cole. No wonder Dad never includes you. Dad was right. There *is* a lot of money there. Enough for bail. Just wait 'til he sees what you did to me."

Was there enough for braces? He shut his eyes and clung to that thought. There had to be. Had. To. Be. He just committed a felony and assaulted a helpless, innocent woman. He hoped there would at least be braces for Penny in the end.

There was no undoing what he'd participated in tonight. It went so bad. So much worse than he ever pictured it could be. Or feel. The moment that poor woman came out and saw them, her fear glistening all over her, and the shaking and nerves she exhibited as she obeyed them, were painfully heartbreaking to witness, much less, cause. Cole realized she'd never feel safe again in what was previously a very safe place for her. Until they arrived to ruin her sanctuary.

She wasn't supposed to be there in the first place. Smash and grab. That was all the plan entailed.

Why would they have so much money on hand?

Damn. If old Dad weren't right. Perhaps they only had a weekly bank run. Lucrative damn business with plenty of cash and a safe in the back.

But no one was supposed to be there. Whoever the woman was, she wasn't part of the plan.

And Everett was definitely not supposed to do *anything* to her.

"You hurt her. You deserve to get hurt." Then Cole stared down at his feet, feeling totally dejected. His entire life was over. He could never face himself again after what he'd just done and been a part of.

"Dad said to make her quiet, and it had to be guaranteed. So I did."

They didn't deserve to have anything good again. Not ever. Never again.

They'd knocked her out. She crumpled to the ground. Helpless and hurt. What if she weren't okay? What if she got a concussion or some other long-term damage? What if no one found her?

Cole panicked. Grabbing his cellphone, he called the police and reported it anonymously.

Then he destroyed his phone.

"We have to get out of here." His tone was flat as he clambered to his feet.

"Why the hell did you report that?"

"So she doesn't die or get paralyzed. You knocked her out." Cole snarled in reply.

Twisted, sick fuckheads. He massaged the stabbing pain in his head with his fingers. How could he live with this? With what he'd just done? He knew better. Of course, he did. He clearly understood the difference between right and wrong. He was twenty years old. He couldn't blame his dad's bad influence or his dimwitted brother's peer pressure. No. Cole was well aware of the plan, he'd been there to help conceive it, and then, he helped execute it. He was involved from start to finish.

They drove out to the ranch and hid their trucks in separate places. Walking casually around the grounds, Cole pulled his cowboy hat down low. No one would look twice at three men walking around with cowboy hats on. When they got closer to the large barn, they took a quick glance around to make sure no one was out and about. Then they pulled up the bandannas they'd tied around their necks. That quickly, they were in disguise.

The door was unlocked and the lights were on. It was supposed to be closed at this time of night; however, after casing the joint for a few days prior, they noticed occasionally people stayed after hours.

At least, now was the emptiest hour of night usually.

Tonight, thankfully, it was only a woman. One single woman. Weaker, smaller, and obviously at their mercy. If one of the ranch hands had been there, Cole was sure they wouldn't have done it. Truth.

That woman. Fuck him.

She was tall and athletic. Gorgeous, really. With long, straight, thick, brown hair and a round, pleasant face. The shock at seeing them there so late at night was obvious by her expression. Then a look of abject fear replaced her shock. Cole's stomach started to churn while remembering the fear he saw in her eyes. He'd never been the source of fear to another human being. It made him feel… terrible. Far worse than he imagined it could. He believed he was prepared to commit the crime and steeled himself to do it. Just one time. For Penny. All for Penny. So she could get her braces and stop the little kids from tormenting her.

After all the hurt she endured just by being the sister of Zack, Everett, and the only daughter of Chance, Cole was obligated to protect her. And to compensate for her illiteracy. Cole chanted to himself that this one time was okay because of the reason he was doing it. For Penny.

But now, it wasn't for Penny anymore.

Now an innocent woman had been terrorized and injured. Really terrorized… by *him*. She would probably suffer from nightmares and flashbacks of the trauma that they inflicted on her tonight.

Not to mention, she was also seriously hurt. Smashing the butt-end of Everett's revolver on her head, she collapsed like a sack of concrete. It was shocking how fast it happened. Her energy, and life force, or whatever held her upright was fine until… boom. It was all gone. She fell as heavily as an anchor on the ground.

Cole knew she would not be okay, even if she fully recovered from what they did to her.

He hated the way he felt at seeing the stark terror in her eyes, all caused by him and his disgusting family. His actions were to blame. His gun was aimed at her.

It was unloaded, of course. All of them were. Cole double-checked to make sure as he couldn't trust his brother or his dad. Cole was confident all the weapons were empty—just in case. The odds that something could go wrong and freak one of them out or panic them were definitely high and not in their favor. The whole fucking, colossally bad idea went from being just terrible to murder one. That was why he had to make sure the weapons were unloaded, right? That horrible ending couldn't be a possibility.

Cole never considered what it felt like to hold the power over another person's life before.

In a word, it was sickening.

He also failed to prepare for the violence directed at the innocent woman who obediently did everything they asked of her. Despite her shaking hands, sickly, pale skin, and the full-on terror he could see in her eyes, she'd done exactly what they asked.

They could have tied her up and left her there. That wouldn't have been too much for her to bear.

Aside from the terror, nightmares and future triggers, no doubt.

But now? Holy shit. It went so far beyond what he imagined to be the worst case scenario.

Now, his guilt and shame nearly made him sink to his knees in despair. Maybe that could staunch the images and deep, dark, appalling feelings of betrayal that left him on the verge of throwing up each time he thought of her.

What if she weren't okay?

They drove to the cheap motel in Pattinson that they booked for a full week. Nothing fishy about them being there. They'd put in plenty of time being out and about, making themselves visible in the area. Messing around town. Vacationing. No one would connect them to the robbery tonight. They were safe in their motel room and all Cole could do was pace the floor.

His brother moaned from the bed. "You mighta broke one o' my ribs."

"I hope so," Cole growled in reply.

"Dad'll break one o'yours for doin' it." Dad had gone back home.

"Dad ain't big enough to hurt me," Cole sneered back. Zack. Everett. And him. They were all afraid of Chance Poletti. Even though he was old and fragile now. Somewhere in his seventies. Thin and frail, he posed no threat to anyone really.

But he was still as mean as a cornered rattlesnake. He would strike anyone for no reason, and do it over and over. Cruel words were his emotional terrorism. They all still cowered from his loud voice. Three strapping men, all bigger and stronger than Chance, not to mention, much younger than he, and still they cowered and submitted to him.

Chance Poletti had full control over all of them.

He started his family late and didn't have his first son until he was past fifty. Then came the other three kids. Four unlucky bastards that carried his genes of immorality. And to add further insult the injury, he decided they had to carry on the shit-assed lifestyle that he'd led for decades.

Cole would have left when he was a teenager and still able to get away.

But for Penny.

Little, sweet, wonderful, good Penny. The surprise child of this screwed-up idea of a family that Chance Poletti wrested full control of.

Why did three grown, huge guys allow a physically weak old man to rip into them like a piranha, tearing them apart and making them hate him while still feeling unable to sever their shocking loyalty to him? That was why they committed his crimes and moral degenerative actions even though they all knew better.

They chose *not* to do better.

Well, Cole tried to do better at least. He was the only one who wanted to avoid being like any of them, but he failed all the same.

Tonight? Cole acted the criminal he was born to be. The suave criminal Chance wanted him to become. He was always destined to fully embrace the outlaw lifestyle, he supposed.

Cole detested himself. Along with his brothers, his father, and sometimes, even Penny. If Penny weren't there, he'd have left the situation he abhorred so long ago. He could have been a loser somewhere else on his own, working at some shitty job, but at least then, perhaps he wouldn't have participated in a physical assault on an innocent woman. A woman whose temple he held a gun to.

Now, there was no going back. No turning this around. He was a fully-fledged criminal. A degenerate. A man with a history of violence from this day forward.

Everett just fell asleep while Cole paced. He paced faster.

What if she were dead?

Cole left the motel room. Taking the truck, he drove back up the Rydell River Valley and the many miles it took to return to the crime scene.

The police were still there. She hadn't been left alone all night, which could have happened if he hadn't called the assault in.

Oh, right. As if he deserved a brownie point for merely calling in the crime he committed on the woman. A crime that could have killed her.

But he saw no ambulance there. Just cops. He drove through the scene, glancing back. None of them paid him any mind. He wished they would. How could they not sense his evilness in driving by? Couldn't they smell his guilt? Didn't all criminals return to the scenes of their crimes to relive the experience? Wasn't he doing that now? But he wasn't relishing or enjoying anything about his crime. Did that mean he wasn't totally a sociopath or psychopath? He felt gut-sick. Then he started shaking. Then he got scared.

So scared of what he'd done and been a party to.

Scared of what it meant for his future. He wondered if he still deserved to have a future after this.

Nothing could relieve him from his guilt.

What he did was so wrong. He deserved to live in eternal hell. A prison cell. And a merciless beating.

He deserved the butt end of a gun being smacked hard on his cranium so he passed out cold on the floor. Yeah. Maybe that was the best solution to abate his remorse.

Hollow-souled, Cole went back to the motel room. He clicked on the TV, searching for the local news. He found it and waited.

Oh, yeah. The shit made the local news hour. He cringed and hated himself while listening to the various versions of the night's event. *Local business owner robbed at gunpoint and left for dead after being struck with a weapon.*

Actually, it was a gun.

And yes, the perps were that heartless.

The victim is in the hospital for treatment and observation. We expect the patient to make a full recovery. Her name is being withheld for her own safety.

Her safety? Were they insinuating the faceless monsters planned to hunt her down and finish her off? Cole stared in shock at the grainy surveillance video of them... especially *him*. He paused the TV and stared at himself. Slowly, the full repercussions and reality of his crime began to wash over him.

"Stare hard at who and what you are now, motherfucker," he muttered out loud.

But at least, the girl would be okay. That was the only reassurance he had, just that. No, it couldn't excuse or lessen his involvement, but knowing she wasn't dead helped ease his conscience.

He reached out and touched the screen. "I'm so sorry." But the woman would never know. Why would she care about what he felt anyway? She wouldn't want to know anything about him. What they did to her was seriously screwed-up shit, even if Cole were truly sorry.

He should have cold-cocked Everett and let the police catch them there. Right in the act. Admitting their participation. Maybe that was the only way to make it right. Or did they deserve retribution? But running away and leaving her lying there? There was no other name for them now except *monsters*. He came from a family of monsters.

And cold-hearted criminals.

CHAPTER 4

*I*T HURT. IT FELT like an elephant was sitting on her head and chest. Blinking her eyes open, the hospital room eventually came back into focus for Jade.

Oh, yeah. She'd been attacked. Robbed at gunpoint.

And assaulted.

The reality of that concept made her shiver. It was something she'd never considered happening to her. Not in the Rydell River Valley. But it did happen. Right there. At her home and place of work. She tried to move around to alleviate her discomfort. Immediately, she felt someone grabbing her hand. She glanced over and saw her mother.

Jocelyn, her tall, stately, wild-haired mother, looked pale and exhausted. At nearly sixty years old, her mother had always dressed with kind of loose, bohemian style. She wore her hair short now with a variety of colors in it. Tattoos covered her arms, although neither of her daughters cared for a single one. Funny that Jocelyn's funky style never extended to either Lillian or Jade. That didn't matter though because Jade always adored her mother.

As her mother adored both of them. "Oh, Jade." Jocelyn's

voice cracked. The emotion in her tone made Jade's eyes fill with tears.

"What happened, Mom?"

"Don't you remember anything?" A sense of alarm seemed to fully engage her mother at hearing that. Then it became more like panic.

"No, I do remember the three men. Their guns and loud words. I also recall being by the safe. I thought they were done with robbing us and then... there's nothing after that..." Her voice trailed off. "What did they do to me?"

Her mom exhaled a soft moan. "They knocked you out. Most likely by using the butt end of a gun. You were totally passed out. Someone called the police and then we were notified. You were still out cold when they found you. The sirens brought us out to the arena. No one knew what happened. To discover it was you, getting knocked out next to the safe... oh, Jade, it was just gut-wrenching. An ambulance brought you to the hospital. They said your vitals were strong. You're so strong, sweetheart. But..."

Jade squeezed her mom's hand. "Yeah. *But.* That had to be terrifying."

"Still is."

The door opened. "Oh, thank God she's awake." Her dad's voice reached her.

"Nothing else happened?" Jade asked softly.

Her mom squeezed her hand. "No. Nothing else. They left after they incapacitated you, or so it seems."

"Who called the police?"

"It was anonymous. But since no one else knew what happened..."

Her heart skipped a beat in her chest. "You think it was one of them?"

"Maybe."

"One was not as aggressive as the other two. The oldest

one did all the talking. He was mean. Another one just followed orders and did the old guy's bidding. The quieter one told the other one to back off at one point..." She shrugged. What? Was she suggesting a nice criminal was holding her up at gunpoint?

Jade scoffed at the very idea of it.

Her dad rushed to her other side. "Baby girl..." he gripped her hand, leaning over to kiss her.

"I'm okay, Dad."

"That's good because I'm so, so not."

She smiled a weak, watery version of a grin. "Okay, me neither then. I'm so not."

There had been several crimes over the years in the Rydell River Valley. There was a mass shooting right in downtown River's End once, in which eight people were gunned down and died. A cousin of sorts, Silas's dad was there and witnessed it all before taking out the shooter. Her dad's cousin, Iris was also the victim of a crime when she was violently raped on Rydell land.

Other tragedies occurred over the decades. A fire destroyed everything many years ago. And just recently, Roman Barrett, a cop and Rydell cousin, was in a standoff in which he ended up shooting the suspect. The suspect had kidnapped a baby boy, holding the boy and his mother captive, and was threatening to kill them. Roman killed him at the last critical second right before the perp could shoot the woman in the head.

That was the woman Roman was now dating. But the whole incident still shocked everyone who lived in the area.

So the residents weren't naïve or sheltered from crime and tragedy, but it still seemed a little more appalling when it happened to Jade at her family ranch. "I never dreamed something like this was possible. I left the door unlocked despite how dark it was. Just because it was night, it didn't occur to me to take even the smallest precaution..."

Her dad's hand rubbed her forehead with tenderness. "All of us do the same thing. No one takes it seriously, not really. But screw all that guilty shit and blame. Tell me first, how are you?"

"My head hurts."

"We've been waiting for what seems like days for you to wake up. Worried about a concussion and possible brain injury. Let's get a doctor in here now; the rest can wait."

She nodded and allowed the hospital staff to conduct a full physical and neurological examination. When they deemed she could, they allowed Jade to talk to the cops about what she remembered of what happened to her. Roman came in and took her statement.

His gaze glistened with sympathy towards her. "I'm sorry, Jade. Really sorry this happened, especially to you. I'll be on this right away. I promise to do everything I can to track down the cowards who did this to you."

"Just don't tell my dad." She smiled through the head fog. "He'll kill them."

"Your father's not the only one. Others feel the same way too. Half my job is spent convincing the Rydell family not to exact vigilante justice." He smiled with tender care at her. "I'm just kidding." Then he shook his head and added, "Kind of."

Jade almost laughed. She was picturing her seventy-eight-year-old grandfather being distraught and preparing to track down the guy who did this to her along with her own father. They were nothing, if not loyal.

Jack Rydell, Jade's grandfather, came from a totally different time. He was the last of a dying breed and a full cowboy. She suspected he'd easily avenge anyone who dared to hurt a single member of his family. Even now.

Jade did have a concussion. Everything else hurt on her too. From her head to her toes, her entire body was in pain.

"You took a hard fall when you passed out. It jarred your body, dropping your full weight on the ground like that. You also sprained your wrist when you involuntarily put it under you to cushion the fall." She looked down and saw it was all bandaged up.

That annoyed her more than anything else right now, knowing she would be temporarily sidelined as a result of that night.

After her parents were given a list of things to watch out for, Jade was finally allowed to go home.

Her sister, Lillian and husband, Matt were there as well as their son, Benny and daughter, Molly. Jade was hugged, clucked over, and fully pampered. Her parents drove her to their place to cherish her and give her the intensive care she required. They had a huge apartment located in the upper portion of the large arena. The same place where Jade and Lillian were raised. It had a private entrance from below and its own garage stall off to the side of the buildings.

Was it any wonder why Jade was so horse-crazy? She was all but raised with horses in her backyard.

But it was still home and the best place to be after an unexpected attack that left her feeling oddly vulnerable and weak… Some people might say, *like a girl*. That evoked a negative meaning of being weaker. Jade never considered herself weak in any way. But now, she felt weaker than she ever did before and she hated that worse than almost everything else about the experience.

She clenched her hand into a fist, staring out at the ranch spread all around her. Whoever did this to her would someday, somehow get payback in full.

Being home with her family didn't ease his guilt and humiliation for what he'd done. Cole couldn't stop the memories from returning. He quit sleeping because the nightmares kept waking him up. He kept dreaming of the girl falling and hearing the sickening noise she made when she hit the ground, like a hollow tree thumping to the ground. He'd wake up after dreaming she'd died. Or was brain damaged. Then the girl became Penny. Penny's face started to appear on the girl's body as if he'd done that to his own sister.

But what mortified him more than anything was the knowledge that he'd done what he did to someone else's sister. And daughter. And, possibly, wife. An innocent woman who'd never done anything offensive to him. Never. And she didn't deserve to suffer at their hands. It was their idea. Their perverse collaboration and performance.

And it was all so he could buy his sister braces?

Oh, yeah, and to bail Zack out of jail. Mission accomplished.

"Surprised to see how much they had onsite that day. But that would have gone better with Zack's help."

"No, it wouldn't have," Cole replied to his dad's rambling. He ignored his brother and dad. He couldn't stomach even looking at them... or hell, looking at himself.

But Zack was released on bail. He came back to live in the overcrowded trailer with them, full of his own tales of horror in lockup.

"I can't go back. I can't live like that." Zack exclaimed. As if living in their trailer and squalor was that much better? Maybe the claustrophobia thing came from the bars, which seemed legit. Cole was certain he'd feel that way too.

But deep in his guts, Cole knew he deserved to be in jail too. They'd all most likely end up there, he expected.

Even Penny probably. How could he prevent it?

Knuckles flashed before his eyes, then snapping fingers appeared an inch from his nose. "What the hell is wrong with you? You lay around here like you're comatose. You sick or something?" Zack asked. He wasn't part of the heist. He laughed when he heard the story about it and knuckle-punched Everett as if to congratulate him. The cocky, little scene made Cole's stomach curdle.

Cole was depressed and felt sick. Everything went back to being the same. Staring at endless filth and observing his family's dysfunction, Cole was sure his entire path forward, along with his sister's, would only be more of this chaotic existence. Penny, the only person he loved and valued would end up getting ruined by the same forces that ruined him. And he was one of those forces now. He was guilty for causing that. He didn't know how to fix it or change it. He'd actually hurt someone physically. Violence was part of his nature now.

Yeah, Cole was sick of his life but saw no way out.

"What do you want?"

"We gotta get out of here. Dad and I. I'm not showing up for court. Or anything else. No hearings. Never going back to that shit hole. They'll convict me for sure."

Cole sat up. His interest in what Zack was saying finally motivated him enough to take heed. He hadn't cared about anything for over a month since the robbery.

"What are you going to do?"

"Run. We gotta run. Dad's gonna help me. We gotta get outta here."

He glanced at his dad.

"What about Penny?"

"She'll have to come with us obviously."

"But… the school will notice her absence. People care about that shit. They'll look for her. What if I stay here with her? Keep things going as usual. You often go away to work.

We'll make good for a while. They won't come snooping if a little girl isn't missing. No offense, but you'll just be another prick jumping bail. But Penny..."

It was a weak lie. No one would come looking for Penny. There was never anyone interested in her before. After being yanked around and moved from city to city, small town to the next faceless small town and across state lines, no one ever showed up to check on her wellbeing. Cole wished they would so he could find her a new home. A real home. And caring parents. Something she could hang onto and trust.

But if the old man went away, maybe Cole could finally get Penny away for good.

How though? Crap if he knew. But their last crime pretty much illustrated how crucial it was for him to get her out before she ended up like him. Like them.

No. Cole figured he'd die on that hill, but Penny Poletti was getting out. She was going somewhere better.

How? He'd spent years trying to figure out a way. What to do. With no family to speak of and no friends to turn to, it was solely up to Cole. The only friends he knew were as bad or worse than him and his brothers and father. There was no one he could trust with Penny. There was no nice social worker or teacher either who might notice Penny's need for better home care.

But now, there was *someone*.

An aunt. *Erin Poletti.*

Erin was the faceless aunt from whom his dad had stolen money. Maybe she wasn't like him. Like *them*. Maybe she wasn't a real Poletti. Maybe she was more like Penny and had the same name but wasn't like any of their personalities.

The aunt was a longshot, sure, but she was all he had. The only possibility. The only chance. He had to take it. But he couldn't figure out how to pry Penny from Chance's grasping claws. Chance would most likely call the cops and report her missing if Cole tried to relocate her somewhere else. He'd say she was kidnapped. He'd do that for sure. He'd get Cole tossed in jail for kidnapping Penny. So Cole had to have a good reason. He had to persuade Chance to give him permission to remove Penny permanently from under his control. But he also had to make sure Chance was in a place where he couldn't call the cops.

This might be it. His one and only opportunity to get the hell away and live differently.

"What're you gonna do with her?" Zack inquired.

"Just keep her here. Like normal. You know. I'll be the cover."

His dad's head shook. At least, he was considering it.

Damn… please. He needed this. Something. He was suffocating from remorse. What he'd done. Who he was. Who he was inadvertently grooming Penny to become.

"Might be a consideration…"

He almost closed his eyes. *Maybe.*

Penny heard the whole conversation. She was on her bunk, and regarded Cole with a tilted head. Puzzled eyes. She knew things. She also knew not to ask out loud. Especially in front of Zack or Everett or Chance. She knew only to ask Cole. And always quietly and privately.

He gave her a quick look. She nodded.

Later.

Penny didn't know what Cole did to get the money to buy her the mouthful of hardware she flashed at him just then. His heart swelled up. That girlish, hideous smile of silver metal was all that kept his heart beating. He'd take her out of this shit hole life. If this worked and they could stay together, it would be great.

If not? He'd get her to… What was her name again?

Erin Poletti. Right? No. Erin *Rydell.* He'd take Penny there and somehow… someway convince them to save her.

Getting jailed for kidnapping or assault? Cole supposed it didn't really matter which one they arrested him for, now did it? Either one was a felony and his destiny.

FINALLY, Jade felt better. Her head was not so achy or tender. She wandered out towards the family barns and found her dad in one of the main ones. Her wrist still hurt so horseback riding for her was out, as well as guiding tours. Those assholes stole a few weeks of her life.

"Hey, sweetie." Ben was busy lifting a large bale of straw. She wanted to rush forward to help him, but couldn't with the stupid wrist.

She came closer.

"Stuff gets heavier the older I get," Ben muttered.

"You're not old." She smiled; her fifty-eight-year-old her dad was fitter than most men twenty years younger.

"I *am so* getting old. Way past middle age." He finished the bale by opening it and spreading contents into several stalls that had pregnant mares inside them. Finally done with his chore, he glanced at her. "Wanna walk with me?"

Surprised at his serious tone, she nodded. "Sure. I'm going crazy in the house and my stupid wrist keeps me from getting to do much more than that except walking around the ranch."

His lips twitched. "You were always an antsy, busy little girl, always staying outdoors even late into your youth. All the running, hiking, riding, water-skiing and I can't remember all the different activities you liked to do. Worrying your mother until she was frantic with all the stuff you did in the backwoods, and usually, all alone."

She snorted as they fell into step. "And how ironic that I was on our own land the night I got hit."

He cringed, and she sighed. "I'm sorry to be that callous. I know how upsetting it's been for everyone."

"It really has been." Sunset streamed in gold and orange hues as it sank in the sky and reflected on the river. The view of the horses was eclipsed, majestic creatures that they were, as the mountains on the horizon were bathed in brilliant, dramatic sunset and russet tones.

"This place never gets ugly, does it?" Jade commented as she observed how well it was thriving in the fading light.

"Nope. Been the same ever since I was a boy. Seems like centuries ago now."

"Why do you keep talking like your all done in? Grandpa's still going at seventy-eight and he's hardly slowed down."

"Because… I'm kinda thinking I'm getting up there."

Startled, she stared at him to see if he were joking. He paused to lean over the tall white rail of the horse fencing. Miles of white rails surrounded them, zig-zagging in and around all the Rydell land. "Dad?"

He smiled as he turned towards her. "Jade?" He shook his head and an odd, kind of tender gleam twinkled in his eyes. "You look like a perfect replica of my mother standing there."

She'd often heard the same comparison. She was apparently a spitting image of the woman who would have been her natural grandmother, Lily Rydell. Lily was Jack Rydell's first wife and the mother of Jade's dad. Lily died of illness when Ben was only ten years old. He sometimes still spoke of her and always with bittersweet fondness.

Apparently, Jade resembled Lily not only in her looks, but also her energy, personality and hobbies. Jade found it interesting to be compared to someone with whom she had no emotional connections. Her grandma? The only grandma Jade ever knew was Erin Rydell.

"What's going on? Why do you seem so oddly contemplative and sad?"

"Not sad. But honestly? What happened to you has really been messing with my head."

"It was a singular occurrence, Dad, instigated by some bad assholes. A freaky, one-time incident."

"Life is so short and it goes by so fast."

She swallowed as she leaned nearer to him. "What do you mean? I don't like how you're sounding."

"I'm sorry. It's just when you get old, you also get more sentimental and aware of your own mortality. And when unexpected things start happening, like watching your dad suffer from cancer, you notice he's looking so much older, and well, suddenly, it feels… I don't know, I guess you just become more overwhelmed by things than you used to be and you start to realize how fast life passes by. And when your own daughter gets assaulted and left for dead, it strikes home how unpredictable and uncontrollable life also is."

"And? What does it mean? You're just talking and feeling worried…"

"I think I'm ready to retire and spend the rest of my life with your mother. And my kids. And grandkids. I think I'm old enough now to do that. And I think I'd like to see you manage the operations and management of the Rydell River Ranch for me."

CHAPTER 5

*J*ADE'S MOUTH HUNG OPEN for several minutes. She was floored by his answer. She had no words to that revelation. Ben used very few words to make monumental statements.

"Dad. What in the hell are you talking about? Grandpa Jack, Uncle Ian, Aunt Kailynn and you all run the Rydell River Ranch. You can't just retire and… and what? Pass the gavel on to me? Announce that I'm the next…"

He grinned, swiping his cowboy hat off and wiping his brow. Yes. His hair retained some of it's original auburn-red color, but it was thinning on the top. But Ben Rydell was very vibrant and youthful in his late fifties. She frowned at his reply. "Announce that you're what? The next Jack Rydell? I can and I think I will."

"Would you quit talking in riddles and making grand gestures? Just slow down and tell me what's going on?"

He nodded. "I'm being serious. I want to retire. I'm tired of managing of this place. All the headaches and hassles and horses. Horses as a business, I mean. Your mom and I have worked for thirty-five-plus years. We raised the two most majestic, intelligent, brave, wonderful women that we could. And now? I'd like to spend some time with my beautiful wife, who, in case you didn't notice, I *still* find fun."

"Does Grandpa know?" Jade was having a hard time wrapping her mind around his idea. She had so much to say. So many more questions to fire at him. But mostly, she wondered how could her dad *not* be such an integral part of the ranch?

Everything he said was true.

"I don't have to ask Grandpa if I can retire, Jade."

"Yes, you do too."

"I'm trying to give you something. This place."

His hand swept through the air. They were meandering on the path but now she believed he'd calculated their destination beforehand, intentionally bringing her right there. It was the same location where her dad's original house used to stand when Ben was growing up. It unfortunately burned down in 2014 in a terrible, devastating wildfire. The same fire that killed Ben's first wife happened on the same night that her older sister, Lillian was conceived. Jade knew all the lurid details and heartbreak of the story. It was her dad's life. Her parents' love story. She knew why she was a full decade younger than her older sister. It took that long for them to make amends and learn about all that happened the night of the fire, along with its aftermath.

The site of the old house became a place of gardens and later, a sanctuary. The insurance money was used for the down payment on the large, commercial arena that now occupied most of the north end of the ranch.

But the view they were admiring now was one she knew her dad took particularly hard. One that transported him back to his childhood. A special spot that no one but her dad, her grandpa, and her uncles really understood. Maybe Erin. She lived for a few years there too.

The view before them was of sweeping grasses and grazing horses that gradually sloped down towards the river. The far left was covered by groves of pine trees and what was now the family housing. The River Rescue was also located on the left where her cousin, Violet and her grandpa, Jack Rydell rescued and cared for sick and abused horses.

To the right of where they stood was the gigantic, wonderful arena that also housed a restaurant and provided stadium-like tiers of seating. That was where they held the horse shows, training sessions, and riding groups as well as the 4H Club.

The various Rydell operations earned them tons of money every year. Jade's dad, Ben was the brains behind that. He was also the one who managed it.

In between those were the resort cabins and grounds.

Surrounding all of that were the tall mountains and above them, Iris and Quinn Larkin had built an eighteen-hole golf course.

Behind them, River Road meandered through the mountains. There were so many trails and paths where they rode horses, hiked and enjoyed the bountiful land that surrounded them. All the decades of work, sweat, tears, blood, heartache, joy, violence, loss, and love were encapsulated here. Where it all started.

"Why me?" Jade asked.

Her dad smiled softly. "Because you're just like my mom. And if she'd lived, she would have ended up running this place. Not Dad. He'd be too busy rescuing horses. He'd have done that no matter what happened. Mostly, I chose you because I know you can do it. And I don't think anyone else can. I can rely on you. I think you could do the work of Jack, Ian, Kailynn and me without batting an eye. Eventually."

"Dad. Crap. Aren't you laying it on a bit thick? I know you get ridiculously sappy about me and Lillian but come on.

I'm just one person. You can't expect me to fill in for *all* of you."

"No. But you could be the next Jack Rydell, the one in charge of it all."

Sighing, she shook her head. "Explain, please."

"What I need is someone to bring all the clashing personalities, managing styles, business entities, enterprises, pet projects and miscellaneous items under one budget. That will require someone to have the final say over where the money goes and all the other shit we have to handle here. Hence, you become the next Jack Rydell. He always insisted he wasn't the leader, saying all of us were equally responsible, but that was bullshit. In the end? Whenever it came down to any decision regarding the future of Rydell River Ranch and Resort, Jack had the final say, always. *Always.* I see that same sense of responsibility and leadership in you. Jade Rydell. His granddaughter."

"Dad... I'm speechless." Jade was overcome by the thrill gripping her, which also humbled her. Being compared to the one and only Jack Rydell was flattering enough, but being seriously considered capable of running the entire enchilada? Well, sure, it was more than flattering. But her dad sounded way too sentimental about her. And them. And all of it.

"Listen to me. I know this place. I was born and raised to live here. Which is why I never left for decades. But no one ever showed up to step into my dad's shoes. Not me. Not Ian. Not Kailynn. No one. He's pretty hard to emulate successfully."

"I know that. I'm a twenty-six-year-old horseback rider. I can't be anything like what you guys want and need."

"Yes, you can. You've got the brains, nerves of steel, leadership genes, courage and you love horses. People respect you because you demand their respect. You just have it all, my darling. I don't know what a person needs to be a boss, but you've got it. You and Jack. You both have it. I never had it."

"Lillian has it."

"Lillian has a sweet charm and ease around people. She also has the book smarts. You, however, have something else… that streak of independent thinking and creativity. Jack Rydell is the only one besides you that I've ever seen it in. I can't fully define what *it* is, I just know it when I see it."

"This is so insane. I mean, what about the uncles and their own kids? What will you do? How will you tell them your decision?"

"Truth?"

"Yes."

"I wanna rebuild the house."

Puzzled, she tilted her head curiously. "What house?"

"The one you should be standing in right now."

His childhood home? "But… why? What will the others think?"

"I don't care what anyone else thinks. Before I die, I wanna see my mother's house standing here again."

"Will you please stop talking about dying?"

He chuckled. "You sound like me and Charlie and Melanie talking to Dad."

"Well, duh. I can't live without you."

He sighed heavily. "I'm almost sixty years old and you'd think I could manage without my dad, but truth is, I can't. Funny how something, even age, doesn't seem to change that. Fear of losing a loved one overrides everything else. But the house I grew up in was the heart and centerpiece of the original Rydell River Ranch. I'd like to see it standing here again."

"Do you plan to rebuild the very same house? Or modernize it?"

"Damn near the same. Maybe tweak a few modern conveniences. It was gorgeous, Jade. Epic. It was really a home."

"But what will the uncles think and Grandpa? This doesn't belong just to you."

"Screw 'em. I'm Ben Rydell and that should count for something, huh? In most families, the first born child of the first born son would inherit the entire place. I'll sit here and claim to be the lord of the ranch as I was born to be."

"Dad! Have you lost your mind?"

"No." He sighed. "It sounded kinda good though. No. I haven't lost my mind. I talked it over with Dad and all the uncles and Charlie. I even included all their wives, so don't give me that look. I'm no sexist. Everyone was fine with it. They even gave me their blessing. They all teared up the way... what's the term? *Full circle.* That's what they said it would be. Coming full circle or something like that."

"But you still haven't told me *why?*" She pressed. Inside though, she was relieved he hadn't fully lost his mind or intended to screw over his entire family.

"Fear. I suppose. Nostalgia. When my dad got so sick and couldn't get up for a few months, it really humbled me. It made me realize my own age. It also made me remember my youth. I realized that now I want different things. Life changes your perspective a lot over time, Jade. It just does. And now I want to rebuild the grand, old house in River's End that a wildfire destroyed. My sister's even offered to help me rebuild it. Imagine that? Huh?"

"Aunt Mel?" That made a lot of sense so it calmed Jade's nerves. Aunt Melanie and Uncle Kyle owned a house building business. Aunt Melanie, Jack and Erin's daughter, physically built the houses too. Jade always had a favorable opinion of Aunt Mel and thought she was not only epic and awesome but also tough and unusual. Jade loved to think her aunt and dad were doing this project together.

"Yes. It seems more than fitting."

"Okay, so you rebuild the house from your childhood and all that. Then what? You're just going to sit inside it with Mom?"

He grinned at his daughter, sweeping an arm around her. "I'm gonna sit right here on my covered porch and watch all you guys work away. I'm also gonna use that damn golf course up there that our family *owns* and I've never found the time or energy to enjoy. I'm gonna… yep, spend all my time with my wife like I never got to before. So yeah. I'm gonna sit around with your mama and relax."

"Ben Rydell occupying the center point of the ranch?" She grinned. "I suppose that could be what might have happened in most families."

His cocky grin faded. "That's not the reason. I just think it's time that I slowed down, and since I still want to be here, I'd like to have that house back. When I saw what my own sister could design and build, the seed in my brain started to grow… why couldn't she reimagine what once was?"

"That's a nice thought. Reimagining the original homestead."

He grinned. "I thought so too. Not my own phrase, I actually saw it on the news for something else and thought it had a sweet ring to it, for this."

"And what about the other uncles? And Aunt Kailynn?"

"They're tired too. The kidnapping of Russell really took it out of Ian and Kailynn. They're ready to retire now as well. Jade, it's not common for people who work as hard as we do to continue straight into their sixties like all of us are doing now. Sure, this work and place are far more extensive than the traditional workplace or a nine-to-five job or even minimum wage work. Sure. I know all that. But even old timers are allowed to stop some time before they die."

"Every old timer except Grandpa."

Ben nodded. "Except for your grandpa. He'll probably die while limping out to his barns."

"Dad." She all but put her hands to her ears to keep the words from entering them. "Don't plant that image in my head."

"I must keep that image in mine. It's the only way I can handle what he just went through and survived. But really, Jade this ranch needs someone, as in, *one person*, to bring it all together. After much discussion, we all agreed the best candidate for that position is you. That is, of course, if you want it."

"You already had… a meeting about this?"

He nodded. His expression grew more serious. "Yes. And we even voted on it. Hunter doesn't like ranching. Landon is… well, Landon, which means, we can't rely on him to take over the operations of a place as complicated as this has become. So Ian's kids are out of the running. Charlie's twins have Reed Ranch if they want to run a ranch or any other ranch they can find from what AJ and now, Asher own and control."

"Dad. The twins have as much right to the Rydell lands and jobs as we do."

He shrugged. "Jade. There are a limited number of jobs here and many family members. Reality can be harsh. *Rydell* being the magic word."

"What if I don't stay a Rydell forever? I might get married, you know."

"Then you'll have to make him or her take *your* name."

She smiled at his solution. Jade never had a boyfriend, nor had she ever brought anyone home. She preferred to stay private about her personal life.

"What about Silas?"

"He's a Starr."

"Dad..." she groaned, thinking of her friend. "He's also a Rydell. And one that's for real, being Joey's son."

Ben shrugged. "He doesn't have it."

"What the hell is 'it'?"

"I honestly don't know how to describe what 'it' is. If it comforts you to know though, I don't have it either. Charlie would have had it if he'd decided to take up ranching or running the resort or anything else we do at this place. But not his sons. Nor Ian's. Nor Shane's girls."

"What about Violet?"

"She's got the horse rescue to deal with. It'll be all hers one day."

"Dad..." Jade's mind whirled through all the different family members whom she found much more capable of doing this. People who were already here. And had the connections. It clicked. "I know. Benny. Benny Rydell is always being called a little version of Jack Rydell. He's the spitting image of Jack and he has the same personality. And on top of all that, he's your grandson." She gave him a long look as if she were disappointed he'd ignore his own offspring. Lillian had Benny when she was very young.

Ben chuckled. "No, one's forgotten him. But he's only twelve. I'm not postponing my retirement another twelve years just waiting for him to grow up. Besides, he's not my first choice anyway. He'll have a spot here, huh? With you at the helm? But... I can't leave everything to him, my daughter. It's you, Jade. You're it. The first choice of everyone who counts." His eyes gleamed. "But most especially, the first choice for me."

She was speechless. Honored. Shocked. Disturbed. Glowing. Her family voted for her, including her uncles and aunts. All the people that raised her and whose authority she always respected and obeyed. From her parents to her grandparents to her uncles and aunts, the choice was unanimous.

"What does all this newfound responsibility entail?"

"To start with? I suggest you begin by shadowing us. Observing all the ins-and-outs of our particular slices of the operations. Then you can establish some way of bringing it all together. You'll be a figurehead. The president. A CEO. The ruler of the kingdom, if you really want to get down to it. As Dad always was for us. He didn't have to flex his power much, but there were times when he did… and no one could argue with him. It was just the way we did things in truth. But as the old timers start to retire, and die, this place needs someone to keep it together. Like glue. It must remain a cohesive endeavor with all the current offshoots and maybe more to come. You'll be the one who makes sense of everything. It'll be hard. There's no doubt about that. You'll have shitty days and be asked to make impossible decisions. You'll make the others mad and sometimes envious. Some won't agree with your choices. Leadership must be earned and it's hard and lonely… but well worth it. But it's time, Jade. It's time for the changing of the guard and you're the next one in line for the honor."

She licked her lips and a wave of apprehension shuddered through her, tingling her spine. "Are you sure I'm up for this?" she asked Ben timidly.

"One hundred percent. Don't worry. No one is throwing you to the wolves. We'll all be right here still. That's the bane, curse, and blessing of being born a Rydell on the Rydell River Ranch. We're not going anywhere. If you need our advice, you can have it."

"What if it goes to my head and I turn out to be an asshole?"

He snickered. "There again, how many Rydells are here just itching to shut that shit down? And who knows? You might find yourself enjoying it. We've all been assholes a time or two over the decades. Every one of us. We don't expect you to be perfect or flawless in this new role. It's enough to know you're getting up each day and trying your best again."

"It's such a massive operation to take on."

"It won't be learned overnight. But given enough time? It will become like everything else does to you, a routine."

"Can I hire some people? To help me? People that I trust?"

"Yeah. You'll eventually be fully in charge of the money. Jade? This is epic. Don't underestimate your worth nor the challenges that you face."

Nerves rippled through her stomach. His words resonated and she knew they were true but also still terrifying. "Do I just… what? Start now?"

"Are you saying yes?"

She shut her eyes for a moment. Then she blinked her eyes open and looked over her dad's shoulder. Spread out before her were acres of land, dozens of horses, a river, groves of trees, mountains, and sky. Now, they were all *hers*. Her entire life and future lay right here from this day forward. Yeah, sure, she wanted it. *Yes.*

She straightened up, looked her dad straight in the eyes and nodded. "Yeah, Dad. I'm saying yes."

CHAPTER 6

$\mathcal{P}$ENNY'S FACE LIT UP when she saw her "dad" at school to pick her up from sixth grade. But instead of her biological, dreaded dad, it was, in fact, Cole, not Chance. Naturally, the smart, savvy Penny Poletti, so accustomed to lying and hiding, knew how to hide her surprise. Showing no real emotion, Penny also knew to stay quiet. She made no exclamations. No asking, why was Cole here? Or calling out loudly, *you're not Dad*. Nothing out of the ordinary. Penny quickly ran up to Cole and greeted him with a hug.

The secretary smiled and Cole smiled tentatively back. Dressed in a hat, a fake beard and the kind of clothes a logger might wear, it was impossible for anyone to determine his age. A pair of sunglasses kept people from focusing too long on his youthful face.

After all, Penny's dad was supposed to be well into his seventies. But did anyone know that here? Penny had only been attending school here a few months. Another school she had to find a way to fit into. Another trailer. Another apartment. Another house. Whatever. Things were never permanent for Penny.

Cole fisted his hands. Unfortunately, that had to continue for a while. The transient, dumpy, poor, unsafe lifestyle they shared. But someday, Cole vowed to change it for her. Somehow. Someway.

Once they were outside the school, Penny started talking. "What's going on?"

Sure, having her older brother show up and claim to be her dad while wearing a disguise might not be normal for most young girls, but it was for Penny. "I'll tell you when we're in the truck." The derelict truck was a dying relic from the seventies. It was a miracle it still ran but that was owing entirely to Cole's endless tinkering, mechanical skills and finagling. It was ingenious what Cole could create without any supplies, parts or proper know-how. Cole somehow managed to keep the rust bucket working for them.

Them, meaning *all of them*. He was kind of stealing it now from his dad.

"Dad got Zack out of jail. That means, he has to hide from the law now."

Penny's face fell. "So we have to move again? But Cole, who will tighten my braces? They won't work if they aren't tightened up all the time." Tears filled her eyes. She'd been moved around, yelled at, ignored, used and abused for her entire short life. She could neither read nor write and her clothes were no better than rags, making her a target for bullying by the other kids. But her only concern? Her braces. The solution to fix her crooked, bucked teeth. His heart ached for her.

"No, Penny, we're not going with them."

He kept his gaze intently focused on the road.

Her fidgeting stilled at his words. "What do you mean?"

"I mean, they left this morning to hide Zack somewhere."

"All of them?"

"Yeah. Won't be back for at least a few weeks."

"And?"

"And you and I are using this opportunity to get away from him. Dad can't easily run to the cops and claim I kidnapped you with a fugitive son on the lam. Most likely, the cops will be investigating him when the court date arrives and Zack's a no-show. Dad'll have to lay low for a long while. He won't dare make any noise about it either."

Her breath caught. "Oh, my gosh! You mean… it's just us?"

He nodded, taking his eyes off the road long enough to smile at her. "Yep. Just us."

Her eyes closed and she flopped back onto the seat. "Cole… do you really mean it? You're not just shittin' me?"

He could only admonish her so often so he matched her grin and replied, "Not shittin' you."

They'd dreamed of this chance, this day, for years. She understood the risk and why Cole couldn't even try to do it before. Chance had legal custody so he'd claim Penny was kidnapped if they simply left. Knowing his twelve-year-old sister was exposed to all these things was another ugly black mark on the Poletti men for allowing them to happen to her. Penny grew up fast and had no childish ideas or illusions. Penny had the viewpoint and world-weary perspective of a burned out loser, because she was raised by them.

"But this will mean I have some huge, crappy requests for you. Listen to me before you agree without knowing what you're agreeing to."

"Anything. I'll do anything to stay away from him." She screamed in an impassioned reply. "Anything so we can just be you and me, Cole. Just us. I can't believe this is happening." Her gaze shot to him again. "It is happening, right?

You're not fuckin' around with me. And nothing else can fuck with it, right?"

His heart swelled with love. He was relieved that she wanted the same thing he wanted. Knowing how much she relied on him and seemed to like him was his greatest reward. She seemed to know the difference, that he wasn't quite as bad as Everett or Zack and definitely not Chance.

"No. It's happening right now. This moment. Here's the thing, you have to abandon everything you have in the trailer. We can't risk going back there as you're supposed to be in school for another six hours."

Cole picked her up just twenty minutes after the bus dropped her off.

That was the head start he needed and counted on.

"Done. Nothing there I want. Just my braces and I got 'em on."

Her and those damn braces. He gave her a smile. "I'm sorrier than you'll ever know that's actually the case. That someone can you rip you out of your home where you have nothing to miss and no regrets."

"Just you. And you're coming with me."

"And the braces. So the two most important things are taken care of now."

Penny let out a girlish laugh. So rarely did she act girlish. Nor did she laugh very often from something joyful, since there was so little of it. "What else?"

"I have a plan about where we'll go. But you'll have to lie for a while. And keep a lot of information to yourself. I'm sorry… it's no way to teach you the difference between right and wrong. But…"

"But other people don't have to escape from their own dad."

"Right."

"I swear to you, I'll be thrilled to lie and stay quiet if we get to live together just us."

"I don't have a lot of money. But I think I know a place where I can get job and start working."

"Where will we live?"

"It's... bad, Pen."

She shrugged. "But it'll still be just us?"

"Yeah."

"Then it's a castle. Where?"

"I found a very old motorhome. The kind you see parked on the side of road with an 'out of gas' sign when it's really a mobile meth lab. It's all trashed up, decrepit, and disgusting. But it was super cheap and I managed to move it. So..."

"Is there a meth lab in it?"

"No. I'm sure it never had a lab inside. I think it was used just to sell the shit."

She shrugged. He hated knowing that Penny knew exactly what *meth* was but was more than ready to accept it just to live with him.

"I swear, it's just temporary."

"Maybe not. If it moves, maybe Dad'll never find us."

He sighed. She just voiced his exact thoughts. "I know. I thought the same thing. Plus, we won't have to pay for rent. Just gas."

"We'll make it nice. You and me. It'll be perfect for us," she vowed.

"It'll be something." He grinned back at her and they fell quiet.

"I could do online school. We'd just need a hot spot for the internet. Besides, I hate school."

"We can't do online school. Neither of us can read the shit well enough to teach you."

She sighed as she stared out the window. "I know. So

fuckin' stupid. I'm the smartest one in every classroom, yet I can't read a first-grade textbook. Dyslexia is so frustrating."

Whatever that meant. Cole simply knew he was just old-fashioned dumb. Instead of being book smart, the Polettis were book-stupid. Stupid was Penny's favorite word, and she loved to use it.

Whatever. Didn't matter. Cole hadn't been to school since he was… thirteen? Fourteen? He couldn't remember for sure. But he'd be damned if Penny ended up like him. Like them. Any of the Poletti brothers was as stupid as the father. Penny *would* graduate from high school.

The ironic thing was Penny wasn't wrong when she claimed to be smarter than all of her classmates combined. In a few years, Cole had no doubts she would fully surpass them all. He just wanted to help her reach adulthood with the least amount of trauma and emotional damage inflicted on her.

So far?

He'd failed miserably.

They rode along silently for many miles. "So… where to?"

"A place called the Rydell River Valley."

"Why there?"

"There's someone who might be able to help us. I just don't know… not yet. Gotta check her out. Them out, actually."

"And why would she or they help us?"

"Can you just trust me on this?"

She snorted. "Of course, I trust you… Dad…" Then she smirked and stared out the window again.

"It'll be different. I'll have full control of our money. I'll buy you better clothes and help you fit in more. I swear. You'll get everything I can give you."

"You always do, Cole. Living without Dad and Everett and Zack, they can't take all the money from us."

Any money he managed to earn in the past was swiftly

snatched by his dad or brothers and promptly spent on gambling, prostitutes and drugs. All of that was done in front of and around Penny. All inside the trailer right in clear sight of her.

"Ah, Penny, someday you're going to really see that I'm only a marginally better person than Zack, Everett and Dad."

She snorted. "Cole. You're so fuckin' dumb sometimes. And I'm not talking about reading. I mean... there's no one else like you. You had no one growing up and yet you didn't turn out like any of them. You didn't have a Cole in your life like I have. I'll never see you as anything but my big brother and best friend."

He smiled. "I'll never purposely leave you. Okay? Whatever happens? I'll do everything I can to stay and raise you."

She smiled sweetly and fully at him. For once, she was looking her age instead of like a moment ago. The seasoned, old woman swearing at all the disappointments of her life was temporarily obliterated. Penny was far too young to be so familiar with so much disappointment.

"You stayed just for me. You hate them too. I know what you sacrificed for me, Cole."

"I stayed because there's no one else I love or care about but you."

"Ditto that."

Silence descended again as he drove the many hours to cross the state. Then he switched back towards the valley he committed the atrocity in. Now, it was the place of last resort, the sanctuary that could save his sister. He glanced over when they were halfway to his destination and saw Penny was asleep against the door. She'd bundled up her thrift store coat as a pillow.

His heart swelled and he knew she would never understand how important it was that he find her a real home. And a real mother or guardian. Someone who would know how to help her instinctively, and care for her, to guide her, and teach her manners and how to behave in polite circles. Someone to help her be the wonderful, special person he knew she should become.

All those positive traits would be slowly strangled and eventually killed if she stayed with Chance.

Or even with Cole.

He prayed the aunt he sought was nothing like them. He hoped she was kind and decent, a woman who would see past the shaggy hair, messy clothes, bucked teeth and foul language, and know Penny was simply a confused, lost, neglected, little girl.

But to Cole, she was the most magnificent person. Wonderful. The best they had to offer. That's why he had to get her out now.

Cole couldn't take care of her. If only because he couldn't teach and guide her properly. Or provide for her. Or be a parent to her. But he was intent on finding someone, somewhere who could be all of those things for her.

Gripping the steering wheel, he made a vow to find someone no matter how long it took.

The starting place? The Rydell River Ranch, of course. He hoped to become their next ranch hand. He had to get the lay of the land first. And spy on them. And meet Erin.

Mostly, he wanted to go there to spy and evaluate Erin Poletti.

Then he'd have to figure out if he could trust her.

He was stressed about getting a job there. He had no horse knowledge or skills with them. He couldn't very well read up on it. He'd watched many YouTube videos on horse care, as well as beginning riding and training. Taking a crash course in all things related to horses and ranching, however, didn't give him the confidence he lacked.

Cole was big, strong, persevering and had a firm work ethic. That would have to be his selling point.

It had to be. Penny's entire well-being was counting on it. Therefore, Cole had to make it come true.

IT WAS night when the old truck's headlights flashed over the garish shell of the ancient motor home. There were doors missing from the outside compartments. Holes were punched along the side panels too and several areas were missing the vinyl siding.

It was right where Cole left it. A side road about three miles up the backroads in the mountains. No houses were close or even visible. Cole prayed it would still be there when he got back. He couldn't afford having it ripped off or towed to an impound lot. Thankfully, it sat there just as he left it.

He had to have a place to take his precious cargo.

Penny sat up when he stopped the truck. "Is that it?"

"Yes. For now. And it's only temporary. Remember that."

"Does it have any lights?"

He smiled. "Yes, it has lights. And we can use the toilet and running water. We're self-contained for a little while, if we conserve the water carefully. Eventually, the toilet and gray water tanks will need to be dumped and our water tank will have to be refilled."

He'd already checked. They tromped out together and entered their new digs. Cole already gutted it. Then he cleaned and scoured it. He used air fresheners and elbow grease to make it livable.

"It's not that terrible." She looked around.

The walls had graffiti all over them. The seats were ripped and the stuffing hung loose. There were only a few boards left to serve as the flooring. Yeah, it was awful. But it wasn't the worst place they'd ever slept for a night. Or lived in for three months.

Six months.

Whatever. Nothing they lived in was considered habitable by most people.

This was. He took her to the back. "There. You get to have the bedroom."

She looked at him with huge, glowing eyes. The thin mattress was covered with a cheap blanket. Cole spread out the thirty-dollar, brand new sleeping bag and pillow as if he were preparing a bed for a queen. It was clean at least. Come winter they'd have to do better as the sleeping bag was so skimpy in stuffing it couldn't keep her warm in frigid temperatures. But as always, they lived to survive *right now*.

She clapped her hands together. "I get my own bed? And… my own room too?" She suddenly spun around and threw herself at him. He patted her skinny back. "It's a sleeping bag pretty much in a closet… but yeah. What little we have here is yours." His heart pinged. She asked for so little. Privacy to change her clothing. Her tiny body was in the throes of puberty and he knew how much she struggled to find some privacy while being crowded on top of each other as they were in the other trailer. Penny was the only girl and four huge men constantly around her was an incessant imposition. Their old bathroom was so small, Cole's wide shoulders kept the door from shutting all the way. How was Penny supposed to blossom from girlhood to womanhood with all that going on around her?

"Are there any mice?" she asked innocently. No squealing or pulling a face. She just wanted to know. She was used to seeing rodents. There were plenty of rodent infestations in the cheap places where they formerly lived.

"Not that I saw while I was cleaning it out. I put mouse traps all around to deter any from coming in."

He'd spent so much money that he couldn't afford, simply because he had to make it better. Penny couldn't live and grow in the worst place she'd ever seen. She deserved to have privacy and a clean home to live in. That's about all he could give her.

"Spiders?"

"None that I saw." His lips twitched. Spiders were the only creatures that terrorized Penny. Cole knew that and killed them whenever she pointed them out. He dutifully inspected her bunk in the trailer, or wherever they slept each night to make sure nothing had crawled into it. Cole never mentioned her fear of spiders to his dad or his brothers because, sick as they were, they'd torture her with the arachnids if they knew she was afraid.

"Will you…?"

He quickly stepped towards the space. "Gladly. Go brush your teeth. I bought you a new toothbrush."

Dollar Store purchases, all of it. But at least it was clean and new.

"What do I wear?"

"I bought these," Cole replied, holding out a pair of pajamas. "After I get my first paycheck, we'll go shopping and I'll buy you something better. I won't register you for school until we can get a few more things."

Her shoulders hunched and dropped. She hugged him again and started crying. "Thank you, Cole. This is… so fantastic." Then she turned and locked the door to the bathroom. Cole's heart ached to know she thought his pathetic attempt at giving her a home could be considered *fantastic*.

Never mind the ripped walls, claw marks on the upholstery, bare floors and stained appliances. He prayed he'd cleaned it well enough for her basic safety. But that was all he could manage right now.

Short notice. No funds.

He waited until she was in bed before using the bathroom and tossing his own new sleeping bag on the old couch.

In the middle of the night, he was startled awake by finding her beside him. "Cole?"

"What is it?"

They whispered because old habits died hard. All these years they often whispered so the others wouldn't know the secrets they shared or hear what they said. They both knew all of it would be used against them, either separately or together. The others mocked and scoffed their unbreakable connection.

His brothers and Chance could only scorn the little girl who got scared or grossed out or hungry. And when no one bothered to feed her for all the partying that was going on, they never had any remorse.

"I'm… it's so dark and quiet here and I've never… been all alone at night."

"Scared?"

"Yes."

He flipped his sleeping bag back. "Mind if I crash beside you? My old back would sure love to get a real mattress under it."

"Thanks, Cole."

He placed his sleeping bag on the outside of hers. She quickly scurried across his and climbed into her own. It was sad but true, they rarely slept alone. Too many of them crammed into small spaces in bunks. And of course, Penny was never alone.

There was no way Cole could trust anyone that his dad or his brothers allowed near her.

What would he do with her while he worked? What if she got scared without him? He lay there, wide awake. He'd planned to leave her right here tomorrow. After scoping it out, there seemed to be no one close enough to notice the old

RV. No fresh tracks anywhere. She should be safe. But nothing was guaranteed. And with no school to attend, what could he do with her?

How could he leave a little girl out in middle of nowhere in an old, mobile drug dispensary?

He couldn't. Work would have to wait another day. He had to find somewhere safe for her to go first. But where?

Sighing, he rolled this way and that. But he was glad to hear her steady breathing and relieved that it was solid and even. Thank God, after the terrible day she had.

After having a terrible life.

Crazy part was: she believed this day turned out to be terrific.

He had to make things better.

But how?

CHAPTER 7

"I'M SO, SO SORRY. This is the best I can come up with for today. I'll find something better soon. I swear." He gave his little sister a regretful smile and insincere reassurance. How much more could he be sorry for? He was constantly making excuses for his shortcomings. Penny would forever be scarred with false promises and a history of men who failed her. There was no way his sister could grow up and be okay. Not after what all of them did to her.

Now, he was leaving her in a park, all alone. That was his version of a babysitter and Penny would most likely have to stay there for the entire day. He didn't know what else to do. They got up early and left the motorhome, driving the old truck. The nearest town was immediately ignored by Cole. The sign said, *Welcome to River's End*. No way. Far too small. Someone would notice a little girl being all alone for *hours*. He needed to find her somewhere she could be but also hide.

All so he could go earn money. Which they needed badly.

Not knowing what he'd have to do if he couldn't find a job and a paycheck made his stomach flip over on itself. Passing the third town on the highway, Cole wondered if it was big enough that *just maybe* no one would notice a little girl being all alone, all day long.

Penny waved her hand around dismissively, saying, "You know, Cole, I've spent every day alone after school since I was... well, since always."

Right. That's because she was neglected and abused since always.

He tried to be there whenever he could. But it was never enough.

"Got your food?"

She lifted her backpack. Cole stocked it with single-serving snacks from the grocery store, pop, water bottles and a prepaid cell phone. As soon as he got some extra money, he intended to buy her a real one. It was essential.

His stomach knotted. The phone was a necessity he couldn't afford but she had to have some way to contact him. And vice-versa.

Damn. The pain climbing up the back of his neck into his head was becoming unbearable. Her cheerful smile at being abandoned in a strange town for the whole day was almost too much for him to bear. She was so used to it, she didn't really consider it that big of a deal. He could tell by her eye roll during his incessant checking and fidgeting with her. His anxiety crippled him.

What if?

What if some pervert found her here all alone?

Or she fell in the river? She couldn't swim, so what could he do? "Don't go near the water. Promise me that. Not even to play in the sand."

She rolled her eyes at him again.

"Penny..." he insisted.

"I promise."

What if a cop picked her up? What if they sent her back to her dad, away from him where he could never get to her again? Officially, he was sure they'd find Chance. Then they'd probably arrest Cole for taking Penny. Fine. But the thought of losing her to a faceless foster care system or, worse still, to Chance?

That was unacceptable.

So was leaving her here, all alone at the Brewster City Park. All damn day.

When she should have been in school.

Cole watched the kids at the nearby school grounds who were just getting there. Lucky, cheerful, little pricks. They had no idea how lucky they were to simply go to school with other kids that morning. His little sister? She couldn't do that. She couldn't read. All she had for security was him and an old drug dispensary trailer stashed somewhere in the mountains.

He was leaving her all alone in a strange park.

"Don't talk to anyone. If anyone follows you or gives you any unwanted attention, head downtown. Go to a residential neighborhood. Act like you know exactly where you are and what you're doing. Act like you always know where you're going. If you leave this spot, don't stay anywhere too long. Move around. But not too often."

She again sighed. "I know Cole. I know. I'm Penny Pearson, I live with my older brother, Cole Pearson because our parents died in a car crash. I'm being home schooled now through the Washington State Online Assistant Program. I can read and write. I'm well-liked and well-fed. I feel wonderful and thank you for asking."

Her cheerful rendition of their cover story was not a new one and it made him cringe. He shook his head. "You're getting far too good at this."

"Lying? Covering our tracks?" She shrugged. "No one else would understand. They'd think I needed to go somewhere else. They'd probably separate me from you. That's *not* what I need. Or they'd send me back to him, and I'd have to live there without you." She fisted her hands. "*Never.* That could never be better than this. No one can understand all the things we have to do to survive. Fuck 'em. We'll make do."

"Pen—"

"Cole. Quit it. I'm fine. I'm a bit older now. We've done this shit before. I got this side of things handled. Besides, look at this town. It's peaches and roses compared to some places I've been left alone. I don't see a single drug deal going on in the alleys, and not one prostitute or any graffiti. So far, I'd call it better than most."

She should not have known about things like that. Or how to say them with such surety. She should not know phrases like "peaches and roses" and what the hell did that even mean? She should not know about what drug deals looked like, or prostitutes and the like, but she did.

Thankfully, she was right. The park was quiet with tall trees and miles of grass. The Columbia River flowed beside it, majestic and calm. The lake looked like a huge mirror this morning as the sun's golden light filled it. The screams of kids behind them at the school grounds filled the air. Traffic was farther off. The elementary, middle, and high schools all shared the same campus. Everything was right there.

The park was huge and very pretty. The play area looked inviting.

But his sister knew better than to stay there. She found a little corner spot at the end of a walking trail. It had a bench, was below the street line, and pretty well hidden from nearby houses and businesses by all the brush.

"I'll stay here until after school when it would look more normal for a kid to be walking around."

"You scoped it out already?" Cole asked. She was savvy about her own survival, just as he was.

She grinned. "'Course."

"Great," he muttered.

"Go on, Cole… we need some money. You said you had an idea. Do it. Find us a big wad of money."

She didn't ask if Cole's idea were legal. She was unfortunately, used to hearing about and seeing all the money her family acquired from illegal practices.

"I'm trying to get hired as a ranch hand at a place called the Rydell River Ranch and Resort. We drove past it on our way over here. It's across from that little town you commented on, River's End. I think I can handle the work. They don't require reading or a high school diploma. And I'm strong. So…" He finally leaked the details as to what he was planning. He was quiet about it because of his ulterior motive: the aunt factor.

Until he realized Penny had no idea or reason to suspect there could be a connection. She knew how hard it was for Cole to find a legitimate job considering his history. Lacking even a middle school education didn't fly too far with any employer. They hired high school graduates, but he wasn't even a high school student.

He looked far older than his actual age. Sometimes that was a blessing, other times a curse.

Today he hoped it'd be a blessing.

"Then go do that. And make a good impression."

He grinned. "Don't act like Chance then?"

"Never." She didn't grin at his teasing. Her face showed all the distaste, revulsion and fear she had of the man who terrorized them all their lives.

Cole put his fist out and she bumped it back. "Never."

HIS OLD TRUCK shuddered and shook as he drove down the pot-holed dirt road heading off the main highway to River's

End. He was surprised such a lucrative, successful ranch and resort area didn't bother to pave the damn road that led to it.

Authenticity?

Probably. Some kind of fake dude ranch most likely. He'd only knew what Chance said to him on the day he first saw it. And the pictures on their many websites. They did lots of things for the community, including a horse rescue. And a resort. And a golf course. What other family had a damn golf course as one of its assets?

The Rydells did.

His aunt's family.

Cole shook his head. What an odd idea. He never before considered how it felt to have an aunt. There'd never been one before. Just Chance, his brothers, and Penny.

The ranch land came into view and it looked the same as it did when he saw it with Chance. All spread out like a golden prairie, the valley floor seemed to glitter in the morning sunshine. Sunlight stretched as far as he could see. There were green fields, blue flashes of river, white fencing and special outbuildings with roofs that matched the resort. Who bothered to match their outbuildings? It was all fancy with cedar-siding, green roofs, and plenty of river-rock accenting all of it.

Then he saw all the horses. So many horses. They lifted their heads, then they lowered their heads, sauntering here and there, a few running yonder, their huge heads bobbing with joy. Big, powerful, strong animals. He all but gulped. He knew what horses were but he'd honestly never been close to one, or touched one, let alone, *sat on* one.

But horses were pretty much the norm out here.

Fine. He'd figure it out eventually. He had to. There was no other choice.

There never was, something he accepted before he came there.

He pulled under a tall, impressive gate sign with fancy writing on it. Most likely the Rydell River Ranch name was inscribed. He recognized the three R's. Who went to the trouble of labeling their home? Rich people were so pretentious and stupid. But he hoped they needed his help all the same.

Knots in his stomach couldn't begin to capture the anxiety he felt. The needless sense of panic that always lodged in his chest was starting to rise and close off his throat. What if he didn't get the job? What if Penny was being spotted by a predator right now? What would they eat tonight? How could he afford the gas to get here? And move the motorhome? To get Penny's braces tightened? What if? What if? The looming paralysis of his new life filled him with doubt.

What if.

But there was no what if now. There was no one else. Never had been. Penny needed and deserved someone who was a role model and a relative.

If Erin Poletti was a halfway decent person she could be the end destination for Penny. But first, Cole had to make sure she was right. He couldn't let Penny know the end goal was to get her in a real home… without him.

Ignoring the paralysis in his mind, he steeled his nerves and ground his teeth. *Man the fuck up.* He could hear his dad shouting in his ears. Along with the snickers and jeers of his brothers. Getting smacked on the head for being such a pussy. And feeling anything deep for another person.

The Polettis didn't feel anything. The Polettis acted out their lives. The Polettis screwed people over and drank to excess and hurt innocent bystanders and scammed everyone and they didn't care. Cole needed that kind of attitude now. Just so long as it never came out in his demeanor.

He shut the old truck down and got out. His grand introduction to the epic entrance of Rydell River Ranch surprised him, it was so quiet. A breeze blew. The far off rumble of tractor was barely audible. A few horses were neighing.

No one came running out to order him off the land. No one appeared with a shotgun in hand demanding who he was. No one appeared... period. Cole was basically unprepared for this and had no idea what to do next.

Should he head down to the barns?

He guessed that was the best approach and started walking towards the closest one. It was next to what looked like a new building site of some kind. Bulldozed land, the beginning of a foundation, but no one was around.

He hoped someone would spot him and come over. Would they ride up on horseback? He supposed that's what people did on a horse ranch.

What could he do until they arrived?

The barn doors were open. What should he do? Just walk in?

Finally, he called out, "Hello?"

Someone replied, "Back here. And hurry."

What? Hurry? Back here? He glanced around. But there was no one else about but him.

Stepping carefully, he quickly followed the grunting sounds he heard. Then he saw a man with a huge bale of some kind of grass. Was it hay? Wheat? Alfalfa? Cole had no idea. He stepped forward and quickly grabbed the other end before heaving it upwards. Immediately, the load was off the other man.

"Thanks... I took on more than I could handle.... Not anymore." The stranger was finally able to see him and Cole smiled at him.

"Who the hell are you?" Then the man shook his head. "Sorry. That was rude. I thought you were someone else when I called out. But thanks all the same. Now tell me, who are you?"

Cole lifted up the bale of grass. "Where do you want this?"

"Up there." The man's eyes lifted to a loft higher up in the barn.

Cole nodded. "You can let go now. I can carry it up there."

The man obeyed Cole and let go of his end of the bale. Cole braced himself for the load and then climbed up the ladder and hauled the whole load up. Obviously, they were stacking the hay bales and he set it next to the first one he found. Then he came back down.

"Wow. You got a strong back. I shouldn't have let you take that all alone. It's an unusually large bale. Someone decided to make super-sized ones and it takes two of us to move 'em."

He wiped his hands on his worn jeans, shrugging.

"So who are you?"

"Oh. Sorry. Cole Pearson."

The man was older, close to his dad's age, but maybe not quite that old. Graying but with a mostly full head of hair. Lean and trim. Wiry. The man put his hand out. "Ben Rydell. So how come you showed up in my barn to answer my calls for help?"

Ben Rydell. Cole stared for a long moment at the older man. If Cole had anything decent or normal about his family, and his aunt married this man's father, Ben Rydell would have been… what? Cole's first cousin or something like that, right? Maybe.

"Uh. No one was around and I wasn't sure where to go."

"For what?" Ben tilted his head.

"I'm new to the area. Heard in town this was a good place to work with horses. I could use a job."

"We aren't hiring now specifically." Ben waved a hand upwards. "But someone with a back like yours sure could come in handy on a place like this. Age is a killer."

Cole failed to grasp what he meant. Was Ben considering him? His heart started to race, hard. It began thumping so frantically, he feared Ben would hear it. Please. Damn. Fuck. He needed a break. He couldn't take another disappointment. Or pick up Penny without a job.

"Should I look elsewhere?"

"Well, I bet AJ and Asher would probably scoop you up in a heartbeat. You remind me a little of AJ, just a bit. But no. Nah. We got a whole truckload of these super-size bales that have to be stacked and stored."

AJ and Asher? He had no idea who they were. "So I could work temporarily? To unload those weird bales for you?"

"Temporarily to start and we'll see how it works out. Tell you what. I think it'll take three full work days to get it all done. You do it, and I'll pay you up front. If it all meets my approval, we'll talk then. Deal?" Ben put his hand out. Cole had to restrain the urge to shut his eyes with relief. *Money.* The man was offering up almost immediate money. He could do three days of work like that. Probably finish it in two. Prove his strong back indispensable for the older Ben Rydell to have around.

He nodded eagerly. "Yes, sir. It's a deal. Thank you."

Ben laughed while turning to walk out of the barn, and Cole fell into step with him. "Haven't had someone that grateful for a while."

Cole nodded solemnly. "I could use a break."

"I appreciate that."

"Where's the truck?"

"Still being delivered. We got a good price because of the wrong sized bales. They delivered one to show me the size difference. I thought I could get at least one up to the loft."

"I could do anything else you need. If you want me to start now."

Ben squinted as they exited the gloom of the barn into the bright sun. "You really have fallen on hard times, huh?"

"Yeah."

He waited for the personal questions. Cruel comments. Excessive demands. But Ben simply nodded and said, "Okay. Come on. I've always got work for someone willing to do it."

Ben led Cole up towards the large arena structure. Horses were everywhere. All around them. He gulped at their pounding hooves and huge teeth. They were so much bigger and mightier up close. Keeping his startled observations to himself, he lowered his gaze. How could he cover for his lack of experience? And horse knowledge? Ben Rydell would know immediately he wasn't a "horseman" when he all but pissed his pants as soon as one approached him. Damn it. They were *so* tall. Surprisingly enormous.

But no, Ben didn't want him to handle the horses at all. Just their... shit.

Cole almost whooped with joy. Ben handed a shovel to him. "The horse stables always need a good mucking." His eyebrows rose. Cole thought this was some kind of Rydell-ranch test. Did the new guy want a job bad enough to shovel the horseshit?

Only too gladly. Cole took the shovel and entered the stall. Empty. He could do all the mucking they asked him to if the stalls were empty.

"Where do I dump it?"

Ben nodded, seemingly satisfied. Then he disappeared and came back with a gray, plastic cart that had two large wheels on one end and a handle on the other. "There are a ton of stalls in this barn. Should fill this up. Then just haul it over towards the corner you see over there. You won't miss where it goes." He grinned and then spun around to leave him.

Alone. To work. That fast, Cole was on it.

He found his rhythm. Scoop, lift, turn and drop. Over and over, he chanted it. He did it with a relish and joy that others might never associate with the task at hand. But it was doable. He had a job he could do.

He just had to prove to Ben he was worth keeping even if they weren't hiring and he didn't really know very much about horses. But maybe they wouldn't notice that. If he could scoop and lift and haul, maybe that could fill enough roles to keep him on.

After he finished cleaning out all the manure, he set the gray cart and scoop back where Ben first grabbed them from. He glanced around. He should have asked Ben where to go after he finished his task.

Scurrying back towards the first barn where he found Ben, Cole scanned the area. Only then did he see him. Ben had a tool belt on and was leaning over to measure something on the building. A woman appeared to be sawing lumber there. Didn't see too many women in the trades.

Cole wished he could join a trade. The wages they made!

But then he remembered all the testing. And school and degrees… not to mention, all the reading, so much reading.

Ben glanced up when he was almost next to him. He frowned and asked Cole, "Something wrong?"

"Uh, no. Just wondered what to do next?"

"You're all done then?" Ben's frown seemed to deepen.

"Yeah. Did I take too long?"

"No. I expected you to take far longer. Okay. Wow… now let's see—"

But the snort beside Ben stopped him mid-sentence. Ben frowned down at her.

"Congrats on passing the Ben shit-kicker test," the woman said to Cole.

Puzzled, Cole remained silent and Ben gave the woman a dirty look. The woman just looked at him and grinned. She was adorable. Short in statue, with long, dark hair and pretty, pixie-like features. She stood upright, and he saw her strong shoulders. She was even wearing her own tool belt. She could kick ass.

"My brother loves to test people on horse shit duty. He believes anyone who'll do that will do just about anything. Too many entitled brats nowadays. They like to hang around doing nothing but playing cowboy on his horses."

Her brother?

Ben evil-eyed the woman again. "Well? Am I wrong? Things today aren't anything like when I was young. Most young people don't know what hard work even is now. It isn't just sitting on top of a horse and riding the trails. There's a lot of care and upkeep involved. Including—"

"The epic amounts of horse waste this place produces." The woman smiled up at Ben and then at Cole. "Sorry, I'm Melanie Rydell, Ben's sister."

Cole had no idea Ben even had a sister. She seemed quite a bit younger than Ben. Melanie put her hand out, and Cole had to shift forward to take it in a quick shake. "Cole Pearson."

She laughed. "He's giving us the look, Ben."

"Sorry?" Cole was just trying to figure out the family dynamics. What did she mean?

Ben snorted.

Melanie let out a funny, twinkling laugh. "You're thinking he looks more like my father than my brother, huh? You're not the first. My sparkling youthful freshness and all. You're right; he's most definitely old enough to be my father. Luckily for me, though, he isn't. Jack Rydell is my dad."

Jack Rydell. The one who was married to his aunt. The one his dad stole money from and fully disdained. *Melanie Rydell*. His heart thumped behind his ribs. Melanie was his cousin.

It had to be real. He was sure of it. They were far apart in age but Erin Poletti had been married to Jack Rydell for the past thirty years. She had to be this woman's mother. His very first, for real, blood-related cousin.

He searched her face and hoped she didn't notice before quickly dropping his gaze. He didn't want to creep her out. What if she thought he was interested in her? Not for what he really came there for… He was desperate for a connection to this place. Now he had a face, a real person, to take care of his sister.

Penny would be her cousin too.

Hope flared inside him.

But he had to keep his cool. He had to quit staring at everything he saw, and acting like each introduction meant anything but that to him. He was just a ranch hand. A laborer to them. He had to keep it all in perspective. He needed more time to figure them out and make sure they weren't pieces of shit like his own family. So far, things were looking up. Hope fueled Cole like never before in his life. These people seemed so nice, which was refreshing. They even liked kidding around.

And they seemed kind. Despite all the mocking and teasing that went on between these two, Cole saw no cruelty. Imagine that.

"You know anything about building or construction?"

"No, sorry."

She nodded. "Well, that's okay. You gotta start somewhere. Grab that length of lumber over there."

He blinked in disbelief. Did she want him to work with her? With them?

She took his hesitation the wrong way. "Yeah, just because I'm a chick doesn't mean I can't order you around. This is *my* housing project. Ben's my bitch on this one. And you can be one too."

Ben sighed behind Cole. "Mel. You can't talk like that. Ignore her. She's just being dramatic. She's accustomed to having average assholes underestimate her. She is, however, an excellent craftsperson and knows all the zoning laws and the subs for the house building trades. So yes, I'm…"

"My bitch!" she called out, grinning at him.

Ben sighed. "I'm her helper. Another laborer. You can join us. You did pass the test."

Cole had no idea he was being tested, but anxiety reigned in his gut. "Test? For what?"

"For me to know if I'll hire you here."

"And?"

"So far, so good."

Wow. The new sensations that flooded Cole were overwhelming. A weird sensation of heat entered his neck and cheeks. Was he blushing? From what? That was almost a compliment from Ben. Cole received so few in his life that… yeah, sure he was blushing.

Cole labored for his newly discovered cousin. All afternoon. He moved the materials, and held the boards, and followed Melanie's instructions while working beside Ben. When they'd finished, Ben asked Cole, "How old are you?"

Cole glanced at him with new suspicion. *Why? What did he want?*

"Uh, twenty-five." Would he buy it?

"Ah. You're just about my daughter's age. Wanna cold one?"

"I don't uh, drink sir."

"Oh? Fine. Then how about a soda?"

He didn't have time for a drink. He needed to pick up Penny. He glanced outside and saw the sun starting to set. He'd been there for ten full hours. But he was proud of all the inroads he'd made. In just one day.

He had to finish the day right.

"Sure. But it has to be real quick though."

He followed Ben into his kitchen. Ben opened the fridge and handed him a cold soda before getting himself a beer. Then he walked out to the deck and took in the horses and river and mountains in the twilight. Damn it. *Penny.*

"So, what's the story?"

Cole looked startled and he sat upright. "Sir? What story?"

"Why'd you show up here today and work all day for me like you did? You did more work than most of my guys can get done in three days. You didn't take any meal breaks. You don't seem to take any breaks at all."

Cole was starving but he didn't dare admit it.

What should he say?

"Not much to tell. Grew up bouncing around with my two brothers and old man. The old man's a son of a bitch so I finally left. But…" How much should he say? Or reveal? Cole decided to try to stick to the truth with this man, since it seemed more prudent. Ben seemed too intelligent and savvy to fall for a line and he'd, no doubt, spot bullshit from a mile away.

"But?"

Well, why not go for it?

"And I didn't graduate high school. I just bounced around with him, doing whatever work we could find. I've done lots of jobs. I just don't have any recommendations. But I can work like I did today, every day. I swear, I will. I just need… a…" Break. A chance. Anything you've got.

"A chance?"

"Yes."

"So you're saying you have no references or the usual shit that employees submit during interviews?"

"No. I'm afraid not."

"Got a criminal past?"

"No. I swear I've never been to jail. Or caught up in the legal system either." That was only because he hadn't been busted… yet.

"Why should I believe you?"

"You shouldn't. I just never had shit. Dad was a bastard. I got nothing to show you but what I can do. And I wanna have more. I want a lot more."

"Why'd you choose to come here?"

Cole smiled, looking around. "What I told you was true. Everyone I run into around here claims you pay more than the other ranches. And also, I mean… well, just look." He spread his hand out. The view was magnificent, more stunning than anything or anywhere in Cole's estimation.

Ben set the beer down. He dug into his pockets and pulled out two hundred-dollar bills. Cole stared at it, his mouth agape. For him, it was a fortune.

"All right, Cole Pearson who has no past, I'll bite. I'll hire you. The work you did today was the equivalent of three days, and maybe even three men. So I'll consider you a bargain but I don't tolerate any shit on my ranch. That includes my horses but mostly, aggravating my family members. Any of them, got it?"

He swallowed. "Yes, sir."

He nodded. "Take your meals at the grill. I'll leave word you're on the payroll."

"Really?"

"You're a big guy, but way too skinny. You didn't eat anything today. Yeah, I think you mighta fallen on hard times. Go over there tonight and eat. I texted my wife. She runs the grill and she's expecting you."

"Could I… possibly take it to go?"

He waved his hand in reply, obviously not caring. *Penny. Food for Penny.* Then Ben Rydell handed him the two hundred-dollar bills. His fortune.

"Good work today. Show up tomorrow. It'll be good for both of us. But if not, no sweat."

Cole lifted his eyes up, his genuine shock evident in them. "Sir, nothing could keep me away." He was staring too hard at the bills in his hand.

"Get some food. And rest. Tomorrow, maybe just do two days' worth of work."

And now he had money. Just like that.

When Cole entered the large arena, he exhaled a long sigh. Wow.

It was like… a grand showcase of something he'd seen on TV. It was huge. Larger than life. Right there.

Then he entered the restaurant at the end of the mezzanine in the large building. A woman walked up to him. "You must be Cole. I'm Jocelyn, Ben's wife."

She was not what he expected. She had purple hair, along with a few other colors. He'd never met a woman her age with hair like hers. Not to mention all the tattoos he saw up and down her arms. She was pretty hot though for someone near Ben's age.

"Here you go, Cole. It's just a roast beef sandwich, an apple and some chips. We were closing. Ben mentioned you didn't eat anything today so I added a little extra for morning." She handed him a paper bag. Cole's throat seemed to have something lodged in it. He blinked at the sudden pressure he felt in his eyes.

Such kindness had never been demonstrated to him before. "Thank you." He meant it too. Sincerely.

She smiled with warmth and friendliness. "Good night, Cole, sleep well."

"Goodnight, ma'am."

Penny.

He turned and ran. Sprinting across the huge arena, he ran down the gravel road and across the horse pasture, past the building site and barn to finally reach his truck. It was already getting dark.

Penny.

At least, he had some money. And some food. But it was so dark and he needed to get to his sister.

CHAPTER 8

THEY WATCHED COLE RUN off, sprinting straight across the whole ranch.

"He's an odd one, that's for sure," Ben said as he tilted his head back and drank a swig of beer. Jade and Ben were leaning on the porch rail watching the grown-assed man run across the darkening landscape. Jade had just come back from leading a long trail ride for the resort, going clear up the backside of the golf course. "Who is it?"

Ben chuckled. "That there's a damn mule, my darling."

"Dad!" She groaned.

He sighed. "I know. That was rude. Sorry, but he's the strongest, hardest worker I've seen here since… well, since AJ's days, honestly. It was nice to see that kind of man still exists."

Jocelyn was walking up to them after closing the grill. "That is one interesting young man." She flopped down. "Was he running?"

"Yes. At full gallop."

"He worked ten hours straight. Mucked out all the stalls in the arena."

Jade blinked, startled. "All of them? No one could do that all alone in a day."

"All of them. He was all finished by lunchtime. It only occurred to me later on that I never saw him take lunch."

"What gives? Who is he?"

"His name is Cole Pearson. He showed up this morning, first thing. I was in Jack's old barn lifting one of those odd-sized bales of hay and it was too much for the old back. He saved the day and shoved it up into the loft all by himself. Said he was looking for work and down on his luck. No high school education or family, or so he claims."

"How old is he?"

"Your age, Jade."

"And he didn't eat lunch? He's big, but no wonder he's so skinny."

"What?"

"I don't know. He asked for a job. Pretty sincere and respectful and he put in a full day here. Did everything I asked. Went above and beyond. Most guys would tell me to go to hell. He even worked for Melanie. Did everything she asked too and without any hesitation."

"He'll work for women then. You were testing him."

"Well…" Ben shrugged. "Sorry to say it but this kind of atmosphere and work can lead to some misogyny. So yeah, it was a test. But pretty soon, I started to wonder if he'd ever say no, or if he'd ever slow down."

"And he still had enough energy to run out of here when he left."

Ben chuckled. "Yeah."

"What's his work history?"

"Says he's a horseman and heard about us in town. Needs a break. So I trusted my gut and gave him one. Figured we could keep him on as a day worker. Pay him in cash. Let him earn the wages tax-free."

"Dad." Jade groaned. Sometimes her dad was so old school. He got around the tax problem by paying the workers under the table. They loved it too. But someday, he'd get caught. Jade had been after him for years to get legal names, work histories, social security numbers, etc. so they could report the wages and pay their taxes and... damn it. What if Ben just hired the next serial killer?

Her dad finished his beer and came closer to Jade. He kissed her forehead like she was still a child. "He'll be lifting heavy stuff and mucking the stalls and all the other shitty stuff that needs to be done. Let him get paid in cash. I might enjoy watching someone work so hard without any damn complaints or any breaks."

"Dad. You're required by law to give him breaks."

"I will. I will. Already set him up in the grill with your mama. See? I'm following all your stupid regulations and labor laws."

"No. You're not." She raised her eyebrows.

"Ah, Jade. You're gonna go all legit on me, aren't you?"

When? After she became the figurehead of the whole place? She still found it so weird and strange even to contemplate. "Just don't want to get sued for nonpayment of wages or harassment or breaking some other labor rules. It's not like the old days, Dad."

Ben sighed. "Don't I know that." He lifted his shoulders. "My old body keeps shouting that to me so I oughta know."

She rolled her eyes. He winked at her before going inside. "Besides, last I heard, cowboys haven't unionized... yet. So let him just earn his wages."

COLE FOUND Penny all huddled up, sound asleep in a small ball. She was still in the cove where he'd left her... *eleven*

hours ago. She was cold to the touch. He hated himself for leaving her alone so long. This had to be the last time. Gently taking her little body in his arms, he lifted her up, despite the soreness in his muscles and his growling stomach. He saved all the food he got from Jocelyn for her.

Penny's eyes opened. "What happened?"

She wasn't even mad he was so late to get her. It was dark. She was all alone in the dark of night.

"They paid me wages for what I did. I worked all day. Told me to come back tomorrow. Might be for longer. I'm so sorry though, Penny. I felt like I had to prove I was worth hiring or something like that. I don't think I'll be so late tomorrow."

She shrugged as he set her in the passenger side of the truck and handed her the bag of food. "Eat up."

She opened the bag and her mouth dropped in surprise. Sticking her hand inside, she came out with a beautifully prepared sandwich that even had lettuce on it. She stuffed it into her mouth and started chewing. Cole's stomach rumbled but he could not deny the satisfaction he got from seeing the sheer bliss on her face. She finished the sandwich in seconds.

Then she frowned at him. "What about you?"

He gave her a fake smile. "They fed me while I was there."

"They did? Wow." She beamed.

He did too.

His stomach was hollow but he was glad. When she finished eating, she pushed what was left in the bag to him. "Want the apple? I can't finish it."

Gladly. He quickly munched on it before stopping to fill up the tank with gas. Thank crap for that. He had no money left that morning. He pulled out the hard-earned two hundred-dollar bills that Ben Rydell gave him. Then he went inside the mini-mart and bought some bread, peanut butter and jelly. They didn't have a working fridge so he had to limit the groceries to nonperishable items for now.

He wondered what the long day alone had done to Penny. How scared she must have gotten, huddling on the shoreline. No one to talk to. Cole figured he deserved to go to hell for sure after what his sister suffered under his watch.

But she beamed like a beacon when he came out with their meager supplies.

"A few more days and I'll find you a Boys and Girls Club or something. You know, like day care for older kids."

"We don't need to do that. I can just stay at the park. I kept out of sight. I was fine."

"It's not fine."

"It's way better than it was with Dad."

"Pen—"

She shook her head. "We're already doing better. We'll get through this."

She should *not* have been reassuring *him.*

But her faith and perseverance shored Cole up. He forgot all about his aching body. And his hungry stomach. He felt glad to work if he could keep Penny safe with him.

He slept like the dead and groaned when the alarm went off the next day. Shuffling his still sleeping little sister out, he left her yet again. In the early morning hours, he packed up her supplies while detesting himself. She curled up with the blanket he brought for her today.

Then he showed up for work at the Rydell River Ranch. This time, a flatbed from a large semi was parked near the barn where he'd first met Ben. When he walked up, Ben grinned. "Glad to see you. Now you can get to work on these weird-sized hay bales."

And that quickly, Cole was at it.

For the next three days, Cole worked eight hours a day, with an hour break to eat at the grill. Ben would hand him a crisp C-note at the end of each day. Cole packed the dinner items Jocelyn gave him and took everything home to Penny. He also bought more supplies. Real ones.

He hoped he worked hard enough to stay on at Rydell River Ranch.

He finished unloading the semi-truck at the end of day two.

Day three was spent unloading lumber that Melanie ordered for her house project.

Then Ben came over to pay him again. "Look, we pay more if we put you on salary. You interested in that? Or you just want cash at the end of each day? That stays off the books and you don't have to pay taxes… so it's kind of a wash."

"I would appreciate the cash, sir."

A damn fortune! And no strings attached? No lying necessary. Just showing up and working was all they asked.

Ben put his hand out. "Okay. Then keep showing up. Someone will put you to work. Someone will pay you at the end of the day, and your meals are included. Don't show up? No harm, no foul. That okay for you?"

"I'll show up, sir," Cole simply replied.

Ben grinned. "Honestly? I believe you."

And Cole did as he said he would.

He worked each day as hard and for as long as he could. They forced him to take breaks. It seemed so nice. Getting meals and breaks? Such a luxury.

When he showed up on Saturday, Ben stared at him and said, "You don't have to work today."

"I'll work every day if you have chores for me? If you're okay with that?"

Ben nodded solemnly. "Yeah, sure, I'm okay with that. We've got plenty of work."

That went on for the entire week. Cole finally had the

funds to buy some clothes for Penny. He enrolled her in school immediately and told the school staff they lost all they owned in a fire, including Penny's school records. He sighed when he dropped her off at the Brewster school. They agreed she should go there so she could return to her little spot in the park cove after school. Cole couldn't get her when school let out. Sometimes, he had to work until almost dark. But she assured Cole she was okay there. At least she didn't have to stay all alone for ten or twelve hours anymore. The relief Cole got at watching her go back to school eased his conscience. Her buck teeth and lack of reading skills still concerned him since she had to be in another new school and deal with new peer pressure, but fuck. She'd be at school with other children now, not all alone in a park. Cole didn't like doing the weird shit he had to do with her. He was uncomfortably aware that it was inadequate.

Cole was almost in a good mood when he turned up for work. Work. It was real now. His life was so perfect, he pinched himself.

He was in the barn being directed by one of the brothers named Joey. It was the first time he was asked to saddle a horse for a scheduled ride. Which horse? They called her Jazzy. He was supposed to use a lead rope to take out the horse and saddle her. It was the first time he'd been asked to do something involving the horses.

How hard could it be to lead a horse from a small wooden stall of the stable?

But when he tried, several times, it didn't work. He started sweating profusely. His nerves and anxiety were making him shake. He feared the horse would kick him. It twisted and turned around the confined space. It obviously didn't like him.

Well, hell. He didn't like it either.

It moved away when he tried again. Cole was unsure

what to do with the mask-like part on the end of the rope in his hand. He had no clue what it was called. He wondered what he'd do when they realized he couldn't even catch the horse. Then they'd know he lied to them. He was shit. He risked everything for this job and now this horse would be the end of it for him.

Then a laugh came from directly behind him and a female voice said, "You're not like any cowboy I've ever seen."

He'd been caught. Now they knew the truth. He all but wilted in defeat.

But when he turned around to see who spoke to him, he was paralyzed with shock.

There she was.

THE woman. The same woman he held up at gunpoint. The same woman he watched fall like a sack of potatoes on the ground before lying there inert. The same woman he should have gone to prison for hurting. There she stood. *Right there.* Across the barn from him.

Cole was so stunned, he was speechless and couldn't move. He forgot all about the horse.

That fast, the horse aimed a kick at him and down he went.

TALL, dark, and handsome could become a reality. Jade blinked at the hot man she spotted across the stable. He had black hair, so shiny it seemed bluish/black. She liked his chiseled features, as well as those big shoulders and bulging muscles.

Her attraction to ranch hands hadn't waned.

She sighed internally. She'd be the boss someday. So she couldn't sleep with any ranch hand that stole her fancy. That used to be the solution to her sex life.

She had no desire for a boyfriend and detested the idea of dating. She wasn't planning to ever get married or have kids. She spared her parents that disappointment, however, because they didn't know. Having a family hampered her lifestyle. Jade wanted to hike and ride and live her life outside in nature doing fantastic shit. Her job allowed her to do that. And her elevated status as JADE RYDELL, the new supervisor and chief on the ranch, might allow her some nice perks for leadership and whatever. But Jade had no room for men in her life.

Although she did like sex.

Ever so discreetly, Jade always found a willing ranch hand to do it with. Naturally, those ranch hands did not work on her family's ranch but elsewhere. There were plenty of orchards in the area and other cattle ranches that had nothing to do with the Rydells. Jade preferred her liaisons with day workers who never stayed in the area. Surprising how many of those there were. Her rendezvous didn't occur all that often. But sometimes, she needed to scratch the itch.

But she could not engage in sex with a ranch hand who was working for her dad. She had to start getting used to this new reality, and needed to make it work for her. Well, soon. Maybe but not yet. It had to work for her.

Especially when she was eyeing the one her dad kept raving about. To hear him talk, you'd think Ben loved Cole. He acted like Cole was the son he never had. Not really, but her dad was having a bit of a bromance with his new hire.

"He showed up for work on Saturday *and* Sunday. I couldn't believe it. Mucked and raked the stalls and..." Yeah, the brute of a man did everything her dad requested.

"Dad, don't torture him."

"No. Exactly the opposite. I just can't stop appreciating his work ethic."

She rolled her eyes. Her dad sometimes sounded so old.

He pissed and moaned about most of the workers nowadays. *Not being tough enough. Not doing the dirty stuff. Now, in his day…* More eye rolls. Snore. Yes, she knew all about his days, when a ranch hand *worked*. They didn't whine and complain.

To be fair, her dad and family did work harder than most other people because they had to.

But still.

So far, the only sight Jade had of the mythical Cole was when he ran across the whole ranch at full tilt. The image still made her laugh sometimes.

She'd been shadowing Aunt Kailynn for the past month. Ian and Kailynn were actually her dad's aunt and uncle, but Jade considered them hers too. Kailynn did all the accounting and made the business decisions for the entire operation. She'd been doing it for thirty-plus years. She was a priceless source of information.

"Do you know how much they fail to report on their taxes? Right now, there are at least three workers earning wages without any paperwork at all."

Kailynn rolled her eyes. "Yes. Jack was particularly keen to avoid taxes whenever he could. Found a special sort of glee in doing so. But only up to a point. You'll get as tired as I am of reminding them about all the local, state and federal laws on taxes. Good luck with that." She smiled with a conspiratorial wink.

"I'll bet Ian at least listens."

She clicked her tongue on her teeth. "Oh? You'd think. Maybe he's marginally better. He listens all right, but…"

"They're so old school," Jade said with a groan.

"Yep," Kailynn replied as she tilted her head back.

"Are you guys sure about this? Me being the chosen one? What about Landon? Or, well, anyone else?"

Kailynn's grin dimmed. "Landon's not even in the running. We all know that. He can't be trusted." She flinched.

"You know…" She was trying to feel out what the family knew. She heard things from Andi but did they also?

"That he can't hold a job? And he's a flagrant womanizer? Yeah, I know my son. You'd have thought he was the one who'd wind up with the Francine fiasco, not Hunter. But yeah, we're well aware that he's no candidate for succession. He can't run this place. You can and you will, Jade."

She flinched at her aunt's honesty. "Are you okay with that?'

"No, I'm not okay…I'm *thrilled* with it. Jade Rydell. Yeah, it's the perfect solution."

Then Jade went out to the barns to watch her dad work.

And the new guy.

The new guy was pretty hot… but also pretty useless. With horses anyway. He was making the horse spin in circles. Jazzy was one of the most docile, well-trained horses and the big strapping man couldn't control her at all. He swore at Jazzy several times. Jade waited for him to hit, kick or try to hurt Jazzy in retaliation for his own lack of skill, but he didn't.

He just kept trying.

She bit her lip. Shit, he couldn't even hold the halter right.

"You're not like any cowboy I've ever seen."

She obviously startled him from where she stood, leaning casually against the door jamb, watching him with obvious amusement.

He turned, then stared at her with a gaping-mouth. Why did he seem so shocked? Was it just because he saw a woman in the barn? Melanie's presence there wasn't unusual, or was it? Jade encountered many a sexist cowhand. But this one seemed entirely mesmerized by her.

At least, he was until the horse aimed a swift kick in the side of his leg. He went down like an anvil.

Shit. She didn't mean for him to get hurt.

Rushing forward, she grabbed the halter and expertly slipped it over Jazzy's head before quickly leading her outside the stall where she couldn't reach them. Then she dropped down and set a hand on his shoulder. "Are you okay?"

Cole shuddered, but rolled to his feet, kneeling. Then he slowly rose. Shaking his targeted leg, he nodded.

"Are you really?" she asked again. "Please tell me if you need medical help."

"No. I'm fine. I was just surprised by it."

Surprised? Blown away seemed more like it. But was it by the horse's kick? Or the woman in the barn?

He rose up to his full height and Jade saw what a big guy he was. He had half a foot on her. Jade was a tall woman, standing six feet. So was her grandma, Lily. Both her parents were tall so Jade was well-acquainted with all the adjectives: statuesque, athletic, handsome... whatever those are supposed to mean to a girl. She cringed at them. Gangly and tall were just as annoying.

She carried her height and weight very nicely with wide, strong shoulders and shapely arms. She liked to wear her thick, brown hair long.

Cole had pitch black hair, but up close, she saw his green eyes. Like jewels, emeralds, that were fringed in dark lashes and far too pretty to belong to the craggy face that owned them. Whew. He was sizzlin' hot. His sultry gaze stayed with her. He nearly devoured her with his eyes widening as they focused on her.

Why the long staredown? Was it due to being in shock?

Did he accidentally hit his head when he fell and not realize it?

"Are you sure you're okay?"

His gaze lifted to her mouth when she asked him again. He nodded, while licking his lips. Was that because of his nerves? She stopped herself from laughing out loud. He was so big and tough looking. Those kind of guys were a dime a dozen around the valley. She'd seen them come and go over the years and nothing changed about them. Big, tough men who could handle horses, tools, and hard, back-breaking work.

But this guy was biting his lip and staring at her, not checking her out. Not glaring at her either. He seemed filled with anxiety, but why? She wasn't sure.

He was different than the others. And they hadn't even been introduced yet. His gaze fell to where her hand still rested on the sleeve of his flannel shirt, which she temporarily forgot.

"I'm okay," he finally answered after an uncomfortably long pause.

She removed her hand discreetly. "You also don't know jack shit about horses, do you, cowboy?" Crossing her arms over chest, she cocked her head and gave him a long, scathing look.

"No, I don't."

Momentarily startled that he didn't deny it, Jade stuck her tongue in her cheek. Interesting guy. His head hung down. Was it from shame? But why would he tell Ben he knew about horses?

"Why'd you lie to my dad?"

His head shot up, and his mouth dropped open but he remained silent.

She smiled pleasantly. "That's right, I'm Jade Rydell, cowboy. I'm your boss and I'm still reeling from what I just watched. My twelve-year-old nephew could have grabbed that docile horse barefoot and without a rope in about thirty seconds. So what gives?"

Cole's head and hands flew up as if he thought he was under arrest. "I don't have an answer for that. I just wanted to work. Any work. I didn't mean to lie. I mean, I shouldn't have lied. I thought I could learn some things before I had to do them just by watching…"

She snorted. "Obviously not. Let me tell you something, cowboy, there isn't anything easy about horses, let alone, the number of them we deal with. You could have been seriously hurt just now. Who do you think would pay for that? Us. We'd be stuck with the bill, you dumbass. You can't fake horse knowledge. They can kick, bite, trample, and buck you off… especially if you're an idiot."

"I didn't know…"

"Because you don't know the first thing about them?"

"Yes."

"What kind of work do you know how to do?"

His shoulders lumbered forward as his head dropped. "Not too many skills. But I got a strong back and lots of endurance."

Something weird tingled inside her at hearing his words. The woebegone look on his face was fascinating. All slumped forward in total submission to her, yet he was big enough to snap her in half if he chose to. Jade found it kind of hot when he appeared so subservient to her. Respectful. Almost scared even.

She sighed internally. Her damn stupid libido was at it again. Always an eye for the ranch hands. They never failed to draw her attention.

She usually went for big, jacked-up, alpha males with drinking problems. Never for quiet, hardworking, subservient men who didn't drink. At least, that's what her dad said.

She shook her head. "Get the hell out of this barn and away from my horses. I'll deal with you later. Better tell my dad. Maybe he'll find you something else to do, cowboy. Because I don't have any positions open for you. I don't like liars or people who'd risk hurting my horses with their own stupidity."

"Yes, Ms. Rydell. I'm sorry. Right away."

He spun around and scurried away. Running again.

Like he did the first night she saw him after his day's work. Running like a felon.

Okay, she laid it on way too thick. Her dad and grandpa might have to chastise her for that one. She was, maybe, flexing. Yes. Damn it. She sighed out loud this time. She'd been flexing her newfound power and sampling her future stature. Chewing out a big, old cowboy so obviously in awe of her was heady stuff. Sure it was. Yes. Demanding obedience could become addictive.

Crap. She'd been such a jerk. She'd have to apologize.

But she spoke the truth: she didn't like liars and no one could mess with her horses. With *their* horses. Jade felt responsible for all of them. If he'd gotten seriously hurt, it could mean a bad outcome for her horses, although it wasn't the horses' fault. Cole would be at fault for being such a jackass.

But most of all, she detested liars. So there was that.

CHAPTER 9

*E*XITING THE BARN, COLE started to hyperventilate. He paused, and leaned heavily against the barn door.

Jade Rydell.

Jade Rydell was the woman he aimed the gun at when they robbed the place. He never knew her name. He didn't know it, but his dad did. Cole shuddered. That's why his dad decided to do it. He purposely wanted to hurt Erin's granddaughter. He wanted to see her skull smashed with the butt end of a gun so he ordered Everett to do it. Chance stood right there and watched it happen.

Cole saw no redemption for Chance. What he did was cruel and unnecessary. Cole detested his evilness and sadistic nature. But Cole was there too. He was just as responsible for hurting the girl that night. Any person who stood by and allowed a crime to occur in their presence was complicit in that crime.

Black spots appeared behind his eyes and his breathing became labored and heavy. Sucking in gulps of air, Cole squeezed his eyelids shut tightly to ward off the overwhelming anxiety and panic he suddenly began to experience.

He had to end his physical response to seeing her.

She'd ordered him to go tell her dad that he was no good with horses.

Penny was the only reason he went there to get a job. He had to do it for Penny. He had to follow through with his plan because there was no one else and no other plan. He had to continue working for the woman he hurt. He had to face her while hoping nothing about him could remind her of that night.

Maybe somehow, he could make up for it without her knowing he did. If he could find a way to show her he was sorry about it even if she didn't know why.

Yeah. He had to do something about that.

Penny. Penny. Penny. He chanted her name to calm his heart and steady his breathing. He had to get a grip and go on.

He was already high-strung from trying to catch the horse and after getting kicked by it, (and that shit really hurt), he heard the familiar voice of the woman he never thought he'd have to face again. Right there.

Unlike the first time he heard it, when she was so meek and cooperative, this time, she was yelling at him.

She seemed as tough as any cowboy, foreman or boss he'd ever worked for. He had to give her that. Cole was standing still outside the barn for many minutes now, and when he realized that, he suddenly straightened up and started sprinting across the landscape. He ran up the gentle slope where Ben worked on the new structure with his sister.

Breathing heavily from the effort of running uphill, Cole bent over to catch his breath, standing in front of Ben.

Ben and Melanie stopped working to stare at him. Ben sighed and said, "Jade called me and said she overreacted when she chewed you out. But she also mentioned you had something to tell me. So what's going on?"

Cole nodded, gulping the air. Melanie slapped her brother's arm and said, "Quit strong-arming the guy. Take a moment to breathe, Cole. Now you can see where Ben's daughter gets her attitude from."

Cole finally quit panting. "Sorry, sir, but I don't know anything about horses and their care. I lied just to get hired here."

Ben stared at him. "Oh. Should I assume Jade observed you with a horse?"

"Yeah, I was trying to put a ropey thing on it."

"A… ropey thing?"

"A rope that has a bunch of loops or whatever on it. Joey handed it to me and told me to grab Jazzy and saddle her up. I tried to but…"

Ben burst into laughter at hearing that. "Jazzy? You don't mean the twenty-year-old mare that's inside her stall over there?"

Well… maybe he did. "Yes, the horse was still in a stall."

"She's nothing more than a big, gentle baby."

Cole bit his tongue to stop himself from arguing the "big gentle baby" just kicked the shit out of his leg. But he didn't, of course, knowing it was his fault.

"So that ropey thing is called a halter. And you shouldn't go near a horse if you don't know that basic principle."

"I got the message, sir."

"From Jade?"

"Yes, sir. I'm sorry. I'll go now. I realize the danger now. Caring for horses isn't like any other job that you can just observe and learn how to do. I didn't realize how complicated it was."

"You could have just told me. I always need help with lots of other stuff that doesn't involve getting near a horse."

"Or a girl," Melanie interjected.

"Or a woman," Ben amended with a quick glance at Melanie.

She smiled. "Cole, they're not firing you. Quit looking so tragic. They can't afford to fire you. Especially now that they know what you *can* do. So relax. Come with me. I can put you to work for the rest of the afternoon. I got all kinds of heavy shit to move that doesn't involve any big, old horses breathing down your neck or weird rope thingies to put on them."

He knew she was teasing him. She was diverting Ben's anger and turning it into humor. She was actually saving him. Cole smiled inside, glad she was a cousin although she didn't even know it. His heart lifted. She was wonderful. Penny would do so well having her as a guardian.

"Yes, ma'am," Cole replied immediately.

Melanie sighed. "Ma'am? No. Just call me Mel. Jade's very strident and she'll eat you alive if you don't learn how to be a little more assertive."

She already did that. Eat him alive, that is.

But Cole was responsible for her getting a concussion. That meant, in his mind, she could do anything she wanted to him. He owed her something.

The astonishment of seeing Jade in person came to him in aftershocks. He worked with Melanie, lifting anchor bolts and prepping stuff as she instructed him. But Cole's thoughts were still riveted on Jade. Jade Rydell.

Beautiful. Strong. Fierce.

The woman he allowed to be abused, hurt, and assaulted. Right in front of him.

Jade Rydell. At least, he knew her name now.

"What did you say to him? He was all but cowering by the time he reached us. Melanie offered to find something for him to do and basically nurse him along."

"I reamed his ass. He was inside a horse stall without even knowing what a halter was. He got kicked when I distracted him. Thankfully, it wasn't serious, but he could have been hit in the head and knocked flat out. Fucking newbie."

"Jade, as a boss, you might try using a little finesse. You'll find it goes a long way to improve your relationship with the workers."

"You and Grandpa don't use any finesse when it comes to dealing with the horses and who's allowed to be near them. He lied to you and put all of them in danger for his lies. 'Course I reacted negatively. I'm a girl but I don't take any shit. And as the next in line, I don't want to have separate rules that apply only to me."

"Okay. Agreed. But seeing how big and tough this guy, Cole appears, he's pretty subservient. Always eager to please and he obeys every order to the best of his ability. Almost like a superhero the way he launches himself into any project. He went into the stall despite his fear because Joey told him to saddle up Jazzy. I honestly don't think he knew any better. He thought it was the same as me asking him to lift that bale of hay. Even though he'd never done it before, he figured he could."

"You really like him, don't you, Dad?" Jade teased him.

Ben shrugged and all but blushed. "Yeah. Okay? I actually do. He tries very hard. Been a long time since I've had a worker be so ambitious, trying so hard that he put me to shame even. Usually, I'm always prodding the laborers and getting disappointed when they put so little effort into it. This guy? I can't keep up with him. It's hard to keep him busy when he's so fast and capable of accomplishing huge tasks by himself."

"Okay. I'll be nicer to him. I told you I overreacted."

"Maybe a little too much bossiness? Huh, Jade?"

She let out a warm laugh. "A thousand percent. That's what I was doing. I kind of love being the boss."

Ben patted her leg. "At least, now you see it."

"I do. I'll fix it on Monday."

"You can do it tomorrow. He works seven days a week. He'll be here, guaranteed."

"I HEAR you're the next Jack Rydell."

Jade grimaced when Asher Reed's familiar voice came over her phone. The words hit strikingly too close to home. Especially after the mind-game she ran on Cole Pearson. "Very funny. Who told you?"

"My dad. I know it's still a secret. They had a big meeting with all the big brass of Rydell Operations and you were appointed the next king, or should I say *queen*?"

She made a face even though he couldn't see it. "Screw off. He wasn't supposed to say anything."

"I know. I know. It's a big-time secret… but only for a while. Dad had to tell someone. Besides, Charlie and Cami already knew and…"

"Then Daisy got word and on and on it goes. No secrets in this valley."

He coughed. "I doubt anyone with a brain would find your secret too salacious. Most would just, you know, assume you were the rightful heir to the fortune anyway."

"Shut up. And nothing's happening for a while."

"Right."

He shuffled around on the other end. "But in all seriousness, you have my congratulations, Jade. You deserve this honor." His tone was deep and sincere.

She smiled to herself. "Thank you, Asher. I appreciate that."

"And honestly? You'll be better at it than any man, I bet."

"And there it is. The chauvinistic pig emerges from his retreat. Does Daisy know?" She ground her teeth together.

He laughed out loud. "If she heard me, she'd squeeze the tiny balls I still have to a pulp. I'm kidding, of course. Truly, you're by far the best choice."

She snorted. "Long live nepotism, huh? Being handed the keys to the kingdom. It feels odd still and weird. I want it though. It just makes me feel—"

"Guilty? Undeserving? Amid so many who missed out getting this massively lucrative kingdom, as you say? I get it. That's why I called you. One ranch king giving advice to the next successor."

She knew he was teasing but she was serious. "What advice do you have for me?"

"The amount of paperwork will bury you. Don't be intimidated though. It's pretty ridiculous. I often wish for a whole day spent in the saddle."

"That sounds perfectly horrible."

"People will also seek you out to complain and vent on. Get used to their bitching. Lots of unhappy workers, vendors, hell, even the people supplying the vendors get pissed at ya. Yep, you're the boss now; the master of the kingdom and everyone's favorite scapegoat at the whipping post."

"And you think I should still do this?"

"Of course, you should." His tone grew serious. "You're calm and knowledgeable. And you listen. You're already a leader at heart so you're naturally the choice because there's no one else in the competition."

She was touched by his kind words. "Do you mean that? Or haven't you dropped the punchline yet?"

"I mean it."

She waited and he added, "I couldn't be considered because, you know, Reed Ranch is my bailiwick but…"

"I would literally sock you right in the gut if you were standing before me now."

"That would not be the action of a leader or even very ladylike."

"This lady will seriously hurt you if you don't stop acting like a chauvinist pig."

"Does this lady think she can outdo me?"

"What? What do you mean?"

"Friendly wager. Boys against girls."

She rolled her eyes. "No one does that shit anymore."

"Ah, dear cousin or whatever you are to me—"

"We aren't blood-related."

He scoffed. "We are too. Uncle Charlie's your uncle too, right?"

"Well, yes."

"Unless you discount me as a family member because of my tragic adoption."

She groaned. "You were setting me up. Of course, you're family. So, what are you proposing?"

"Whoever earns the most money exclusively from the income on their ranches in a year wins the contest."

Holding the phone away from her ear, she gaped at it. Then she slowly brought it back to listen. "Hello?" said Asher. "Did you almost hang up?"

"No. I was speechless. You're betting that your profits from the Reed Ranches will exceed those of the Rydell River Ranch and Resort?"

"Yep. The men represent Reed Ranches all the way."

"I'm going to tell Daisy."

He sucked in a breath. "You wouldn't dare. If you do, there's no bet or competition."

"I'm not participating in the competition. Besides, it's not fair. Like comparing apples to oranges. And I don't even run this place yet..."

"Cattle are much more profitable than horses. The upkeep alone for horses proves that. You know it and you just admitted Reed Ranches are mightier than the old Rydell River Ranch and their tired horses."

"You little prick. Your cattle are not better. They're just bigger and smellier. We've been in the horse business for forty years and you've been raising cattle for what? Maybe two years. We have a brand name. We have a loyal following up and down the west coast, not only for our foals and training, but everything else in horsemanship. You can't compete with all the Rydell operations."

He chuckled. "Then, it's a bet?"

She realized he'd goaded her straight into it. Pride cometh before the fall, she well knew, and here she was. "If you promise not to tell anyone I bet against AJ. Or any of the other Reeds."

"You're on. No one will know. Just a friendly bet between cousins. Two ranchers. Two entrepreneurs. Kingdom rulers. Reed and Rydell. Friends, sure. Right? Just a small bet between friends."

She let out a long laugh. "Yeah. Sure. But..."

"Yeah, but..."

"I must insist we get Mack, Justin and Tyrone back. Or, failing that, at least one of them has to come back. It wasn't fair that your dad stole them from my grandpa."

"Nope. Jack gave them to us fair and square."

"AJ was sad at the time so Jack had to do something."

"Jack did *not* have to. Besides they're way happier to run their very own ranches than be part of the labor force working on just one. For you guys."

"But you left us without any decent foremen. It'll take several years to make up for the loss of all three of them."

"Are those violins I hear playing? Maybe you'd better man up, little cousin." He snickered to himself.

"Oh, my crap, Daisy will kill you someday."

"Hope so. And I hope it's all in our bed."

Jade scoffed as she also laughed. "You know, you can use Isaac and Ethan for jobs. My dad decided they have to go Reed."

"Luckier for it."

"Our families are so ridiculous."

"Yep. Totally. And when you need an ear to vent about it? I'm right here. 'Kay? All bullshitting aside. That's why I called you. It's tough shit and not many will be too sympathetic, considering the nepotism and opportunity you're being handed. But they also don't understand how hard it is. How isolating it can be. Not to mention, so damn exhausting and difficult. Again… don't slack on the paperwork…"

She squeezed the phone. "Thank you. I guess I was due for some annoyance and a pep talk."

"We all need those at some point."

CHAPTER 10

"SO I OWE YOU a small retraction, huh?"

Cole glanced up when Jade Rydell came strolling up to him, speaking before he'd even noticed she was there.

Retraction? Cole was ready to ask her if that were as much of an apology as this proud, fierce woman could make in her attempt to admit she was wrong? But he'd never talk back to her. He'd take anything she needed to say or doled out his way.

"No, Ms. Rydell. I lied and failed to see the danger I was putting myself and the horse in. I appreciated your lecture."

She stopped a few feet away from him. He stared at her for a second and averted his eyes. No. He couldn't dare make eye contact. She had such warm, bright, vivacious eyes. Full of vim and verve, all kinds of know-how and guts. Meanwhile, what was he? A yellow-bellied coward who allowed his old, decrepit father to have her knocked out with the butt of a gun. No, Cole owed *her;* she could never owe anything to him.

Maybe someday after Penny was safely in a better

arrangement, he could atone for what he did. Let her know he was one of the perps that night and take his penance.

She sighed and said, "Damn it, cowboy. You're supposed to glare at me and say something rude, or contrary, or sexist so I don't have to make the retraction."

He blinked. "Sorry, what?"

She grinned. He didn't mean to look right at her face but he did for a moment and his entire insides brightened with joy. Wow. Her smile was wide and engaging; it made him want to grin back. "Dad was right about you. I don't need to use a heavy hand all the time. Being an asshole is not how I want to be. You got the message loud and clear, and without my lecture."

"What did you mean by the other thing you said?" He tilted his head to keep looking at her until he remembered the night he attacked her again. He flushed and quickly turned his head away.

"Because big, buff ranch hands are a dime a dozen. Most of 'em are transients, passing through on the way to their next gig and most of 'em are full of themselves. Some of 'em even argue and swear right to us rather than admit they're wrong or they made a mistake. Add in a reprimand *from a woman* and they blow up for no reason at all." Her shoulders bobbed up and down. "Well, I've been treated differently as a woman in this business, and it happens too often to count. In response, I default to my alter ego, one that must be taken seriously and most of all, heard and listened to. But you aren't like those types and you don't need that kind of treatment. So I'm offering you my retraction, or half of it anyway." She grinned cheekily. "The other half is on you for being so stupid as to lie on the first day."

He would have laughed if anyone else said that to him. But how could he kid around with this woman, the human being he was indirectly responsible for harming? And all for the most selfish and terrible reason. To rob her. To take her money from her. For the sake of money. And the sin of greed.

"I can't imagine mistaking you as someone without authority." He glanced at her and then away.

Her head tilted, and her hair slid down over her elbow. "That's a refreshing way to put it. I'm glad to hear you think that but—" she shrugged again, "lots of men don't. Sexism is still very much alive and well with those types."

"Yeah. Lots of men are still scared of what women can do."

She smirked. "True." She tilted her head. "So what's the real horse situation? Are you afraid or just inexperienced with them?"

"I'm fully terrified." He shrugged. "To be honest? I didn't know I was before. That's because I'd never been that close to one. So I guess I'm inexperienced *and* terrified. Thought they were fine from afar. But up close? No. Nope. That's an entirely adrenaline-pumping experience."

"Lord. I guess the only urban cowboy in town must've found us, huh?"

He gave her a little grin. "Yeah. That's one way of describing me."

"Okay, there's plenty for you to do without ever going near the horses. But some time, it might be worth your while to get used to being around them. The longer you work here, the more you'll have to see and take care of them. Riding horses is kinda the schtick for a cowboy." She gave him wink.

"I'm not really a cowboy, Ms. Rydell. I just wanted to work at the place that paid the best wages in the valley."

"You could have just led with that, you know. No one would fault you for wanting to make a good living."

"I clearly realized that about the same time I caught Jazzy's hoof in my side."

She crossed her arms over her chest. "You bruised up pretty badly?"

"I suppose so."

"If you went down when the horse tagged you, she must've gotten you pretty good. And you lied *again* about it." Her voice trailed off.

Clearing his throat, Cole rose fully upright from where he'd been kneeling. He was trying to scrape off something hard and crusty he found embedded in one of the stalls of the many horses. "That's because my boss was standing there and I'd already lied once."

"What if you were actually hurt much worse than you first realized?"

"I wasn't though. I'd have spoken up if I were."

One of her boots tapped the floor. "Got an answer for everything, huh, cowboy?"

"Shouldn't I?" he snapped back before he realized whom he was talking to. "Ms. Rydell," he softly added.

She looked up. "No one uses Mr. or Mrs. around here."

"I do," Cole replied firmly.

Her shoulders shrugged. "Okay, cowboy. Have it your way. But there'll be no more lying about your skills or getting hurt or covering for your shortcomings. Come out with the truth and we'll deal with it together. Got it?"

He liked the way she chastised him, since he was wrong and deserved it, but she didn't yell at him when she spoke. That made it easy for him to respond to her authority and reparation without taking it personally. "Yes. Got it. But—"

"But?"

"Never having to deal with the horses suits me fine. I don't really need to be a cowboy, if you don't need another one on the ranch."

She smirked as she pushed off the half wall she'd been leaning against. "Oh, cowboy, we always need more. There's about to be another big exodus from here before we have to train a new generation of ranch hands to run this place. So horses will definitely be in your future if you decide to stay on here."

"What do you mean by *exodus?*" Cole asked. He needed more information. He wanted so much more than what he could glean from overheard conversations and the other workers. Most of the workers couldn't care less about the Rydell family dynamics, none had the undying interest that he did. He had to restrain the urge to grab whomever he talked to and shake as much information as he could out of them to satisfy his need for more.

She stepped closer. "Jack Rydell was the original owner of this place long before it expanded into all you see today. He's now in his late seventies and confines himself to the River Rescue. He'll probably do that until he takes his last breath. He had cancer last year, which threw everyone into a tailspin. My dad, along with my aunt and uncles who run this place, and have for decades, are getting ready to retire. I think they all kept working because it's a way of life more than a job. The original foreman here started his own business, Reed Ranch Enterprises, which my grandfather endorsed and even shared some of our younger employees with. There are a couple of cousins and friends who are long time ranch workers here too, like for the past four decades, and they're also getting ready to retire. Things are kind of coming to a head now. It's not happening tomorrow, but probably within the next year."

"Pedro?" Cole met him as the current foreman. He was a tough, exacting man that Cole easily responded to. His clear-cut directions and expectations of what he wanted out of whomever he spoke to made Cole's job easier.

"Yeah. He and Jordan want to retire as well. Caleb, Jordan's brother retired recently. It's time to bring in some new blood." She started to step away. "Learn how to handle a damn horse, Cole Pearson and you won't have to lie in order to get good wages again. Start here, and don't be surprised if it turns into a lifelong endeavor. We're loyal to our workers and we must be pretty decent to work for because most of our workers reciprocate in their loyalty back to us."

Saying that, she sauntered away. Cole's heart was beating hard in his chest with a new sense of longing. Anticipation. Stay here? Loyalty is reciprocated? Work at a permanent position. It was the dream of a lifetime.

But he lied and cheated to get hired here. He had to continue doing that. He let one of the main honchos of the Rydell family get injured in front of him. He couldn't last long here.

So he had no reason to learn how to handle horses. Ever. Even if it seemed like the best dream come true for a fleeting moment.

Back to scraping something questionable off the stable floor.

~

"Hello, am I speaking to Chance Poletti?" The crisp woman's voice on the other end of the phone line made Cole stiffen, and the broom he was using to clean one of the massive concrete slabs was promptly forgotten.

His stomach twisting, he knew it couldn't be good news. Whoever called his cell number believing that Chance would answer meant it could only be bad news. Shit. *Penny.*

"Yes, this is he."

"Penny was caught fighting. Is there any way you can come to the school right now?"

His shoulders slumped. Damn it. Of course she was fighting. Just like three times last year, when the real Chance took the call and drove down to take her home. He acted contrite to the school administration while fist-bumping Penny behind their backs. One of the times, he even bought her an ice cream to celebrate her victory. Usually though, he never bought her anything.

"I'll be there in half an hour." Sticking the phone in his pants pocket, he scanned the landscape for any movement. There. Shit.

He ran towards the figure he saw ducking into the barn. Jade. "Excuse me," he called after her. "Ms. Rydell?"

She whipped around as a small smile came to her lips. "What's the emergency?"

"Family thing. Can I go? I'll get back as soon as I can and work late tonight. I swear."

Her head tilted. "Sure. Of course, you can. I was just kidding because you were running. Again. But go right ahead. You don't have to come back tonight. Things happen. Plus, I don't think you've taken even an hour off in a whole month."

He flashed a smile. "Thank you, ma'am."

She waved her hand. He turned and yes… ran again. That seemed to amuse her. Why?

But when he tried to start the truck, the old rust bucket wouldn't turn over. Probably the starter dying out. He knew how to fix it but he couldn't do it in the snap of two fingers.

Penny.

Shit. His whole life revolved around Penny. He sighed as he ran towards the horse stable. Ben was there, Jade had also shown up and Melanie was working on the foundation.

"Everything okay?" Ben asked when Cole stopped dead in his tracks. Tongue-tied, he wondered what to do? Ask to borrow a vehicle? He glanced towards the arena and noticed a few work trucks parked nearby, newer models than his, of course. No one had any reason to trust him. They had nothing on him and he could disappear without a trace. Why should they trust him?

But he had to pick up Penny.

"My truck won't start. Needs a new starter. But I have to be somewhere soon…"

"Here." Ben dug into his pocket as Cole spoke before tossing a set of keys to him. "Take my truck. It's parked alongside the arena. Rydell River Ranch logo on the side of it."

"I can't drive your truck."

"It belongs to the ranch. It's a work truck. You work here. It's fine. Go."

He gaped at Ben, then at Jade. "Just… I… how do you know I'll come back?"

Ben's lips twisted. "Because you're asking me how I know. Besides, how far can you get with that distinct logo emblazoned on the side?"

"But what if I…"

"Quit trying to change my mind and go. Take care of your family thing."

Cole gulped at the kindness and decency of the gesture. They didn't even ask what the emergency was. How serious it might be or anything else. They just accepted what he said. Whatever he had to do was his business and they didn't ask any questions or need to know if they deemed it worthy of this favor.

A large lump lodged in his throat. How many people ever did him a favor? None. He nodded solemnly and said, "I'll be careful. Thank you. I hate to bother you about it but—"

But he had to get Penny.

"Go on. Run down there. You know you're dying to." Jade said but her words softened with a smile. She always had a smile of amusement towards his penchant for running, one that he didn't think he deserved.

They didn't even ask if he had auto insurance. What if he wrecked their truck? But Penny was the most important factor now. He had to risk it. He smiled, turned and ran. Fast.

The truck was nothing less than magnificent to Cole. Leather seats, a working radio, smooth, purring engine and working shock absorbers. It slid down the road like it was on silk.

There were three more days of school left before it let out for summer. Why couldn't Penny manage to suppress the urge to throw a punch at someone for another three days? She knew how much was at stake. Then again, she was only twelve and had been jacked around all her life. She'd also been relegated to sitting alone in a park for hours on end, and well into the evening way too often. She'd been cursed, blamed, neglected, starved, unwashed, and uncared for amongst other terrible things and scary people all her young life.

Naturally, she didn't always make good decisions.

He parked the truck and sprinted across the playground to the school office. He kept the cheap pair of sunglasses on and wished he had a hat. Hopefully, no one would look too carefully at him or be surprised by how young Penny's "father" was.

His heart pounded in his chest. There she was, so small and tiny, Penny was sitting in a chair in the principal's office, her head bent down. Her little legs were still too short for her feet to reach the linoleum floor.

Cole addressed the man outside the office at a desk. "I'm here for Penny Poletti."

The man nodded. "You may go in."

Penny's head lifted when the door clicked. Her face blossomed with hope and then shame when she met Cole's gaze. He gave her *the look*. Not a fatherly look of anger and disappointment, but more like a "little buddy, what'd you do to us?" expression.

"I'm sorry, but my father's tied up at work. I'm Penny's older brother, Cole. Can you tell me what happened?"

The woman rose to her feet, coming forward as Cole did the same. Their hands met in a casual shake before the woman nodded and, with a tightly drawn face, she said, "A teacher heard some kind of altercation. She saw Penny on top of another girl, hitting her, and pulling her hair. The other girl wasn't doing anything but defending herself and trying to block the assault."

Assault? They were twelve years old. He side-eyed Penny.

"She was too doing something. She said... she said terrible things to me." Penny exclaimed.

"Is she okay?" Cole interrupted, ignoring his sister's outburst. "The other little girl, I mean?"

The principal nodded. "She's a bit scratched up. But yes. Mostly okay. However, this can't go on, Mr. Poletti."

"No. Of course not."

"There are only three days left of school, and normally, three days of suspension would be my disciplinary action. But I think that's a terrible way for Penny to end the school year."

"Yes. Indeed, I fully agree," Cole nodded, his hand over his mouth as he pretended to fully and seriously consider this woman's opinions and synopsis. Oh, sure, like this would be the worst way for Penny to end her school year? At least, this time Penny controlled the situation and fought back. But Cole had to continue to play the game. So he played down his true response and gave the principal his attention. "I think she needs to be taught a lesson. Whatever you think is fair."

"How about summer school? Penny is quite far behind

the other children. I looked into her testing results and I'm afraid she's behind grade level."

He saw Penny's little fisted hands turning white. Shooting a sharp look at her, he telepathically begged her not to jump up and announce how stupid the school was for not being able to teach her. She was below grade level because no one ever bothered to teach her the material. Cole blamed the faculty for doing a subpar job, not Penny. Her mouth opened and Cole gave her a wide-eyed stare, all but falling to his knees. *Please, Penny. Don't.*

She pursed her lips and looked out the window. "Do they offer summer school to children this young?" asked Cole.

"The belief in holding kids back a grade is no longer popular. Not sure I always agree with it, but that's the new standard. We don't have funding for it this summer. But she would benefit from some helps. Maybe she could find someone to help her comprehend the material? A tutor perhaps?"

There was no extra cash lying around for that. Cole wondered if this conversation had anything to do with Penny's poor behavior.

He threw up his hands. Being honest he said, "I'm afraid there's no money for that."

"Ah, of course. I could ask around."

"I appreciate it. But what about the fight?"

The woman sighed, biting her lip. "Two-day suspension. Penny can come back for the last day of school."

His shoulders dropped and he grew quiet now. In his most sincere voice, Cole said, "Thank you. Really. Thank you. The move here has been tough on her. We'll talk to her and suggest other ways to work things out without reacting in such a negative manner."

"Please do that, Mr. Poletti. Your dad will need to sign the form I send back with you…"

Sure. Fake daddy Chance will sign it. He nodded and finished all the usual banalities of light conversation.

Only when they were both seated in the Rydell truck did Cole finally look at her. Penny gaped at the truck. "Wow. Look at this fancy shit."

He gnashed his teeth. "Not now, Pen. Can't you even talk like a normal little girl? Maybe just try for once? Or pretend you're contrite after being caught in the act? Can't you just be... sorry for your action?"

She crossed her arms over her chest. "I'm not sorry though. Why should I pretend to be?"

He sighed wearily, pressing his hand on the bridge of his nose. "Then answer this: what was so infuriating to make you attack a girl and make me risk losing my job, and us being found out and having to live with Chance again? Huh? What could have possibly been worth all that?"

Her mouth opened into an O and her bottom lip started to tremble. "I—I didn't think of that. Or anything like that happening." Big tears rolled down her cheeks.

Cole's entire demeanor crumbled and he hated himself for talking to her that way. She was a little girl who got mad and reacted the only way she knew how. The entire world should not always rest on her weary, narrow shoulders.

"Hey, Penny, I'm sorry. I just got freaked out. It's okay. Everything will work out."

"What about the truck?"

"I'll take you home and drive back to the ranch."

"Can I come too?"

"No. We need to lay low still. The less people who know us the better. More people mean more chances for them to ask questions."

"I know. I just don't wanna be alone again."

She was so often on her own. "I don't want you to be alone either. But it's best if I take this truck back. They loaned it to me with no guarantee or reason to believe I'd bring it back."

"But you will."

He sighed. "Sure... *this* time. But if we had to suddenly escape to keep you safe, I'd take it in a heartbeat. So I'm not that great of a person."

"Dad made us this way." She stared forward, folding her arms dramatically over her chest.

He smiled. "Yeah, Dad didn't make things very easy for us."

She side-eyed him. "It'll get better. We'll make it better and we can be like those good people. I won't fight again. I just get so mad sometimes that it bubbles out of me before I can stop it."

No freaking kidding. She was too young and innocent to rise to that level of anger. He kept that reality to himself. "Someday, Penny. I'll show you the ranch and introduce you to the people who live and work there. I swear I will."

And you can meet your cousin, and your aunt and maybe someone who can help you channel your anger in better ways. Ways Cole didn't know about. "But today, I have to go back to work."

"Yes, okay."

She nodded and fell quiet. Finally, when he pulled next to the RV, she slid across the seat, opened the door and looked back at him one last time. "I'm sorry I put us at so much risk today. I'll be more careful, you'll see."

Shit. She was just a kid carrying so much guilt. "No harm, no foul. It's okay, Penny."

"It wasn't. But I swear I can do better."

Then she sprinted inside the horrible box on wheels Cole provided to serve as her pathetic home. She made herself a PB and J for lunch or snacks or dinner because they still didn't have a refrigerator. Cole didn't know when she last ate.

Cringing at the gas gauge, Cole refilled the truck and drove back to the ranch. Finding only Jade in the arena, he quickly approached her. "Here are the keys to the truck. Thank you again, for the loan of the vehicle."

She flipped around and caught the keys he tossed her way. Tilting her head, she asked, "Everything okay?"

"Yeah, just some personal business I had to take care of."

"I was referring to your truck."

"Oh." The sensation of heat creeped into his face. "Uh. No, I think it's the starter. I'll need to get some parts."

She looked at him more closely. "Hey, cowboy, how do you intend to do that? I mean, first you have to find the parts somewhere out here and then you have to fix it?" She tossed the keys back his way. "Keep the truck until you find all the parts you need. You're allowed to use that one until you get it all straightened out."

He nearly bowed under the weight of her trust in him. What the hell were they thinking? How could they trust a guy with their twenty-thousand-dollar-or-more truck, when they didn't even have his real name on file? He gave them no address so they had no way to find him if he decided to take off with it.

"It'll only take a day. I'll start right now."

"Take two days off. Just come back with our truck."

He started to flip around when he stopped dead and kept his back to her. "Why?"

She held a clipboard in her hands. Cole had no idea what she'd been doing. Taking inventory or something? She was scanning the tack room and shoved the board against her chest. "Why what, cowboy?"

"Why would you trust me?"

"Why shouldn't I?" she countered. "Any reason not to?"

"You realize Ben hired me as a day worker? I get paid in cash."

"Cash that you seem to appreciate. You'll have to come back here to get more of it."

"Keep my wages until I return the truck. At least, then you'll have some leverage."

She gave him a half smile. "That's not a bad idea. But I find it interesting that you feel the need for me to have some sort of collateral."

"You shouldn't trust people so easily, that's all I'm saying." His tone sounded grumpy now. The growing trust and kindness made him remorseful about lying and cheating, but most of all, being present when she got hit on the head.

Her smirk lifted higher. "Maybe you should learn how to trust them more. Take the truck."

"Thank you, Ms. Rydell. The kindness extended to me by you and your family never goes unnoticed."

Her smirk slowly dissipated. "I knew that somehow with you. That's why I didn't hesitate."

She should have though. He wondered how to convince her that she should better protect herself, her family and her assets.

But right now he needed the truck. He'd considered a bus and hiking up to the motor home but that would take hours in the darkness. And as always… Penny came first.

So he drove the truck into town and found the parts he believed he'd need. He had to spend cash he really didn't have but getting his truck running again was crucial.

Returning to the ranch, he brought out the used starter he found at the junk yard. Using his lunch hour, he tackled the fix. He was halfway into it, and under the truck when he heard footsteps approaching him.

Peeking out, he recognized Jade's cowboy boots. "You know, we have an entire mechanic shop. Right here. Rydell

Rides. My cousin, Iris runs it. I'm sure she can help you. Or at least put it on the lift."

He shut his eyes and wondered. They had a mechanic's shop right there? How did he miss that?

Scooting out from under the vehicle, he sat up, resting his elbows on his knees.

"A lift? Right here?"

"Yes. It's over there." She pointed to a cluster of outbuildings. He didn't even know which one she meant.

"You know that's…"

"Creepy? Strange? More fodder for the Rydell cult?" She flashed a smile. "That's what my brother-in-law thought when he first came here with my sister. He was pretty sure there was some weird shit going on and feared we might keep him somewhere on the compound against his will."

"I could see how those thoughts started."

"Really. Do you want to tow it to the shop? Iris will come down and get it for you."

"I—I shouldn't waste the cash."

Jade kneeled before him. Leaning close, he jerked back when her hand moved towards him. She lifted her hand showing the dead pine needle she pulled from his hair. "Might be more comfortable without that. She won't charge you. Again, have some trust."

Trust. That word again. They were always offering it to him. Nodding, he slipped his foot underneath him and sprang upwards as Jade rose also, but she was slower. Standing face to face she nodded. "You seem surprised each time I tell you something."

"I am. Not much of anything where I come from."

"Really? Which is where?"

"Literally everywhere."

"Military family?"

He looked far over her shoulder. "No."

Silence followed his terse answer. Then she said, "Okay, well, let's go talk to Iris."

Iris was standing beside a large, old van when they entered the brightly lit, domed, three-bay mechanic shop. It had shiny tools, three car lifts and endless tools that nearly made Cole salivate when he thought of having access to them.

"Yo, Iris." Jade called over the empty space. There were two other guys working at their own work stations.

Iris turned around, a woman with short, black hair, striking eyes, and a quick smile. She fist-bumped Jade when they got close enough. "Jade. Long time no see you in here."

"How's Irene?" Jade asked as she glanced at Cole. "Iris just had a baby a few months ago."

Iris's smile was huge. "She's a lot of work. Makes this all look like a sweet nap. But... everything's great."

It seemed for years that Iris, who'd long been married to her stupid-rich husband, Quinn Larkin did not want any kids. It surprised everyone when she popped up pregnant last year.

"So what's up?" Iris flipped her gaze at Cole.

"His truck died out in the arena south parking lot. Could he get it hauled in here and finish his repairs?"

She eyed him over. "You know how to fix it?"

"I've always had to make things work. Not a lot of resources, so yeah. Besides, I'm pretty sure it's just the starter."

Iris nodded. Jade rolled her eyes. "Once more, new language speak. I'll leave you guys to it. I got some fun horses to mess with." She made a face at the tools behind Iris.

Iris grimaced back. "I'll haul it over here and throw it up on the lift. I got some extra time. Can help you if you don't mind."

"I don't mind." What would she charge?

"She means for fun. She's not charging you. Iris comes in here basically for fun. It's her hobby. Her passion and joy. She's on maternity leave right now. And here she is. So don't feel guilty 'cause you're not putting her out. She breathes this shit like air."

He eyed Jade. It was like she could read his mind. Her words let his conscience and ego relax. But how did she know?

Iris had a husky laugh. "I'm on maternity leave. Irene is sleeping and Quinn is right there, and… hell yes, this shit is super fun." She rubbed her hands together. "Come on, cowboy let's go see what you got here."

He groaned, casting a glare at Jade. Why did this person, who was totally unrelated to the horse operations, and whom he'd never laid eyes on before use Jade's nickname for him?

Jade threw her hands up when she noticed his evil-eye. "Iris calls all the ranch hands *cowboy*. It wasn't from me I swear. She detests anything to do with the horses and makes fun of us horse people. So…" She grinned before flipping around and scurrying away.

Iris laughed at Jade's retreating figure. "True that." She gave him along look. "Were you offended by me calling you cowboy? I mean, most guys ignore it and don't even realize I said it. I don't mean it as an insult."

"It's only an insult from her." He waved toward Jade's figure. "I lied to get on here and said I was good with horses but I'd never been near one. She saw me when I couldn't grab what was apparently their calmest, oldest, all but comatose horse, and it kicked me. Since then, she decided to—"

"Endlessly rib you? Yeah, that's our Jade. And know this too, if she bothers to rib you, consider it a compliment. That means she likes you. She won't bother with people she finds dull, boring, rude, distrustful and so on. If you lied to get hired and she still gives you shit over it, count it as a win," Iris said as she flashed him an impish grin, adding, "cowboy."

She was impossible not to respond to. But the distinct pounding of his heart after getting Jade's ribbing was... what? A sign of his affection for her?

And how did that make him feel? He liked it but maybe way too much.

"So what should I call you?"

He snapped back to the present when Iris's voice interrupted his fantasizing about Jade. "Oh, uh, sorry. Cole. Cole Pearson." He put his hand out.

Iris took it and gave him a strong handshake back. Then she rubbed her hands together. "Okay, let's go get the flatbed and see what you got."

She was quick, efficient and a bottomless well of knowledge. There wasn't anything she didn't seem to know how to do, wrangle, or fix. His ancient truck was no more to him than an ugly rust-bucket next to all the newer vehicles on the ranch, but Iris snorted with joy when she saw it. "Ah, damn, haven't worked on something like this in a long while. Love the old shit. No stupid computers or sensors. Just old school bones and parts working together the way they were designed to and should."

Iris seemed to love spending two hours to help him figure out how to rebuild the starter from the junk yard and make it work. She didn't offer up any new expensive part that would have made it far easier. She just helped him get the used part in.

An hour into it, he glanced at the clock. "I have to get back to work."

"Nah. I let Jade know we almost had it fixed. She said to go ahead and finish."

"I'll work late then."

Iris paused, wrenching the block. "You like the ranch work?"

"I like any sort of work."

"Why do you know so much about this stuff?" she waved toward the vehicle.

"I always had to keep our family's vehicle running. Just kind of learned it."

"Hands on?"

"Yes." He bit his tongue to keep from saying it was the only learning he had.

"Your outstanding work reputation precedes you. If you ever get sick of the smell of horse shit and Jade bossing you around, give me a shout. I can give orders with the best of them but my work is hella more fun." She grinned and it was huge. Almost sighing with pleasure, Cole eyed the wreck of his truck they were about to test start. If she liked what he did with this, she'd have an orgasm over how he jerry-rigged the old motor home and got it to run. He was a proud that he managed to get that shit-bucket back on the road. But there was no one else to appreciate his genius fixes. He found it slightly disconcerting that she knew about him before this day.

Iris's veiled job offer totally floored him. Staring open-mouthed at her, he waited until she finally glanced up and asked, "What?"

"No one's offered me a job before."

"Well, then no one's ever seen you work your magic using only a wrench on a piece of shit metal junk heap."

How he'd love to work there. Glancing around, it almost made him forget his troubles. But Iris's shop wasn't where Erin Rydell hung out. And he couldn't interact with his cousin, Melanie there. He needed to take care of Penny first. The whole purpose of his job there was to find Penny a connection and a new home. Cole's biggest fear was when the day arrived that his past and his sins caught up with him. He needed to be ready for the consequences.

"But Jade will have my ass."

"Why? Why would Ms. Rydell mind?"

Iris flashed a wink and grin. "Who do you think told me about you? Nobody stands on ceremony around here. Jade runs the grapevine."

A jolt traveled through him. It was a stretch for Cole to imagine Jade mentioning him with so much positivity.

Iris let out a laugh. "Well, I see Jade has some interest in keeping you. Put my little seed somewhere in your mind and we'll see if it grows. If things change, come see me."

His heart was ready to explode. All these unsolicited compliments flummoxed him. Never the reality he could even imagine. "I'll definitely keep that in mind, Mrs. Larkin."

"No. I'm Iris. You call me that again and I'll throw this wrench at you."

He flashed a grin back. "Okay, Iris. Ms. Rydell doesn't protest like that."

Iris snickered. "That's because my dear cousin, Jade gets off on you, the big, hulking tough guy deferring to her. She won't admit it but that girl thrives on power. Now fire this sucker up and let's see what she'll do."

Cole turned the key in the ignition and it started up with a hum and a clarity of purpose he hadn't heard in years. They'd not only fixed it but improved it too. "Damn."

Iris nodded. "Damn." They shared a fist-bump and Cole liked the sense of congeniality he shared with a near stranger.

He pulled his truck back into the parking spot and trotted over to the arena. This time, he searched for Ben, Pedro or Jade for his next list of tasks. *Jade*. The things Iris said made him smile. She had Jade nailed. The women did enjoy bossing around the guys. He'd witnessed Jade telling them what to do and telling them off if they grumbled or complained at her.

He also liked Jade. Stopping dead, he frowned. What did it matter if he liked her or not? Or Ben? Or any of them? He was literally the monster from the dark, especially for Jade. He'd become the source of pain and triggers she might suffer in the future. He was evil. And he was here again, using her. Using them. No matter what, he could never downplay his role as the monster in the dark for them.

Cole was no ordinary worker, and he was thrilled to know they liked his performance, and him. Hearing that Jade was singing all his attributes to others at the ranch didn't matter to him. The only thing that did matter was Penny. She was the reason for his moral compass.

CHAPTER 11

THE NEXT MONTH WAS SPENT bickering and sharing work, amidst bursts of trying to show Cole Pearson that people could be nice. And he didn't have to grovel for it either. Jade witnessed his general unease with the most… what could she call it? *neighborly* of actions. Literally, that was all they'd done for the man. They provided for a few of his needs like any good neighbor would.

But seeing Cole's incessant politeness and the way he got so churlish when he was offered any help was something Jade liked to tease him about. That and knowing he couldn't handle a horse yet. Or stand to be near one. The jeering at him didn't come exclusively from her, but from several other ranch hands they currently employed.

In all honesty, Jade wanted Cole to learn about the horses and become more comfortable with them. His work ethic was unparalleled and he never refused a task assigned to him. No job was too big, too grunt-like, or too distasteful for him. Cole simply didn't comment or complain. He worked through most of the meal hours. Usually, he took his meals home with him and often was the last to leave. He showed up like clockwork, at the exact same time every single day. Taking his cash at the end of the workday, Cole never forgot to say a humble thank you.

It was Jade's job to pay him so each day he looked for her before he left. She was always the first to see Cole, and the last to see him.

Oddly enough, Jade found herself always looking forward to it. She counted on their little, private interactions that usually lasted only a few minutes. There were lots of teasing and suggestive looks and just… fun. So much fun. Learning her dad's job was exhausting for Jade. Not only because of all the physical work he accomplished every day but also the paperwork and things he did behind the scenes. Ordering supplies and feed for the immense volume of horses housed on the ranch was an ordeal in itself. They couldn't begin to grow all the different kinds of food the horses required. Then there was the veterinary care, both standard and emergency. An entirely different budget was dedicated to the needs and maintenance of the River Rescue horses.

"If not for the resort, we'd run into the red every month," Jade noticed one afternoon when Kailynn was giving her an overview of everything.

"Yes. Exactly. Ian's expansion is what saved this place. They would have ended up having to sell off sizable chunks of land just to keep the core of it, a much smaller version, working. Yeah, it takes tourism and merchandising nowadays to keep the original idea afloat."

She blinked. Sometimes the cost of buying so much poundage of feed and supplies not to mention, miscellaneous expenses, was extraordinary.

Kailynn patted her hand. "Wait until you spend some time with Joey and Hailey. You'd be amazed by the numbers they run at the resort. Or Violet and Finn at the horse rescue. Or Pedro's budget for the orchards."

There was also the huge, commercial arena. It was an entirely different entity, managed by Ben and someone named Douglas. "Why can't everyone just stagger their retirements?" Jade finally grumbled to no one in particular.

"I think because we all kind of hit a wall. When Jack got sick last year, and then all that trouble with Russell and Francine…"

Jade grabbed her aunt's hand to show her support, while nodding that she remembered.

After all, it was only last year. That was when they saw Grandpa Jack get cancer and undergo the harsh treatment to cure it. Last September, Kailynn and Ian's grandson, Russell, was kidnapped from their own house. The villain behind it was Francine's old lover, who later turned stalker. He ended up being shot dead. But the lingering shock and gloom still hovered over the ranch in the minds of all who endured it.

Flash to the present, and the latest scandal, Jade's attack last April.

"We need an entirely new fleet to come in."

"Yeah, Jade. That's what we're looking at."

She all but gulped out loud, and a headache started to squeeze her head with unexpected pressure. Sighing deeply, she said, "And this is where I come in?"

Kailynn nodded. "Yep. That's where you come in."

The pressure increased painfully. The agony sometimes go so bad she suffered from stomach aches, and found no relief. She wished she could run like she so often witnessed Cole doing. The little interactions they daily shared soon became events she anticipated with joy. The whole point of the entire Rydell River Ranch and Resort centered on the horses. Then came the ranch. Then the name. Then other people.

Cole was fast becoming Jade's next project.

∽

"I don't think you know the meaning of the word, cowboy," Jade jeered behind Cole. Never backing down or even suggesting she might be wrong. Cole knew she wasn't always right.

He had some pride, after all. Not a lot. Not very often either. But once in a damn while, couldn't she just be generous and give him something to feel proud about?

Sure, he let his brother smack her on the head. He knew Everett hurt her. Knocked her out cold. And then they robbed her. But she didn't know that. Cole had it etched in his brain forever. But she didn't. He couldn't imagine what she might do or say if she did know.

"You can't ever be wrong, can you? You're always right, no matter what. Or is it just because you're a woman in a predominantly male business that makes you—"

She stepped right up to him and got in his face, pushing her finger in his chest. "Makes me what, cowboy? Huh? Say it." She glared at him while pressing her index finger right in the center of his chest. Then she taunted him in a soft, almost feminine whisper, suddenly so at odds with her former rude words, "I dare you."

Their original argument concerned how to proceed with fixing the roof of an outbuilding that was worn from age. Ben instructed them to repair it and this time, Jade was Cole's co-worker on it. She had no more knowledge about how to do it than he did.

Cole clamped his mouth shut. Then he impulsively grabbed her wrist and shook her gently, saying, "No."

"Are you afraid? You're always afraid, cowboy. Why is that?"

"I don't need to answer that," he spat back.

Her eyebrows rose along with her chin and surprise

shone in her eyes. Or was it hurt? Maybe. But Jade Rydell submitted to no man. She was above correction and every other human on earth. No one could hurt her feelings, especially such a lowly worker as he. No way.

They didn't move. Now they were caught in a heated, glaring, stare-down contest. Her lips curled up as his gaze squinted hard at her.

Then… what?

What happened?

He was holding her wrist to stop her from pointing at him, then his hold suddenly tightened and her breath caught in a weird moment and either he pulled or she took a step but they both moved forward. He didn't know how. And would never know.

That fast, her body fell towards his and they connected. In a blink. Now, she wasn't his superior anymore. She wasn't superior to him at all in fact. Cole seemed to become the man he never was with her before. Taking her wrists in his hands, he jerked her forward and lowered his mouth on hers. She was tall but couldn't quite reach him, and had to stand on her tiptoes until their mouths met.

Cole's kiss wasn't soft or gentle; it was hard.

No teasing of lips in a sensuous manner, but rather, two mouths crushing together. It was instantly a spray of sparks from the brewing inferno that sizzled between them. Ignored until now. But it was always there just the same.

Her mouth softened under his and a little moan escaped her. His heart started pounding at the sound she made. Coming from Jade, it was so soft and wispy and feminine, like nothing he ever heard from her before. Her head tilted and her lips separated before their tongues found each other.

He released her hands and grabbed her waist to bring her closer to him. Something odd and compulsive took over his entire body.

He was fine. Arguing one moment and blazing on fire the next.

She grabbed his head and tugged on his hair. Her fingers caressed his head as her mouth opened wider. Their tongues explored each other. It was instantaneous. Hot sparks flew. There was a definite fire smoldering between them.

His entire body was ready to burst with emotion. He stepped forward. He had to, being compelled by something dark and deep and unusual inside him. He pushed against her, stepping between her legs. She stumbled backward but didn't try to stop or release him. Instead, her hands moved lower to grab his shirt and crush it in her hands. She released a soft *oof,* when her back hit the rail of the empty stall.

It was dark, shadowy, and gloomy in the barn.

Her fingertips scraped his scalp and his entire body seemed to react. He grunted and pushed his hardening dick towards the only thing that he cared about. Like a caveman. He acted stupid and lost. He pushed his body towards Jade's body. Her long, solid, beautiful figure.

Their mouths kept twisting and their lips were crushed together. Suddenly, Jade withdrew from him and stopped gently licking his mouth. His entire body all but ejaculated right then. *Jesus.* What was that?

It was good. So damn good, Cole groaned and all but devoured her mouth and she whimpered in response.

He grabbed her shirt. Pulling and tugging in a graceless motion, he finally got the material between his fingers, but it wouldn't give. In a swift reaction, he simply yanked it hard and the blouse instantly split in two, buttons flying. Jade let out shocked gasp but Cole dropped down and stuck his mouth over her lace-covered breast. The hot, tight, bead of her nipple in his mouth aroused her and she loved it when he used his tongue as well as his teeth and lips to encircle the pebbled tip. The material of her brassiere was getting soggy but he kept sucking and biting her. It wasn't really hard and didn't hurt her but he seemed to devour her and she willingly submitted to him.

Her head thunked back and she sighed, "Oh. Oh. Cole…"

She tousled his hair and he lifted his face long enough to grip the flimsy material and push it up. Her breasts popped forward towards him. Two perfectly round handfuls. Naked. He paused to stare at them, right there. The white globes seemed so proud and firm, standing off her chest. But not so heavy that they drooped, not at all. Her nipples looked like buttons painted pink and rouge. They were beading from the cool air on the wet tips.

Cole never looked at a woman's naked breasts before. Not right in his face like now. His body reacted. Heaving upwards, he began wanting more of her.

Caveman. Animal. He was both.

He grabbed one plump bosom in his hand and pushed it into her chest, letting the hard, little bead on the end touch his palm and hand. While he licked the other one, Jade uttered little sounds that made him want to tear her apart.

He released her so his fingers could manipulate her some more. He teased the little bead, making it come out as if it were seeking someone to play with. He kept doing that and she whimpered more. She liked it. He peeked at it while his mouth was around her other one. She was beautiful. So perky and bright and her hard nipple was elongated and very tight. It was so malleable.

Cole had no idea sex could feel like this.

He couldn't begin to think. He just had to do something.

"Did you bring a condom?" Words. She said some words to him but he only wanted to play and pet and maybe even fuck her beautiful tits.

"Cowboy?"

He released her nipple barely a moment to mutter,

"Yeah?" But it was muffled and came out more like "Yeph?" Cole went back to it. She gripped his head and moaned some more as he sucked a little harder this time.

Why would he bring a condom? Who knew this would happen? His brothers said he should have one with him at all times. That's the only reason he did, to convince them he had plenty of his own women to screw.

"I need it."

What? She needed what? Him? His dick? Okay. He'd never had anyone say she *needed it* before. So he kept sucking and licking and biting her tits. He switched sides when he felt her hands groping around in his jeans pocket. Then she took out his wallet. Why?

Oh, yeah, the condom?

For sex?

He almost jerked back. No. He couldn't do that. He shouldn't… but when his eyes opened again the heaven surrounding him was too tempting to refuse. Two naked, glorious tits were in his hands and his mouth so… He shut his eyes again.

He felt her hands moving and wrestling around. He didn't care anymore. He was in heaven and doing something he'd never done for the first time in his life. He could die happy doing this. Exactly this.

But she was still fidgeting and then he felt the back of her hands on his bare stomach. He was startled and pulled back to look down. Her hands were working on the tab of his jeans and shoving the zipper down.

Down.

Like to expose his dick?

What was going on?

He glanced forward and noticed her jeans were already undone.

"A little help over here, cowboy," she muttered. Her face

was down-turned. Her tits were fully exposed and her shirt looked ragged from his stupid impatience with the buttons.

He swallowed hard. Shit. No. They could not do this. Not. Ever. He already hurt her. He was violent. He should go to prison for what he did to her. He would eventually. He also needed the job he had with her family. They were his family too. Kind of. No. But she was moving ahead… and he needed to stop. They had to stop. Then—

Her hand touched him. As she was working on the zipper, the back of her knuckles grazed the length of his hard, aching dick.

He jumped in response.

Damn.

Damn.

He'd never felt anything so wonderful. Nothing like his own hand. Like nothing else. It was sheer electricity and heavenly and… and…

Her fingers were pulling off his jeans and boxers. Now his dick was openly exposed in front of her, the barn, and the outside air. He was not naked. It was naked and poking out but the rest of his clothes were still intact. It was right there. Wedged between them. Shock made him go still. Inertia paralyzed him. Puzzled by his inability to move, he almost asked what was happening?

Until she grabbed him. She, this hot, beautiful, fierce woman touched him. Her hand was firm and sure as she lifted his naked penis that practically stood between them and stroked it.

He didn't ask her to. He didn't even want her to. Not really. It never occurred to him to ask her to hold it. He never guessed that she would.

Then she was using her two hands and rubbing him until his hips leaned forward. Hard. Towards her. Those magical hands were giving Cole the most beautiful experience. He'd never imagined anything could feel so good. Her gaze was on him, and she was looking at his dick. She knew what she was doing. She watched her hands holding his dick. Moving and tugging him until his hips pistoned forward.

He shoved his hand to the wall above her head to hold himself upright. Gritting his teeth, he cursed as his hips jackknifed toward her again. "Fuck me."

"I'm trying to. But you have to hold still," she muttered. She smiled and chewed a little on her lower lip. He shut his eyes and surrendered to the delicious sensations her touch created.

Her hands moved some more and when he looked down again, he was happily surprised to see he had the condom on.

Sex anyone?

Now she wanted to have sex with him?

But...

They should talk first. Clear things up. She might not even know his first name. It wasn't right. So far from what he should be doing. He was evil. A bad person. He could not have sex with her. He could not...

She shoved her own pants all the way down before her boobs swung right into his view. She paused long enough to take her boots off along with her jeans. Then she rose and stood before him. Well, actually she was sort of under him. He still leaned against the wall, his dick sticking out straight as an ice pick, poking her body.

Now she was naked. Standing right before him.

He swallowed as he blinked in astonishment. She was beautiful. Long torso. Long, muscular arms. Such sexy, strong arms. Her stomach was smooth, and then... there it was.

He all but gulped. That special part was beautiful too. Her lady part. Her whatever she might want him to call it.

He stared down as she continued to stand before him.

RIVER'S EDGE

"Cowboy?" Her voice was low and husky.

Oh, no. Now she wanted him to do something. What? He just didn't know if he should. No. He knew he shouldn't. But what if…? He tried to forget all the bad things he'd done and all the reasons he had for doing them.

But also, he'd never done *this* before.

Her hands touched him again and his hips followed, seeking her warmth. He was filled with a kind of joy he never knew. An unearthly magic. It was sinful. It meant everything.

Then she set him right in that spot. The spot that was now naked. He sucked in a breath of air and tilted his neck back. Shit. He practically came right then. He was just looking at where his condom-tipped end touched her.

She squirmed. "Something can be said for drawing things out, but… c'mon, cowboy. Oh, oh, Cole! Fuck me."

So he did.

Without thinking. Without reason. Without any morals or conscience, he simply pushed his hips forward.

And buried himself deep inside her.

He was so far inside her. He couldn't believe how far. To the very end. To the hilt. All the way. She let out a shocked, little "Oh!" and he had to shift forward. He jerked a little bit to see how it felt. Her body bobbled on his and she let out a little cry and then a moan.

His legs were between hers and then he just shoved himself inside her. Hard. Keeping his hands on the barn wall for traction, he went in and out, over and over. Like a jackhammer. She was so soft. So wet. So perfect. He had no idea anything so perfectly wonderful could exist in this world of imperfection. Not this. This was nothing *but* perfection. He pounded her some more and his brain felt lost. His thoughts were scattered. Until they were gone. For once in his miserable life, his pointless, useless thoughts were irrelevant. This was only about feelings. Feeling good. No great. Omnipotent. Spectacular. Fantastic.

He rammed her body into the wall as she let out a squeal of delight. He gripped her waist and held her there as his body jerked when it spewed and convulsed inside her. His neck fell back and his teeth were bared. He had enough awareness not to scream out but that was about it.

He had no idea sex could be like this. It was the greatest thing that ever happened to him his whole in life.

He wilted downwards.

∼

Jade blinked with surprise.

Did he just… come?

It was barely three strokes. He'd started out so… promising. So hot. He was inarticulate for sure. After ripping off her blouse, he all but mauled her. Not unusual for Jade anyway. But he acted like a brute: using brute force, at a brute height and with a brute mass. His compulsion for her was a heady factor too. It turned her on.

He'd been so busy staring, reveling, and all but playing like an enthralled teenager with his first crush. He loved being with her. That was obvious. He didn't realize she was undressing them until she touched his dick. And then all bets were off.

The man seemed unfamiliar with his own dick. Glancing down as if someone else placed the dick between them, his expression might have made her laugh if she weren't so turned on. His very lack of finesse was, oddly enough, the thing that did it for her. Was it because he was so unusual?

But when she touched him, he all but bared teeth and pounded the wall. Obviously, she overwhelmed him. And then he'd stared at her as if she were the only woman alive, making her the best, greatest, most beautiful naked woman alive.

Wow. She was nice looking but not that spectacular.

He felt different as soon as he entered her. Never moving his hands off the wall, he didn't even bother to touch her as his hips pumped like a piston and he filled her up epically.

She blinked again. Was he already done?

Her body was still strumming. Despite his lack of finesse and speediness. Crap. That reckless speed. But her body was still primed and ready. She deserved something that felt good too.

"Finish me off, cowboy," she suddenly demanded.

She felt his head lift, and he seemed startled. He glanced down. "What?"

"That was too quick. Touch me."

He waited a long moment before moving his hand down between her legs. Where he'd been a beastly brute just a few moments ago, now, he was strangely unsure and filled with trepidation. His fingertips stalled, caressing the top of her legs until he… suddenly jammed them into her again.

She let out a grunt of surprise as he pushed her body against the wall. "Crap!" She gasped. While immediately grabbing his wrist with her hand, she said, "Easy, now."

He instantly let her go. Like she was poisonous or radioactive. "I'm sorry. Shit. Shit. Shit. I'm such a brute. I'm sorry. I didn't mean to hurt you. You said… no, it doesn't matter what you said. I just… don't know how to do it. I'm sorry. I just don't know how to do this."

There was the man she recognized.

Not the oddball caveman who overcame her without any care for her needs. That was the man she never saw before. Puzzled by what he didn't know how to do, she froze when she heard movement outside.

No.

Her entire body felt paralyzed. No.

Someone was in the barn.

She lifted her hand and covered his mouth. He jerked back in surprise. She shook her head frantically. He heard something then too and suddenly, he swiftly dropped down, pulling her with him. He twisted so she was sitting on his lap and slid back into the corner where it was even darker.

Then they held their breaths.

Who could it be?

She had no idea. No one spoke. There was just the sound of movement. Rustling. Finally, she started to relax. There didn't seem to be anyone looking for them. Or more specifically, looking around like they thought anyone was out there.

Please don't let anyone come down to this end. The consequences of being discovered were too terrible to imagine.

But time passed and nothing approached them.

She noticed him more closely.

She was on top of him. Still naked. Her bottom was over his crotch. His big body cradled her and she felt small and diminutive in his arms. She loved the sensation. The inside of his arms chafed the sides of her breast. He was still fully dressed but for the hard dick she felt beneath her. He didn't even move. He was barely breathing.

But time kept ticking. They were, so far, unnoticed.

She started to succumb to his hold.

She let her stiff back relax and kind of melt into his hard, big chest. She felt him glancing down. Was he surprised? Judging by his movements, she seemed to surprise him a lot.

His hands were still around her and she was right there on his warm thighs. She lifted her hands and pulled herself upwards. Quietly. She was after all, fully naked.

She pushed his hand on her nipple but he didn't move at first. Finally, she had to bite her lip to stop herself from whispering or sighing. She was still unsatisfied by him. And it had been a long time since he came. She'd been sitting on his hard dick, still naked, and her ungratified body was still rushing with passion and wanting a climax of her own.

His fingers moved over her breasts. She shut her eyes and let her head fall back on his shoulder. She was close to his chin. He finally lowered his mouth to hers and she all but fully sighed at the bliss of it. He strummed her nipples over and over. They were hard and achy from her desire; the delicious combination created a form of pleasure-pain.

His mouth was different this time. Calmer, because he was still trying to keep quiet. His tongue finally slipped into her mouth and she encouraged him, lifting her breasts up.

She put her hand over his and worked his hands like they were hers, while gently pushing downwards. He didn't respond at first until she pulled his fingertips and he started to grip hers. She set his hand between her legs. His mouth explored hers, and he felt the soaking wet, puffy, swollen lips in her nether region that were eager for this touch.

He slid a finger along her in a slow, soft outline of her. So unlike the way he was earlier. He seemed more gentle now. Almost reverent.

He did it again and she was almost embarrassed by how wet he made her. Damn. He was totally lacking in any finesse. Too quick. She should have considered him terrible in bed. But, to her pleasant surprise, apparently, that did it for her.

He played with her this time. Just like he did with her breasts earlier. She wasn't sure what else to call it. He set a finger deep inside her and she bit her lip, rising up to increase the pressure. She was ready to cry out and beg for more. Harder. Faster. But she couldn't speak.

Or even move around.

This was so bad. So naughty.

So hot.

She started to whimper and wanted to flip over, straddle him, and take him on her own terms. Or let him take her.

He kept moving inside her but not where she needed the stimulation. She moved her hand down there and found the spot she wanted. It was oddly erotic as his exploration of her stilled when he felt her hand competing with his. His hand moved towards hers. She lifted his and set his fingertips right where she needed them. All the while, their tongues smashed and kissed harder and he dallied as he increased her wetness. She spread her legs wider. She felt wanton and shameless.

Both of their fingers were inside her and she could only whimper. She had to. She released his mouth and bit her lip as she undulated. Silently. So damn silently. She pushed up and felt the pressure of their fingers. She rubbed her own clit while he was inside her. And it made up for everything. She whimpered again. She couldn't stand it. Her head thrashed involuntarily.

Her insides were boiling. Not percolating. Not building, but quickly becoming a full-on inferno.

Her heels found the ground and she dug them in for traction.

She had no idea sex could be as exciting as this.

She was sobbing. And ready to release herself. She needed the climax that he earlier denied her.

Then she jerked as hard as she could into the pressure of his hands and grabbed his shirt, stuffing it into her mouth as she came in wonderful waves of bliss. Her body undulated against his to capture every last drop of the experience.

Did she scream? Blood was rushing through her veins and all around her; so she wasn't sure what she was doing or how she felt. She was temporarily deprived of all senses until she epically came on the man behind her... But someone else was inside the barn with them.

She hated having to bite this man's shirt to keep herself quiet.

Finally, the wonderful orgasm ended and she was exhausted. Her entire body collapsed over him. Sweat soaked her skin and dripped under both breasts. But too fast it started to dry and a tremor shuddered through her body.

He pulled her towards him and she slung her arms around his neck before burying her face against his chest. Pulling up her knee to her stomach, Jade fully cocooned her body into Cole's.

Quiet and peace.

She could still hear the far off noises though.

She shivered. And then… she fell asleep.

CHAPTER 12

*J*ADE SLEPT IN COLE'S arms.

He gulped as he gripped her tightly and stared down at her in utter amazement. Her eyelids were down and her delicate lashes touched her cheek. He let out a deep breath that he'd been holding for the last hour.

The person who came into the barn was off doing something. Shit. Cole was stressed they'd get caught, but somehow, the more time that passed, the more they got used to it.

He stared down at her. She was...

Glorious. Spectacular. Breathtaking. A supernova. He had no idea women could be like that.

Or that he was so deserving as to have one.

There was so much on his mind. He was overheated. Overstimulated. Overwhelmed.

But still, she felt so warm and right and lovely in his arms now.

She was soft and sweet, not like he'd ever witnessed her being before.

None of what happened was normal for either of them.

The sex was wrong. He suspected he blew it, and then she outright said it and of course, he wanted to fix it. But when she showed him with her own fingers… well, yes, then he realized he'd done it all wrong. That turned out to be so sexy and erotic, even better than her naked breasts.

He had no idea.

It was so soft and so, *so* wet. No idea it could feel like that. All the deep folds and the hard nodule that she herself so frantically touched. Was that her clit? Had to be it. He didn't know. Until now.

He wanted to do it better. Slower. Longer. Make it right. He blushed now in the dark as she lay against him. Sleeping. Calm. Quiet. He felt ashamed when he heard her say he went too fast.

It felt like forever when he filled her up with himself. But she seemed to think there was something he missed. That's probably because his brain was so ablaze with fire, no wonder he missed it.

It was epic.

And horrible.

Finally the barn was silent. Who the hell was in there the entire time? When all of this bad, inappropriate behavior was going on?

Cole's entire life was bad and inappropriate. That was partly why he hadn't had sex before. Living in fear, he tried hard not to be one of the crude, soulless assholes the men in his family were so gifted at being. It was so much easier not to do the act than to worry about the pitfalls involved.

Cole didn't want women to cry because of him. He'd witnessed that before and often. Sex with his brothers always occurred right next to him, or below him, or on the bunk beside him. He heard the women moan and groan and the sloppy, gross noises their bodies made.

He knew at a young age what his dad, and later, his older brothers were doing with women.

He watched the women cry too. Heard them whimpering as if the very act hurt them. But most often, they wept when they were all but ejected from the living space when it was over.

Cole was a singular person and indeed, very different from all the other men in his family.

And now, he'd done it. With the woman he worked for. Inside a barn. And with someone else there.

He'd hurt her also at one point. Not on purpose. In his haste to fulfill anything she asked of him, he lost himself. But still. He'd felt her body flinch and her critical words pierced his skull.

Glancing outside, he also knew it was getting late. He *had* to go.

Jiggling her sleeping, naked body in his arms, he said softly, "Ms. Rydell?"

A small smile touched her lips but her eyes didn't open. "You might have to start calling me Jade after this, cowboy."

He liked her snarky humor. That boldness he admired but also kind of feared. Jade's undeniable confidence in who and what she was. Her place in the world. Her standing. Her power over it. They could be intimidating to some people.

He frowned at her smile. What if she kept calling him *cowboy*? Although it started from a point of disdain and mockery, she persisted in using it as almost a pet name for him. But what if she really didn't know his name?

"You *do* know my name is Cole, don't you?"

Her eyelids popped open and that fast, her bright, inquisitive, fearless gaze found his. The same moment she opened her eyes, she flipped around so she was straddling him. Her shirt was still on her shoulders, but the front gaped open as he looked at her.

That was because he *ripped* the buttons off it.

Acting like a possessed, out of control, feral animal.

Just like his father.

Regret made his heart contract. He grabbed the two gaping sides of Jade's shirt together and covered her, his noble attempt to restore her modesty. He gulped when he had to lift his gaze from where his hands clutched the fabric over her. Her knowing, bright gaze was fastened on him and he needed courage before he could look at her.

He got startled when her hands cupped his face. "I know your name. It's Cole."

He nodded with her hands still holding him as well as her gaze. "Oh? Okay. Good."

A small smile curled her lips as she rubbed her thumb along his lower lip. "You must know my name is Jade, right?"

"Of course I do." His eyebrows furrowed in annoyance. "Of course, I know your name."

Well... good. They established that fact at least: they knew each other's first name. He frowned at how inappropriate this was. He couldn't comprehend how much he risked being here with her right now. The valuable things he earned and worked so hard for were suddenly threatened for the sake of feelings. For the sake of a forbidden act.

He risked Penny's safety and security. As paltry as that was for her.

Jade used her knees to rise and she moved closer to him. Her lips touched his as she straddled him, hovering only a few inches above him. He had to tilt his head back as her mouth touched his in a soft, closed-mouth kiss. She licked his lips and ran her hands through his hair, using her fingers like a brush.

But her mouth was still planted on his. Cole let go of the loose fabric that encircled her waist and felt the soft, silky bare skin of her waist and back. She was intoxicating when he held her in his arms. To rub and feel her skin was a thrill Cole luxuriated in and relished.

She all but purred at him. Then her mouth released his and she tilted her forehead to set it on his. They were cross-eyed staring at each other. She sighed.

"Well, we may have blurred the lines here..."

He gulped again. That was an understatement. But the only one to suffer for it would be him.

He'd, no doubt, be fired. He expected that. For doing this. Yes. Of course she would. She had every right. She wouldn't want to remember all the nasty things they did. They probably weren't as enjoyable for her as they were for him to begin with. To her, he was just another cowboy, one who'd served his purpose in more ways than one. Of course.

He suddenly pushed her off him and lurched to his feet. With one hand, he grabbed his jeans and slid into them before he ran away.

He didn't want to hear the words. He didn't want to admit his actions. He knew what he'd done with her. Or, should he say, *to* her? Despite how bad *he* was and how wrong *it* was and all the many consequences that would invariably ensue, Cole honestly liked it.

He didn't want to admit how much he liked it.

How much he wanted to do it again. And again. And again.

Shame engulfed him and the heat crept up his chest and pooled into his face. He'd thoroughly embarrassed himself and would lose his job for it. His one livelihood. His sister's only chance out of hell. And for what?

Dirty, disgusting sex. He shuddered as he ran full speed towards his truck. The dawning sensation that he was now one of those creeps who perverted women with sex made his heart and his head pound. He'd done it in a moment of poor judgment. Now Penny would lose everything for his one moment of… glory.

Jade landed to the side of where Cole set her before he (again) fully ran away. Was he running from her? From what they did?

She stared in open-mouthed shock. She'd just been getting around to making sense of what happened here. Everything was so unplanned and unsought. Not to mention, unexpected. She'd been hunting for the right words to describe it and kind of wondering if she might like to do it again. Things were very confusing, to say the least.

But Cole was something else. Intense. Shaken. Worried.

Jade nearly knocked her head against the barn wall. He'd been horrified by what they did. He'd had sex with his boss. Jade could be considered a—a sexual aggressor. A sexual harasser.

Oh, damn. This was bad. The knowledge and guilt made her cringe after that. She gripped her torn shirt and got up. Blushing furiously, the heat was intense in her cheeks. Jade never had sexual relations with anyone here on the ranch before.

Who was she kidding? Sex. Dirty sex. Rammed up against the barn wall sex.

Sex she'd fully instigated and… oh, damn.

With her favorite employee?

And the oddest one of all? Cole *was* odd.

He simply ran. Like he did so often. Sprinting across the land after his job was over for the day. Especially if he worked a late shift. Why all the running?

He made her laugh. It was so quirky. Such an odd thing for a grown adult man to do. One might expect it from a youth or a child, but only because they're eager to go somewhere and like to run at full tilt. But Cole did it so often that it made Jade wonder what inspired him.

He was strong and handsome but very unsure of himself. Ridiculously unsure. Her legs quivered and he seemed to tremble with them. During their entire encounter, he was unsure and insecure.

He was utterly fascinated, however, by her boobs.

She glanced down. She considered her boobs the most ordinary part of her. Small and compact and fine. Sure. But Cole elevated them to the status of a celebrity. Staring and touching, gripping, and playing. He seemed to be content to do that for hours.

Strange response.

She reached over and hunted for her clothing items.

Talk about a walk of shame. She grimaced. Cole did the *run* of shame. Only the obvious for Cole Pearson.

Ms. Rydell?

In the most vulnerable moment, in the afterglow of sex, why did he choose to call her that? He must've still felt humbled by her power and authority over him.

Jade *was* guilty of sexual harassment then.

She gulped. That was a crime. She broke the law.

She let out a small cry of horror. She'd hurt someone who'd never done anything to deserve it. He was so kind. Hard-working. And ridiculously industrious. So concerned about her and always proper and polite. Even then. At their special moment. The most tender but strange moment. She was naked, lying against him and he still called her *Ms. Rydell?*

Her throat got a sudden lump in it while she busily tried to sort out her clothes… and her dignity. Dignity didn't mean very much to her only an hour ago.

She cringed as she stared at the empty horse stall. At least, they weren't in an occupied one. And it had fresh straw and no horse dung. But as reckless as she'd been, would she have even slowed down to allow for such temporary obstacles? Probably not.

She'd seduced him. She hurt him and embarrassed herself and him. Had she committed a real crime? She knew it was something unethical, but would she go to jail for it?

Rising to her full height, and clutching her ruined shirt, she stuffed the used condom into her pocket and stuck her hat back on her head. Lacking pride, she walked out of the terrible place.

She was responsible for this. She had to face the consequences.

Worst of all, she so obviously proved she was not the ideal candidate to be next in line to Jack Rydell. Look at what she'd just done. She was morally weak and corrupt. She just demonstrated that.

Glancing around, she quickly started to cross the pasture when someone called her name. She died about five deaths from her own self-disgust. Her dad was calling her.

She ripped her hat off and stuck it over her chest, placing her other hand under it in order to keep her shirt closed. The hat covered enough that her dad would probably not realize that it wasn't buttoned. In case he asked, she'd say it got ripped by the wind when it blew so wild and hard…

"What?" she said loud and sharp. She was hoping he'd stop rather than come all the way up to her. He paused and spoke to her from a few feet back. Thank goodness, the shadows lengthened the yard.

"Cole ran off. He didn't come to pick up his day's wage. Anything going on?"

Ran off? Yeah. *Literally*. Away from her. And any discussion. But he always ran off so this was nothing new. As for his money, she knew he needed it. And he never forgot to pick it up before.

Weak, horrible, and as far from a boss as she could possibly be, she shook her head. "No. I haven't seen him."

"Shit. I'm sure he needs the cash. Something must have gone wrong."

"What do you know about him?" She asked, her head tilting and her heart hammering. Why start a discussion with her father, while trying to hide her ripped shirt and a dirty condom in her pocket? She was just as disgusting as her behavior. But she also wanted to know.

"Same as you do. He's a mystery. Doesn't like to disclose much."

"Does that bother you? What if he's a criminal or something worse?"

"Could be. Wouldn't be the first we hired. You know, AJ was a criminal once upon a time too."

Yes, her dad and his theory that Cole was the latest version of AJ Reed. Meaning what? That Cole would be the next budding foreman who would honor an almost life-long loyalty to the Rydell River Ranch? Her dad definitely insisted on loyalty. That's why he was mentoring Cole.

The truth struck her in the chest like an arrow through an apple.

Yeah. He was. Her dad loved Jade and Lillian. Sure. But the zest he displayed in the way he went about helping and working with Cole was unparalleled.

Huh. She didn't really foresee that. And she found herself a little bit offended. Now she was cringing at what she ruined.

"Do you have any idea where he stays? You could take it to him."

"None whatsoever."

"Cell phone?"

"No…" Then his eyes brightened out of nowhere. "Mel. She got it from him because she calls him for help whenever she has heavy things for him to lift. She calls him from the ranch to do the work on her building now and then. She has his number."

Ben spun around to go get it. Jade let out a breath.

Great. Good. Now her dad could pay the man whom she sexually harassed at work today.

She flipped around. She wanted to shower. Change. And repent.

She had to fix this.

COLE'S BITTERNESS gnawed at him. He lied about his real last name. So it didn't matter what she called him since she didn't know what his real name even was. It wasn't his first lie either. He lied about the worst mistake he ever made. He could have given her closure and identified the criminals who attacked her. He could lead her to all the culprits, help her get her revenge and justice. And all of them were guilty and deserving of the fullest punishment. Including him.

But Cole hid from her and lied about it and then did this?

He was almost offended when she referred to him by her little pet name again.

What was he going to do?

Anxiety gnawed at his guts. He had to slow down or a cop would pull him over. He could not afford to have that happen. No license. No proof of insurance. At least he had a place for Penny to go for the summer. He drove to the local equivalent of a Boys and Girls Club. It provided after school activities and for summer, full-day child care at affordable prices. At least Penny would be safe and busy. Not rotting away all alone on some hidden gravel walkway avoiding grownups, cops, city workers or any other basically decent people who would wonder about a young girl left all alone for hours on end.

His head ached from all the self-recrimination. But today it was worse. Just pulling into the parking lot to pick up Penny, he went still when his cell phone rang. He glanced down. No one ever called him. What if... it were Chance? Could he have located them already? He didn't recognize the number.

"Hello?"

"You didn't pick up your money today. Are you coming back for it?"

Ben's voice didn't waste any time with pleasantries. Cole was so freaked out, he literally ran away. Leaving Ben in the lurch.

"Uh, I'm sorry I just left. I—"

"You're not on salary here. You can leave anytime you want. No need to be sorry. But you did put in a full day and you deserve to be paid for that. Where are you? I can have someone bring it to you."

"I—I" Cole stuttered and leaned his head on the steering wheel.

"You, okay? If you need something... just ask."

He jerked upright, blinking hard. Ben Rydell was... what? Checking on him? Why did he care? Cole never had anyone ask him if he were okay, except his little sister. He gulped as his own self-revulsion blocked out everything else in his mind. He'd defiled this man's daughter, in the barn, on his land and now he was checking on *his welfare?*

"I'm... I just messed up something. Personally. And I..."

"Where are you? I'll bring it over. You don't need to come back."

It was more like he *shouldn't* come back. "Brewster. Getting dinner."

Cole needed to explain so he said, "I'll come in tomorrow morning. But I probably… need a few days off… you know, to take care of my personal thing?"

"Of course. We owe you that. Man, you worked for thirty-five days straight. You're owed a few days off. So take them. And I'll be pleased to see you when you come back."

"Thank you, Mr. Rydell."

He let out a deep laugh. "How many times am I gonna tell you? No one calls me Mister anything. It's just Ben. And Jack and Ian and Shane. The list goes on. None of us goes by Mr. Rydell."

"I appreciate that sir, but…"

He sighed. "You seem to prefer Mr. Rydell. Okay. When you quit calling me that maybe you could just, you know, stay on as my employee? Huh? Consider that seriously, cowboy."

Startled at Ben's use of that moniker, he stared at the now dead line of his phone. Why did he say that? Did he know what happened? But if so, why would he ask him to stay on? He tried to swallow the lump in his throat. What was he going to do?

CHAPTER 13

HER CLOTHES CHANGED, JADE left the house. Bursting into her sister's veterinary practice the next morning, she thought she had a grip on herself but suddenly broke down into tears when her sister's gaze met hers.

Astonishment filled her sister's eyes. "Jade? What happened?"

"Can I—I talk to you?" Jade croaked over the unexpected tears.

"Of course." Lillian quickly came forward and wrapped her arms around Jade. She felt Lillian tilt her head slightly and figured she was motioning to her husband who also worked with her, to leave. Matt quickly walked out of the room. Luckily, Jade barged in on them before they were scheduled to open the veterinary clinic. After taking one look at her sister, Jade started crying like a child and was grateful she didn't break down in front of any witnesses.

It might have looked funny that her tiny sister was holding her up. Lillian was much smaller and shorter and Jade felt like a giant hovering over her. Both in height and breadth. But Jade clutched her much older sister close to her and sniveled pathetically.

She cried for many minutes and Lillian just let her get it out.

Finally, Jade started to calm down and released her sister. Rubbing her nose with her sleeve, she shook her head as she turned and flopped down.

"What happened?"

"I can't bear to tell you. Everyone will hate me."

Lillian came over and sat down beside her. "Well, now you *must* tell me. Did you do something to me?"

"No. It wasn't to anyone specific in the family." She shook her head and choked on another wave tears. "But specifically, *to* the family. And to someone who didn't deserve it."

Lillian put her arm around her shoulder and tugged her closer. "Okay, Jade. You're really going to have to explain now. Tell me everything."

She peeked at her regal, lovely sister and the images of all the unreal, dirty things she'd done yesterday flashed through her mind. She groaned and buried her face in her hands. "I can't tell you. It's… it's about… sex." She whispered the word as if she just sacrificed an innocent animal on an altar.

"Okay. Sex. You do realize I've had it before. I even had a baby because of it once. Jade, you're twenty-six years old. I hoped you're having it and liking it. But you aren't exactly the kind of woman who sits around gossiping over sex and munching on junk food. I always respected that about you. You can talk to me about anything, you know… including sex." She whispered *sex* in a mocking way. Turning her head, Jade caught Lillian's small smile.

"I had… really inappropriate sex."

Lillian laughed. "You realize how Benny got here, right? How much more inappropriate can sex get than that, huh? I had to tell Mom and Dad while I was still considered the pristine, good girl. I had my first one-night stand and I got knocked up. I'm sure whatever you did pales in comparison to that. You just see me as I am now. You don't remember what an awful, awkward time that was."

Jade inhaled a shuddering breath. "I-I think I seduced one of… one of the workers. And it happened in… one of the barns. During the day. The work day. With the nicest of all the workers. And now I think I might be guilty of sexual harassment or something equally as inappropriate. And when it was over, he ran off and then…"

"Ran off? You must be referring to Cole."

"How do you know about him?" Jade whipped her head up curiously.

"Because Mom keeps talking about Dad's bromance with the new ranch hand who runs to his truck every day before he goes home. Mom thought it was cute. Especially since he's so big and tough looking. She gives him all his meals and she thought when he first showed up he hadn't been eating enough nutritious food to sustain him."

Her mouth dropped open and Jade simply stared at her sister with incredulity. Her entire body jolted as her sister's words registered in her brain. Since when did her mom think he wasn't eating enough? Shutting her eyes, her wet eyelashes stuck to each other.

Oh, damn. She had no idea. Jade thought he was just another worker. Not that he came to them from a place of poverty and hunger.

"He lied to get a job here. Said he was good with horses. He's awful. Scared to death of them. Clumsy and horrible around them," Jade went on to explain.

Lillian nodded. "So I heard. They thought he was pretty desperate when they offered him meals. He takes most of them home." Her sister's hand slipped onto Jade's shoulder and tossed her hair off. "So… what happened?"

"We used to have fights. Sometimes. You know, like silly, fun ones. Now as I look back though, maybe not. What if I were already sexually harassing him and he only submitted to me because I'm the one with all the authority and power? He was just hungry for food, not for me." She shook her head.

"Jade. Slow down. Okay? You met him and liked him. You two spent extra time together then?"

"Yes. We were working together more often. I like to make fun of him. And goad him. And he kind of does it back. But then, he gets all reticent. I see why now. He had to keep his job to keep himself fed. I-I underestimated what a good job like the ones we advertise could mean to someone. You know, we usually get guys who love horses and the ranch lifestyle. That's what they choose to do. Not something they *must do* to survive."

"I wouldn't say that's always true. I think it might be a source of survival for some and a lucrative income for many others. Don't forget how privileged we are."

The mild rebuke fully stabbed her gut with pain. "I did for a minute," she whispered confidentially. "I thought we were flirting. He's very big and handsome. I liked his smile and the way he acts. I did want him. But it never really occurred to me. No. I don't sleep where I work. Even I know better than that. Even I have some standards. I mean…"

"What, Jade?"

"I decide whom I have sex with, when, and if I have sex. In the past, I just picked up a ranch hand or cowboy around town and had a quick fling. I don't like or want anything serious. And that worked fine for me. Scratched the itch when I needed to. I started doing that when I was nineteen or thereabouts."

"I used to wonder about things like that sometimes. But you're not like most women so I didn't grill you for information. You're allowed to have sex whenever, however, and with whomever you choose."

"But this time, I chose a Rydell employee." She shook her head. "I have to tell Dad. I can't be the next in line to run this place or whatever they mistakenly keep trying to groom me into being. I'm corrupt. And immoral. I probably did it subconsciously to sabotage the whole thing. I tend to cave under pressure."

Lillian leaned back and let out a small laugh. "I think you'd tell Dad so he can take over the role of the boss for this one employee. That way, he isn't working, quote-unquote, for you. Takes out your dynamic. You tell Dad as the adult woman you are now. And the leader you're about to become. Don't grovel or apologize for being an adult to your daddy. Got it?"

Startled by her honesty, Jade stared in shock. She felt speechless after listening to her sister. "What? You want me to just act like I'm not ashamed, or mortified, or remorseful?"

"Yes. And you're not giving up this place. You still have to keep shadowing everybody so you know all the things you need to know. You had sex, Jade. The only person you owe any explanation to is Cole. And that's strictly between you two."

Jade shut her eyes. "I don't even know how to find him."

"You'll figure it out."

She breathed hard. "I can't tell Dad."

Lillian let out snort. "Why not? I had to. I was about your age too. When you think of all the shit Mom and Dad pulled when they were our ages?" She let out a shrill whistle. "They can't be too judgmental." Then she knocked her shoulder into Jade's. "Besides, they won't be. They'll worry about you being upset and try to help."

"I've never been ashamed of sex before. It's always been, you know... just fun. I like things to be uncomplicated."

Lillian snorted. "I hear that. Until the pregnancy test told me different. At least, you won't end up with a little Benny... right?"

She smiled. "No. We used a condom. He had it on him. Luckily. I guess he was more than ready for a cold screw against the barn wall."

"Tell Dad as a responsible adult who knows you acted wrong in that moment and want to fix it. The rest is all your business."

She suddenly turned and grabbed her sister in a hug. "Thank you. I thought you'd be horrified at me."

She patted Jade's back. "I don't think you've ever needed a big sister moment."

She wiped her eyes. "I think I might need one all the time. This whole ranch thing? It's so much more than I bargained for. I'm always intimidated. Always scared. What if I can't be the next Jack Rydell? I don't even know how to be Jade Rydell."

Lillian rolled her eyes. "The drama of this family. You're already Jade Rydell, so nothing changes there. It's the land. The horses. The job. Calm down and relax. Learn it day by day. As anyone learns a new job. I mean, on the first day of vet school do you think I took a scalpel to a dog's belly and spayed her?"

Jade winced. "Ooh. Your job sounds so gross. But you make a clear, real and dramatic point. It took you a decade of schooling to do what you do now."

Lillian laughed. "Exactly. It's also hard, complicated, and brimming with new knowledge that I must continue to learn in order to keep up. Day by day. Year by year. Decade to decade. You aren't special in that. And Rydell is just a name. A *last* name. Calm down and go hang out with the horses. And Jade?"

"What?" She leaned against Lillian like her back was

broken. All clingy and freaked out, she hung on the solid words of advice hammered into her by Lillian.

"You slept with this guy because you're feeling vulnerable and overwhelmed right now. You never learned how to reach out to others. You react instead of acting. You do. So consider that. And you only act when there's a reason or an emotion behind it. So probably not a good idea to try out another cold screw against the barn wall."

Her sister's advice saved Jade's sanity. Her guilt began to abate. Her consolation started to sink in. But Jade knew it wasn't over yet. She still had to face the consequences. She left her sister and headed back to the ranch, easily finding her dad supervising the new house site. Why he felt the need to rebuild his childhood home now, so late in life, still mystified her.

But her mom just explained it by saying, "He's going full circle. That kind of thing. Not a mid-life crisis but a legacy with his name on it. Grandpa Jack's illness really freaked him out. That's saying a lot. Ben has a hard time talking about it though. He speaks through his actions so this is like a love letter from him to his dad, his mom, his youth and to us."

Jade remembered what Lillian just said to her, regarding the family's opinions of Jade, and it jolted her to think they were confident she could handle things in stride just like that.

"Dad?"

"Yeah," he asked, not looking up at her. She sighed.

"I need to talk to you and it's important so you can't be doing something else."

He dropped the hammer he held in his hand and immediately lifted his gaze and studied her. "What happened?"

She gulped. "You've had some pretty tough conversations before. Right? With Grandpa? Like when your first wife died and later, about... Lillian?"

He frowned but nodded. "Yes. What is it?"

"I did something that Lillian said I shouldn't be ashamed about or feel the need to apologize... but I still feel ashamed and I am apologizing."

"What did you do?"

"Not what. Who." She pressed her lips together and closed her eyes. A furious heat made her face red hot. "I'm sorry, that came out wrong. Too harsh. I'm stressed and humiliated and embarrassed."

He sighed deeply. "This is about sex, isn't it? Couldn't you just tell your mother?"

"Ordinarily, yes, and I'd far prefer to do that. But this time?" She sucked in air for courage and shoved her shoulders back. "This time, it concerns my actions and the consequences of doing it on my job, at this place. Our place of business." The kingdom, the legacy, everything with a Rydell brand. Everything this family bled, sweated, and wept for.

But Lillian reminded her it was just a brand: a name and a business. Maybe Jade needed to get a better perspective.

Ben dropped his shoulders and rolled his head all around. Then he sighed and said, "All right. Lay on it on me. Who is it? Why do I need to know?"

She would have laughed at his tragic facial expression and the way he seemed to brace himself if not for her flaming embarrassment. "Cole."

She bit her lip and failed to hold his gaze. She stared at the burgeoning foundation of Ben's... what did Mom call it? A love letter to Jack Rydell? His youth. See? Lillian was wrong. Everywhere Jade looked, the Rydell legacy was alive and well and it was a big deal.

"Okay. So that's why he freaked out yesterday."

"Yes." She cleared her throat. "I think I'm in trouble for sexual harassment or something. I think I freaked him out and... it wasn't his fault. He didn't do anything... he didn't..."

"I don't need any details."

"I didn't initiate it. It just... happened like..."

"I know how those things happen even when we don't initiate it."

"Right." She turned away. "I'm sorry, Dad. I know, this is not what you had in mind when you considered grooming me as the heir to all this. I abused a solid position of power for nothing. No good reason. I just... did."

"Is he quitting now?"

"I have no idea. He left before I could say anything. I don't know how to find him."

"No one does. Except when he's here. What lucky timing. There he is now."

Her stomach twisted with revulsion. Turning around, yes, Jade saw Cole pull into the parking area. "I talked to him yesterday. He mentioned something personal was going on and asked for a few days off. Of course, I agreed but asked him to come and pick up his pay. I believe he needs it."

"What do I do now?"

Ben gritted his teeth. "Well, you can't tell Cole Pearson what to do anymore. I will. You're no longer his boss so you need to consider all the consequences before you act next time."

She gulped with chagrin and shame. Her dad so rarely spoke that way to her. He never had to. She was pretty self-sufficient and usually well behaved... most of the time.

"I'm going to pay him. We'll finish this conversation later."

Shame consumed her. Dismissed in obvious disappointment by her father, she deserved it. But she still felt like shit.

And there he was.

Her gut told her this was it. Cole Pearson left no address or contacts. Nothing written down to prove he worked with and for the Rydell River Ranch or any of its tangential companies. He wouldn't stay on now. He would soon disappear. That made it far easier for her. Better for her.

But it wasn't what she wanted.

Jade just wanted to talk to him. Her dad ran over and met Cole's truck. Cole didn't get out. Panic rose in her throat. This was it.

She had to follow him now or she'd never resolve the mistake she made. This terrible, hurtful thing she did. Her decision firm, she quickly circled around and ran towards her small truck. It also had the ranch logo on the doors.

Lillian was right. Jade often forgot how deep and real and pervasive the privilege into which they were born was.

And Lillian was also wrong. The Rydells were far more than a business. They were a heritage family. One Jade still wanted to be a member of. But only if she didn't hurt people to get there.

She pulled out after Cole's truck, staying far enough back that he might not notice her. The bloom of dust indicated where he was, and when he turned right to head out of the valley, so did she. When he signaled to turn off the highway, so did she.

Off they went. Way off the road. Turns and twists across many single-laned, forgotten, backcountry, unpaved, rough roads. Goodness where on earth did he live?

He must have assumed there was no traffic. For if he glanced at his rearview mirror, he'd have to notice her. There was no one else, and lots of road. But he just kept going.

So did she.

She knew she was doing a bad thing to make up for a worse thing.

CHAPTER 14

IT WAS... A MOTOR home. And a really bad motor home. Did it even run? Didn't appear so. Jade shuddered just staring at it. Long and mostly white, but with lots of holes and missing doors and busted-in dents and scratches all over the vinyl siding.

Ick.

She gulped with revulsion. She couldn't even consider calling that heap of plastic a home.

They gave Cole food because he seemed too skinny and in need. She was sure of that now when she saw where he lived.

Why was he parked so far out? The gas he wasted to get here must have posed a huge expense. But maybe it didn't run anymore. If that were so, how did he empty the tanks when necessary? Did he just use the woods for a toilet?

She was such snob. But the motor home alarmed her. It looked straight out of *Breaking Bad*. Really. She expected Walter White to come out in his mad, crazy, meth-making underpants.

She really had no background knowledge of him. And her comparison to the old series about making meth along with all the crimes that followed, had her stomach quivering.

But no. Cole presented too in need of basic resources to be what one visualizes as a typical drug dealer.

Unless he was poor from using drugs.

That would be sad. Jade would not judge or turn away from him… not just yet.

His gaze found hers through the windshield of her truck. She shut her truck off and silence descended. It lasted so long, it became tedious and horrible. The eye glare between them persisted too.

Courage. Grow up. Act your age. Face this.

She broke the stare and got out of the truck.

She waited for an explosion from him. *What was she doing there? How dare she follow him? Who told her to show up there?* Instead, he eyed her wearily before nodding.

"Would you like to come in?"

He was so formal and polite. Like he were standing on the threshold of a grand, ornate mansion. Like it wasn't such a piece of shit RV.

What did she expect? Because he was poor and lived here, he couldn't have any manners?

"I would. I need to talk to you."

"I figured that when I saw you following me."

"You knew I was?"

He nodded. "There's no one for miles out here. Of course, I noticed."

"Why didn't you pull over? Or get mad?"

"You obviously thought it was important enough to follow me."

She swallowed and dropped her gaze. Ashamed. Again. "I did. I am. I'm sorry, I didn't know how else to find you.

You're like a ghost. There's no way to get in touch with you. I'm so glad someone had your phone number."

"Are you shocked by where I live?"

"You do live here then? You didn't just lead me here to get me off your tail?"

"I live here."

He stepped to the side as she took the three steps up into the RV. She licked her lips and made every effort to control her reaction without revealing her revulsion. Her snobby, crusty, bitchy disgust. For she had it in spades.

Ripped up walls, missing handles on cabinets, and everything she saw bashed in with dents and holes. The couch was stained and ripped, but it had a neatly folded up sleeping bag and pillow on it. Weird.

She didn't want to even touch the couch. Or the chairs. Or any of it.

She was horrible.

Was Cole a former drug addict? Was he fresh out of prison and seeking all options? That was the clichéd story that this place, this RV, said of its occupant. Jade just hoped he wasn't the one who did all the damage to it.

"Is this temporarily your home?"

"One would hope so. Just for the near future."

She perched on the end of the stained couch. He stood in front of her, his arms crossed over his chest, his hips leaning against the unfinished counter. It was stripped clear down to the plywood.

He seemed as though he were protecting himself instead of being angry at her uninvited presence. His expression was puzzled and his head tilted. "Why did you follow me home?"

"We have to talk about yesterday."

"I'd rather not. I get it was wrong and all that. But I'll stay away from you from now on. I swear I will. I still need the job. It pays very well."

"Oh, Cole your job isn't at risk. Not at all. I swear to you. I just talked to my dad; he'll be your boss going forward. I'm not anymore. I'm just another worker with you on the ranch."

His face blanched at her comment. "You talked to your dad? Like, you told him... what I did?"

"*We*. What did *we* did. And honestly? I think anyone would blame me more than you."

His mouth popped open again and he shook his head. "You told more people?"

"Not people. Just my dad." Well, that wasn't really true. She sighed. "And my sister. 'Cause I didn't know if I should tell my dad. I didn't know what to do. So... yeah, they're the only ones I told."

His handsome face grimaced. "So your mom must know. And your sister's family?" His head shook. "But why?"

She flipped her hair back. Fingering the ends of it, she sighed. "Because I didn't know what to do. For real. I was a mess. And I thought maybe it was like..." She dropped her eyes and looked at the ground.

"Like what?"

Her knee jiggled. "I was afraid I'd sexually harassed you."

He snorted. She lifted her shame-filled face. "You called me Ms. Rydell in the same polite tone you always use when I'm being your stupid boss."

"Because you are. And..." He rubbed his hands on his hair. "I don't know what to call you or how to talk to you. I was just 'cowboy' to you and you liked telling me what to do." His shoulders lifted. "I didn't know how far that extended... beyond... that moment."

She rubbed her hands on her face. "I did. You respect me because I have power over you and... then I... I was pushing you to..."

"You can't push me to do anything. I'm way stronger than you, no matter how good you might be with horses."

"Sexual harassment doesn't refer to physical harassment. It's a dynamic of power. I have it over you, therefore I was the responsible party, speaking in the metaphorical sense. Because you submitted to my power over you. How could you say no? What I did was so wrong, now that I realize it. I didn't until my brain started working again."

"My head wasn't working at that moment either. Not at all."

She could not face him. Her shame engulfed her and reddened her face. She closed her eyes and finally opened them to look at him. "I'm so, so, sincerely sorry, Cole."

"I really didn't expect you to follow me and apologize for having sex. I have plenty of regrets for my own reasons, but you didn't do anything to me. I mean, the parts I'm worried about are what I did to myself."

"You just said all I do is basically call you names and order you around." Her horror fully filled her. Is that why he'd done it? He was afraid of her? She'd been so bossy to him, he took it as just another order to follow. She scratched the back of her hand. She was feeling itchy all over. Like her skin was stretched too tight.

Her behavior was impulsive.

"You do and you did. It was your job and mine. That's who we were until... just about then. I mean, I was worried about doing that with a Rydell. Any Rydell. But specifically, Ben's daughter and then... you went and told him?"

Somewhat confused, she tilted her head. "Cole, I have the power to fire and hire. As much as my dad does."

His lips puckered up as his eyebrows scrunched and surprise reflected in his eyes. "I didn't know that. So I don't see how it could be sexual harassment."

"Oh, crap. I went from bossing you around in the barn to forcing you to sex me up against the barn wall."

"Again… no."

She took in a shuddering breath. "Okay, so you don't think I used my power to control you."

"I'd have just said no. I should have said no. I wasn't afraid of you."

"Okay. Then why'd you run away?"

His face tightened as he turned to do something else. "I had to be somewhere."

"Then?" Her tone squeaked higher. She was offended. Yes, she was totally offended, even though she didn't have the right. "Then" was referring to the time when she was almost totally naked against him.

"Yes. *Then.* It wasn't like I planned to do that."

She pushed her hands to her face again. This was excruciating. She'd never found it hard to face her sexual partners after the deed was over. But then, how often did she have sex with someone she barely knew, and then try to talk to them? Casual sex was easy. After the sex, it was all done and they purposely avoided seeing each other again. In fact, Jade never had a partner return to the valley after they'd done it.

She barely knew Cole, but she'd seen him every day for hours and was used to being around him. It was an odd feeling now to have a working relationship that was usual for the circumstances. She did treat him like his boss or foreman and he responded as her worker. They weren't a guy and a girl dating. They were a boss and an employee. She had no idea how to treat him as a man. A sexual partner of her choice. Now he was no more than a stranger before her.

"I've never done that before. I mean, at the ranch. In fact, I've never had sexual encounters on the ranch grounds before."

"Me neither," Cole replied with a lift of his shoulders.

She had to smile at his quip. "I'm struggling here. I don't know how to talk to you or treat you. But I need to figure out what to do and say to you now."

"Why? We did the wrong thing and we can never mention it again."

She jerked her neck back. "Is that what you want?"

"What I want most is whatever will allow me to keep working there."

He was hungry. He needed food. The place she now cringed at sitting in was his home. Yes, of course his needs were far different from hers.

"You're welcome to come back today. Now. My dad knew about us when he paid you. I literally was still telling him about it. He was mad at me, not at you. So knowing that, did it mean nothing to you?"

Cole shuffled at her words. The length of his silence made her finally peek up at him. "You don't like me. It was just a stupid, impulsive moment and you regret it for the job hassle but not for anything about me specifically."

That was okay. He had it right. But already, that hurt. She wanted him to care more.

"It would have meant something to me."

His wording was so strange. "Would have?"

He nodded. "If things were different and I was different and you were just another girl... yeah, it would have meant a lot."

"But I *am* just a girl." She rolled her eyes. "A woman."

"Not to me. You're Jade Rydell. You take care of endless horses and give orders to a half dozen grown men who are all bigger and stronger than you and they obey whatever you say. You come from a family that has things my family never even knew about. You're bright and smart and beautiful. I don't even know why this thing happened. Considering it was with me." He swiped his hand around as if to encompass the motor home around them.

Her breath caught. Rushing to her feet with a clenched fist, she exclaimed, "I'm not the ranch. I mean, I am. I kick ass at my job. You're right. But that doesn't mean I'm not a girl. A woman. Someone you could maybe... *like*."

She hated being called a girl. She found it condescending and yet, here she was, doing it. "I didn't, and I don't know anything about you. Don't you see? That's my regret. That's the huge problem. And I'm crazy attracted to you and confused and hurt and..."

He moved off the wall he'd been slouching against when Jade said the word *hurt*. His gaze landed on hers. "I didn't mean to hurt you. I just have no excuses. I forgot for a moment how big I am and I wanted to do whatever you asked..."

She unclenched her fist and tilted her head as her confusion addled her. What was he talking about now? "I'm sorry, what?"

"You know. When I hurt you."

She calmed her tone and her racing heart. "Why do you think you hurt me?"

"When I didn't make you finish. I was trying to do it how you wanted and I hurt you."

Finish? She'd never heard anyone refer to an orgasm like that. She tucked a hand over her mouth. "Um. I meant when you ran off without talking to me. That's 'cause only a moment before, I was lying naked in your arms. Remember that?"

"Every moment." He breathed softly and his head shook. "I didn't know that hurt you. I was confused. And I had to go anyway. I'm sorry. I thought it was something I didn't do right. And I thought it hurt you because you flinched."

Every moment, every part of this had been so awkward. And kind of bad. But she still did it. What in the hell?

He was so quick. He reminded her of her first time with that guy who jack-hammered into her without realizing it was over…

Her breath gushed out as she gasped. "You were a virgin." She didn't say it like a question but rather, a statement. She remembered how his fascination extended to every part of her. His haste to see her boobs. She thought it was just sexual haze, sure, but he was so eager to see them. So eager… period. Clumsy. Strange. Unsure. He didn't do anything right.

And way too fast. And when she encouraged him to touch her, he did it fully wrong. He was a virgin with girls too, not just with actual sex. Maybe that helped explain why all of this was going so badly. Even trying to talk about it was painful.

His gaze jerked away.

Regret fully sliced through her.

"Why? How? I mean, Dad said you're my age."

He turned from her and flopped down on the stained couch, leaning forward to keep his head down. "Religion."

She gasped. "Oh, no, this is so much worse than I thought."

He snorted. "No. Not religion. That would be the easiest and least embarrassing answer."

She licked her lips. What should she say? She asked, "What's the harder one?"

His shoulder shrugged. "Just never met the right girl. So it didn't happen."

How could this gorgeous, big man reach the age of twenty-five without it happening? "Are you that picky?"

"I have no idea."

"I'm not exactly considered eye candy for men. How could you choose me?"

His gaze flipped up to hers, and his eyes went wide. "You're the most beautiful person I've ever met."

He then looked back down and clasped his hands together.

Something weird made her heart flutter. She was the most beautiful person he ever met? She wasn't just a sexual partner? He saw her as a woman? And he found her interesting? How flattering.

Her heart pounded harder in her chest. She shut her eyes. She had no idea how much she wanted to be told that. It felt nice to know a guy thought that about her. Two days ago, if someone asked her about it, she'd have said, no, she didn't want that or like being thought of like that. But this guy was so puzzling and strange, it was nice to know he thought that about her.

"But what about the condom you had in your wallet?"

He snorted. "Old habit. I have two older brothers that I lived with until recently. Couldn't have them thinking I was so lame."

"If you considered it lame to wait, why did you?"

His arms were loose but his anxiety showed in his tapping toe. "I didn't like how they did it. We always lived in close quarters. I witnessed it with them way too much. Couldn't avoid it, I guess. I hated that part. I want to be as different from them as possible. Seemed a way to make sure I never hurt anyone. Besides, I also preferred a more private place."

Her mind whirled. Where and under what circumstances were he and his brothers raised? "When you say you didn't want to hurt anyone. What do you mean by that?"

"Most of the girls were usually crying when they left or crying during sex. I didn't like that."

She gripped his forearm near her. "And you thought you hurt me?"

"Yes."

"Is that why you ran off? Because you regretted it so much?"

"Well, that would be the top reason. Next, would be the stupidity of doing it at work, and third, doing it at a job I need."

"You didn't hurt me. You just didn't... do it right, so it surprised me. I swear, I'm fine. I'm a healthy, strong girl."

He didn't even try to smile and she sighed. "This should have never happened. Knowing it was your first time, I'm even more sorry."

He shrugged. "You had to have known. I'm sure I didn't do it right. I mean, just knowing about it is not the same as doing it."

She bit her lip to keep her smile from showing. "Have you ever seen a naked a girl before? Or touched her boobs? Was it all new for you?"

He didn't answer. But his loose shoulder shrug told her no. "Did you like it?"

His gaze slid to her hand, then away. "How can you ask me that? How could I not? I had no idea. I just..."

"Just what?"

"I was too fast and too hard and I lacked finesse. It happened all so fast. And knowing there was someone in the barn with us also made it wrong. I just didn't want to do it so wrong especially with someone there."

Just like his brothers. He didn't say it but the words lingered between them.

Jade wanted to yell at herself. She'd destroyed this man's highest illusions of his self-image and sex. People just assumed all young guys had sex. Lots of it. But did that mean they couldn't have issues like girls did? Of course, they could. Given how he described it, he must have lived at home in crowded circumstances until now. And then she and he did it in the worst way possible. And let's not forget about the person in the barn.

"Okay this had to happen. The job situation being number one. We agree. But in that moment I was… fully gone… I was over the moon for you. I'd never wanted anyone so badly and sex was on my mind. I wanted you so much, I lost track of everything rational. I wanted you so bad, it hurt. I've never reacted that way to a man. Honest to goodness. And then… yeah, it was too fast, and things were a little odd, but I still wanted you." Her words came out in a rush and without pausing. Flipping her hands up, she finished with, "I'm not a sleazebag and I've never done something like that with anyone else even close in proximity. Not like what you describe your brothers did. I was just as taken with you and just as…"

He peeked at her as she spoke. Hot-cheeked now, she said, "I wanted you to touch me until I came so bad I could not stop myself from… from making you do it. That was all on me. You didn't do anything wrong. I should have known that was not the right way to do things."

"It's reasonable to assume I would know how to do some things."

"Is it? Why? I should have slowed down. Or asked you."

"After I was so bad why would you want me to keep touching you?" His puzzled tone revealed his genuine confusion.

"Because I'm that attracted to you. Why do you think that ever even happened?"

"Why did it?"

She tilted her head and stared at his profile. "Why? You're clearly out of my league. Looks wise. But you're funny and you make me laugh. You show up every single day and work like no one I ever knew before. I respect you like hell at work. I hope I can use that to explain why it happened. And I... like you."

"Because I seemed like a good partner for screwing you against the barn wall?"

She bit her lip. "You actually do look like you've had a stable full of women, or men, depending on your preference, with your good looks and hot, blazing body. But I'd never considered us doing that. It was literally in that moment. I felt this desperate desire for you then. I've never been one who goes overboard with sex. I like it a lot. Don't get me wrong. But never have I felt like I *needed* it."

"How do you usually have it then?"

She smiled. "It's fully calculated. I usually know when it's been a while. I just find a ranch hand I don't know who doesn't live near our place, and is transient. I usually hook up at a bar. I flirt for a while. Get a motel room. Have sex and never see the guy again."

"So you came here only because you had to see me again."

"No. I came because I'm filled with shame and guilt for what I did. From start to finish, that was not how sex feels or works for me."

He glanced at her and then away. "I'm sorry it was so bad for you. I've done nothing but relive it with increasing shame. But then for me..."

"What? Please tell me what it was like for you."

"Everything. I never knew anything could feel as wonderful as that."

She smiled at his sweet statement. So naïve. Like something a young kid might say. She found him so puzzling. He looked like a grown-assed, experienced man. And yeah, like he could fuck anyone stupid against a barn wall. But he was so unsure. Clueless. Humble. Sweet.

Still hot.

Even if he lived in the motor home from hell.

"Do you think I'm like the women your brothers pick to sleep with? The ones that made you so averse to having sex?"

He jerked upright and whipped his head around. Immediately, he said, "No. Never. You're a much higher caliber than any person I've ever met. You're everything wonderful."

"No, I'm not. But maybe we could try to determine what I am with you and vice versa."

His eyebrows furrowed. "What?"

She took a deep breath. "What if we did it again? Now we both know each other's names and if you need any coaching, I'm available to help you. I still want you, but not as your boss and not in an otherwise occupied barn."

He went perfectly still. "You... really want to do that again? With me?"

"I want to make sure your first experience is one to remember."

"It... I told you, for me..."

"No. You don't know what it can really be like. Let me show you."

"But... why?"

"I don't know. I'm so attracted to you and we've already done it wrong. I want to do it right now. Change the whole thing around. And the job is irrelevant."

She ruined it and wanted to fix it.

"Here?" He glanced around and his nose scrunched.

"Can you put the sleeping bag out?"

"I don't have anymore condoms."

She shut her eyes. "I do."

"You planned this?"

"No, I always carry them in my purse, which I brought today."

"Oh."

What did *oh* mean? She had no idea. He was no player.

Not even a spectator in the ball game. It made her heart soften. "Can I?"

"Can you what?"

She didn't know. She stood on her feet and gulped down her nerves. Moving towards him, she straddled his lap. "Kiss you?"

He stared at her and nodded. "Yes."

CHAPTER 15

SHE WAS THERE. JADE Rydell had followed him home. There was no more hiding where he lived. She must have had something to say to him, considering what he'd done to her. And he figured he'd lose his job no matter what, anyway.

There was simply no way to hide the motorhome she now stood in front of.

He told her things he'd never considered discussing with anyone. He didn't know anyone to talk about the things they did. He didn't expect she'd want to hear about his thoughts and feelings. Much less, his opinions. Again, no one ever asked Cole for those.

He wasn't sure what to make of the things Jade said.

Except for her guilt over sexual harassment. No. He'd have refused if he didn't want to do it. He didn't realize she could fire or hire him but figured she'd use her dad for that. Although it wasn't his main concern. He *wanted* to kiss her and touch her. So there were no power dynamics involved, like she was so worried about.

What he didn't expect was for her to acknowledge what

she did with him. He'd spent half the night awake reliving it. Thinking how bad it must have been for her. Mostly, he was hung up on her flinching and his failure to do what she asked of him.

But having Ben hunt him down to pay him his wages, and then finding out Jade followed him here?

His mind was blown by both incidents. The father/daughter combination. He was still ashamed for how he'd acted with the daughter and how bad he made sex for Jade.

Except she came to him.

Daylight flooded the space. It was bright and cheerful unlike the RV that was dismal, dumpy, gross and depressing. He jerked his head back. "You can't have sex in a place like this."

She smiled softly and cupped his face with her hands. He had to restrain a groan. She had such soft hands. He'd never been caressed with soft hands before. Or any woman's hands. "Yes, I can. It's your place. And I did it with you in an occupied barn yesterday, so things are improving."

She slipped back and grabbed the hem of her own shirt, lifting it upwards and his body reacted. Intensely. His dick was engorging with blood as inch by inch, more smooth skin became visible.

She wore a beige bra. Lifting her shirt over her head, she caught her hair in it before she released the clasp. He swallowed when she reached around her back and undid her own bra. Slowly, the straps loosened and slid down her arms. And then the mounds of her breasts appeared. His heart started beating hard. Too hard. Sweat made his palms slick. He stared and watched as the fabric fell away, revealing her breasts very slowly.

They were the most perfect, fleshy globes he'd ever seen.

"Have you never...?" her voice interrupted his reverie. He was dazzled by his sudden sense of want and anxiety.

"No. Not until you."

"It's nice to know you don't try to hide it. I'm glad for that. Here, give me your hands."

He stared at his sweaty fist in his lap and looked up at her. "Did I do something else wrong already?"

A soft, little laugh escaped her lips and she shook her head. Her tits swayed a little as she replied, "No. You watched me so reverently, that's what tipped me off. Now give your hands to me."

He stretched out his hands, palms up towards her. She took them in her smaller ones. "I'm going to show you what *I* like. That doesn't mean it's the same for everyone."

Her fingers were cool and smooth on his. She was a tall, poised woman but his huge hand dwarfed hers. He didn't try to resist her, and allowed her full control, gulping when his gaze kept landing childishly on her chest. He couldn't help it. They were so pretty and round with the bright, bold tips so tightly compressed and pouting up.

She took his hands and pressed them to her breasts from below. Then she pushed them into his hands and let him assess the weight of them. She shuddered and her eyelids fluttered. He was surprised he could tear his gaze away from her sexy breasts to care about her facial expression but he did want to know how she felt.

She guided his thumb to her nipple. He didn't need further instructions. He wasn't that clueless. Doubling his movements, he used both of his thumbs to graze the very tips of her nipples. She jolted and he felt her pressing, almost unconsciously, against his jean clad leg. "Yes. Like that. Do it for a long time. I really like that."

He didn't have to be told twice. He kept brushing, swiping, and swirling his thumbs over the ends of her nipples while his hands cupped her breasts. Her eyes closed and her mouth opened as a full gasp was expelled by her.

After several long minutes, she used her hand with his and arranged his fingertips into a type of steeple. "Pull on them. Hard."

He did as she commanded, stretching them out together and she moaned as her head tilted fully back, while pushing her proud, little tips toward him. After several minutes of that wonderful building anticipation, she grabbed the back of his head and pulled him forward with a gentle tug. No teaching was required now, he immediately clamped his mouth on one of her overly sensitized nipples.

"Yes. Oh, my God, yes," she gasped. No further encouragement was needed. He sucked, licked, and gently nipped the tip of it. "You're a fast learner." She championed his efforts with her breathless voice. He switched sides and replaced his fingers with his mouth.

He seemed to be getting something right.

THIS WASN'T Jade's first rodeo, so to speak. And it didn't seem fair for her to hog all the intense, orgasmic crescendos and feelings. He deserved it more than she did.

She rubbed his silky hair in her hands, loving the softness of it. The ends were blunt and kind of hacked up. He needed to get a decent haircut. But not much could hamper his good looks. Finally, she grabbed the strands of hair and tugged back gently. He lifted his face. "Did I do that too hard?"

She shook her head. "No, it was perfect. Let me show you some more things."

His eyebrows lowered as if he were concentrating on a college entrance exam. "Me?"

Licking her lips to stifle her laugh, she nodded. Even now,

he seemed so surprised at anything pleasant being directed his way. Even her.

She leaned off to the side and sat on the sleeping bag. "Take your shoes and socks off. I can't work with those on."

Bending over, he started untying his lace-up boots.

She did the same, slipping her cowboy boots off and then peeling off her socks. "Shirt."

Twisting to the side, he gave her a long study. She smiled. "Trust me. Shirt."

Still sitting, he pulled his torso upright and grabbed the edges of his plain black t-shirt before lifting it off. His skin was paler than his arms and neck, and he had sparse black hairs on his stomach. Jade looked at his flat nipples and shoulders. He was strong and muscular but not ripped. His muscles came directly from the kind of work he did. Not from a gym. He wasn't the type to target areas of his body to create sculpted planes. She particularly liked the wide, bulk of his shoulders and the way his neck emerged from it with a thick band of muscle.

He tossed the shirt beside his leg.

She scooted forward and rose to her knees. "Can I kiss you now?"

He side-eyed her and nodded his head. "You can do anything you want to me."

Her peal of laughter came out too loud. Embarrassed, she slapped a hand over face. He grinned at her. She threw her hands up and said, "I'm nervous."

"*You're* nervous?"

"Yes. It's not often—"

"What?" he prodded.

"It's embarrassing."

"It can't be worse than not knowing what to do or how to do it."

"I haven't done it twice before."

"As in, you only give a guy one round?"

She bit her lip, finally admitting that with a nod. "Yes. Only once with one guy. Some guy I know I'll never see again. So…"

He tilted his head. "So… again, you can do anything you want to me."

"You should never give anyone that kind of open permission."

"I'm not giving it to anyone. I'm giving it to you."

Her heart skipped and she felt weird. "Just me?"

"Just you."

"Okay. I'm kissing you now." She leaned over and kissed his mouth. Starting chaste and easy, she slid her dry lips over his. He turned his head and she sighed at how soft his lips felt. When she finally released him, she began peppering kisses down the side of his face, cheek, chin and neck. Some errant hairs tickled her lips, left over from shaving too quickly. His skin was warm and smooth and she could feel him swallowing. He tilted his head back, seeming to enjoy her little trail of kisses.

She slipped her hand to the top of his shoulder and kissed it. Then she leaned forward and began licking his nipples and he jumped the first time he felt the touch of her tongue on them.

"Didn't expect that," he said softly.

She kissed him some more and moved down over his stomach. His muscles flexed and his breath seemed to catch as she kept slipping lower and lower, her long hair sliding down his skin and spreading out over his nether region in wild disarray. She felt him threading his fingers through the ends of her hair and twisting it.

She lifted her head and brought her hands down to his jeans *finally*.

The old motor home was insanely bright with the afternoon light. It wasn't like her to be shy. But it wasn't like her to have sex in the daylight either. Usually, she did it in a motel bed, after lots of drinking and at night time. Murky atmosphere. Names mentioned but never remembered. A little conversation and not much else. No real connection. No secret looks or smiles or even thoughts like she'd shared with Cole so far.

It wasn't exactly making love, but for her it was the most intimate she'd been with a partner. She was amazed to find sex with Cole so nerve-wracking, but also tender.

She gripped the heavy buckle of his belt and quickly undid it. Tugging several times until it slid off him, she dropped it to the floor. Next she grabbed the waistline of his jeans. His chest rose and fell more rapidly.

"Lift up," she commanded and after loosening it, she pulled the zipper downwards. His penis rushed out, all hard and hot, bouncing upwards towards her and clearly eager for freedom. His legs strained and his butt came up as she worked the jeans down far enough so she could grab his hardened length.

He surged towards her while his butt plopped back on the seat. She grabbed him with both hands and he sucked in a deep lungful of air.

He'd more than earned his share of pleasure.

She kept one hand gripping him while she pulled upwards. While pumping him, she kissed his chest and he made soft sounds of gratification. Watching her hand on him made her heart beat faster and she finally leaned forward to climb into his lap.

Her lips touched the tip of his penis first. She held him still, pointing upwards between her lips and her hot tongue gently lapped the end of him. He let out a happy sound, something between a moan and groan. Her hair slipped all around her as her hands kept gripping it, while his hips pushed upwards towards the heat of her perfect mouth.

She hadn't done this very often. But the grunts Cole made indicated she really nailed it. She licked him and took him down her throat and held him with hands.

As she predicted before, he wouldn't last long, which is what she was counting on. Feeling him starting to strain, he muttered, "Oh, damn."

She felt him coming and released him from her mouth. She could not swallow his semen. Quickly lifting her head, she kept her hand working him and set her mouth on his. He leaned over her, jamming his tongue into her mouth, and taking her head with his hands. He rubbed and caressed the back of her head. Her hair would be rendered a literal rat's nest after this encounter.

He moaned into her mouth. He was lost. Gone. She knew she was overwhelming him.

She pushed his penis against his stomach when she felt him ready to come and kissed him right as it spurted out.

He let out a moan. She kept kissing him as he held her face in his hands. His eyes were shut and he seemed almost in a daze. His mouth devoured hers.

She finally slowed him down and kissed him once, twice, three times before he finally released her.

His head flopped dramatically back on the headrest. He didn't move. She curled against his side. Doing her best to keep his goo off her, she leaned her head on his shoulder and kissed it. "Sorry, but I don't like to swallow."

His head didn't move. "Don't apologize. You just gave me the greatest experience of my life."

His eyes still shut; his hands hung limply his sides as he was so spent, he couldn't move. A giggle came out of her mouth. She slapped her hand over her mouth and tried to suppress it.

His mouth smiled although his eyes remained closed. "You have such a pretty laugh."

"It was a giggle. And I *don't* giggle."

His eyelids opened, and he said, "You just giggled with me. I should probably ask you why, but I'm afraid I don't care."

"You. You're so…"

"Quick?"

She did laugh this time. "Yes, but I knew you'd be. I was counting on it. I can't do that for very long. It'll make the next part better."

"So were you like… prepping me for you?"

"Yes." She smiled and he understood. "And you were so…"

"Grateful? Amazed?"

"No. I was going to say, relaxed. I don't think I've ever seen you that relaxed."

He finally lifted his head. "That was not relaxed. That was me after losing my head. That was… the polar opposite of relaxed."

She leaned forward, pulling his head down and kissing him long and deep. "No. Okay then, you were unstressed. Right here. And you didn't run off."

"If you want to do *this* with me, I won't run. I swear."

"You might when you have to return the favor."

"Return the—" He paled so fully, his mouth looked strained.

She quickly rubbed her thumb over his lips. "Forget it. Not today. I was just teasing. Kidding. Only when…"

"When? Are you suggesting this could happen more than just today?"

She gave him an odd look. "Of course, more than today. You caught that part, at least. I hope you want to spend more time with me."

"I want you," he answered immediately.

She leaned over and picked up his discarded shirt, which she placed on his stomach and used to soak up the mess they'd created. His hand clamped her wrist. "I got it."

She allowed him to finish wiping off his stomach and she got to her feet. She was trying to ignore the boards on the floor below her and cringing when she thought about what her bare feet might be touching.

"I'm sorry."

"For what?" she asked while looking down to unsnap her jeans.

"The flooring. And the rest of the RV."

She lifted her gaze to his and held it for a long moment. "I'm not sorry." She was lying, of course. But it was entirely worth it, and necessary and the kindest thing to do. She chose that over saying the brutal truth.

Then she tugged her jeans downwards along with her underwear. One foot came out and she used the other one to hold the pant leg down while she pulled her other leg out of it.

Naked.

She faced him and he quit talking. His eyes glimmered like hot coals as they started on her neck and slowly journeyed down her body, all the way to her toes. He spent some extra time staring at her middle.

"Cole?"

He didn't raise his gaze from her.

"Just let me enjoy the scenery for a while. It was so fast last time. Confusing."

"Confusing?"

"I wanted to look at everything at once. And touch and feel and kiss you all over. And then... when the actual sex happened, I wanted to die while doing it. Nothing ever felt so good to me before. I didn't know it could be so fantastic. It happened so fast and spontaneously that I just got... overwhelmed and wrapped up in the moment. Just let me take some time to look at you now."

She tilted her head and considered the care he displayed while examining her naked figure. "You've seen naked pictures before, right?"

"Porn isn't anything like this, Jade."

Finally. He said her name. It sent shivers down her arms. So did his intense and thorough inspection of her. She fought the urge to cross her legs or tap her foot when her nerves started to show. "I can't… just stand here like I'm on display."

He sighed and rose to his feet, dropping his jeans down. She bit her lip when he bent down and pulled his legs from his pants. "Did you just sigh at me?" Jade asked him.

He turned around, now naked as she was, and towered over her. "I did. I was really enjoying the view of you ."

"What do you think of the view?"

He lifted a hand to her face. "I think it's the best view I've ever had the pleasure of seeing."

She stepped forward until they were toe to toe. "I don't know the best way to do this."

"Well… I doubt I have any opinions."

"Do you like to control things? Or would you rather I led you?"

"For this? I'd be grateful if you led me through all the steps."

"Okay."

She set her hands flat on the middle of his chest and slowly pushed them upwards to loop around his neck. He had to bend down a few inches as their mouths touched and they picked up right where they left off. He held her much harder against his chest and finally seemed to respond with more confidence and poise. His mouth parted and he filled hers with his demanding, pleasure-seeking tongue.

She let him kiss her until he could do it no more. It seemed like all he wanted was to dally with her and take his time learning the skills. He also wanted to experience it fully. Jade couldn't remember getting so much attention on her body, her needs, and her responses before. It made her feel self-conscious as well as empowered.

She finally turned and tugged on his shoulders. Cole got the hint and turned immediately until he was beneath her so she could straddle his middle. She took her lazy time inspecting the enormous body she saw laid out before her. Wide, square shoulders that were well-rounded by defined muscles. She admired his biceps and his thick wrists. His neck was also very square and ropey. She caressed his wide chest, tracing his sculpted pecs and the way his waist tapered so nicely as the muscles of his abs and sides like corded bands. She touched, prodded, rubbed, and felt his entire chest. She was also discovering what he liked. The texture of his skin intrigued her and she liked the way it stretched over his expansive chest.

"Have you always been so buff?"

"No. Just sometimes. Depends on the work I do. Most of the work I do is outside. Usually lifting all kinds of shit."

"Before you came here, what were you doing?"

"Threw freight at a distribution center."

His voice warbled when both of her hands slid upwards, in tandem from his waist to his shoulders. He shuddered and fully enjoyed the sensation. Her hands slid over him and she felt the warmth of his body rising. Silky smooth. Hard as steel. Filled with grace. Steady as stone. The contradictions Jade observed in Cole made him even more alluring to her.

He looked like Hercules but he was a virgin. Usually quiet and liked to run everywhere he went. Strong but filled with anxiety.

Leaning forward, her lips kissed the spot where a thick

band of muscles rippled between his neck and shoulder. Jade licked, kissed, nibbled, and worked her way towards the soft plumpness of his lips.

Then, the electricity between them fully exploded. Turning his face to meet her lips, Cole's hands wrapped around her bare back and he pulled her tightly down on his chest. His mouth felt hot and he hurried to kiss her again. Her body was perfectly aligned over his.

She started dripping on his thigh and his erection prodded her thighs.

"Let me get the condom," she whispered between kisses, her own tone breathless. She tilted off to the side, searching for her purse. Finding the desired object, she popped up and handed it to him.

She rolled on top of him as their mouths fused together once more. Opening her legs over him, with little fanfare, she carefully lined him up to her wet, hot entrance before leaning back to let him slide inside her.

She moaned into his mouth when he so easily filled her up. Thrusting her hips toward him, she fully enveloped him. His long groan was deep and heartfelt.

Jade intended to fully demonstrate all the joys of sex to Cole, but to her surprise, she got so turned on, she began to seek her own satisfaction instead of worrying about Cole's. She lifted her hips and her tongue smashed into his, while her body once more hovered over his.

Sighs and moans from both of them filled the small space. It no longer mattered if Jade came into contact with the fabric of the couch beneath them. Or that it was hot and stuffy in the RV and the dust particles kept swirling aimlessly around them. It didn't matter there was no proper flooring or that they were uninhibited and loud. The act itself became the only goal. She was lost in time and space, something that never happened before to her. She loved how Cole felt inside her warm, wet, swollen center that, with each thrust, surged with a gratifying release. She grunted when he slammed his hips fully into her.

She impaled herself directly over him and he let out a startled cry of surprise and unbridled ecstasy. She grabbed one side of the couch for leverage before she started pumping herself over him. So lost in her own pulsating rhythm, she could only obey her greedy, primal need to have more of him buried inside her. Fuller. Harder. Deeper. She wanted him to consume her from the inside out. He zeroed in on that spot inside her that responded to him with every touch, push, and stroke as her body worked over his, her tits bouncing, hair swishing, and her eyes closed. Every part of Jade was lost to Cole and at the mercy of his body.

After several more minutes, her body exploded in a rush of blinding, wonderful, light and joy that stretched from her toes to her scalp and her fingertips. Damn. It curled through her like adrenaline, starting deep in her guts and swirling through her bloodstream and out to her extremities. She pushed hard against him as the aftershocks subsided.

She suddenly felt him grabbing her waist, holding her steady before he rammed himself up inside her without any finesse, clumsiness or hesitation.

Yeah, Cole figured out real quick what he wanted. He also knew how to get it and he wasn't shy about taking it.

She leaned her hands flat on his chest to ride out his orgasm inside her. His mouth hung open, his eyes shut and he let out a long, gasping groan that seemed to make him shudder.

She was staring at him before his eyelids blinked open. He stared up at her, still unseeing for several seconds. Only when his body started to relax did he lift his big hand to touch the side of her cheek. He pulled her mouth down and planted his lips on hers.

"You're a fast learner," she commented dryly, speaking between kisses. She felt his lips twisting up into a smile.

"I had an excellent teacher."

She kissed him again before flopping down, exhausted, on his chest. His big hands stroked the bare contours of her back and she let out a soft moan at the tingling that followed the rub.

Her head twisted to the side, right over his heart she could feel the pounding of it until it started to regulate. Their skin cooled down and his penis withdrew from her. She slid to the side and he wrapped his arms around her. She lay still for a long while, content and relax, almost draped over him. His hands slipped from her shoulders down to her bare butt as he kneaded all her muscles. She let him know how much she liked it with a few moans of pleasure.

It wasn't long before she felt him hardening again. Smiling, she tilted her head up, placing her hand under her chin. "Really, cowboy? You ready to ride again?"

He grinned, sheepishly, and with a lazy ease that he lacked the first time. He was starting to get used to her. "Anytime you're ready…"

There's something to be said for insatiable virgins…

They did it three times in as many hours. The third time, Cole put his arm around her waist and rammed her from behind, diving into her dripping wetness over and over again. Trembling, she used her hands when she nearly collapsed forward, and tilted his target upwards for easier access. He finished by slapping her butt until she was screaming into the sleeping bag underneath her. She bit into the corner of it to muffle her screams.

White-hot. Blistering. Ceaseless. They both enjoyed the wild, primal onslaught that ensued and the shattering, screaming orgasms that left both of them trembling. She collapsed face first and he did too, falling to the side of her.

His lips touched her ear before they both melted into a big puddle of wonderful feelings and treasured memories.

He was intoxicating. Totally new and different for her.

He adored her too.

He touched her everywhere. Rubbing, massaging, holding. He didn't stop. It was like he could not stop touching her, as if he needed to memorize every part of her and her body. There was no part of her he didn't touch. He licked, sucked and rubbed all of her parts, from the pads of her feet to the mound of joy between her wet, now aching legs.

She had bite marks, hickies, and razor-burn from the bristles on his chin. But Jade got so much sexual pleasure she feared she'd pass out from sheer ecstasy. She even slept next to him... once. Only to be aroused by his magical hands abrading her nipples in soft circles of exploration.

Finally, she closed her legs and pushed her butt against him. "No more or I'll never be able to walk again."

He jerked back in horror. "Are you really hurt?"

She let out a husky laugh. "Screwed raw, cowboy. I'm burnin' and stingin'. But it's a great condition to suffer from. One that I have to say is new for me too."

He kissed the side of her face while she kept her eyes closed. "I'm sorry. You feel so good to me."

Her eyelids flipped open as she tossed onto her back so she could see him. She pushed away the hair that kept falling over his forehead. "Yeah. I get that. So do you."

His gaze stared at her. "Really? Despite all the newness?"

His eagerness was intoxicating by itself. Plus, he did exactly what she said when she moved his hand or shifted him here and there. He responded instantly with enthusiasm and an insatiable desire to please her.

"Yeah. That was... hot. All of it. And pretty unusual for me. So it's new for me too."

He kissed her mouth. Then, his regret gleaming in his eyes, he said, "But I have to be somewhere soon."

She smiled up at him. "That's good. We can't seem to stop and I won't be able to work."

He eased off her and she finally sat upright, wincing. He noticed it and set a hand on her lower back. "I can't stop. I mean… unless we're stopping because this was just another accident?"

She found her shirt and slipped it over her head. She stopped dressing herself to answer him. "No, Cole. We're going to do this a lot more."

"Like… in secret?"

She stood upright, shaking her head. "No. There's no reason to keep it a secret. It's already known. But we could start dating?"

Stepping into her jeans, she looked down as she rushed the last question from her lips. She was a new at this, just as he seemed to be.

"Us?"

She looked upright. "Well, why not? We get along okay. We talk all the time. We definitely have sex figured out right. So… why not?"

His head nodded and he stared down, as if in thought, but even he was surprised that it made him feel suddenly shy.

"Cole?"

He stood up and stepped towards her. "Yes. Anything you ask me or want from me, my answer is yes."

She slid her hands up his chest and looped them around his neck as she gave him a theatrical groan. "Never give anyone that much permission. I told you before how much I like bossing people around. You could regret giving me that kind of trust. You can't trust people. I might take advantage of it."

His head tilted back and his teeth flashed in a laugh. It was a rare treat for Jade to see him acting so young and relaxed. She stared at him, eager for more moments of happiness and ease. "I think I want you to take all kinds of advantage of me." His boyish, hot smile and twinkle in his eyes made her heart swell.

Oh, damn. This might be much more than she'd ever contemplated before.

"Don't be weird when I see you tomorrow," she commanded.

"Only if you promise not to be either."

She nodded her head. Fair enough. She deserved that warning. Setting her hand out with her pinkie sticking up, he glanced down and gave her an odd look. "What? Pinkie promise?"

"Yep."

He grimaced but twisted his pinkie around hers and then pulled her forward, kissing her lips. "I'm glad you followed me home today."

She surprised herself when she swatted his ass and gave him a flirty smile. "Oh, yeah, cowboy, sure you are."

Then she turned to leave and with huge, matching, happy grins, they walked to her car, where they kissed one more time before she drove off.

What had she just started?

CHAPTER 16

"OKAY, COWBOY LET'S SEE if we can't actually turn you into one." Jade Rydell's voice came up behind Cole as he was busy hauling feed to the next group of horses. Startled at her coming up to him right there at work, he whipped around. Weren't they supposed to be hiding this?

"Ms. Rydell, I thought…"

She glanced around, stepping right up to him, and stood with her booted toes touching his booted toes. She was not touching him however. Although it felt like it. And then she shook her head. "Don't ever call me that again."

"I thought…"

"We're co-workers. Jade and Cole. Remember? Co-workers talk and give shit to each other for fun, and work together. They do not get all breathless and confused or put Mr. and Ms. before their names. Especially ranch workers like us."

Like us. Those words were the greatest aphrodisiac Cole could ever imagine. Or dream. Being a real ranch worker, with Jade, on the same ranch.

He nodded. "So we can interact?"

Her lips tilted up. "Yes. There's no shame in having sex. On our personal time. Not on our work time. We only crossed the boundaries once. We won't do it again, since neither of us liked how that felt. But it was great otherwise, just not at work. Right?"

Her voice was strong and sure and he stared at her. Was she ever unsure about anything? Did propriety even matter to her? It was hard for Cole to imagine his opinion mattered to anyone. But to someone like Jade? Someone so beautiful. Poised. Assured. Smart. And confident? That meant the world to Cole.

"Right. If you think that's best."

"I do. Plus, this is a *working* horse ranch. So you need to know how to get on one." Her smile returned, big and bright as she added, "Cowboy." Then she winked and turned away.

Was she flirting? Cole never engaged in that kind of fun before. But her words registered and made sense to him so he followed her. "Wait. You just want me to get on a horse?"

Walking swiftly across the yard, she glanced over her shoulder. "Well, soon, but not yet. First, you have to learn how to approach one."

He rushed over to her and said, "But Melanie told me to stack all these windows in the storage room. It's gonna take me hours. Learning how to approach the horses isn't working."

She stopped dead and flipped around. "We're the Rydell River Ranch. We teach people to ride, probably a half dozen or more a day on average. That includes you, and you'll still get paid while you learn. You deserve that and you've earned it. When will you realize you won't be kicked off the job if you take a lunch hour? Crap. If it makes you feel better, consider it time served for all the bathroom breaks, lunches, Saturdays and Sundays you worked right through."

She kept walking.

Distraught by his indecision, Cole followed her. "Jade!"

She didn't stop until she came to one of the paddocks. He didn't know the name of the horse enclosed there. They had so many horses, Cole couldn't keep track of all their names.

"What?" Jade replied.

"I'm… also… terrified of them."

She shook her head. "So I gathered. Although I can't relate to that kind of phobia, I promise to be gentle with you. Far gentler than I have been with you."

He blushed as she no doubt intended. Funny part was: she blushed too, even though she said it. Then she let out a groan of frustration. "You've made me feel all weird now and I never did before."

"About what? Riding?"

"No, sex." Her gaze flitted to him and away. "I keep feeling like it's all new to me too. But riding isn't new at all. It's just work. Okay, I promise to go slowly. And seriously, you might love it. A lot of people who are initially afraid of horses and aren't even interested in riding find it completely different when they try it."

He sighed. "Kind of like sex."

She happily giggled. He'd never heard her laugh like that and it affected not only his heart, but also his dick. She was so intriguing. Worldly. Comfortable in her own body and mind. And so adorable telling him he made her feel something different than she'd felt before.

Damn, if only she knew. She was completely new to anything he'd ever felt.

"That was funny and true and I can't believe you said it. Here."

She pretended to do a full body shake. "Okay. No more. We must behave like student and teacher now. The only concern on your mind from now on is horses," she added sharply when he opened his mouth. He wanted to add something to flirt at work with suggestive innuendoes. It was oddly hot. Foreplay of a sort.

"No more joking. Strictly ranch stuff. All right, what do I do, teacher?"

She sighed deeply and her shoulders sagged. Was it from unhappiness? Alarmed he asked, "What? What did I say wrong now?"

"Nothing. I was disappointed in myself. All I could think about was teaching you things by bossing you around. I'm ashamed to admit I like it and I didn't know how much I liked it until now."

"Is that a bad thing?"

"What if no one likes it as much as I do?"

"What if I like it?"

He turned away before she could see his blush. Or his massive hard-on.

Minutes passed, she was busy roping the horse. She walked it through the open gate towards him. Stopping in the corral only a few feet from him, she said, "Okay, cowboy, back to work. Now are you afraid to be near this horse?"

"I was only ever close to the one that kicked me."

"That was a bad introduction. But I hope you learned to always be aware. Even the most docile horse will kick or flinch when they're startled. They have a fight or flight reaction, and their first instinct is always to run. So they don't usually try to kick you. But the result's the same. Never act scared with them. Be respectful and observe their moods. Their energy. And they will react the same way to you. They can smell fear so don't let it cross your mind."

He glanced at the docile, quiet horse beside her. Its head was dropped and it seemed to merely be foraging for tasty morsels in the scrub and dirt. Jade held it by a loose lead rope. It didn't pull or try to get away.

But the animal was so *big*. It was dark black and its back was higher than her breasts. Cole had to wonder how high its head reached. He gulped.

"I can't imagine getting on the back of one. I'm not sure it's worth all the stress."

Jade, who could ride before she could walk, gave him a soft smile. "Cole, I swear to you it's worth it. It's so incredible. You explore the world in a brand new way with this big, majestic animal between your legs. It feels... I don't know how to describe it. It moves and sways over the land so effortlessly, like you're floating or gliding. It feels so good... and not scary at all. Like being part of something much bigger than yourself. You're controlling an animal that trusts you and allows you to control it. The horse agrees to let you direct it where to go. It responds to you because it trusts you. It's an amazing gift for these huge, intelligent creatures to bestow on us. I mean, deer don't do that. Most herd animals are unwilling to be trained and corralled and asked to do all the things we do with horses."

He blinked in surprise at her speech. She glanced at him when he became so quiet. Then she flinched and gave him an uncharacteristically shy smile. "You're surprisingly easy to talk to."

He'd never been told that in his life.

"You really feel that way about the horses? That's why you like doing this?"

She shrugged. "I do. I don't think I've ever explained it like I just did to anyone before. But yes, I really do. It's like something deep inside my soul that calls to me. I can't imagine my life without it every single day. I know how stupid lucky I am too. I mean, look how hard you have to work. You do it just to earn a paycheck. But I'd work with horses no matter what, if I never made a dime doing it. I know I'm privileged and ridiculously indulged."

"No. I don't hate what I do for money... I didn't grow up with much in the way of a decent family and I never had any hobbies or sports. I never knew anyone who loved something as much as you love horses. You're unlike anyone I know. I'm glad you get to do this and that you love it so much." He cleared his throat and looked away.

Silence followed his comments. When he looked over at her, she was staring at him. The back of the horse was between them. Her eyes were big and... what? Misty?

"Cole?"

He wondered where her nickname and sarcasm went. She sounded breathless. "I think I could teach you a lot of things that you'd end up of loving to do."

His heart beat faster. What? No. What did she mean by that? He was not as adventurous as she was. He liked to enjoy good things. But what did she mean by that?

Sex. She liked him for sex. Why not? It was amazing. Perfect. Far beyond anything he deserved. Sure.

Jade just stared at him.

He dropped his hands to his sides and turned fully to address the horse. "All right, Jade. What do I do first?"

She shook her head. "I suddenly don't know. I've never actually met someone who was so afraid of horses before. I've taught tons of newbies, mostly ranch or resort guests, who want to ride but don't know how. The ones who pay to learn aren't afraid of horses."

"Could I possibly help?"

Startled, they both jumped a little and turn around as one. The woman's voice was unexpected since neither of them noticed her in the vicinity. She must have heard them talking to ask that question.

"Grandma!" Jade exclaimed in a way too high-pitched, little girl's voice. He'd never heard her sound like that before.

Grandma? Cole's heart started jackhammering in triple speed. His palms were instantly slick with sweat from his nerves. Shit. *Grandma* had to mean the woman was Erin. *Erin Poletti.*

No. Erin Rydell. But she was still Erin, Cole's aunt.

Cole knew nothing about Erin or Jack Rydell when he arrived at the ranch. The idle gossip from the other workers allowed Cole to glean some information. They had a house on the south end of the ranch, with their own personal barn and horses. They didn't often spend time on the main part of the ranch, where Cole did most of the physical work.

But after working for Melanie, he wondered if she might be the best person to find a home for Penny. He'd already watched her demonstrate her heart and bravery as well as being badass. Penny was badass too.

So was Jade.

Cole tried to ignore the jittery nerves roiling in his stomach. He didn't expect to feel so emotional at the thought of knowing his aunt. His real family.

He dropped his gaze to the ground and it landed on the tip of Erin's boots. He slowly scanned upwards with his eyes. She was quite small in height. Jade dwarfed her. Thin, and wearing jeans with a sweatshirt, she looked like most of the women on the ranch. She was sixty-eight or so, if his calculation were right. She was still rather spry and fast though, almost like someone his own age.

His aunt had black hair that she tucked up in a cowboy hat. But her face really knocked Cole for a loop. It socked him right in his gut. Older, with more wrinkles and paler but... Damn, she could have been Penny.

He blinked a few times.

He had no idea. Melanie resembled Penny too, but only a little. Erin was more like a clone. Even separated by a half century, the resemblance between his sister and his aunt was undeniably striking.

Erin was the only decent Poletti, who smiled with kindness at her daughter and then turned towards him.

"How did you know what I was doing?"

"Your dad mentioned it. Growing up on the back of a horse, you're not the best teacher for someone who fears horses. Someone who overcame their own fear of horses might be better at it."

Cole couldn't gulp down the lump in his throat. He was shocked Erin was there. Her voice was soft and kind. His brain got all foggy and dizzy. Did she come over to teach him how to ride? She was a stranger to him. He was just a ranch hand with a phobia of horses. Why would she care? Why would any of the Rydells be so damn decent to a stranger? A worker. He was just a worker on their ranch.

But they treated him better than his own father did.

"Well, I was hoping I might have some sensitivity and not be a monster about it." Jade's voice interrupted his thoughts. Casual. Easy. This meant nothing to her. Just a normal day when her grandma walked over to see her.

Cole fisted his hands at his sides to keep his anxiety at bay.

Erin chuckled. "Yeah, because a little finesse goes a long way. Honey, you're an amazing leader and you're so tough and fierce, you can wrangle cowhands double your size. But as for being sensitive to the frailties of others, maybe not so much. Bull in a China shop. That's our Jade."

Cole laughed out loud. Startled by the echo of his laughter, both women turned towards him. Jade's demeanor hadn't changed: boundless, frenetic energy. She was like that with horses, work, and sex. Even when they did it in the barn, she couldn't stop herself despite knowing it was wrong. And she also knew the barn had another occupant. Bull in a China shop.

He shrugged when he saw her scowling at him. "That's so true about you."

"Well, at least I didn't throw you into the stall with it to get kicked again." She growled back, her eyes flashing.

Erin stepped between them. "Let's try some finesse, honey. That's my specialty. How about it? I've got some time this afternoon. Let me do this and you can take over tomorrow. It takes more than one lesson to overcome fear."

Jade glared at him for a moment and then gave the end of the lead rope to her grandma. "Well, fine. Don't want to step on his tender toes with all my mean, horrible, bullying ways." Then she stomped away in anger.

Surprised, Cole watched her leave. Erin merely laughed again. "Don't worry, she's just high-spirited. Quick to boil over, quick to simmer down. A lot like her grandpa."

Cole turned his full attention to Erin. She was the very reason he was on the ranch. His damn throat felt constricted. "Jack? That's Jade's grandpa, right? Your husband?"

"Yes. You haven't met him yet?"

"Nope, but I heard a lot about him… and you."

Her mouth lifted into a soft small smile. "I hope it was nothing too terrible."

"No, just the opposite. Legendary status."

She scoffed. "Well, it's bullshit then. We're just a bunch of ranchers that are getting too damn old to do it anymore. Now, it's Cole, right?"

"Yes."

"Cowboy to our Jade?"

She knew. Her eyes twinkled as she assessed him. That's why she was there. She was checking him out for "their Jade." He was sure of it. He rubbed his sweaty hands on his thighs. "Yes. But only sarcastically." He flinched.

Erin stepped closer to the horse and rubbed its head. The horse lifted its head up and looked across the stable, curious about something it saw or heard. The quick motion and change of the horse's posture made Cole jump back. Erin was totally hidden by the height and breadth of the huge animal. He could no longer see her. She stepped under the horse's head so she could see him.

Erin noticed his shocked expression at her action. "Yes. I understand now. Not too used to them, are you?"

"No, ma'am."

"Call me Erin." She waved a hand around.

Cole knew in thirty seconds: Erin was nothing like Chance Poletti. His heart expanded in his chest. She spoke in a soft tone. She showed him kindness even though he was a stranger. How well she knew Jade and how to handle her. That appealed to him. The way she gently stroked the horse. There was care, concern and genuine love in everything she did to those around her. Be they persons or horses.

He almost fell on his knees. He wished he could tell her everything. Who he was. Why he was there. And Penny. All about Penny. He wished he could beg her to take his sister and teach her to be just like Erin. So Penny would know that good people did exist in the world. Penny needed to grow up like Erin Poletti, not *him*. Not the other Poletti.

He asked, "Were you always able to walk around them like that?"

"No. I was terrified of them when I first got here. That was a lifetime ago. Hard to picture an old lady like me but I was about your age when I first came to this place."

"You remember the first day you came here? Then you weren't a Rydell, I guess. Duh. I mean, most women take their husband's name when they marry."

Startled, she looked up at him. "No one's ever asked me that before. I mean, most of the folks in this valley have known Jack and his family for over a century. No one ever thought I was a Rydell until Jack married me. No, my name was… well, I haven't used it in many decades. It was a shitty last name from the shittiest time of my life."

Cole knew. He shared that thought. He was stuck with it forever though. For a moment, he tried to imagine not having that Poletti stain on his name, his reputation, and for the rest of his life.

"I know how that is."

Her gaze focused more clearly on him. "This place was a lot smaller then. With only the barns right there, the fencing from there to there, some sheds, and the main house when I first came here. Less than half what you see now, excluding the resort. And yet, when I first saw it, I thought it was the most beautiful place God ever created on earth. I didn't know people lived like this."

His heart skipped a beat. Yeah. Yes. Exactly his opinion. "I —I literally thought that too. When I first pulled into the driveway. I never thought I could… get a job and work here."

"Jade and most of the kids here now don't know what it was like in the old days. For which I'm glad. Their appreciation or lack of it doesn't affect the way I always felt about it. This place. The horses. The Rydells. They kind of saved my life back then. I always wondered if I hadn't found this place, would I have survived? But I think you might understand what I mean."

How did she know? Did she sense their blood relationship? Did she get a whiff of the reeking evil spawned by Chance that surely resided in him? Cole was her nemesis. Cole had no doubt about that after meeting her.

She was everything decent; and Chance was everything satanic.

"I do. I understand that."

She smiled. "These horses, however, scared me so much, I

almost peed in my pants. So I'll teach you the way my own husband taught me."

"Was he your husband when he taught you?"

"No. Learning to ride was kinda how we found each other, to be honest."

"How did he start?"

"Gentle and easy. He asked me, would you like to come closer? Let's start there. Nothing else. Just sharing the space with the animal. They always know you're there. They feel you. The anxiety inside you right now? This girl knows all about it. But they don't necessarily do anything about it, you know? They just accept it because that's how you feel. But when you start dealing with them, then they might care about how you feel."

He didn't expect his first horse lesson to be about how the horses felt about him. He stared open-mouthed at her. "I had no idea it was so complicated."

"I remember how surprised I was to learn they weren't all animals with the exact same personality. They're dynamic, interesting, and very different creatures. All of them. That was my first surprise. More like dogs and humans than a herd of sheep."

So Erin Rydell taught Cole for another hour. He listened to her carefully as she simply spoke about horses in general. Then she talked about the one beside her. She was full of funny stories in how she first dealt with them. Lulled by her easy manner, Cole soon relaxed but was unaware of himself until she suddenly let out a huge smile.

"Now that your nerves are calmed, if you want to try putting your hand out and letting the horse see your palm, put this in your hand." She produced a carrot.

Sure as shit, the horse's big, long teeth came towards his hand. His heart hammering, he stared at it, big-eyed until the horse gently mouthed the carrot. He didn't dare move a muscle. After the horse lifted the carrot from Cole's palm, Erin laughed. "There, Cole. Congratulations on your first healthy interaction with a horse." And she genuinely admired him for it.

His first on purpose, interaction with a horse and he didn't die. He counted it a win.

CHAPTER 17

"GRANDMA, WHAT THE HELL was that? Why did you all but strong-arm me out of there?" Jade shouted as she stormed up to Erin.

"I've heard a lot about your cowboy. Wanted to get a feel for him myself."

"My c-c—" Jade pressed her lips together. "He's not my anything."

Erin smiled with a knowing maternal look that was also kind of chiding. "I was young once. You're not the only one to find the barns... interesting places to hang around."

Her entire body jerked upright. No one knew that. What? How? But... Oh, god, Gross. Was her grandma talking about her grandpa?

Had they done it in the barn too? "How did you—" Jade slapped a hand over her mouth in horror.

Grandma merely shook her head. "No one told me. I just suspected. I heard a rumor from your mother. Figured out where things might happen, considering where you spend all your time."

Jade was blazing so hot, she feared she would incinerate.

"Grandma," she groaned as she rubbed her knuckles into her eyes.

"Jade, honey, he's very handsome. He's kind and gentle and he looks at you as if you're the only woman he's ever seen. He's also poor and was pretty hungry when he came here. I just wanted to see for myself. You're worldly and awesome and you do know cowhands. But you were never like him. The daughter of a landowner might not always understand someone who isn't so fortunate."

"What are you talking about? Like I'm somehow clueless and he's using me? Or I can't understand his lack of resources? Or… what?"

"As if I wanted to make sure he wasn't using you."

"Grandma."

"He's not. He's very unsure, and sweet, and docile. He's also smitten with you. I thought he might be using you but I think, sweetheart, you need to tread gently with him."

She blinked. Well, yes, duh. She'd deduced that about the same time she was sitting on his lap teaching him how to make her happy. She hadn't forgotten his hesitation and concern. But being warned about it by her grandmother? That was odd, strange and inappropriate.

"You thought that about him too? He's big and tough looking, but there's something…"

"Vulnerable and tragic about him?"

"Yes." Wide-eyed, Jade stared at her grandma. "Yes, that's it. I couldn't find the words."

"He's been through a lot. Something happened to him before he came here."

Jade bit her lip. "More like you."

"Yes."

"And I'm a spoiled jerk who grew up like this." Jade waved her hands towards the ridiculous wealth surrounding them.

"Yes. Thank goodness. No one would wish my life and

upbringing on anyone they love. But he didn't have any of this."

"He's—" she thought of the ugly RV, but hesitated to say anything. She didn't want to upset his privacy. She'd already violated it. He said he wasn't a convict or druggie or anything else nefarious, but what if he were?

He was too kind. Funny. Sweet. Tough. Hot. There were so many contradictions to figure out with him. About him.

"I like him," Jade finally admitted to her grandmother as well as to herself.

"I had a feeling. After you told your dad about him and didn't want him fired."

"I would never do that."

"It would have solved it. No one would have known. But you didn't. You took responsibility and suffered personal humiliation. You also look at him like…"

"Like what?"

"Well, even old ladies know what *that look* is."

She licked her lips. "I've never felt this way before."

"I know. We all know. You're lucky."

"How is that lucky?"

She shrugged. "Because you *are* vulnerable. It's hard to be like that, isn't it?"

"I'm terrified of it."

She nodded. "I know. For you especially."

She glanced around. "He… was a virgin." She blushed furiously. "I was afraid I ruined it for him. And yet, he's so worried about me."

"He's opposite to you. That could have benefits sometimes."

"Do you think it's okay? Dating him while he works for us?"

Erin had a small smile on her lips. "Was it okay your grandpa dated me while I lived here? I was also stranded and needed a job like Cole seems to. So, hell yes, I think it's okay."

"I don't know that much about him."

"Maybe he can't talk about it; or isn't used to talking about it; or can't trust you; or has a secret to hide."

"Why didn't you tell Grandpa everything?"

"I had a shameful secret in my eyes."

"What if he has one too?"

Erin shrugged. "What if he doesn't? I guess you might start by getting him to open up to you. If you really want to know."

Instantly, she replied. "I really want to know."

"Then ask. Talk to him and ask him questions. Find out about his life. His wants and needs and opinions and past. Ask, Jade, and see what he says."

"I'm scared of what he'll say."

Erin smiled with an other-worldly kind of knowing. "Or you already know the answer and that's what's really scaring you."

She glanced away. "Or that."

"Your grandma talked to you about me?" Cole asked Jade while she and he were in the middle of building a new fence. After almost an hour of work with little personal communication, Cole couldn't resist asking her. His interaction with Erin made him feel like he'd known her for years. But that had to be all in his head.

"She did. She guessed right about us. And, get this, I think she was trying to tell me she and my grandpa had a sexy barn episode too. Gross. But I think she understood things… and she was checking you out to make sure you weren't using me."

"What did she decide?"

"That I might be using you."

He jerked back, looking startled. She shook her head. "No, she doesn't think you're the typical, jacked-up asshole who might try to use me."

"Those were her words?"

"No, her words were: *you seem very nice.*"

Very nice. His aunt believed he was very nice. The good things this family said about him really touched him.

And if Erin thought he were nice, maybe she'd like Penny even more.

He wondered how to broach the subject. And what to say. He dreaded risking the anonymity he and Penny got to enjoy in the valley. His biggest fear was someone finding out he wasn't Penny's legal guardian. Any official or bureaucrat could probably track down Chance.

Keeping Penny to himself outweighed Cole's ability to trust these people that had proven, so far, to be *nice.* What little Erin said of her upbringing was reminiscent of Cole's own. So Cole doubted she'd report Penny's presence on the ranch to Chance Poletti. Maybe no one would question it if he claimed Chance was dead and he was now her guardian. The best of all worlds would be if he could infiltrate Penny with women like Erin and Melanie while still remaining her brother.

He might have been a shitty provider for Penny, but the alternative of not having any control over her wellbeing left him frozen and inert.

He couldn't find the answer yet. Like always, he was too busy with the here and now. Sleep. Work. Shop for food. Do more chores. Everything for Penny.

Today, they needed to stop at a laundromat to wash their dirty clothes. Lacking an extensive wardrobe meant they had to wash their clothes often. Cole also needed to start up the monstrosity they lived in, go to the nearest town, and visit the state park with an RV dump. He had to empty the sewage tanks and refill the water tanks with fresh water.

Every time, he had to do this, his stress level soared. What if the RV broke down and he couldn't get it back to its parking spot? So far, no one but Jade knew where it was. Nobody but she had ever driven past it. The dust was too thick for anyone to hide their tracks. Hiding. Lying. Hedging. Keeping quiet. That was how he and Penny survived. They had no one but each other to turn to when their father neglected, abused, hurt and terrorized them.

Although it was more of the same, everything was different.

"You're showing up for work tomorrow, aren't you?"

Startled by Jade's words, Cole glanced over. "What?"

"Horse training with Grandma? She's planning on it. She'll probably keep at it until you're comfortably perched on the back of one. I think she compares your arrival here with her own."

He jerked upright. "How so?"

Cole was holding up a plank so Jade could hammer a nail in it as they continued their random fence repairs. When he moved, she dropped the hammer and got up. "The way you insist on keeping quiet about your past. No background history. Both of you were about the same age. Common fear of horses. All alone. She had the same experience."

"I'm not helpless though. I can work and pull my own weight," Cole said defensively. Why was he snarling at Jade? He rarely sounded so sure of himself. But he didn't want to be a pathetic burden on the Rydells or this ranch, especially in front of Jade. He liked knowing his aunt felt a connection to him and had a desire to help him though.

"No. Of course not. I don't think she believed she was either. It wasn't her fault."

"What do you mean?"

"My grandma had a rough past. Her mom committed suicide and she discovered her body. She made her way here despite having very little welcome or any assistance."

"Why did she come here? Where was she from originally?"

"Seattle area. She moved around a lot. Her mom's mental illness and death really messed her up." Jade shuddered. "I can only imagine."

Who was his grandma? Cole didn't know her name. He wanted to ask Jade but it seemed an odd question to ask after the macabre facts Jade described. It would seem unimportant to anyone else, but for him, it was the most pressing question. Drunk or high, Chance often spoke of his bitchy mother offing herself. But Cole never remembered hearing her name. He frowned. Why had he never asked her name?

Probably because he didn't feel a connection. Relatives were faceless and meaningless so why name them? But knowing he had an aunt and a cousin with faces and personalities now made Cole eager to know more names. Who was his grandma? Whom did Erin know? What was Chance like back then? It was impossible for Cole to picture the mean, gnarled man he knew as anything close to young. Was he better in those days? Did old age, trauma and disappointment warp him into the miserly asshole he was now?

Cole couldn't ask because Jade wouldn't know. He'd never had a connection to his past or relatives or family history. He never needed one. He came to the Rydell River Ranch for Penny, not for himself.

"Did she have any other family?"

"One brother. He worked for my Grandpa Jack. But actually, my Uncle Joey hired him. Apparently, Grandpa hated him. Detested him the whole time. He still calls him obscenities on the rare occasions when his name comes up in conversation. It's pretty humorous to see how Grandpa describes him."

Finally. Cole got a glimpse into his father's youth. It seemed more than odd. He nearly snapped out an order at Jade demanding she tell him everything she knew. Why did she use the word *humorous?* If Jack detested Chance so much, it was for reasons that Cole understood all too well. There was nothing humorous about the way Chance behaved and probably mistreated his sister. If he were anything like he was now, he must have always been sociopathic.

Chance didn't abuse his children by hitting them. He used cruel words, insulting names, and sadistic pranks. His filthy hands didn't have to touch them.

Chance used a different kind of torture.

"If she didn't like her brother so much, why'd she go to him?"

Jade shrugged and turned before dropping down. She grabbed the board he let go of and held it with her knee before preparing to nail it on. Cole felt useless, his hands on his hips.

"Because she had no one else and nowhere to go. She hoped he could give her some help. But then he—"

Jade was struggling to balance the board with her knee while hammering the next nail into the wood, so Cole sighed and grabbed the end of the board before holding it for her. She glanced at him with a small smile, and picked up the hammer. They were in a new pasture that was recently added to the ranch. It was not near the main ranch area. Most of the ranch and resort hugged the Rydell River, taking up prime valley floor space. The new land was separated by a hump of small hills with a primitive trail to reach it. The land was too sloped for building but ideal for grazing and keeping livestock. A year-round creek flowed through the center of it. They were building a new fence without any power tools or electricity. No power sources meant no nail guns. They were left with an old-fashioned hammer and nails. Excavating the holes for the posts with a post-hole digger, they had to fence it in and nail the rails. This fence wasn't all white like the main ranch. It was weather-treated wood but unpainted and designated for the "back pasture" now.

Together, in the heat of the day, Jade Rydell was hammering nails and setting posts with Cole. She earned his respect. The whole family deserved respect for raising a granddaughter and daughter who knew how to do such a thing with him.

"What did he do?" Cole pressed Jade to know the true story his dad wouldn't tell him about his sister.

"He abused Grandma. Grandpa said he was cruel and mean to her all the time. He called her names, made fun of her, and did mean pranks that weren't funny. Grandma was and still is terrified of snakes. Grandpa tells one story of when he was working in the barn, and a blood-curdling scream interrupted him. He ran towards it as any decent person would and what did he find?"

Mean. Cruel. Sadistic. Chance. Cole could imagine it perfectly. "What?"

"The pervert had my grandma pinned under him. He'd bruised her up and held her wrists while dangling a live snake in his other hand all over her. She was phobic about them. I mean, who does that?" Jade pounded harder on the rail.

"That's pretty sadistic," Cole said quietly, picturing his own scenario. His little sister was screaming. Only eight years old, her little, skinny arms were like sticks and so fragile and weak in Chance's hard grasp. He held her when she pushed, kicked and beat him with her legs. Why? Because he was holding a spider. A huge, juicy spider that he hid in his palm. He was taunting Penny, laughing and making fun of her. He was preparing to drop the spider into her hair when Cole showed up. Cole knocked his old man's hand away from Penny. Chance was pissed and snarled at him. But Cole made a big enough distraction to allow Penny to run.

She always ran. Just like Cole did.

They had a pact. Run and regroup later. Always. No matter where he and Penny lived, they secretly scoped out meeting spots. Get away first. Meet after that. Since Cole was bigger, he told her to never look back or wait for him. He'd get away. She had to run as long and as far as she could.

When Cole got away from Chance and his jeering, he found Penny a total mess, trembling and nearly hyperventilating. All because of the threat of the spider. She was that afraid of them.

Just like Erin was afraid of snakes. It was chilling for Cole to comprehend such antisocial behavior and sadism but it seemed to be a pattern. Three or four *decades* of a pattern. How could one person remain so unpleasant for so long?

Jade nodded at him. "I'm glad you see that."

He tilted his head. "It's hard to believe anyone couldn't. But I know how some people can be."

Jade straightened her back, setting her hands on her hips, her elbows out while frowning. "Those brothers you told me about? They remind me of Grandma's brother."

He frowned in respond. "Yeah. Lots of assholes out there."

Jade nodded, watching him solemnly. "Yes, there are. But in my experience, those assholes are in the minority."

He snorted. "Not in mine."

She didn't respond. He stared at the pile of boards they still had to nail—boards he'd spent days dragging up there. Driving an old pick-up, he left the stacks at various intervals along the new fence line. Holding another board in place, he waited for her. She stepped forward and dropped to one knee beside him. Their faces were at eyelevel. This little ritual was repeated over and over. They switched off as to who held the board and who hammered. Taking turns. Jade gave as good as Cole. It was epic to him. He'd never had a work partner, especially one like her before. Chance or one of his brothers were the only ones who helped him, and they didn't work, so there were no comparisons.

Instead of pounding the nail, she dropped her hand onto his forearm. Staring at her gloved hand, he looked up to find her gaze on him. Sympathy shone in her eyes. "You're not that way though. Whatever they, your brothers, are, you're not like them."

He clenched his teeth. Why was she so nice to him? And always that way? Every time she complimented him, all he wanted to do was grab her and kiss her, or maybe he should shake her. He wasn't deserving of any compliments. Wait until she found out what he participated in. What he'd done to her. What he'd watch get done to her and by whom. He didn't help her. Unlike his aunt, he wasn't victimized by Chance and his brothers. He was part of them.

"You don't know anything, Jade." Feeling grumpy for his own guilt, the sharp words he snapped came back as anger toward her.

"No. You're right. I don't know much about you. None of your history. I don't know what your brothers did or didn't do. All I know is: you're not like them."

"How could you know that?"

"From every interaction I've had with you. Or my family's had with you. You can't fake it that well for that long for that many people."

"Jade, no offense but you were raised here. These are your people. You don't have much experience with what the rest of the world is like and humanity sucks. People are assholes. They hurt, lie, steal, corrupt, mock, abuse and murder each other. You can't expect the rest of the world to be like your family."

She let go of the hammer and nails while she turned towards him. He grabbed the board and set it aside. She slipped onto her knees and simply leaned forward, putting her arms around his neck and tucking herself up against his chest. Startled to have her suddenly in his arms, Cole had to shift his body to brace her weight. He landed on his ass while she scooted forward to crawl onto his lap.

What in the hell? Jade Rydell never did this at work. Acting so girlie. So clingy. Like they had sex or cuddled or touched every day.

His gaze darted around. Her lips touched his in a soft, quick kiss. "There isn't a soul around for miles. So tell me something. Tell me about your family so I can get an idea of all the assholes that are out there comprising the majority of humanity. Tell me something personal, Cole. Something real and true about *you*." Her tone was soft, encouraging, and sweet. Womanly. Less Jade Rydell, kickass ranch hand co-worker and more like someone unsure, curious, and wondering about him. Who cared about him before? Who wondered about what he went through? Or what he thought? Or felt or experienced? Cole found that pretty heady. Completely thrilling coming from a creature like the one who just crawled into *his* arms.

Where should he start?

Your grandma? She's my aunt. That snake thing? My father, who's her brother, did that to my sister too, you know, he abused her by scaring her with a spider, her biggest phobia. The sister I kidnapped and hid from everyone. I'm afraid she'll get taken from me and have to go back to my asshole father. I'm afraid I'll go to jail for kidnapping and assault.

I assaulted you.

The words were right there. On the tip of his tongue. The

impact they held made his entire body shudder. She felt it and her arms simply tightened around him. She was comforting *him*. Her attacker.

He had to tell her the truth.

But he was an asshole too, the spawn of Chance Poletti. His arms tightened around her and he squeezed all the comfort she was offering him against his chest. He buried his face in the spot where her neck joined her shoulder and breathed in the sweet scent of her skin. Salty from the heat and sweat. Outdoorsy fresh. That was Jade.

Jade was someone he hoped his sister might become. "We never lived in the same place longer than five months."

She jolted at the words he said. "Who do you mean by *we?*"

"My father and my two older brothers." Lie and evade all the details. He couldn't add Penny to his family yet.

"Why did you continue to live with them so long?" He blinked before he remembered she thought he was twenty-five years old. Not twenty.

That alone was probably a deal breaker.

He shrugged his shoulders. "Better the devil you know. They were all I had. It's intimidating to be fully alone in the world. I've just tried to survive. Survival was my only goal."

"What made you leave them now?"

He closed his eyes. The indelible image of this woman crumpling to the ground after being whacked by Everett flashed in his mind. "They hurt someone who never did anything to them. I just couldn't stand their wanton cruelty anymore."

"What'd they do that was so cruel?"

Her inquiries were so innocent. She just wanted to know Cole better. He wasn't even a man yet, or barely a man but she didn't fully know that. The boy she was sleeping with. But Jade wasn't just sexually attracted to him. He knew that now. She inexplicably enjoyed him, seemed to have true, caring feelings for him. She liked him.

"One of them hit a woman."

Her head lifted and she stared at his face. He couldn't look down. One of her hands reached up to cradle his chin. "The same reason you didn't have sex. Because you didn't like how they treated women?"

He shuddered, thinking of the most important female to all of their lives: Penny. "No. I really detested the ways they treated women."

She suddenly flipped up and turned around. Now facing him with her legs straddling his trunk, she used both hands to cup his face and locked her eyes on his. Jade didn't have a clue about the dark, evil side of humanity. The side that Cole knew. She was innocent, optimistic, and sweet. Not quite naïve but almost.

"You're nothing like that. You believe that, don't you?"

His gaze darted towards her temple, then returned to her sincere, caring face. "I try not to be. But I can't always escape or ignore the disgusting upbringing I had."

She leaned forward and her lips touched his while her fingers still cupped his face. Gentle. Sweet. Reassuring. Caring. He tilted his head toward her touch. Right now, it meant more than the kiss even.

Softness. Kindness. Tenderness. Sharing. He didn't know how badly he wanted it, not until Jade started touching him.

"You're big and tough. You're also unsure and willing to learn. You hold me with a sense of care and insecurity. You're never aggressive. Some say I am, but that's my style." Her lips lifted in a small smile. He couldn't help smiling back at her. Yeah, she was kind of aggressive but only from eagerness. "You treat women well, not how the assholes in your family do. I can attest to that."

He shuddered. No she could not. How he hated lying to

her. Once she knew the truth, he dreaded knowing how it would taint and defraud this moment with her and every other honest one they shared.

He soaked up her soothing words like a dried out, crusty sponge dipped in water. He needed her. Her words. Her touch. Her reassurance. Her curiosity. He wanted all that and more from this woman. To feel wanted and desired.

"Tell me something else. Something good." She kissed his mouth again. He wasn't used to the attention she gave him. Her gaze was bright as she stared at him. Her lips were so warm and tasty. He could surrender to her like a toddler in a loving parent's embrace. Having never experienced that, however, he could only guess what it was like.

Penny. Penny was all the good things he cherished. But there was no way to even tell Jade about her without having more questions and more lies.

"Being here. With you. That's the good something."

Her eyes glimmered with grief, for him. "Oh, Cole, you kind of break my heart saying that. Are you serious?"

"Yeah." His tone was as heavy as his heart.

She leaned forward and her lips engaged his for several, long, heated moments. She paused and then said, "I do know a little bit about assholes."

Startled, he blinked to clear the wonderful fog her attention always created around him. The *good* feelings that were so rare. So damn rare and new.

"Last spring," she began, and his entire body froze. Shit. She was going to tell him about what they did to her. Something he shouldn't know about. But he did. Intimately. "I came in late after leading a late riding tour. It was only eight or eight thirty, but it was dark out."

It was eight-eighteen, to be exact.

"We keep money in the cash register in the concession area of the arena and there's also a small safe."

Yes, the safe. It held three thousand, two hundred and forty-eight dollars.

A small fortune. Cole took two thousand dollars. He bought a motor home that didn't run and some parts to jerry-rig it. He also furnished it with a few odds and ends to make it more habitable for his sister and filled it with a tank of gas. After parking it where it now sits, he virtually kidnapped his sister from her school.

He also put five hundred dollars down on his sister's braces with the money from the heist. He took Everett's share too, after threatening to beat him up if he told Dad about it. Oddly enough, Everett didn't argue with him.

The rest of the money? Chance used it to pay the bail bondsman for his brother, Zack to get out of jail.

Jade shook her head and went on, "I didn't even lock the door. So stupid trusting. You're probably right about me. I never considered something like that happening here."

Her guilt was evident in her voice.

"Whoever did it probably counted on that. Could be why they chose this town. It's not your fault for not locking the door. They'd have just busted it down."

"You're probably right."

"How many were there?"

"Three men. They wore cowboy hats and covered their faces with bandannas. Pretty common disguises in this area."

Yeah, Chance and his bros weren't complete morons. Cole's stomach cramped up as she spoke and he remembered.

"What'd they do?"

Her entire body shuddered as the memory of it returned. "They all three aimed handguns at me. I can't explain but some kind of force of inertia made me freeze. Terror immobilized me… I couldn't move or speak at first. They just wanted to rob the place. I didn't fully comprehend that. So stupid, I thought, what do they want?"

He swallowed. Remembering her standing there frozen in front of him. He'd blocked the memory temporarily but he remembered quite clearly now. Jade was standing there, just staring at the guns.

"I forgot to put my hands up until one of them yelled at me. One of them was old. Really old. I could tell by the wrinkles around his eyes and his white eyebrows. He was the loudest and meanest and probably the most dangerous, I bet."

She was right and had good intuition.

She shook her head as if to loosen the stuck memories. "Anyway, they were there to rob us. I finally went to the register as they told me to. Shit, I couldn't think though. I could barely make my fingers work to open the till even though it was second nature for me normally, but I just couldn't think. The stress of seeing three guns pointed at me. All I could imagine was what would happen if one bullet…"

Her entire body jolted and she leaned against *him* for comfort and strength.

The level of self-loathing Cole felt on hearing Jade relate her side of what happened that night was unparalleled. He imagined Jade being Penny.

Penny wasn't really prone to crying a lot, but when Chance and his brothers got vicious or scared her, she did. Their behavior changed when they were high or drunk. Then it became wild and unpredictable. Cruel words and pranks became funny to them. Having sex in the trailer was their idea of a good time. Scary, loud sex that was utterly repulsive for a teenage boy to see, but downright gross and ominous for a little girl to witness, became the norm.

Wrapping his arms around her, he held her tightly against him. One hand stroked through her silky hair. "What did they do to you, Jade?" he asked, his mouth right next to her ear.

She shivered at his words. "They knew or guessed about the safe. Ordered me to go back there. My nerves made me so clumsy I took out a display with a loud noise and made a mess. I thought the old geezer would shoot me. For real. His eyes were soulless, murderous. I—"

"You didn't know how to react," he filled in softly.

She trembled. "No. Of course not. But it was terrifying to feel so weak and useless. I was at their mercy. There was nothing I could do. One of the younger guys tried to calm the old one down."

Fuck him. So he's the real hero of the story, right? Cole tried to keep the bile from rising in his throat while remembering exactly what she described. Cole knew how she looked, but not how she felt until now.

"Anyway, we got to the storage room and I was terrified that they wanted to gang rape me."

He let out a gasp. He never knew that little tidbit. He had no idea that even crossed her mind. It was so clear to him why they went back there, but yeah, how would she know? How could she know the limits to their debauchery and evilness? They held her up at gunpoint. Yelling at her. Robbing her. Why not rape her?

"Damn, Jade..." he said and his tone was hoarse.

"They didn't though. They wanted the combination for the lock on the safe. I was shaking so bad it took me a few tries before I could open it. I kept waiting for one of them to shoot me, or hit me when I messed it up. They were definitely stressed but I was terrified."

"And you got it open?"

"I did. And the—what should I call him? The one who wasn't so trigger-happy and didn't scream at me took the money out. The joy I felt at that moment. I thought, 'Oh, that's what they want, just money.' I was so relieved they were only robbing me. I thought everything would be fine. And over now. It sucked but I thought it would finally just end. But…"

His stomach cramped and he feared he'd puke. "But…?" he said quietly.

"But that's all I remember until I woke up at the hospital. One of them hit me in the temple with the butt of their gun. At least, that was what they told me. I passed out and woke up at the hospital."

"Jade…" Cole's voice sounded as tortured as his soul. What could he say? How could he ever ask to be forgiven? She'd know the truth someday and remember this moment with him. Then she'd detest him as much as he hated Chance. He would be the real villain of Jade Rydell's story.

She leaned against him. "I sprained my wrist when I fell on it. Being off work for a few weeks really pissed me off. I suffered because of what they did and it made me furious. They made me a victim and I'll never forget that feeling. It changed the woman I am and how I see the world. So really, Cole I do know about assholes. More than you think."

He wrapped her biceps with his hands. "You were never their victim. Jade…" His words failed him. His apologies were empty. He was a failure.

She touched his chin. "I didn't tell you to make you upset. But I do understand bad things. And it even happened to me. You were telling me things that affected you. I want you to know the things that affect me. If… you want to know?"

He sucked in a breath. She wondered if he wanted to know her better? He wanted to inhale her and keep her with him always. Never leave her. But she had no idea what a terrible guy he was. He said, "I want to know all about you."

She smiled softly. "Now you know something about me. I don't like to feel weak."

"You're the strongest person I've ever known. Mentally, emotionally, and as a leader."

She gave him a little grin. "I like hearing that. I can't be the strongest physically speaking though. Stupid girl genetics."

A small laugh emerged from his mouth, surprising even him. She was so funny. And so earnest and sweet. She twisted her mouth at the word "girl."

"I really, really like your girl genetics."

He deserved to burn in hell. That was his fate and future. Jade suddenly rose up on her knees and leaned over him, using her mouth to devour his. He eagerly joined her. When his hands landed on her waist and started to inch upwards, he waited for the lightning to strike him dead. Cupping her breasts in his hands the way she liked, he used his thumbs to rub her tightening nipples and she sighed into his mouth. He deserved to fry in the electric chair.

Jade shared her confidences and insecurities with him. She wanted to comfort and be a part of him. The Cole she thought was down on his luck. The same age as her. A grown-assed man who was nice and kind and unsure.

Not the Cole that terrorized, attacked, and left her for dead.

She suddenly ripped her mouth from his. "You want to know the irony of the entire episode?"

"What?" He was startled as he stared up at her. His eyes were dilating with intrigue.

"One of them called the police so they would find me. That's the sticking point I almost can't let go of. Why? Why would they knock me out and then call the cops to get me some help?"

He couldn't tell her the answer. Because he was the devil.

She sighed and leaned back towards him. "I guessed it had

to be the quietest one. The one who didn't knock me out or yell at me. But why?"

Because he was slightly less psychotic than the others? Not much of a defense, however.

She smiled and leaned on him, kissing his face and hair. "Cole?" she sighed softly.

"What?" he sighed back.

"Lie back."

He could not do this with her now. Not after what she confessed unwittingly to him.

"I don't have any condoms out here, Jade."

"I don't need them. Just do it now. Please."

And God help him if he didn't do exactly as she asked.

CHAPTER 18

COLE WAS, FOR ONCE, sitting down and eating. Jade blinked. Had she ever seen him eat before? No. He opened up a brown paper bag for the lunch that was prepared by Jade's mother. Biting into the sandwich, he devoured it in three bites. Next came the banana, and he was about to inhale the cookie when he noticed Jade watching him. He slowly lowered it and a blush started to stain his neck a deep red. "Hey." He looked up at her. "Sorry, I was... I mean... I was really hungry."

Jade sat beside him. He was sitting on the newly poured foundation of the future house of her parents. His legs dangled as he straddled the short cement wall. She sat the same way, facing him.

His eating wasn't so much gross, as it was desperate. Watching him, she realized he was well-acquainted with hunger.

That thought startled her. Jade never spent a single day, not even an hour, or a few moments feeling hungry. There was always food available to her. Her parents' cabinets and refrigerator were always brimming with her favorite dishes.

Her aunts and uncles and grandparents were the same way. Anywhere she went, there was always food offered to her. She always had plenty of access to an assortment of tasty treats.

Her heart thumped when she saw how hungry a man could be. In this country. Nowadays.

Was he starved as a kid too?

"Were you often hungry growing up?" He jerked his gaze up towards her, but didn't reply. "Cole? I get the feeling you had to survive with only the basics, if you could get them."

He looked away. "Yeah. I sometimes went hungry."

"Still?"

"Well, no. I work here now."

Oh, shit. She could have made him lose his job, which was the only bridge between him and his hunger.

She was a hopeless, entitled asshole.

"Were you starving when you came here?"

"I don't remember."

"Cole." She tilted her head, and her eyes were penetrating. "You know what I mean."

"I was low on cash at the time, so that's a likely possibility."

"Why? Didn't you ever work before you came here?"

"I did. But at the time, I was getting away from a bad situation."

"You don't want to tell me about it."

"No."

"But you'll have sex with me," she grumbled.

He nodded. "You started it. But no, I don't want to talk about my life, not even with you."

His words chilled her. She rubbed her arms and crossed them over her stomach. "Do you only want sex with me? Don't you like me at all?"

His eyebrows lifted. "Of course, I like you. I like you more than anyone I've ever—"

Her eyes grew large and he suddenly ended his sentence. Then he stuffed the cookie into his mouth. "You ever what? Met?"

He sighed, munching the cookie, and nodded finally.

"You don't want to talk to me though?"

He chewed some more. "No. I didn't say that. I don't want to talk about starving or any other shit from my crappy past. I'll talk to you about anything else if you're interested."

"I'm sitting here so I'm interested. Way too much probably. I don't understand it. I've never had anyone act so cagey about their history before. It kinda worries me."

"How so?"

"The mobile meth lab you live in... I mean, there *are* red flags... I can't fully say."

"It was never a mobile meth lab. It would have been too hazardous for human habitation if it were."

She shrugged. "I was just being dramatic."

"It was used as a mobile drug dispensary. The previous owners just sold drugs out of it."

Her mouth dropped open but nothing came out. "Oh. Okay. That's a huge distinction, I guess."

He finally smiled. "I was just messing with you. I know what you meant. I live in a piece of shit. I have nothing to my name and you're wondering what the hell you were thinking when you fucked the weird guy in the barn who jacked off like he was still sixteen."

Whoa. Cole never acted or talked like that before. She swallowed. "Well, yes. Something like that. But no, you're not *the weird guy*. Not at all."

"You should be wary. I'm nothing, Jade. I have no future for you. We both understand that. I'm a transient ranch hand that can barely stand to be near a horse. I'm like every one of the guys you pick for your one-night stands. This is just lasting a bit longer because, for some odd reason, you seem partial to sixteen-year-old jack-offs." He smiled again.

She shook her head. "None of that is true."

"All of that is true. You're real. You get stuff. Don't forget that."

She rose to her feet. "So you were often hungry and had two brothers. You didn't have sex because it disgusted you when you witnessed it with your brothers. You also had a crappy father. You worked sometimes, but desperately wanted this job. You live in a retired drug dispensary. That's the basic plot for you, am I right?"

"Some of it."

"Is the rest worse?"

He glanced away, letting his eyes scan the land. "Yes. Far worse."

"Cole?"

"Jade, there're lots of things I won't discuss because I'm ashamed of them. Don't kid yourself. You don't need to stick around for any of that shit."

Then he got to his feet and, (sigh), ran over the grassy land towards the barn. Always running away when the conversation got uncomfortable and ugly.

There was so much she didn't know about him. So many layers she couldn't fully comprehend because he was so different from her. His past and his present were unlike anything Jade ever knew about. The longer she hung around him, however, the more she wanted to know about him. It soon became an obsession that consumed her.

A feeling of dread accompanied that obsession. Jade feared she might be falling in what other people called *love*.

Could you love someone you didn't really know?

With a sinking feeling, she knew the answer to that. Yeah,

you could. How did she know? Because that's what happened to her.

∼

"Ben, could I see Cole's employment application?" It was Jade's grandmother's voice.

Ben glanced up from what he was doing. Each horse on the ranch was due for their yearly vaccines. Lillian was the one in charge of that. Jade assisted her. Jade looked up when Erin entered the barn to help them. "Why do you want to see that?" Ben asked. For some reason, Ben seemed to be hedging. Jade already knew there was no employment application for Cole along with a few other hands. Something that always bothered Kailynn and Erin.

"Because we need to make sure all the employees are accounted for. If Jade takes over someday, we need to collect all our paperwork and codify all the applications. We have to quit fudging on a few things."

Ben straightened upright. "Ah, hell Erin, he's just a day laborer. I just pay him as we go. I don't have anything on him."

"Ben Rydell," she scolded him. "You know better than that. He's young, new, and since he's been sleeping with your daughter, don't you think you should make sure he's not a felon?"

"Grandma!" Jade gasped.

"Erin!" Ben thundered.

Lillian burst out laughing.

Erin simply folded her arms over her chest, raising her eyebrows with a serene expression. "Well? It's true."

"Oh, my gosh." Jade wilted as she covered her eyes.

"Erin! Stop it."

"Oh, come now, Ben we've all been young and had our

flings in the barn. I remember catching you and Jocelyn out there looking a little piqued when I came to feed the horses more than once…"

Jade completely covered her ears. Lillian mimicked her.

Ben groaned.

Erin smiled. "My point being: there is no judgment here. But we need to make sure our files are up to date and the applications are all properly filled out and buttoned up. It's not the old days anymore. From here forward, Jade won't have the simplicity and ease that we enjoyed all those decades ago. She'll have to follow up on everything, right down to the letter. You know the saying."

"I think you're nit-picking. Are you, by any chance, mad at me?" Ben tilted his head and his expression looked injured.

"I think you need to check Cole out some more."

"He works hard. I had no idea that…"

"Jade works with twenty men a day; is it really such a shock that one might end up as her boyfriend?"

Jade dropped her hands. "Grandma. I swear you'll make me die of embarrassment."

"Boyfriend? I thought it was just a singular incident?" Her dad's voice sounded distressed. He glanced at Jade and then averted his eyes quickly.

"Jade, do you want to fill your father in, or should I?"

"Cole's not my boyfriend."

"No it's much worse. She's in love with a ranch hand who isn't really a cowboy."

Speechless, Jade's mouth dropped open and she could only gape at her grandma.

"It's more than obvious now. We need to make sure he's legitimate."

"He's not my boyfriend." Jade's protest was weak and whiny, even to her own ears. "And I'm sure things are fine." Her voice wavered.

"Are you, Jade?"

"He's just hit some hard times…" She looked at the corner of the big building.

"Well, then, there shouldn't be any trouble getting a few basic facts about him."

"Right. I'm sure." Jade had no argument to object any longer.

But when her dad gave a long, strained look, she felt five years old again. Stupid family.

CHAPTER 19

"Cole?"

He glanced back when he heard Erin's voice behind him. Smiling with pleasure at his aunt, he appreciated her gentle, caring tone. She was always so unassuming. "Hello, ma'am. Is it time?"

They proceeded with the next lesson to make Cole a "real" cowboy. Jade teased him almost every day about it and often inquired how his "cowboy school" was going.

"I wonder first if you could do me a favor?"

He set aside the saddle he was busily rubbing with saddle soap. It was one of almost fifty he had to maintain. "Of course. What do you need?"

"Your real name."

His heart instantly lodged in his throat. *They knew*. His guts started to turn liquid. And worse, Jade was standing beside him doing the same task. As she so often was. She heard her grandmother. "P-P-Pardon me?" Cole's eyes darted to Jade, then to Erin. *She knew*. How? Why the polite inquiry? What else did they know?

"Yes, I need your full name. We have to get a full employment application filled out on you. This isn't like the old days and we can't keep paying you under the table. We need to fill out the proper paperwork and, I'm afraid, that includes taxes. We have to report the wages we pay for our taxes. But to compensate, we'll raise your daily wage so your take-home amount is the same."

They were so fucking decent to him. They just wanted to cover their own asses as employers. Any other worker would jump at the chance to stay on and be a real citizen, a tax-paying adult. He couldn't, of course, do that. He had to provide false information and after they ran the background check, they'd all know he was a liar.

He'd be long gone by then though. But what about Penny? What was his plan? He still didn't know.

"Uh, sure. Yeah. It's Cole Rodger Pearson, my last known address is Colville. I recently moved and don't have a permanent address yet. Social security card will take a little longer. I lost it and I have no idea where it might be. Unfortunately, I can't remember the numbers. But I know I have it tucked away somewhere. Could you give me a few days?"

"Sure." Erin said with an easy smile. "Could you also read and sign this liability form?"

His stomach soured at the word *read*, but he said with a smile, "Sure. Just let me know when and I'll come by and do it."

At least, he could sign his name.

Erin brought it with her. Surprised, Cole stared at the folded page in horror as she removed it from her pocket. "Here. It's important. Read it carefully. It releases us from any accident or injury liability."

"Sure. Sure. Legalese. I get it." No. He had no idea what something like that would say. But he took it and scrawled his name on the bottom line.

"That's the print line."

He glanced up.

"Pardon?"

Erin's voice was cool and gentle. "Where you signed, it says *print name here*. Not *sign here*."

He frowned. "Oh, right. Here." He signed the line below it. What did it matter?

"You need to read it over, Cole. It's a bit stingy and benefits us in the long run. I want you to be fully aware. So please read it."

He tried to keep his smile casual. Shrugging, as if it were no big deal, he pushed it back to her, and said, "I trust you."

"You shouldn't. Not at all. We're a substantial corporation now with deep pockets and many facets. We would probably win in court against a single person or entity. We have lawyers on retainer. Daisy Rydell, as a family member, will make sure we win. So please read that right now, before I take the signed copy away."

His smile slowly faded. How bad could the waiver be? Geez. He took it from her and nodded. Then he wandered over to the nearest stool and sat on it. He pretended to read it carefully. His eyes were glued to it, and he slowly scanned the words. What the fuck? How long would something like this take him to read? He recognized some words. Only a few. But he really didn't have a clue about what it said.

Lifting his gaze, he was shocked to find Erin staring at him. She was watching him read it. She really took this paperwork and liability seriously. "All right. I'm done. I read it. It's signed. Everything's fine."

"Tell me what you read. I need to know you understand all of it."

He frowned. "This isn't school, ma'am, and it's a contract, not a book report. I told you it's fine. I have no further concerns."

She smiled softly. "No further concerns? What about your opinions? Perhaps you have questions?"

"Grandma, what is this? What form did he have to sign? I never heard about anything so serious or anyone else having to sign it." Jade asked, stepping closer.

"Oh? You should read it over too, Jade. You need to know this stuff."

Jade huffed. "Well, duh." Jade leaned forward to look at it.

He handed it to Jade, relieved to get the stupid form out of his hands. He was also glad Jade distracted Erin from her inquisition. She was scarier than a drill sergeant.

Moments later, damn. Jade seemed to be a fast reader and lifted her head, her expression was completely puzzled. "What—what is this, Grandma? Some kind of joke?"

"No. No, unfortunately, it's not a joke at all."

Her face blanched. "But why did you have Cole sign a recipe for instructions on how to mix your favorite cupcakes?"

A recipe? What? Cole's body went still.

"Cole, did you realize you were signing a recipe?"

He licked his lips. "I didn't want to hurt your grandma's feelings. I thought she'd given me the wrong paper. Maybe had a senior moment."

Damn. That was smooth. Better than he expected from himself.

Her eyebrows jutted up. "Oh, you're pretty quick on your feet. But not for one second do I believe you thought I'd slipped in my faculties. You had no idea what that paper said."

Jade's confused expression followed Erin and then returned to him. "Wait. What is this?"

"I'm sorry, Cole. But I suppose it's your pride that won't let you be honest. I didn't know how else to find out. I get it. I was the same way as you. When you came here, your life hadn't been going very well. I also know that feeling. You're dating my granddaughter now and that's my reason for making it my business. I know you can't read. I also know what it's like to have that problem and the reason why you can't."

Jade gasped. With a horrified expression, she looked at him and then at Erin. "Grandma! How could you be so fucking mean?"

Cole stared at Jade when she screeched. He didn't expect her to come to his defense. Meanwhile, his entire face burned and turned crimson as he fisted his hands at his sides. He wished Erin were forty years younger and a cocky dude so he could…

No. He didn't hit people. He didn't believe in violence. That was too reminiscent of his father.

No.

He rubbed his hair. They knew. Jade knew. He was doomed.

And yeah, it was really fucking mean.

"I didn't do it to be mean. I only did it to keep him honest by admitting it so we could move past it," Erin replied.

Past it? There's no getting past dumb.

Erin ignored Jade. "Remember when I told you about my arrival here? And I mentioned your age?"

Erin had his brain buzzing. He jumped to his feet and backed up a few steps. He was not listening or caring what the old, fucking, mean bitch, had to say. He didn't care that she was his aunt anymore.

"Cole, I couldn't read either when I came here. Not more than a few words on any page. Couldn't write much better. I know how dumb you feel. How humiliating it is. But let me tell you something: you can't fix it if you don't admit to it. So…" She shrugged. "I don't suggest waiting three years like I did before you learn how."

Wait, what? There was another adult in the world who couldn't read? Most seven-year-old children could read.

Jade's face went from confused, to shocked, to appalled, to full pity. He detested that more than anything. She'd never looked at him with such sad eyes.

"I don't fucking care if I can read or not. I don't need an old lady playing tricks on me to make me into some kind of joke. Thanks, but forget it."

"Cole Pearson!" Erin snapped. "Do not raise your voice at me or call me an old lady in that tone again. No. I will *not* forget it. *We* will *not* forget you. Jade cares about you and that's the reason why this must be addressed at once. I'd do the same thing for any other worker on this ranch, never mind, you. Especially you."

He paused although he was about to walk away. He fought the urge to flip her off. He just stared open-mouthed at her. Did she just scold him?

No one ever scolded him like a naughty child. Not even when he was naughty. He was stunned when she called him out on his illiteracy and then scolded him. Temporarily, he even forgot he was pissed at her for humiliating him.

He evil-eyed her and ignored Jade. He couldn't bear to see her pity for him.

"What do you want me to do?'

"Try a structured literacy program to learn how to read. The same kind I did. You're either dyslexic or you have ADHD. All that means is: you need an Orton Gillingham based literary program in order to learn. It's not your fault. Remember that. You live in a country in which most of the states don't address dyslexia with the right type of remediation. We have a systems that's been proven for thirty years or more to work. I can't fight the system that failed me and you, but I know a method that will help you learn to read. Same as I did."

"We're not the same."

"Oh, yes, Cole, we are. I arrived on the ranch here when I was twenty-six. I knew all the same evasive phrases and half-truths to get by. How else do you think I picked up on it with you? Concealing the great secret and shame of my life was a full-time job and effort. No one, not an educator or a Special Ed teacher or anything the public school had to offer could teach me to read. I was that dumb. Oh, I know the schtick you and I both used. If I didn't, I'd have had Ben kick you off the ranch a long time ago. I knew you were lying and telling half-truths to avoid detection. I wasn't sure why, but it's far better than the alternative."

"Which is?'

"You could have been a felon, or a domestic abuser, I don't know. But this is something that we can deal with."

His burning anger and flushed face went all the way to the tips of his ears. But Erin's words made sense to Cole. It blew him away that she was onto him so quickly. *They* were onto him just as Jade was. But Jade accepted his half-truths, thinking his life was a terrible tragedy. And it kind of was.

If what Erin said was true, it would be a good cover for why he lied. It solved some problems but also made new ones.

Then... the truth hit him like a Mack truck. Erin was his aunt. Fuck. No wonder she had the exact same problem he did. It must be hereditary.

He eyed her with extreme disdain, but finally asked in a tight voice. "How come you couldn't read?"

"I have dyslexia. I bet it's the same reason for you too. It's neither rare nor hard to spot. In fact, it's really common, prevalent, and easy to detect. I mean, getting a formal diagnosis' is helpful but it isn't necessary in order to fix any reading or spelling issues. Far more important to find the right kind of reading program. Specific interventions that have been scientifically proven to work. Not the balanced reading curriculums or or whole word approach that have been endlessly proven *not* to work with dyslexic learners."

Her bitter words came from a personal understanding. Something deep inside him wanted to reach out to her, sensing that she might understand him more than he understood himself.

"Cole, is it true?" Jade's soft tone came from his side.

He clamped his jaw so hard, he feared it would shatter. But Erin explained it all so well. Maybe they wouldn't grill him for his real name and social security number. All the stuff he was still trying to conceal.

"Yeah. It's true."

"Why didn't you just ask him?" Jade turned to her grandma and her expression seemed puzzled.

"He'd probably lie and say he could. Or that he was a slow reader. Most people just lie. Cole would have probably lied and left us."

Her eyes widened as she whipped her face to his. "W-W-Would you have done that?"

He pressed his lips tightly as he glared at his aunt. "Yes. I would have done that."

Jade looked from Erin to Cole. "But why? Why wouldn't you…"

"What, Jade? Fix it?" Cole snapped. "If I could fix it, I would have done that when I was seven."

Jade shook her head. "No. I'm sorry. That came out wrong. I know about this. My grandma told me and my aunt made a career teaching dyslexic students how to read. I just… I'm sorry, I never ran into people who had it, being out and about. Most of the dyslexic students I met were brought here to my aunt."

"They all had concerned, involved parents or guardians or someone that cared. If you don't have that luxury, you sit in school where they *don't* teach you, but you say they are, and you don't get fixed. You internalize your stupidity, and call yourself dumb and ignorant, and it's shameful. That's why, Jade."

Erin described it exactly. His gaze pierced Erin's heart. "I guess you're telling the truth."

"Of course, I'm telling the truth. I was twenty-nine years old before I learned to read."

He tilted his head. "But you can read now?"

Jade kind of gasped. Erin nodded, and her eyes held his. "Yes. I can read well now. You can learn how too. It takes time, and it's no quick fix and all that, but if you don't start now, when will you? If the school system just taught it to the kids who needed it from kindergarten, then people like you and I would never have to suffer so much. Nor would we drop out of school because we're unable to read. Which, I bet, happened to you."

His jaw clenched. But he still needed Erin for Penny. In case Chance showed up. Most likely even if he didn't.

"I dropped out."

"What grade?"

He slid a glance at Jade and his balls seemed to shrink up into his body. "Eighth grade. Didn't see the point of going to high school when I couldn't spell, or even read the assignments. Kindergartners could read better than me."

"Sight words, no, spelling patterns are the worst." She smiled sympathetically. "You need to learn the spelling patterns and the rules to know what the letters are saying and why they change. You can learn, Cole."

"I can't afford it."

"I think we can help you with that."

"I've made it this far."

"Not very well, you were hungry when you got here."

"I was having some problems at the time."

"I followed my brother to this place because I too was having *problems*. I was also hungry and I had no one but him."

Wow. The impact of hearing how his father got here nearly blew his mind. His heart thumped. "Why did you follow your brother?"

"He was all I had. I had no money. No way of getting a job. Filling out the fucking job applications."

He shut his eyes.

Jade smacked her hands together.

He rolled his eyes. "Yeah. Fucking job apps are a real pain. Couldn't have been all bad since you had your brother, at least." He held his breath as he skirted the subject.

Erin snorted. "Chance fucking Poletti never spent a single minute making my life better. He mocked and abused me at every turn, and talk about being mean. He was the worst apple at the bottom of the barrel and my very last chance. Forgive the pun."

The name. His father's name. Hearing her say it was startling. Knowing how well she understood his sadism, abuse and malice made her a kindred spirit.

"What happened? How did you end up staying here?"

"He stole my car, all the cash I had, and my duffel bag of clothes, right down to my bra. I was sleeping in bed and he simply took it all. I never saw him again. The police never found him. He left me as helpless as a newborn kitten. Jack bought me my underclothes that very day; that's how poor and needy I was. I gave new meaning to the word *pathetic*."

Chance had been doing the same thing for forty-two years. Cole's heart pounded. Cole knew exactly how she felt. He'd been left behind and mocked by his dad doing all of those nasty things. Stealing. Stingy. Horrible. "That's a cold mother fucker."

"He was a cold, sadistic mother fucker. I honestly hope he's dead now. And I say that with no guilt in the least. The day I stopped being a Poletti was truly the greatest relief and liberation for me. I was finally no longer associated with a bag of shit."

Because being a Poletti made you a bag of shit.

That was why he had to get Penny out. But Erin was so bitter about her brother. Of course, Cole understood why. But now he feared she'd automatically hate any offspring from him.

But Penny wasn't like any of the men in the family. What if Erin could meet Penny somehow? If he could introduce Penny to her as just some kid? A kid named Penny Pearson with a dyslexic brother who couldn't read or get a decent job to support her. And what if she couldn't read for the same reason? What if they saw Penny in a non-Poletti context? Cole was sure they'd see her potential and want to help her. Then finally, he could tell them the truth and they'd love her by then and want to raise her.

Then Cole could go to jail and they could keep Penny.

He shuddered at the thought. Glancing at Jade, his regrets flooded him. But it was also the best and only plan he could think of. He had to get out of this mess with a modicum of decency and be sure Penny would be taken care of.

"What do you want me to do?"

Erin's shoulders dropped and her eyebrows rose with her delight at hearing his question. "That's an excellent beginning."

He didn't look over at Jade. The pathetic sympathy he'd already seen on her face made him cringe.

CHAPTER 20

"PENNY. THERE *IS* A way for you to learn how to read."

She looked up from where she was throwing rocks into the little stream near where they parked the motorhome. "Duh. I've told you about it. I've told *them* about it. But none of them do it. They stick me on computers or hand me their 'grade level passages' and tell me to read them. I obviously can't read faster if I can't fucking *read* in the first place. When I tell them that, they tell me I'm not trying hard enough."

"Well, I met someone today who's dyslexic and she can read now. She knows how it all works."

"Obviously, we're both dyslexic. I've been telling you that too. It runs in families."

He bit his lip. "How do you not feel… stupid?" Moronic. Retarded. Dumb. All the words his brothers and Chance constantly used to taunt him so often that he internalized it.

"Because I can talk well. I can understand anything spoken to me and retain it. I know I can learn. I just can't read. So it's a learning disability. I'm not stupid."

He grabbed her in a hug. "I wish I were more like you."

"Dad made sure you couldn't be." She lifted her eyes to him. "You took all the ammunition he had so he didn't fire his mouth off at me."

Cole did. He eagerly took the brunt of the jeering, trying to get them to leave Penny alone.

"We'd have to tell them you're my sister. I dread doing that. I think it's almost a phobia for me now. But we maintain the rest of the lie: our last name is Pearson, our dad is dead, our brothers are useless."

"Do I get to see the ranch then? And go there with you?" Her big eyes were enough to make his heart twist. All she wanted was attention. Normalcy. To hang out with her brother.

"Yes. But you'd be there strictly to learn. You'd have to spend lots of time with this woman. You'd have to also be careful about what you say. Maybe try not to swear all the time. I mean, it'll be like school but much more intensive."

"I can keep my mouth shut when I need to." She stuck her tongue out at him.

Cole felt old when he smiled back. Old and tired of failing his little sister.

"Always. Don't forget that. It seems like it will never end. The lying, I mean."

"Whatever. As long as we're together and away from Chance, it's worth it."

She was the more mature one. *Whatever.* That's how Penny handled everything that happened to her. She had no mother. *Whatever.* The woman died. *Whatever.* Penny had to sleep in a sleeping bag with brothers who drank, used drugs, smoked and had sex in front of her. *Whatever.* That's just how it was. She couldn't read or write. She never had privacy or decent belongings. Her dad was cruel to her. Her brothers mocked her. Kids at school bullied her. *Whatever.* That was how she lived her life.

The only thing Penny didn't say *whatever* to was her teeth. She needed the braces. And that was why Cole embarked on this whole adventure. Even Penny had a breaking point.

"I don't need to read, Cole." But her hungry eyes said otherwise.

"You do. Obviously, you do. School would be better. Life would be better too. But mostly, your entire future will improve. You don't want to be like me, Pen."

"I would rather be like you than any president or millionaire or whatever else you consider successful."

He reached over and ruffled her hair. "But I can't read, which limits all my choices for us. If you could read, you could read for both of us."

Her entire face brightened. "I could. I didn't think of that. Yes. I could totally do it for us. If someone would just fuckin' show me how, I *know* it won't take me long."

"The swearing. Please. Little girls don't talk like that."

She evil-eyed him and he had to laugh as he lifted his hands up in surrender. "Little boys don't either. I meant, little kids in general. Good manners are important."

"Good manners, my ass. We don't feed hungry kids, or teach dyslexic kids how to read at school, when it's their job. Or punish all the mean dads. But I need to have good manners. Our entire value system is ass-backwards."

"How do you even know what things like value systems are?"

"I told you I'm the smartest one in the classroom. I just can't read." She eyed him with a smirk, adding, "Yet."

"You'll do it then?"

"I'll meet the lady and see if she's as pointless as every other person who promised to help me."

"They did try."

"By doing useless things. I told them it wasn't working!

They didn't believe me, but blamed me! Or they told me I needed to try harder. How could you not be more angry?"

"I think they worked with what they knew and had at their disposal."

"But it didn't work." Penny's voice cracked. "They blamed us. They made it our fault." Penny's voice rose with emotion. Penny had the same educators that Cole had. They were all very nice but totally ineffective. "Think of a word that starts with the letter C and could fit the meaning of this passage." Penny mimed the familiar instruction and then all but spat her derision. "What horseshit. You want me to guess what I can't read? How is that teaching me to read? Find the word? How many words do they think I can memorize? As smart as I am, that's a still a small limit."

His limit was even less then hers. She was that smart and he was desperate to get her out. The dysfunction and the lack of resources they struggled with before could be at an end.

"I might know the way out, Penny."

Cole had to try. If Erin could meet Penny and get to know her, maybe Cole could finally come forward and admit who Penny was to Erin. Maybe then, he could find a permanent solution for Penny's welfare.

"Fine. I'll meet her and let you know."

Penny didn't allow anyone to blow smoke up her ass. She was more than familiar with disappointment and frustration.

COLE SENSED Jade's presence before she said anything. Leaning over the stall, he was doing the unglamourous but necessary job of mucking the stalls. They boarded dozens of horses. Many were being trained for various specialties: from reliable trail horses to dressage to jumping to barrel-racing and other sports.

He didn't look up or over when she spoke. "What?"

"Say something. Why won't you acknowledge me? I didn't do anything to you. Grandma did. I'm sorry for how she handled that. But you can't just ice me out because you feel… well, see? I don't know how you feel."

He threw the rake harder, scooping up the horse manure and slamming it into the rolling cart beside him. "I was pissed off. It was no one's business. Pretty shitty thing she did. It was also the truth. So what do you want me to say? You can fire me now. But I need the job still."

Her boots clunked on the planks of the wood floor in the stall. "Cole?"

"What?" he snapped. "Wanna fuck me against this wall? Haven't done it in here yet."

He didn't look at her but he felt her halt. Was she shocked? Appalled?

"Cole?" This time, she said his name in a soft, almost soothing voice. "What are you mad at me for?"

He shoved the rake handle away and leaned over the mess in the cart. "Because I'm subservient to you in everything. I couldn't even screw you right. It's just one more thing for me to feel inferior about. Big, dumb, old Cole."

She touched his shoulder. "No one thinks you're dumb. But even if everyone did, I wouldn't, and I don't."

"Just let me take a few days to get used to everyone knowing."

"You mean *me* knowing."

He pinned her with his gaze. "Yes, mostly you, Jade."

"Why? Why was I not the one you would tell? The one you…"

"Ask for help?" He snorted. "Do you have any idea how many programs I went through? For years, Jade. Public schools are required to help us. Teacher after teacher. At least eight of them tried to teach me. From the regular classroom to all the magical courses. Special Ed. The Resource Room. Title Services. Take your pick. None of them taught me a fucking thing."

"The same stuff happened to my grandma."

"So? Knowing that doesn't fix it."

She looked to him and then away. "I didn't mean I'd be the one you call to fix it but the one you just… you know, come to."

He straightened up, twisting around to look at her. "What do you mean? Come to?"

Jade shuffled her feet and fidgeted with her hands, wringing one with the other. What the hell? Why was Jade so full of nerves? "Like, if I were having trouble or being attacked again, if that happened now, I'd tell you about it. I felt let down by the world. I didn't know things like that could happen. It messed with my head. If that happened today, instead of running to my mom and dad and sister, like I did at the time, I would come to you now."

His breathing escalated as she spoke. Damn. What kind of an example was that? He was acting like a pissy jerkoff to her about something he lacked. Nothing she'd done to him, of course. Jade was decent and funny and kind and full of fire. He was hurt because he felt like less than a man now in front of her. She wanted him to know his vulnerabilities endeared him to her, and she hoped he'd seek her out as much as she would him.

Trying to regulate his breathing, he finally admitted, "I've never had anyone to rely on."

"Never?"

He shook his head. "No. No mother. Father was a joke. Who do you think mocked me the most of all? Why do you think I learned how to conceal my deficiency? Most of all because of the taunting and torture my dad and my brothers gave me. One could read perfectly. The other is like me, but not as bad. But he never gave a shit about it. Not like I did."

"Cole, I don't know much about you. I doubt you realize how little you tell me or share. I just want to know you better. I really want to. Forget about your father. I just care how you feel. I want to know *you.*"

She did too. Glancing at her, she was standing there, her spine straight, her hands splayed at her sides in a beseeching gesture. Tears filled her eyes. "Let me, please. Let me start to know you, Cole. It doesn't have to be fast. But just let me."

She moved herself against him. Ignoring his hands-off, clenched jaw and fists, and stiff posture, she simply put her arms around his waist. Her face burrowed into his chest. She was hard to keep at a distance. Or even at arm's length. She was still his boss. And his nemesis. And the victim who could identify him as her attacker.

Cole wrapped his arms around her and clutched her tightly to him. He leaned down and set his lips on the top of her head and held her. All she wanted was to give him comfort. He could feel it in the strength of her arms when she squeezed them around him. Taking a deep breath, he tried to relax. Was she relieved? Yeah, he was glad too. She didn't move for a while. Way too long.

When she lifted her head up, she smiled at him. "I think I could fall in love with you, Cole."

His heart raced. He tried to swallow the sudden lump in his throat that filled him with dread. And with hope. And with longing.

"Jade…" He breathed her name almost desperately.

She smiled easily and lifted her hands to cup his face, running her thumb along his lower lip. "Don't answer me. I just wanted you to know how I feel. It's not a declaration. Or a requirement. Just so you know."

He closed his eyes. The gift of Jade was too much. He'd

never deserve her, obviously. He wasn't a good enough person for her, not morally or emotionally. He could never be free of the shit that marked him and his life. Like father, like son.

Cole had no idea what to say.

So he thought of the first thing he wanted to share with her that meant something real to him. "I have a little sister."

Penny. Shit. There it was. The words flipped out of his mouth. Unexpected. Unplanned. He was still debating whether or not to mention Penny. But now? He'd already started it. The reveal that would eventually lead to a jail sentence for him and the departure of Jade. But hopefully, he could find something to last forever for Penny.

Jade's eyes nearly popped from her head. "Y-Y-You have a little sister? Where? Around here?"

"She lives with me."

"In the motorhome?" Her eyes were wide as saucers now.

He couldn't help smirking at her reply. "Well, not outside in a tent. It's marginally better than that."

"What? Why? How come I didn't know this before? Why all the secrets? Where is she?"

He sighed. "This isn't the time. Okay? I need to work. And think. Can we talk tonight?"

"But where is she? Where is she all the time when you're here?"

Okay, he'd said too much and blown her mind. "She goes to a boys and girls center."

"How old is she?"

"Twelve."

"You have a little sister and all this time... she was *right* here?"

"Well, not *right here*. She's never been to the ranch. She's a little bitter about that."

"Why not just tell me? Us? Why?"

"I don't share my life much. I told you before. It's always been us. We keep to ourselves. Dad's dead. Brothers don't count. It's just me and her."

She stepped back and started pacing. Then she stopped and froze. "The running. That's why you run when you leave to get her."

"Always."

"She can read. She does all the reading for you guys." Jade nodded as if that made sense. If only.

"No. She doesn't. She has the same problem I do. That's why I told you. I need Erin's help. For her."

"For her." Jade repeated, giving him a puzzled glance. "But what about you?"

"I need to work. I'm already hopeless. But not her… she isn't like me, Jade."

Jade seemed to snap out of her shock and reverie when he said her name.

"Bring her here. Tonight. We'll meet with Grandma. Of course, we'll get her all the reading help she needs. Of course we will. Damn… all this time…" She kept shaking her head.

"Tonight?"

"Yeah. Duh. No more wasting time. Tonight. Come back and text me when you get here." Jade's tone was crisp. Business-like now. Getting shit done was what Jade did and when she was fully at her most shining best. Jade liked having a clear-cut goal. A point to move towards. And just like that, they left the soft, squishy, heart-felt Jade. He liked her both ways. But he needed her like this for Penny.

"Fine. Tonight. About six-thirty or so. I need to get her some dinner first."

"Right. Feed your little sister. Yes. That's quite important. That's where all those bagged meals from the restaurant go, isn't it?" she asked, sounding almost pissy about it.

"Yeah. It is. Better food than I'd buy."

"And what do you eat, Cole?"

"I eat fine, Jade. I just eat cheaper stuff."

Her lips pursed. "Bring her here at six. We'll all have dinner at the grill. No arguments." Then she flipped around and was gone.

Gone.

And Cole was coming back. With his little sister.

His stomach felt rancid. It was all starting now. He was slowly losing control of the situation. The final, terrible conclusion was fast approaching. The end that would be the best thing that could happen to Penny.

So it was finally happening.

For Penny.

The anthem of his life. What would happen when he was sent to prison for assault and Penny was no longer a worry? Jade would, no doubt, abandon him. He'd lose his job. There was no one else he cared about.

What would keep him going then?

CHAPTER 21

$\mathcal{C}$OLE WALKED IN WITH a black-haired, little girl beside him. He dwarfed her. She was both skinny and short. Her hair was a shaggy cut like Cole's. Poorly brushed. Her clothes were worn and stained. But they seemed clean.

Cole gave Penny all the meals he didn't eat there.

But wouldn't the school provide meals for low-income families? Wouldn't the daycare do the same? Was he so used to going without food that he naturally fasted? What did he say? That the quality of the Rydell food was better than what he provided himself.

Jade thought of the motorhome and shuddered to think this little girl lived in it. She remembered the busted door on the refrigerator. She didn't really think about it at the time, but now realized since it didn't work, they couldn't keep any perishables in the RV.

They looked shaggy, raggedy and adorable standing together. Cole's height, breadth, and brawn contrasted to Penny's diminutive frame. But the way they both held themselves clearly showed they were related.

Right then, however, they were both stressed. Unsure. Confused. Distrusting.

But at least they showed up. Jade stopped studying them for a moment and gathered her wits. Things were getting a bit too dramatic over the last few days. After the great reveal by her grandmother, that could have probably been handled better, and Cole's jerky, asinine reaction to it, she actually told him she loved him. Crap. What was she thinking?

And his response? He told her he had a little sister who was right there all this time.

Stunned? No, there were no words to describe her emotional response.

But the few personal reasons that he missed days at work now made sense.

Jade sucked in air and wished for more courage. Why was she so nervous? It felt like bugs were living in her stomach. Her perception of Cole was rapidly changing. He was still a complete loner and tough, yet oddly sweet and earnest. Learning that he had a drastic reading problem and a little sister were huge revelations. She now understood why he was always running. She didn't know why Cole insisted on secrecy. Why not just tell her the truth?

"Here, take this out to them. I'll slip away through the back," Jade's mother said when she came up behind Jade.

Jade took the tray her mom arranged for them. Several different popular dishes were served. From pulled-pork taco wraps to chicken strips and an elaborate chef salad. "Yeah. Obviously, Cole's not used to being in crowds, getting attention or watching his manners."

Jocelyn rubbed her hand down Jade's hair. "He hurt your feelings, huh? Not telling you about the reading problem and his sister?"

Jade blinked with surprised at her mom's soft tone. "Yes. I

guess he did. Just my feelings. I told him personal things that I felt, which I—"

"Which you just don't do."

"Exactly. Which I don't do. And he won't tell me the usual facts people share with each other?"

"Ask him. Keep at him."

"I will but he was so strange about hiding his reading problem and little sister."

"Then give him more time. All the signs of trauma are evident."

She blinked harder and straightened up. "You're right. And I can be stronger." Pulling her shoulders back, she carried the tray towards the main part of the grill.

Cole and Penny hovered together at the entrance. "Come in. Sit down." Jade called as she set the tray on a table between them. Cole's demeanor vacillated between appearing fully uncomfortable and acting surly. No smiles. No quick kisses on the mouth as he sometimes did. But that was always when they were alone. So no surprise there.

Jade didn't even know the child's name. Startled, she blinked as the girl stared at her with wide eyes. She was not shy, wilting or averting her gaze.

Jade put her hand out. "Hi, I'm Jade."

"Penny." That fast, she knew Cole's sister when she pumped her hand and revealed her name. Penny Pearson.

Feeling odd, Jade waved toward the seats. "Sit down. My mom made some popular choices."

Penny glanced at Cole, who nodded, still unsmiling. Jade didn't miss the interaction between them.

Penny selected the chef salad. Surprised, Jade watched her eat it for a few moments. She scooted the tray towards Cole. "Take your pick. I like all of them."

Cole grabbed the chicken strip basket. Keeping his head down, he tore into it. Jade sighed with distress. What was happening? Why was he acting so awkward? Was he stressed? He almost seemed mean.

"So Penny, what grade are you going into?"

She again looked at Cole while stuffing more bites into her mouth. He nodded. She looked back at Jade. "Seventh."

"Do you go to school in town?"

"Yeah."

"Do you like it?"

She shrugged. "I'd like it better if the bitches would back off."

Startled, Jade blinked several times but had nothing to say.

Cole stopped eating and shot Penny a sharp look before snapping, "Pen."

Penny sighed. "She asked, Cole. And that's the truth."

"What... ah... what do the bitches do?"

Cole finally looked at Jade and she gave him a little half smile and a shrug. It was as though she were saying *what are you gonna do?* So Jade went with it.

"They're always dissing me. About my teeth mostly. But when school ended, I stood up for myself so I think it'll stop when I start next year."

As she spoke, Cole shook his head.

A tender sense of sympathy filled Jade. Yeah, that age could be a pretty harsh phase. And having a mouthful of crossed, crooked, bucked teeth with braces on them wasn't much help.

"We need a better orthodontist. The one in town doesn't tighten them well enough. Do you know a good one?"

She'd never been asked such a question by a child before. "Uh..." Jade looked to Cole for help. He was almost shutting his eyes in horror at the topics of his little sister's conversation. "I'm sure my mom would remember mine. Want me to ask her? We actually went to Wenatchee for them. Pretty important, huh?"

Penny nodded. "Right. But damn. Isn't that like, really far?"

"I told you to knock it off," Cole admonished her harshly.

Her pixie face fell. "What did I say?"

"Damn and bitches."

"But those aren't bad words."

"Yes, they are."

Empathizing with the inappropriate yet very sweet girl, Jade reached over and touched Cole's hand. "Hey, it's okay. I don't mind. It's not like we're in school and I'm her teacher."

Cole jerked his hand away from hers. Startled by the adamant reaction, Jade withdrew, feeling hurt. Cole's gaze was only on his sister. Penny was staring hard at where their hands barely touched.

Her little face shot up to Cole.

What was happening now?

Her face was filled with tears. "How could you?" she whispered. All signs of the tough-talking, truckdriver language were gone.

How could he what?

Cole fidgeted in his seat. He threw the half-eaten chicken strip down. "Later, Pen. Not now."

But Jade had a feeling no one could tell this dynamo to wait for later, especially if she were upset. Clearly, something must've triggered her. What? The food? Was she remembering a familiar incident?

Penny shot to her feet then and accused Cole, "You had sex with her, didn't you? How could you. How could you do *that?*" Then Penny ran away. Going out the door, she scurried down the stairs.

Cole merely leaned back, holding his head. "Fucking A."

Did he really tell his sister about sex? Or at least, identify the girl he did it with?

Jade was confused. And what she found puzzling was moving fast to becoming disturbing.

"What just happened?"

"This was a mistake," Cole replied.

Jade grabbed his arm. "No, really? What just happened? Why is she so upset? How did she figure that out? And why does she care so much?"

He pushed two fingers on the bridge of his nose. "She and I lived in the same house, so we witnessed the same stuff. It turned us both sour on the subject. We agreed it was gross and pointless. She obviously assumes I still think that. I have to find her."

He spun around. Jade stood there all but sputtering while her heart contracted. These two seemed so sad and lost. Everything in their lives revolved around survival. Rushing after Cole, Jade started down the stairs. Cole was already calling her name. "Penny! Penny!"

She followed him. He went out through the large arena doors and scoured the area. "There." Jade pointed towards the river.

"Fuck." Cole stormed. "Penny can't swim."

Sprinting into a full run, Cole started after her. Jade tried to keep up but she couldn't. She was out of breath when she finally caught up to them. Cole had Penny in a full hug, pressed against him as she struggled furiously. She was red-faced and angry. Yelling. Pushing him.

"How could you? You promised. You *promised* you would never be like them."

"I'm not like them." His voice was calmer but loud enough to hear over hers.

Hanging back, Jade was entirely unsure what to do. Then

Penny's tear-stained, red, angry face found Jade and she asked, "How could you let him?"

Utterly confused, Jade stepped closer. Cole all but growled but Jade ignored him and kneeled closer to the crying, upset girl. "How could I let him what, honey?"

"Let him do that... do those disgusting things to you? Why would you even want to?"

"*Penny.* Please stop." Cole's voice sounded strangled now.

Looking up at Cole, Jade shook her head and put her hand up. "What do you think he did to me? Do you think he hurt me?"

"Yes. Of course. It hurts."

"No, sweetie, it doesn't. Not when you want to do it. And we wanted to do it. It's okay when two people discover they..."

Penny swung her face around. "Don't you dare say *love each other*. That's just a load of horse shit."

Jade pressed her lips together. Okay, she definitely knew about sex. It was happening all around her. How fucked up is that? Shit. Jade never heard of adults having sex with kids in the same room. It was predatory. It was a form of abuse.

That's why Cole didn't do it. Because he'd been in Penny's shoes. So he abstained from it and chose to remain a damn virgin.

"Let me speak, Penny." Soft and soothing couldn't cut it with this little sailor. She spoke sharply at her. "Shut up for two seconds and listen to someone else for once, okay?"

Her little back snapped upright as she crossed her arms indignantly over her chest. But her mouth finally stayed shut. Tightly. She was purposely silent now. Jade rolled her eyes. It reassured her, however, that Penny still had some childish reactions inside her.

"You clearly know what sex is?"

She nodded her head and Cole turned three shades of red. "You witnessed it?"

She nodded. "My dad and older brothers used to do it. I tried to plug my ears and shut my eyes, but…"

Jade shuddered. "I see. That's pretty horrible. And it's not right. Most adults would never do that kind of thing in front of a little kid. So you and Cole agreed not to do that with anyone? What you think of as sex?"

"Yes." Penny whispered this time and bit her lip. "Why would you want that to happen to you?" She gazed directly and unblinking into Jade's eyes. Penny was quite a pistol.

"Pen—" Cole started to interrupt, nearly groaning her name. Jade put her hand up and shook her head.

"She needs to hear this. From a woman. Not from you."

Jade looked back at Penny. "Nothing like that was ever done to you?"

Penny's head shook vigorously.

"Okay. Good. And you understand what I'm talking about is strictly for adults. People way older than you. I'd usually never discuss this subject with a young girl like you. But you aren't getting the whole story. I'll tell you about it if you come back to the grill and finish your dinner. No use letting the food go to waste, is there?"

Penny shrugged but the gleam in her eyes reflected her interest. "Let's go."

Cole shoved his hands into his pockets. His bleak-eyed expression indicated his absolute horror at this entire conversation.

They walked quietly back to the staircase and ascended. Their food was waiting where they left it.

Penny sat down and swung her feet back and forth as she downed half a cup of pop. "So you really want to hear this?"

She shrugged. "I guess so. I wanna know why?"

Right, why. What do you say to a kid? "Well, simply because it feels nice."

"How could *that* ever feel nice when it's so terrible?"

"When someone is nice to you and you like that person, then it's a nice thing to do together…"

"Just because you like them makes it not as gross?"

Jade bit her lip. "Well, yes. When you're old enough, and you have a real connection with someone special, it's as good as candy and not like what you've seen before."

"You like Cole doing that stuff to you?"

Cole slumped down and put his hand to his forehead, shaking his head. He was dying inside of mortification. Jade was too. But she held onto the bold girl's attention.

"I don't know what kind of stuff you mean. But I like what we do together. Yes."

Penny stuck a bite of lettuce and chicken in her mouth. Chewing, she asked, "Why?"

"You really like that word."

"How else can I learn?"

She smiled. "True enough. But on this subject? People like to be private about it and only discuss it with adults. I hope you don't repeat anything about me and Cole to anyone else. That's not fair to us. Is it a deal?"

Penny eyed Jade, then slowly put her hand out. "Okay, deal."

With the hand shake of a promise, she nodded solemnly in response. "Okay."

"What do you want to know?"

"Why does it feel good?"

"I honestly don't know why. I guess because your body responds to certain things. But you're not old enough to understand all that yet. When you're old enough, I promise to tell you, if we're still friends."

"Then it really doesn't hurt?"

"No. But it can. You're not wrong about that. When sex is wrong, it can hurt you. I'd never do it again if it hurt me."

"So you really do want to do it with Cole?"

Talk about getting to know his sibling. "I do. I really want to."

"And he doesn't hurt you?"

"Never. Not once."

Cole leaned forward. "Penny, please stop. This isn't fair to Jade."

She gave him the evil-eye. "You lied to me."

"I did not. I wasn't doing it. I hadn't done it when you asked me."

Jade bit her lip at the almost childish response from Cole.

"You didn't tell me you started doing it. You didn't tell me about *her*."

"Well, I didn't tell her about *you* either."

"But…"

"And Jade's right… this stuff is way too old for you."

"But Jade already told me about it."

He threw his hands up. "I don't want to talk about it anymore with you."

She bit her lips. "But you always talk to me." Real fear flashed into her eyes. "Will you only talk to her now?"

"No. Of course not. But I prefer not to discuss this subject with you."

"Can I ask Jade then? If I have more questions?"

Cole shut his eyes as if he were suffering great pain. "What more questions?"

"Well, when will I get my period? How does that work?"

"Your…" he sighed. "I don't know when."

Jade snorted. "You'll bleed every month and hate it. What were you going to say about it?" she asked Cole. "How much do you know about it?"

"Nothing." He gave her a cool look. "I'd have to figure it out."

Oh. That was more than she expected from him. "Well, ask away, Penny. That, I can tell you about."

"Does it hurt when you bleed?"

"No, not usually. Unless you have a heavy flow."

"Do you?"

"No. I have a pretty light one."

"What does that *mean*?" Oh. Jade sighed. She was blessed with an older sister, a mother, a grandmother, numerous aunts and so many cousins. She knew about menstrual flow and PMS and all the fun puberty stuff ever since she could remember. It was simply part of their conversations. By the time it happened when she was thirteen, she'd long known what to expect. Still it shocked her. Jade ran to her mother in tears and her mom held her. Of course, they were already prepared and had all the right supplies.

"The flow refers to how much blood comes out and how fast. One of my aunts soaks through a whole pad or a tampon almost every hour for the first few days of her period. She's got stupid heavy flows. I can go like, three hours. Typically, the first three days are the worst of it. The first day is always the worst for me."

"How does it start? Does the blood gush out everywhere?"

"No. Well, I guess maybe it depends. I started with some brown spotting in my underwear. So I just wore a pantyliner so I'd be ready."

"Ready? How?"

"With pads and tampons. There are other options too nowadays. If you don't like the pads and tampons, we can check those out."

"We?"

Jade shifted, now uncomfortable at her presumption. "Well, if you're around. Sure."

She flipped a glance at Cole. He was turning a lovely shade of green. He pushed his food away, and she tilted her head. "Too much period talk, cowboy?"

He whipped his gaze up to her and she shrugged. "It's a fact of our lives. I don't see why you should be shielded from the thrills. Plus, you'll need to get over it for her."

"Right. I never really thought about it that much before."

"You know, I've had it while you've been around me." She didn't add that was the reason why they didn't have sex for a few days.

"Of course you did. I mean... I guess so." He finally threw up his hands. "I don't really know."

"Back to me." Penny interrupted. "So the flow determines the number of pads you need. But where does the tampon go?"

She grinned when Cole groaned and put his head down. She patted Penny's hand. "Most likely you won't start with tampons. But it goes where the blood comes out. It starts in your uterus, drips through your cervix and comes out through your vagina."

"*Jade.*" Cole moaned almost in distress.

"It's her body. She likes to know how things work. She *should* know too. There's no shame in it. Now is there?" She gave him a look.

"They were teaching Sex Ed at school in the fifth grade but I ditched it."

"Sounds like you shouldn't have. Especially living with all guys," Jade replied sweetly.

"She experienced enough. I told her if she didn't want to go, what's the harm?" Cole answered.

Interesting. Even a few years ago it seemed he was making choices for Penny.

"Is that where the sex happens too?"

"Yes. It is."

"Interesting," was all Penny answered as she slurped more pop and took another huge bite of salad.

"It is, actually. Nothing shameful or gross about it. It's not like that." She gave Cole a *Grow up.* look.

Penny saw Erin walking up to the grill.

"Hey, Penny? My grandma's walking up here now. Could we please not continue this conversation in front of her?"

"Sure."

Jade rose. "Hi, Grandma. Come meet Cole's little sister. This is Penny."

Penny didn't get up but stuck her hand in the air and bent her fingers. "Hello."

Cole got up. "Hello, Mrs. Rydell."

"Hello to all of you. Enjoying some dinner?"

"Yes. And lots of small talk," Jade said with a secret smile at Penny and a wink. She giggled and then nodded.

"Yep. Just getting to know each other."

They let her finish eating as they made idle chatter. This time, it wasn't private or intimate. Jade met Cole's gaze a few times. He was unreadable still. He puzzled her.

Finally, Penny pushed the food and drink away. Then she asked, "So are you the one who's dyslexic too?"

Erin turned her attention to the bold little girl. "Yes. I am. Are you dyslexic?"

Penny shrugged. "No other reason to explain why I can function normally otherwise but can't read basic words or sounds."

"You know what it is then."

"Clearly. I live it."

Erin smirked. "It isn't such a curse once you know about it and learn how to read. There are gifts and strengths that come with it. But let's start with fixing what makes it hard."

"Reading. Spelling. Writing."

"Yes."

"Are you some kinda teacher?"

"No."

Penny crossed her arms over her skinny chest. "Thank crap for that. Don't need another lecture about trying harder or working on my comprehension even though I can't read the fu—the words."

Erin tilted her head. "You've obviously had some tough times, but you also seem things clearly."

"I'm not stupid."

"No. Definitely not. And very mature for your age."

Erin had no idea how mature but Jade kept that to herself.

"What's going on then?" Penny asked, almost belligerently.

Erin leaned forward. "My sister-in-law taught dyslexic kids for almost thirty years. She'll let me use her materials. Or she can teach you. You'd have to come here on a regular basis and work with me. But you'll be able to read at the end of it."

"Of course it will work if someone would just show me why the letters change sounds and maybe, what some of the sounds are."

Cole shook his head, trying not to smile. He was obviously well-acquainted with his sister's intelligence, as well as her smart-mouthed comments and confidence. Jade hadn't met someone so young who knew so much. But she also found Penny kind of amazing.

Erin's eyes gleamed. "That's exactly what you need. I can do that."

"Well, then fine. Let's do that."

"You're refreshing."

Cole snorted. "You say that now…"

"When do you want to start?" Jade pressed.

Penny shrugged. "Now? I'm not getting any younger sitting here."

It was impossible not to laugh. "Okay. Yeah. Let's go to my house."

They started to rise but Cole sat there. Penny gave him a look. "Come on, Cole."

"I'll talk to Jade and come down for you later."

Penny scowled at him. "You read worse than I do. You need this too."

He glared at his sister. "This is all for you."

"Cole… you really should learn too."

He gave Jade a snarling look. "No."

Erin pressed her lips together. "That's exactly how I pictured this. That's why I found you out the way I did."

Penny flipped around and simply sat down. "If he's not doing it. Neither am I."

Jade almost rolled her eyes at the childish gesture but envied her brilliance.

Cole shoved her shoulder. "You don't get a choice in the matter. I told you to."

"You're not my father." She snapped. He jerked back as if she'd just jabbed him with a hot poker. He glanced at Erin and then at her. Why? It seemed a legit, immature comeback from a little sister.

"Don't push this, Pen."

"I won't do it. Not unless you do too."

He shut his eyes. "But I… can't."

Jade's heart kind of broke.

"You think you can't. You're not dumb. It's dyslexia. I've told you this. That lady just said so too. She seems to get it."

"I don't have the time."

"You're not doing anything but sitting here right now," Penny pointed out reasonably.

He glanced around. "Not normally."

"Well, then, we'll have to make the time." Erin said crisply.

"Penny's right. You need to do this too. It's just as important that you learn to read too."

"She'll be much faster. She's much smarter than me."

"It isn't about intelligence. It's a brain difference in how print information is taken in and stored. What determines how long it takes each individual is usually correlated to their severity of dyslexia, not smartness."

Jade was glad her grandma did everything but chide him. And she'd pressure him too.

"Why can't you just be in the room? We can start there?" Jade asked, trying to get Cole to at least show up. Persuade him to listen in. Maybe he could figure out he needed it too.

"That's right. Do that. I won't sit there if you're not there," Penny threatened. She was hardcore with her snotty bribery.

Truly, Penny needed to be put in her place, but in this case, Jade agreed with her.

His jaw ticked and he clenched it while crossing his arms protectively over his chest. "Fine. If you're going to be this juvenile about it, I guess I'll have to sit in with you like a baby sitter."

Lord, the squabbling. But Cole got to his feet and walked out.

Erin shrugged, her gaze pinned to his retreating figure "It's pride. Embarrassment. Much easier to face this as a child. I refused to deal with it for three years."

Penny jumped up. "How stupid. You claim it actually works, why would you avoid doing it if it works?"

"Because when nothing else worked, I thought it must be me that was the problem, not the programs or the people trying to help me. Most of them were very nice."

Penny gave Erin a dirty look. "Really? Failing me? Blaming me? Telling perfectly normal talking and acting kids like me to *try harder, when I was trying!* When I tried harder, and it didn't work why didn't someone find another way for me? You did!"

"I didn't. Again, my sister-in-law did. She's a teacher and a kind one."

Penny didn't give an inch. "One who went out and discovered the answers."

"Come on, let's go learn some answers for you two," Erin said, her mouth twitching. Yeah, Penny was hard not to like.

But Cole's reaction to her suggestion? Not his finest hour.

CHAPTER 22

CORNERED, THERE WAS NO choice. Damn Penny. She knew better than to argue right in front of strangers.

Especially in front of their damn aunt.

And Jade.

Cole's face got so hot, it could have melted snow. He was so embarrassed for the entire evening. From Penny's freak out to Jade's description of their sex life. Seeing how Jade managed to engage Penny so fast was pretty amazing to Cole. In the past, Cole was the only one who could do that. He felt tongue-tied and stumped.

But Jade picked up the slack and seemed to know what to say.

When she brought up *periods*, Cole was nearly floored. He didn't know about those things. No. He knew it would eventually happen, but had no clue how to discuss it with Penny or what to buy for her to use. What were the chances they'd still be living here?

Now he was about to follow his aunt into her house. The way Penny mentioned fucking Chance so cleverly in front of them all to get her way disappointed Cole. She was fast becoming a manipulative brat. Cole had no idea she was so nonchalant and capable about it.

That's how she persuaded him to go there with her. But what choice did he have?

His reading problem was a long buried and, he hoped, dead issue. Sure, when it popped up it was annoying and humiliating. But now, Penny had arranged everything for him. Insisting he go to Erin's house for what? To be tutored by his own aunt?

Erin's house was as grand and clean and comfortable as all things Rydell. Screw them. Cole was embarrassed and grumpy. He wished they'd never agreed to come to dinner.

If he'd had any balls, they'd probably climb back up into his body.

A hand suddenly slipped into his as he stomped down the road. Startled by it, he stopped dead to see Jade standing there.

"Cole, you're being very difficult and immature."

"That was humiliating."

"My take on the sex, the facts of menstruation, or Penny's dyslexia?"

"All of it. But mostly the second issue. I would have figured out what to do about her periods when the time came."

Jade's hand was still holding his. Why did she bother with him? And so easily shower him with affection? He liked holding her cool, slim hand in his. "Really? That's strange after you seemed a little green around the gills when I mentioned mine. Maybe we need to have a more in-depth discussion soon."

"What do you mean?" His voice wavered. What else did he do wrong? He couldn't read. Or properly help his sister, or be a mother to her, or teach her to read, and he was terrible at sex.

"Hey, Cole, if I have to suffer through it, why shouldn't you know about it too?"

"Suffer through what? Sex?"

"No, silly, my period. The blood that flows each month. The cramps. The tenderness in my breasts. The gnawing hunger and unexplained mood shifts. All of that."

He stopped dead. "Is it really that uncomfortable? That intrusive?"

"For me. Not for everyone. It can be far worse for others."

"You mean, this is what I have to look forward to with Penny?"

Jade's face softens. "You really love her, don't you? I mean, I love my siblings too but Penny's more than that, almost like your daughter."

"Friend or sibling, not my daughter. I'm all she has left for a father figure. I've taken care of her ever since I knew about her."

"Which was… when?"

Should he tell Jade? He never told anyone anything true about Penny. But Jade wasn't trying to hurt him or take anything away from him. Especially Penny. "Five years old. She lived with her mother until then. When her mom died, she went under the custody of our shared father and he became her guardian. That's why she's such a good person. Her mother loved her very much and took good care of her. If only her mother had made better plans for Penny's care in case she died. She was killed in a car accident. And then Penny moved in with us."

"Did you know her at all before then?"

"I knew *of* her. But I didn't know her. Dad never visited her or paid child support. To Dad, we were all just pawns for his scams or targets for his abuse."

"So when Penny came to your household, you took her under your wing?"

"I had to. She was so small and sweet, and that shy smile. I knew she was better than all of us so I had to protect her. I just failed at it sometimes, and I still do."

Jade's hand gripped his to grab his attention. "You never failed her. She just showed you that. She adores you, Cole. She was jealous when she discovered I'd come into your life. I was someone she didn't know about and wasn't involved with you two."

"I never realized how upset she'd get. But you're right, there's been no one else but us. No friends. No mentors. No guardians. No teachers. Just Penny and I against the world."

"She's extraordinarily worldly, sharp, and intelligent, but Cole, she's still a little girl trying to find her way in a grown-up world."

"I agree with all that, yes."

"She's also quite exceptional."

Jade saw it and Cole's relief flooded him. Jade understood what he struggled and fought so hard for. "She *is*, isn't she?"

"Yes, she really is." He finally risked glancing down at her. Jade's mouth twisted into a warm smile. "I think you both are."

"Jade... I'm really not. Penny's the one with the brains. Did you miss the reason why I have to sit through Penny's tutoring session because she'll only do it if I'm there?"

Jade's arms suddenly encircled him and she pressed her body against him. "That's because you need to read too. I don't think you're dumb or weak or stupid even if you think I do. I think you're—"

"I'm what? What can you possibly gain from knowing me? My inspiring conversations? All the sparkling fun I can provide? I can't offer you any of that. I have to run home to my disgusting, barely habitable RV to live with my little sister. There's no fun there. We don't do anything out there but survive. What can I possibly offer someone like you?"

Jade's body bolted upright with the tension in the air. "Why do you need to offer me anything? Maybe I just like you, Cole. Maybe, I enjoy the person I see inside you."

Agitated now, he shook his head. "You don't see anything inside me."

"I simply care about the person I know. As you are. You might not care about him, but I do. And no one can tell me otherwise." Hands on her hips now, she tilted her head, and raised her eyebrows as if to challenge him.

"You don't really know me, Jade," Cole replied in a quiet tone, trying to cool down his emotions.

"I know how you make me feel."

"Jade, I need to sit with my sister now. I'll always be doing something with my sister somewhere. She's my number one priority. And always will be."

"So what? I wasn't asking you to put me first."

Jade was too good a person and impossible to win an argument with. Grabbing his hand again, she said, "Go and sit with Penny. Listen to what my grandma says. You're only a prick if you don't use this opportunity to improve yourself. Or are you embarrassed about it? Are you afraid I'll mock you? How could you think so little of me?"

He snorted. "Because everyone in my family did. It's the reaction I always get. I don't talk to anyone else."

She pressed her lips tightly. "Well, that sure as shit isn't how anyone decent would react to you, Cole. I would never do that to someone I cared about. Or someone I'm involved with. Why would you think I could ever be such a dick?"

"Because that's what always happens."

"Then you definitely need to make new friends. I'll be the first. We all want to call you our friend."

His heart ached with longing. He wanted everything Jade

could offer him. The bitterness of his remorse never left him. Someday, somehow, Jade would learn that he'd been one of the assholes that robbed her. That would be the end their friendship, no matter what. He was sorry that it had to go that way.

He wished he could have Jade in his life forever.

Cole entered Erin's house and felt relieved not to spew anymore lies.

COLE SAT behind Penny and off to the right. He could hear Erin and saw what was on the propped-up tablet before her. She gave a simple explanation for what she wanted Penny to do.

It was all about sounds and making them. Cole knew the alphabet and mentioned to Erin both he and Penny did.

"You could learn to read without ever knowing the *name* of the letters. It's the sounds they make that is where the problems start. And it gets worse when the letter sounds start changing. You have to first know the most common sounds to mastery, and then be told *why* they change sounds, and what they change to. This first two levels of this program, what we are doing is *all* about sounds to symbol recognition problems."

Whatever. None of what Erin was doing seemed usual or familiar.

Say the word and Penny did. Penny would bring down three separate colored tiles on the iPad, and then she'd say the three sounds while pointing to a tile for each sound. Then Erin would change one sound and Penny would have to repeat the existing two sounds with the new sound added, and then blend it all like a word.

Erin nodded. "Excellent. Here's the next one."

Cole leaned forward as he wondered how this could possibly help Penny read the text of her grade level? And they needed to get on with it. Feeling stressed, Cole listened and watched for a long while. He had to bite his tongue to fight the urge to voice his recurring doubts.

At the end of the hour, Erin sat back and stretched out her arms. "That was an excellent, introductory lesson, Penny. We'll continue from there next time."

"When?" Penny's arms crossed over her skinny torso, and her eyebrows shot up as if she were an authority figure questioning Erin.

She really was precocious.

"I suggest we work together at least two hours a week. That's the minimum for growth and retention."

"Is more often better?"

"Yes."

"How many days a week can you spare?"

"Penny. You can't ask for more time. Let Erin tell you when she's available," Cole scolded her.

Erin nodded. "If you're willing to work with me and Allison, she's my sister-in-law and a retired tutor, we can work four to five days a week."

"Fine." Penny's tone reminded Cole of an approving teacher. Rolling his eyes, Cole rose to his feet, anxious to escape.

Erin swiveled in her chair and her gaze pinned him. "Sit down."

His neck and face started getting very hot. But he did as he was told.

"Did you listen to Penny's session?"

"Yeah," he grunted.

"Okay. Then let's get started with you." She did the same lesson for Cole and he responded. Reluctantly, he reached forward and slid down one of the stupid colored tiles as she requested.

He noticed she repeated the same sounds several times. Frowning, he did what she asked, but why was she repeating everything?

Cole continued to obey her instructions, moving the tiles around and saying the sounds as he touched them. What the hell kind of game was this? How did it relate to reading?

Again, Erin repeated the combination of sounds he was saying. He noticed the book she worked from was quite slim. But Penny seemed to get through more than half of it. He didn't even get through a third.

It was hard for Cole to concentrate. Fuck. What did she say? He tried to remember and his brain went totally blank.

When she repeated a sequence of sounds for a third time, he pushed the iPad at her angrily. "Why do you keep repeating everything?"

His voice came out too aggressive. Horrified by his own behavior, Cole rubbed his hair and leaned forward, staring down at the floor.

"Because when you repeat some of them, they're out of order with the wrong sound inserted. We simply re-do it until you correct it. It's okay, Cole. It's all part of the process. This is fixing a foundation weakness you never developed. You never stood a chance of putting accurate letters to your sounds, beginning to blend them together, and then reading left to right to start sounding out syllables in longer words. " Erin spoke in a cool, soothing, but firm tone.

"You didn't repeat the sounds with Penny. Not as often as you do with me."

Erin nodded. "Correct. She seems to have the phonemic awareness. Some people have it. Some need to learn it. Nondyslexic people usually acquire it organically. But it seems Penny either had it already or someone must've taught her. It's also indicative of how pervasive dyslexia is. Penny's probably on the *milder* end of the scale. *You* might test more towards the severe end. That's how it was for me." She indicated the slim book before her. "This thin, little book exhausted me when I was learning to read. It literally has to rewire your brain. Pretty important stuff if you don't have it. If you do? You could whip right through this."

His head spun with all the new information. "So this stuff is what most people can do? But it's so..."

"Confusing? Exhausting? Yeah, it is when you don't get it."

"But Penny can do it?"

"Yes. But it means nothing, Cole. Just differences in the levels of dyslexia. I was more like you."

"What does it mean for Penny?"

"It means she'll get through this stuff and the program at a different pace then you. That's all it means."

He smirked. "While I'll be on the slow end of the program." So went the story of his life.

"Most likely. It's not an exact science. I tutored but not consistently. Allison can explain it. Typically, if the first level is too hard, too exhausting, or too prone to mistakes, then the dyslexia is considered more severe. That just means it takes longer to get through it. We try to move as fast as we can but as slow as necessary. It's just the way it goes."

He didn't raise his head. "How does this help me?"

"Later on, when you blend sounds together, you're learning the basics for decoding. You need that to read. You need the segmenting sounds for spelling. Cole, if you don't have this stuff down? You don't stand a chance of reading."

"But Penny does?"

"Penny *will*. Just keep bringing her here to see me or Allison."

"I promise. I'll bring her here."

Erin nodded. "And since you have to be here with her, why not continue to learn yourself?"

He waved a hand. "You just said…

"I was explaining the differences in the condition. But Cole?"

He jerked when she said his name with a scolding tone to it. He grunted at her.

"You'll learn how to read too."

Penny came up beside Cole and slipped her hand into the one that hung limp at his side. "Please Cole? Will you do it too? For me?"

He'd do anything for Penny. He hoped he'd proven that. But this felt like one thing too far. Her big eyes stared up at him, brimming with hope. "Fine." He managed to answer. He was unable to feel grateful or hide his annoyance. No. He didn't want to do this at all.

And fuck. He was tired.

But this was far different than a day spent hauling odd-sized hay bales or learning how to handle a horse and saddle.

COLE CAME out of the tutoring session with a grim look to his mouth. Penny trailed him, and she was also quiet.

Jade jumped to her feet. Startled to see her, he flipped around and said, "You waited all this time?" His expression became a deeper frown.

"Yes."

He didn't meet her gaze, and kept fidgeting with his feet. "Well, we have to go buy some food. Penny said she was still hungry, so…"

Striding quickly, Cole was almost running. Penny's little legs hurried to catch up with him. Sighing, Jade jogged after him too. His ego and pride were bruised. He didn't often exhibit such traits but holy shit. This brought it all out.

"Cole!" Jade called while almost skipping backwards alongside him. "Would you stop?"

As if he pulled an emergency brake, he almost skidded in the dusty lot. "What?"

"You're being a complete ass to me. I didn't do anything to you, might I remind you."

"I just didn't expect you to wait around for two entire hours."

"So? You're treating me badly just because I waited for you?"

His entire expression melted. "I'm not trying to do that."

She crossed her arms over her chest. "Well, you are. Your problem has a solution but I didn't cause your problem, I just told you there was a solution. I don't care about all the extra things you feel about it."

He shut his eyes for a moment. "I don't want to talk about it. Okay? We established what it is. I'm seeking the solution. But with you? I really don't want to acknowledge it now."

"Because…?"

"Because it humiliates me. It might seem trite to you but it damages my pride. Can we leave it at that?"

"I don't think any less of you."

He threw his hands up. "I do. I think a lot less of me. It affects my self-esteem."

She whipped her head back. Oh. Shit. Okay. She was too understanding and caring. The best thing she could do was not discuss the fact that Cole had to learn how to read.

She glanced at Penny. "While I was waiting, I was wondering where Penny goes after school on non-school days."

"The local youth organization helps with low-income child care."

"Couldn't Penny come out here to the ranch? She could work with Grandma then, and have dinner."

He shook his head. "I can't drive to the school and back on my break time."

"Yes, you can. You're allowed to get her. I'm giving you that allowance."

"I didn't ask you for special privileges." Cole started walking.

"Fine. Then use your lunch hour. Everyone gets a lunch hour. No special privileges there. Take lunch at three instead of noon. What about that?"

He whipped back around and she finally grabbed his attention. Penny started jumping up and down. "Oh please, Cole. Can't I do that? I'd much rather be here."

"I can't keep an eye on her. What's she going to do for all those hours? Run wild all over the place? You have no idea how curious she is and all the trouble that she can get into."

"She could come out to the barns and learn about the horses. As you well know, there's always one of us around there."

Penny went wild at hearing the word *horses*. "Oh, Cole. Please. Please. Please. I know I won't be afraid. I wanna see the horses. Can we go right now? You get to see them all the time. It would be so much better. Please." She bopped all around them as she danced and shrieked.

Cole gave her a look of annoyance. She merely smiled back. "Penny, go over to that fence and wait there," Cole ordered. No smiles. No joviality. Sometimes, he acted younger than her and even deferred to her. But definitely not this time.

"When it comes to Penny, please don't bring things up in her presence that I haven't approved yet. It makes it much harder to say no if I need to."

Ashamed, she nodded. "I've only been around Benny as his aunt. But I'm more like an older sister who gets into mischief with him. Raising Penny makes you an authority figure. I'm sorry I didn't see that before."

He nodded. "I guess you probably didn't." He pressed his hands on his neck. "I'm so lousy at relationships."

"Not with Penny though. You're stellar in that regard. Right?"

He finally released a small smile. "No. But I do try."

"Then keep trying with me and I'll keep trying with you, okay? That's the only way things like this can work. We're different people. I'm not used to being a caregiver for someone younger. I like being the fun aunt. I see now that's entirely different for you."

"Look, if it's okay to bring her here, then yeah, that might be way better."

"Plus, she can work with Grandma so you guys don't have to be here as late."

"Right. But shouldn't I clear that with someone? Your dad? Erin?"

She sighed and hunched her shoulders forward. "You really haven't fully grasped things yet, have you?" She held up a hand at her wording. "Sorry, that sounded shitty. What I meant was the power dynamic going on. You see, just before you came here, we had a big family meeting between all the ranch owners: Ian, Shane, Joey and Grandpa Jack, along with their wives and my parents. Several things were discussed. The older folks are fully ready to retire. They agreed to have one figurehead. One leader, instead of all of them. Whatever. And for some reason, they chose… me. I'm it. I'll be the future authority figure with the final say-so on all things Rydell."

"All things Rydell… You mean the ranch?"

"The ranch. The resort. The orchards. The mechanic shop. The golf course. The last two are owned and managed by Iris and her husband, but they're also under the big umbrella. I'm like the… umbrella holder. Or I will be soon. Until now, my grandfather, Jack Rydell, ran everything. They're kind of making me his replacement."

Cole didn't reply for a full thirty seconds. "Orchards? You guys own orchards?"

She almost laughed at his response. "Yes. All those trees across the river, near my Uncle Shane's house? They replanted them about seven years ago. Now they grow organic apples, along with pears and cherries. They added more varieties to prevent crop diseases and the like. You didn't realize that land was ours?"

"No."

He stared at her. "You're destined for great things. I'm not surprised they picked you. Your leadership? Yeah. Your decisiveness. Check. Knowing your mind and saying the hard things, no issues there."

She waved her hand around. "The point to my conversation is this: you can take an hour and pick up your sister and bring her here. She'll be closer to you, better supervised and able to get all the tutoring she needs."

"Because you say so."

She smiled. "Cole, I could have said so long before today. Last May was when they asked me." She shrugged. "Just for your information."

"I guess it makes sense for Penny to come here. Okay. And I appreciate it."

"And Cole?"

"What else do you have to say to fully blow my mind today?"

"The grill will provide dinners for both of you. Go with it. Do it for Penny. You take your food home to her anyway. Now you can both have dinner together."

His shoulders fell forward. "Thank you."

She smiled. "You look like I just told you I plan to strangle you during our next sexual encounter."

That made his face whip up, and his eyes blinked in astonishment. She grinned. "Have you forgotten about us? Or have you decided there is no more *us?*"

"I haven't decided anything. It's all on you."

She tilted her head. "I guess you don't see you have as much clout as I do. When we're talking about us being together, we're equals. We're partners. We're… friends. At least I am. Aren't we?"

He nodded. "Yes. We are. We're friends. You're the only real friend I've ever had."

He broke her heart when he said that. "Okay then, friend, bring your sister tomorrow and I'll introduce her to Benny after her tutoring session and we'll see how they hit it off."

He turned to leave, taking Penny's hand as they walked away. She could hear Penny blabbing a mile a minute, insisting that she get to see the horses. *Right? Right, Cole?* She begged and chatted until her little voice faded away.

Jade's heart ached.

Jade cared a lot about a guy who could not read. With an eighth grade education. Imagine that. Oh, and the little sister. She was his everything. His motivation for living. Why he always ran across the ranch and took home food for her. Sustaining himself on far less than his giant frame required for nourishment. He was complicated. Secretive. And most of all, private.

Now, he was also a parent.

For all intents and purposes, Cole was a father to Penny. Penny and Cole were a package, a two-fer, and inseparable.

Jade's heart felt fuller, heavier, and more tender. She found it easy to love Cole.

Love?

She stopped dead.

Did she love Cole?

Jade had never been in love before. Were these jumbled, squishy, confusing, joyful feelings part of being in love?

Fuck. She feared it were so. Disturbed by her revelation, she jogged back to her grandma's house.

"Did he actually sit down and do it?" Jade peeked in at her grandma who was just tidying up the desk where she worked.

"He did. Begrudgingly." Erin set down a white book she held. "He's pretty profoundly dyslexic. This was extremely hard for him. At some point, he knew I was doing repeats for him in ways that Penny didn't need any. Not that I'm comparing them. Not at all. It's strictly a determination of how people take in new information and then retain it. So, this is pretty tough for him to conceive, and he'll probably take three times longer than Penny before he can read."

"Do you think he'll stick to the program?"

Erin's hair swung on her forehead as she tossed it back with a nod. "No idea. Penny wants to come back… a lot. He agreed to come for her. So maybe he will. Because of her. But stay out of it, Jade. He doesn't like you seeing him like this. He's ashamed."

"So I gathered. We just had a whole discussion about it. He was angry that I waited and asked him about it."

Erin shook her head. "I was just as phobic as he's acting now. I didn't want anyone besides Allison to see me in that state. Magnify that a hundred fold when it came to your grandfather; and we were married at that point. I felt so stupid and no one could talk me out of it. Cole reminds me of me, to be honest. It was just as hard for me as it is for him. Mostly, because I refused to accept it could actually work. When so much doesn't work, when everyone claims it should it grill into you that nothing will ever. I was *that* disbelieving. I didn't want anyone seeing how hard it was for me. And more so, the ones who most wanted me to read."

"Wow. Okay. I promise to stay out of it. I just wanted him to know I care about him, and want the best results for him."

"Let him have this."

"Okay. I said he could take an hour to pick Penny up from school and bring her here every day. She can start tutoring with you at four o'clock. Would that work?"

"Yes. And then Cole can come by when he finishes up his work."

"I thought I could introduce her to Benny. And maybe show her the horses and see how she reacts to them. I have a feeling she'll be fearless."

Erin's mouth twitched. "Benny and Penny?"

Jade blinked and then started cracking up. "Shit. I didn't think of that."

"It's too funny. Benny keeps telling me to call him Ben. He seems to be swiftly outgrowing our nickname for him."

Jade flinched. "I hate to see him grow up. He's so special."

"So is Penny. She's a wonderful, little girl. Haven't met one like her before. She's so confident and opinionated, and she swears like a truck driver. She kept catching herself, and I have a feeling Cole probably warned her. But her curses kept slipping out. Half of them were so frequent, she didn't even notice."

Jade flopped into the chair Penny and Cole used. "They're both unusual. I literally had no idea Penny existed, much less, that Cole was practically her father. He's that private. And he always overreacts if you do or say anything nice for him. He'll kill himself working without asking for any help. Even gives up his lunch hour. He's like no one I ever met, Grandma."

Erin quit moving and replied, "Oh, Jade… You must be in love with him." She said it as a statement not a question.

"What? No." Jade protested, but even she could hear the waffle in her tone. "Shit. Grandma, I just might be. The things I feel with him... are pretty big stuff."

Erin moved to sit on the edge of her desk. "You're ready for big stuff. He's a good kid, Jade. I agree he's quiet, and confused when anything nice happens to him. Especially anything that helps Penny. I have to give him credit. I doubt most brothers would take care of their little sister as well as he does. My useless brother never would. I hate digging up my old ghosts, but I really admire him. He forfeits his meals and provides anything she needs. Anything in Penny's best interest. It's a fascinating dynamic to see. The way he cares about her means he's capable of very strong feelings and putting his loved one first. If you can work through his trust issues, and accept his devotion to Penny as a positive without thinking it interferes with the relationship between you two, I think he could be worth pursuing."

Surprised at her grandma's thoughtful evaluation, Jade replied, "Even though he's sleeping with me, Dad liked him right off, since the first day when he cleaned out all the arena stalls without any help or complaints."

Erin let out a snort. "True. Your dad never said a bad word about him."

"But Cole doesn't tell me much. He's almost secretive."

"Yes. Or maybe just private? I don't know which one. I was too. The reading thing could be the reason. It had a lot to do with why I always quiet."

"Life seems to move in circles."

"Honestly? I had the same thought. Here I am, tutoring students with dyslexia, which I resisted for so long, and so desperately needed. Now, I'm teaching someone who resists the program as much as I did. Interesting. Life is so crazy."

∽

Cole eventually learned how to sit on a horse and stay upright. When he finally managed to accomplish that, everyone who saw it applauded him. It was the first time he rode a horse all the way around the arena without falling off. Then came the jeers and whistles but Cole flipped them all off. Jade was overcome with joy. He looked awkward and uncomfortable on the horse's back. No rhythmic swinging of his body with the gait of the horse. Cole was stiff and tense, his mouth frowning and his knuckles turning white as he gripped the reins tightly.

"Look at you. You're finally a real cowboy." Jade smirked while staring up at Cole on the large mare when he accomplished his first solo ride. He gave her a dirty look and glanced around.

"When we're alone, *cowgirl,* I'm gonna spank that rude ass of yours."

She let out a happy, girlish laugh and blushed.

"You'll have to catch me first. All I gotta do is get on a horse and walk faster than my grandma and I'll beat you."

"Funny. You're such a jerk." But his eyes gleamed with emotion. "However, I like the idea of spanking your ass."

"New fetish developing?"

"One where I have the upper hand? How 'bout I use it to cover your sassy mouth?" He smiled, his eyebrows rising at the innuendo.

"You'll be galloping with the herd and corralling them in no time," she laughed.

He rolled his eyes. "If I could just stay on the back of the horse, I'll call it a win."

It was during one of his horse lessons that Penny came out to the stables. Scrambling up the rails, she liked watching Cole. Penny had endless questions and soon became well-acquainted with Jade, Erin, Ben, Melanie, Cole, Pedro and all the other workers. She had no issues about discussing any subjects and would ask whatever she wanted to know without any inhibition. It took days before she could convince Erin to put her on a horse. Unlike Cole, Penny learned with so much ease and grace that made it seem like she was born on the back of a steed.

Penny soon loved the horses, the Rydells and her tutoring sessions as much as Cole tolerated them without further distress.

When October arrived, Penny was thriving. She had an endless number of people for company, who happily gave her answers and explanations to satisfy her incessant curiosity and energy. She bounded around the ranch, springing and skipping with every step and it didn't take long before everyone knew who Penny Pearson was. She talked to everyone.

Penny was finally getting the chance to develop her own ideas, express herself and fully engage with others. It enriched her personality and gave her a sense of joy that was lacking before. Cole smiled to see Penny's destiny becoming much brighter with every day.

CHAPTER 23

*T*HE DUST WAS CHOKING, clouds of swirling, fine powder seemed to be everywhere. Stinging the eyes, as gritty and harsh as gravel, clinging to the sheen of sweat on everyone's skin. Through October, the whole valley was in the grips of a never ending, exasperating summer. It hadn't rained since mid-June. Several wildfires were burning and smoke kept drifting in and out of the valley basin. In some spots, the dust was six inches deep. The only hint of fall were the cool nights and mornings. That meager temperature drop in the air lowered the river temperature every week. To tolerate the hot afternoons, people dipped their toes in the river and waded. It was quite numbing to the skin and a sharp drop from the hot air.

The sun baked the people as much as the parched land.

Cole was unmindful of the heat and just grateful he could manage to stay on the back of his horse… Sometimes.

He was still a cowboy-in-training, not quite a useful cowhand yet. He had to pinch himself sometimes to make sure he wasn't dreaming.

Jade Rydell would soon take over as the King, Queen,

President, CEO and any other titles of leadership to this fantastic operation of theirs. Cole was glad she still seemed to like him.

His heart leapt with pride at the thought of her.

And his sister had moved to level three of Erin's reading system. She claimed Penny hadn't known several letter sounds accurately and consistently when isolated. Level two solidified all of them and taught all the short vowel sounds.

He had yet to move out of the first level where it was only sounds.

The tutoring sessions were working for Penny at least.

Penny loved her afternoons on the ranch. She and Benny got along well and never tired of finding things to do. She was allowed to feed the horses, talk to them, and go out into the barns to hang out with whomever she found there.

Outgoing, confident, bright, and happy, the exceptional Penny Poletti almost instantly carved out a place for herself at the Rydell River Ranch. The Rydells instantly accepted her, especially her own aunt.

Erin really liked Penny, and never tired of mentoring, guiding, and teaching the child with loving affection and patience. Cole didn't miss it every time he sat in on her tutoring sessions and when Erin so diligently engaged in Penny's chatter as she skipped and danced all around her aunt in the barns. Erin answered all of her incessant questions and never complained. There were no rude comments. No lame excuses to get away. No name calling. No neglect or abuse. Erin was the ideal mother-grandma role model of authority that Penny never had.

That was why Cole was so torn. How could he tell Erin the truth now? How could he shatter the illusion that he was a self-sacrificing, nice guy raising his little sister? Being down on his luck wasn't his only failure.

Penny was innocent though.

Cole's sins were unforgivable. And definitely illegal.

But he didn't know how to fix it now.

He never felt more nefarious, selfish, or lowly than he did now. He loved everything about his life on the ranch. He practically worshiped the Rydell operations, not only as a successful enterprise that he was proud to contribute to, but also for the people. The family provided him with such a wonderful place where he and Penny could come everyday. Cole worked seven days a week and Penny spent her weekends in this heaven on earth. She never tired of exploring the area, talking to the people, and learning about nature. But her favorite part was being with the horses. That was where she could usually be found.

Penny always sought out Erin first. Then she looked for Ben. Jade's sister lived nearby and Penny often joined her to hang out with Benny. Some days, she trailed the various ranch hands because she liked them and found them interesting. They were an endless source of information and answers to Penny's intelligent questions.

After years of living in a place where she had to entertain herself, Penny thrived. She blossomed like a beautiful flower. The Rydells embraced her with open arms.

Penny was still unaware of her blood relation to the Rydells, namely, Erin.

Cole needed to tell the truth and turn himself in. Penny was safe with Erin. Cole was convinced after spending so much time with her, that Erin would do the right thing by Penny.

But he always chickened out. He shied away from outing himself. He needed more time... (or so he convinced himself).

More time? To what?

More time to lie?

More time to deceive a woman he never should have

touched, befriended or spent so much of his time with? His biggest sin was making love to Jade. He couldn't stop now.

Time passed and Cole enjoyed the best life he'd ever experienced.

THE HORSES WERE skittish and danced around in the blowing dust, unsettling the fine powder. The vegetation was destroyed by the drought and nothing could anchor the dirt anymore.

"Cover your mouths and noses." Jade yelled to the crew who were working to corral a small herd of horses. They were retrieving them from one of the distant hillsides where they were allowed to graze. The blowing dust sped up their return to the main pastures and barns. Jade slid the bandanna she'd tied around her neck over her nose and mouth.

As a little girl, she used to giggle at her dad when he had to tackle the task during dust storms. "You look like the bad guys from an old western."

Now she was one of them. But it was necessary, especially during one of the worst dust storms she could ever remember. She tugged on the reins to bring her mount around and headed towards the opening in the fence where they wanted the herd to go. The land was directly above AJ and Kate Reed's original house.

"Bring them on." She called out to the ranch hands skirting the pocket of horses and forming a moving fence to funnel the agitated horses where they wanted them to go. Horse hooves bucking and dancing everywhere, they emitted distressed whinnies and moved with increasing energy. They didn't appreciate the sudden departure from a hilltop they'd been occupying so peacefully.

"Steady. Bring them closer together." Jade yelled loudly.

Slowly, the horses and ranch hands all began to cluster towards her, like a choreographed ballet or a living organism. She swung the lasso in her hand around without alarming the horse at the lead. As she idly twirled it in the direction she wanted the front horse to go, she clicked her tongue and calmed the front steed down. Below her, a small army of other mounted ranch hands were guiding the horses across the River Road, the only other barrier to grazing pastures on the land above the Reed home.

Her gaze kept scanning around. She was busily guiding the horses, counting them, and noticing the movements of all the other ranch hands. Naturally, Cole was trailing at the end of the herd. Still the novice, still awkward, but always learning.

Her amateur cowboy still made her heart beat faster and a stupid, sappy grin filled her face as she watched him use one hand to hold on while doing his best to flank the horses. But in the end, he clung to the saddle horn just to stay seated on his horse.

Turning his head, his hat fell back, and his bandanna was over his nose like everyone else. Jade's eyes drifted over him and his mount and she tilted her head. Something niggled at the back of her mind. *What was it?*

Cole looked different, but also familiar. Why? How could that be?

Slipping past her, he lifted his eyes to hers. Perhaps because he sensed her staring at him. What was so compelling? Even puzzling?

But when his eyes met hers, everything inside her completely froze.

She was instantly horrified. What the hell? He looked… so similar… to…

It was him.

Cole was one of the men who robbed and hurt her.

The one who held back. And didn't hit her. Or yell at her. But he was there all the same.

Fuck.

Jade's heart skipped a beat. The sense of betrayal she felt was so sharp and intensely penetrating, it was like an arrow piercing her heart.

Cole was right there working for her family every day. For months. How did she miss it?

Now that his face was covered like it was that night, she instantly knew who he was.

No doubt, her eyes were big as saucers as she stared at him incredulously. He suddenly jolted upright in the saddle and his gaze was riveted on hers.

Her thoughts raced. What should she do? She was temporarily prevented from doing anything since she had to finish the task at hand. Her dad was right there too, directly behind Cole. They had to get the horses securely relocated.

And then what? Would she tell Ben? He'd kill Cole. She was sure of it. She had to… what? Talk to him? Consider the best way to approach him?

First she had to finish the task.

Forcing herself back to the chore, she urged her mount to get beside her dad, and together they brought up the rear of the herd.

It took another good half hour before all the horses were safely corralled into the barns and stalls.

THE DARK, dusty barn was alive with horses' neighs and whinnies but it didn't muffle the sound of their collective boots clomping over the concrete floor as they stopped behind him. He didn't have to turn around to know exactly who it was.

Jade, Ben, and most likely, Jack. Cole was glad Jade was smart enough to ask for help and not confront him alone. As far as she knew, Cole could be violent and dangerous.

Because she finally knew exactly who he was.

Why did it take so long? After almost six full months of constant, daily contact, until today, she'd never hesitated or wondered about him. Cole fully expected that to happen when he first showed up on their ranch and got introduced to her. But Jade never so much as blinked. She never displayed any kind of recognition and assumed she'd never laid eyes on him before. The first time he spoke, Cole feared she'd recognize his voice. But not once did she demonstrate any realization of his true identity.

Not once.

Until today.

Today, with a bandanna over his mouth, covering the lower half of his face, exactly as he looked the night he robbed Jade. When he looked up at her in the dust storm, Jade's gaze was overbearing. She was evaluating him.

Her head tilted and her eyebrows furrowed. She'd been figuring it out. Trying to determine what was different about him. He just happened to look at her when her brain hit the jackpot and realized precisely who he was.

But the herd of horses were too dangerous and loose to act on her discovery. She couldn't stop to let her personal revelation fully germinate.

Jade had finally placed him from her memory of that awful night, and now she was ready to see him punished for his crime.

Cole expected Jade to get her dad, her grandfather, and the cops.

"You were part of the three men that attacked me." Icy tone.

He nodded as he fully swung around to face them. "Yes. I was always sorry for that. I didn't know it would go like that."

"So you don't deny it?"

He dropped his hands to his sides and let his shoulders slump in defeat. "No. I saw the moment you recognized me."

"We could just kill you and no one would know."

He nodded, lifting his gaze to the soft statement spoken by Jack Rydell. He didn't like his granddaughter being hurt. "You sure could. No one would ask about me either. There aren't many who'd miss me." His heart twisted. *Just Penny.* Damn. Poor Penny. She deserved so much better and always did. "But I'd prefer it if you'd just call the police. They'll arrest me."

"No one's going to harm you." Jade's voice interrupted the posturing being performed by the men in her family. She crossed her arms over her chest. "You won't try to stop us from turning you in? I thought you'd run."

He shook his head. "I can't stop you from doing what's right. There's nowhere left for me to run." And what about Penny? Always Penny. He had to do what was best for her. Someone had to.

"Why did you come here? What do you want from us? What kind of game is this?" Ben asked Cole. Behind the two men and Jade stood Jade's mom, Jocelyn, and her grandmother, Erin.

Erin. She was the only reason he came here. She was his last hope. Cole wished she'd take pity on him. Or would she side with her husband and urge him to do as he threatened? After all, that was fair punishment for what he'd done to Jade.

"It was no game. I needed a job. You guys paid the best in

town. I didn't know who Jade was, or that she'd be here until the moment I met her."

"Why'd you stay?"

"Because Jade didn't recognize me and I did need a job." But the real reason was Erin. He had to save Penny and he just couldn't figure out how to proceed.

"Fuck that. There must be more to this. No way did you end up here by accident." Ben snarled.

Cole sighed. "No, you're right. It was no accident."

"Jack. Ben. Call Roman before you two do something stupid." Jocelyn called out from behind them. Roman Barrett was a cop that the family adopted, or something. Cole didn't know the details about it. Jocelyn made a reasonable and correct suggestion. They should do that. Cole didn't blame any of them for doing the right thing.

Cole licked his lips and said, "Yes, you should call Roman. I'll confess to everything. I can tell you who I was with that night, and where to find them. I'll do all that. I have just one request."

"Oh, screw that. You don't get to ask for anything." Ben thundered.

"I know I don't deserve anything from you. But… could you please let me have a moment with Penny? She doesn't know about any of it."

"Not our problem, asshole. We'll call Child Protective Services because she's *their* problem now," Ben concluded as he stepped forward. "Go call them, Jade."

Jade hesitated before she started to move. Cole felt desperate. *Penny*. He had to save Penny from a horrible foster care situation. "Wait. Please. For Penny's sake, let me have a few moments of your time."

"It's not our fault her brother turned out to be a piece of shit. You're lucky if all we do is call Roman." Now Ben was getting closer to Cole.

Desperate for them to hear him, Cole finally had to use his last line of defense, and also his last chance. "Erin. Please, hear me out. About Penny. She's really Penny… *Poletti*… your niece." He stared at Erin as he said the words.

Erin stayed behind them all, quietly. So this entire debacle revolved around her? She was the real reason he came here? And the reason why he stayed?

Cole watched his words ripple through Erin. Her eyes grew brighter, her mouth dropped open and she jolted upright before she shot forward. Jack grabbed her when she moved right in front of him.

"Then who are you?" Erin snarled.

He regretted this so much, but there was no other choice. "Cole. My name is Cole… *Poletti*."

Erin's eyes shut and her face crumbled. "No. No. Don't say it. That name. That fucking cursed name."

"I'm sorry."

She shuddered. "You know Chance fucking Poletti?"

"Yes. He's our—" How do you admit your greatest embarrassment was being the offspring of a sperm donor? But it also explained everything there was to know about him. "He's our… father."

CHAPTER 24

*E*RIN'S BODY SEEMED TO crumple as if buckshot were hitting her.

Cole couldn't even look at Jade. *Jade.* He'd never had her. The time he shared with her was literally like touching the sun. What could he say? He deserved to lose her? He couldn't lose the greatest person he never deserved. But it felt just as devastating.

"Chance... has... kids?"

"Four of them, that I know of."

"Oh, fuck. Just call the police. No fucking Poletti is allowed on my land." Jack suddenly stepped forward in front of Erin. He was snarling like a rabid dog. Nearly screaming.

The old man was angry. Rage-filled. Cole flinched and waited for a fist in his guts or his face.

But he needed to stay coherent a little longer. He had to secure a stable home for Penny.

"Please just let me have five minutes to explain things."

"There's nothing coming from a Poletti mouth that I'll listen to," Jack hurled out. "You assholes assaulted my granddaughter. You'll *all* roast in hell for that."

"You're right, Mr. Rydell. You're right about all of us. Except for... *Penny*. You're not right about her." He looked over Jack's shoulder to Erin. "She's your niece, Mrs. Rydell. She's not like... us. Or me. Please, Mrs. Rydell. Please, I must make sure she's taken care of." He begged her. Pleaded with her. Nearly dropped to his knees and knelt in her presence. He had no pride, and nothing to live for or prove. He just had Penny.

"My niece?" Erin said in a quiet, dazed tone. She shut her eyes. Everyone fell silent after she spoke. Even Jack. Then she blinked and said, "That means... I'm also... your..."

"Aunt," Cole supplied, linking them, despite her dismay. They were connected by blood. That changed everything. "The only thing I care about is that you're Penny's aunt. She needs you. Please. I'm not defending myself for anything I did. I was there and that makes me a criminal. I'll testify to everything we did. I'll gladly go to jail. Arrest me. Do all of it. You have me now. But I beg you to let me just have a few hours to... to figure out what to do with Penny."

"Why? Why did you come here?"

"Because of *you*, Mrs. Rydell. I came here because of you. We have no one. Penny has no one but me. I didn't know about you until last spring. Chance never told us. I didn't know we had family, let alone, a woman. Penny needed someone. I knew at some point she would need much more than I could provide."

"Why not just ask me? And tell me who you were? Why all the lying, sneaking, and manipulation? Why the ridiculous theatrics? Why... *Jade*? How could you involve her in your scheme?"

His body rippled as her words registered. Jade stood off to the side of her grandparents, simply stunned. Her eyeballs darted back and forth from him to Erin.

"I didn't come here with an endgame or plan. We were in

trouble. We had no money. All that was real. But I didn't know you. I wondered if you were anything like Chance. I had to see for myself. That was my only intent behind all of this."

"Except you knew who Jade was."

He wilted. "I never knew her name. I didn't know anyone was in the arena that night until I first laid eyes on her. It's why I seemed so awkward around her for such a long time." He glanced Jade's way, imagining what she might think.

"What did you intend to do? When were you going to end the charade?" Erin's tone conveyed her complete bewilderment by his actions.

"I don't know. Penny—"

Almost as if he conjured her, Penny's head suddenly popped into view. She was behind the barn door. "What's going on? I saw a lot of grownups running into here."

Her tone was squeaky. Girlish. Innocent. And curious. Always curious and wanting to know everything that was going on around her. Shit. But she had to find out no matter what. Cole hoped to get an hour with her to explain it. The thought of disappointing Penny nearly cut him in half. Knowing that she'd compare him to their father left him feeling nauseous.

But here they were.

Penny walked in when all the heads swung to her but the barn remained ridiculously silent considering how many people were in it. The Rydells surrounded Cole in a half-moon arrangement.

"Cole?"

He glanced around but no one tried to restrain him. "Come here, Pen," he said softly as he dropped to one knee. Ignoring the harsh, judgmental looks around him, he decided to be strong. She'd remember this day, this shitty day when her entire world morphed, yet again, from decisions made by the shitty adults who fucked up her life so epically.

Uncharacteristically quiet and timid, she stepped into the collective gloom of the barn. She walked slowly towards Cole, her gaze shifting around to all the people who'd been so kind to her and shown her a way of living and being a family that she'd never enjoyed before. Her gaze skimmed over Jack to Erin and finally landed on Jade.

But most tragic of all were the doubts Cole saw in her green-tinted eyes as she stared up at him. The same cat-green eyes as his... and Erin's. He'd noticed Erin's eyes were just like Penny's.

"Why is everyone so serious?" Penny innocently inquired.

"They discovered some bad things today. I need to tell you about them, okay?" He took her shoulders in his hands and smiled with a sadness that didn't convince her everything was all right.

"They know?" she whispered. Her gaze was solemn and serious as she kept eye contact with Cole. "About us, I mean?"

He nodded. They exchanged a long, understanding sense of disappointment. "But there's a lot more. Some things you didn't know."

Her eyebrows scrunched together. "You kept secrets from *me*?" Her voice cracked at the thought of betrayal. He knew what it meant to her. More than anything. He was the one who shared everything with her. Even things no little girl should know or be exposed to. It was how they survived despite Chance and the rest of the world. Until recently.

"Yes, Pen. Very bad secrets. I'm sorry. I'm so sorry." His voice cracked again. Penny's lip trembled and she blinked several times to stop the tears from filling her eyes.

"What's going on?" She glanced around. "Why's everyone acting like this?"

He felt her anxiety. He decided to rip the Band-aid off. He

had to own it. Admit everything. No waffling or circumlocution.

"I did something bad when we were still living with Dad and Everett. I committed a crime, honey. Now I have to face the consequences. Like I should. Okay? I deserve them."

Her eyes wavered with weariness. "What'd you do?"

He sucked in a breath of air and held her gaze but kept his voice gentle. "I robbed this ranch. I was part of it. And... Jade got really hurt when we did it. They have to turn me in to the police now. And I want them to. It's the right thing to do, Penny."

Her eyes grew larger as he spoke. Her head swiveled towards Jade and then back to him when he said her name. Her mouth twisted up and then she started shaking her head. "What happened to Jade?"

Cole loved her kind, little heart for worrying most about Jade. "She was hit on the head and knocked out. She went to the hospital. What we did was very wrong. And we deserve to be punished for the crime."

Penny stared hard at him. Then she looked around, confusion in her gaze. All at once, she suddenly whipped around and hurled herself at Jade. Jade, of all people. Her little body trembled with sobs. "It wasn't Cole. He didn't hit you. It was Everett. Please. You can't let bad things happen to Cole."

His heart lifted before it broke at the dramatic reaction she had. "No one will let anything bad happen. It's the right thing to do, Penny," Cole assured her. But Penny was leaning against Jade, sobbing piteously.

Jade looked down, flabbergasted to find the little girl hugging her waist and burying her face into her stomach. Penny was relegated to her visceral self. It was a testament to how she felt about Jade and Cole.

"NO!" she screeched loudly. "I'm sorry, Jade, I really am,

that you were hurt, but it wasn't Cole. He'd never do anything if he thought you could get hurt. He didn't hurt you." She was so adamant, Cole's heart swelled with love for her undying faith in him. No one else on earth had that kind of allegiance toward him. "Please don't let them take him to jail."

So many details flooded Cole's brain. Chance would find out their location. He'd surely take custody of Penny again and this time, Cole couldn't do anything about it because he'd be in jail. There was no buffer to protect Penny from Zack, Everett, and Chance. Cole had a feeling they would all get away with it as long as Cole paid the price. They would band together against him. He knew that instantly.

Penny suddenly pushed Jade off her and ran towards Cole, hysterically flinging herself into his waiting arms. He braced himself, when he saw her launch herself at him. Sobbing. Incoherent. He knew the reason why. All Penny could see was her favorite way of life suddenly being ripped away from her. Foster care lay ahead, if she were lucky. Chance, if she weren't. Cole would be locked up with no power or ability to help her. The happy life they led for the past six months was so much better than any for years before.

Penny's sobs echoed through the barn and Cole simply held her and let her wring herself out. Her little torso was jerking with the violence of her shaking. She kept repeating, "Please don't take him from me" and "I know he didn't do it! I know he's good."

Finally, her outbursts trailed off. Kneeling at her level, Cole held her against his chest and kissed the top of her head. When she was too exhausted to protest, she started to quiet down. She kept clutching him tightly. The sudden silence of the barn was ominous. Cole didn't lift his head to observe their reactions.

Erin cleared her throat. "So I'm gathering Chance is still alive? He must be if he were the master mind of this robbery? This child is confident you didn't hurt anyone without having a clue it ever even happened."

He lifted his gaze to Jade. Regret shone in his eyes as he looked at Erin and answered her. "Yes. Chance is still alive. Unfortunately."

"Who knocked Jade out?"

"Everett did. Dad said so." Penny ripped herself away from Cole's chest. Her tears were drying but she had streaks down her face. She clutched her fists at her sides and faced all of them, standing in front of Cole like a shield. If the circumstances weren't so vile and threatening to Penny's safety, Cole might have grinned at seeing this tiny child defending him. How dead on serious she was.

"How do you know?" Erin challenged Penny.

"Because Everett is a weak son of a bitch who's never had an original thought in his life, and Dad is a mean son of a bitch who uses Everett as a weapon." Cole once said those exact words to her.

"Dad, being Chance Poletti?" Erin continued, her voice calm and cool.

"Yes. But that's not our fault." Penny screamed again.

"But what I did was our fault, Pen." Cole set a hand on her shoulder but she jerked free.

"NO." She seemed to zero in on Erin, not realizing the connection yet. "You can't let them take him. They'll... send me back to *him.* They'll put Cole in jail for the rest of his life for kidnapping me... but... but he had to do it. Don't you see? He *had to.* I don't know why he did something bad with the others, but if he did that, he had to. He *had to.* He always did everything for me. Everything."

He sighed. She spilled the beans. Cole couldn't expect her

to keep his secrets anymore. It was never fair to burden her with his crimes.

"Enough. I've heard enough." Erin suddenly yelled. "Cole, grab your sister and both of you come into my house. We'll sit down and figure this out now."

Penny started to argue, but Erin held her hand up. "No, young lady. Enough. Into my house. Everyone."

Cole grabbed Penny in his arms. It was more than decent of Erin to invite him to her house and let them have some time to explain. He needed to know what to do with his sister before he fully ruined her life.

JADE'S HEAD swiveled on her neck. How could this be happening? She recognized one of the men who attacked her. She was sleeping with him. And believed she was in love with him. She figured out the disgusting history between them but not until that crucial moment.

She panicked at first, expecting Cole to run away. That's why she galloped her horse towards her dad as soon as the herd was safely returned to the Rydell property. She didn't stick around to even see the last gate shut. Jade went full tilt after her dad, gasping out the story while still sliding off her mount. Ben held her in his arms as she spoke, and she trembled so hard while telling him, she was a mess. But Ben immediately grasped what she was saying. Cole was one of the perps.

Ben yelled at Pedro to take care of her horse. Then he got his phone out and texted a bunch of ranch people, or so it seemed.

Her grandparents and her mother were alerted and they hastened toward the barn where Cole had ridden into.

They found him quietly going about his task of unsaddling the horse and putting all the tack away. The horse was neatly tucked into the stall and fully brushed down.

He didn't try to defend himself. Jade's brain buzzed like a swarm of bees were inside it.

Cole was one of the perps. He admitted it. She'd prayed that her memory was wrong. She wanted Cole to snarl at her angrily and ask why she would say such lies? How could she think such terrible things about him? How dare she? But no. He was contrite, sorry, and almost destroyed, but he was honest.

She wanted him to demand that she trust him. She wanted to end up regretting and having to defend her actions. She wanted to be wrong.

But she wasn't.

Poletti. Aunt. Penny. Chance. Her brain spun until it hurt.

Until Penny entered the barn. Screeching, screaming, crying, sincere, and vulnerable Penny. She threw herself at Jade. She was so sure her brother couldn't hurt Jade. She wanted Jade to what? Defend Cole? Say what he did was okay? What was his end goal? Jade couldn't articulate it.

Then she remembered the last issue Cole mentioned.

Kidnapping.

Now the entire group were shuffling out of the barn, walking together, but also apart towards her grandparents' house. Cole carried his upset sister like a little child.

He was her parent. Her caregiver. Her hero. Her everything.

That was a role he played. He also played the role of a kidnapper and robber. The role of the caring brother clashed awkwardly with his other roles.

The unspoken solution was impossible. Cole couldn't just take Penny and disappear. Not now. He had no escape plan. No. Cole walked to her grandparents' house obediently. Jade walked behind them. Watching. Shaken. And unsure.

"Sit down," Erin ordered Cole. He sat down on a loveseat with Penny beside him.

The others entered the room and took seats like it was any other family get together. Her parents sat on the couch, and Jade sat on the chair opposite Cole and Penny. Her grandma sat in her recliner with her grandpa beside her. He was holding Erin's hand in support. Obviously, he knew this was hard on her.

"Where is he now?" Erin asked without preamble. "Where's my brother?"

"At this moment? I don't honestly know."

"Is he planning to show up here?"

"Not that I'm aware of. He doesn't know we're here."

She shuddered. "But your presence could bring him."

"I hope it won't." Cole was leaning forward and staring at his feet.

"Wait. Wait. Wait." Penny pressed her little hands on her temples. "How do you know our dad?" Penny asked Erin. Calmer now, her girlish voice contrasted with the serious conversation. It seemed incongruous.

"He's my brother," Erin said simply.

Penny jolted upright. "What?" she whipped her head around and stared at Cole but he kept his gaze downcast. "Then... does that mean we're related?"

"Yes. I'm your aunt."

She nudged Cole's arm. "Did you know that?"

Jade's heart hurt at the innocent inquiry. It was so honest and real. For as worldly as Penny was in situations that seemed far beyond her grasp, she still reminded them sometimes that she was only twelve years old.

Cole tilted his head and smiled at her. That small smile touched Jade and her weak heart swelled with emotion.

"Yes. I knew. That's why we came here."

Penny nodded. "Because you had to see if she was like

him." Her sneer when she said *him* indicated her true feelings for her dad.

Chance Poletti. Jade heard her grandma mention that name when she spoke infrequently about her past. Normally upbeat and in a good mood, Erin was fun and loving towards all of them. Occasionally, however, she got morose. From a few conversations, Jade pieced together the real history behind her grandma's mood swings. Her parents filled in some of the pertinent information.

Erin was twenty-six when she came to the ranch looking for her brother, Chance Poletti. He worked for the Rydells as a ranch hand. She was instantly distrusted by Jack, who had a long history of conflicts with her brother.

Erin remained an unwelcome visitor among the Rydell brothers, as well as her own. Much later, Jade's father, Ben revealed her secret: Erin was illiterate.

After her mom committed suicide—Erin believed her mom suffered from chronic, untreated mental illness—she left their small apartment after her mom's creepy boyfriend kicked her out. She'd only sought her brother, Chance, out of necessity.

Chance was mean to Erin all her life. Jade remembered her grandfather recalling the encounters he witnessed between Chance and Erin. "Sadistic bastard, who never spoke a kind word to her in my presence. She claimed he never physically hit her, but I saw him manhandle her enough and the vitriol was more pronounced than anything else."

Chance promptly robbed the ranch, taking Erin's car, her luggage and all the money she had left in the world. He stranded her on the Rydell River Ranch and left with the Rydell family, who unwillingly allowed her to stay.

Erin later fell in love with Jack, and she made her home there.

No one had never heard or seen Chance since then.

Erin hoped and believed he was dead.

Erin's presence was the only reason Cole came there for a job.

"Yes. I had to check Mrs. Rydell out before I could expose you to her."

"But you know she isn't like Dad. She helps me read. How come you didn't say so then?"

Yeah. Jade endorsed Penny's question.

"Because of what I'd done to Jade."

Penny literally rolled her eyes. "You didn't do anything to her. Everett did that. And Chance."

"I was there to rob her. I took the money, Penny."

Penny stared up at Cole and then gasped, slapping a hand over her mouth. "You did it… for these," she said, indicating the braces. Tears filled up her eyes once more.

"Yes. And to get the RV." Cole's gaze stayed on her. He took her hands away and held her face between his big hands. Jade's heart climbed into her throat. "But that isn't your fault. I still chose to do it."

Penny looked around. "He did it because I needed braces. I begged him for them. I cried and cried. People were always mean to me at school. Not only about reading but also for how I dressed. I used to ignore them, but my teeth got so awful, I couldn't take it anymore. I mean, just look at them." She turned around and made a giant grin, to fully show off her grid of hardware and her crooked, buck teeth.

"Look," she ordered everyone, pointing toward her mouth, and it was impossible not to look. Jade realized that her teeth, not her illiteracy, were the most devastating flaw she had. At least, they were to this little girl.

Cole knew that so he tried to fix it.

Erin sighed. "I appreciate how much he wanted you to not feel self-conscious about your teeth. But there's still right and wrong. He should have found a decent job and worked until he got the money."

"Where? With what? He's only a kid too." Penny hopped on her feet, getting argumentative now towards Erin.

A kid? Penny's wording puzzled Jade as well as the others in the room, judging by all the raised eyebrows that followed Penny's announcement.

"How old are you, Cole?" Jack finally asked.

Cole sighed heavier than before. "Twenty."

Jade's eyes almost popped from her head. Cole was just twenty? Not twenty-six like she believed?

He was barely out of high school.

Shit.

Cole sat upright. "I'm twenty years old. I quit school in eighth grade. I knew I couldn't do any of the work when I got to high school. I was flunking every single subject that year, except my cooking class. I was used to failure. And that was despite having the special classes, resource rooms, reading assistance, and all the fancy terms that go with it. None of it could help me but I did try. I knew how hopeless it was by the end of that year. I started doing all the odd jobs I could find. I knew money was more important for me than getting an education. Chance moved us around all the time and we never lived anywhere permanent. Chance didn't think it was his responsibility to feed or clothe us."

"Cole did that." Penny suddenly inserted in a passionate tone. "He did all those things for us."

Us, meaning the two of them, Jade suspected, not the whole family unit.

Eight years was all that separated Cole and Penny. When Cole was fourteen, he was doing that? Taking care of an eight-year-old? The unusual closeness and bond Jade witnessed between him and his sister wasn't her imagination. They'd been living like two kids against the world.

Kids.

Fuck.

Twenty years old.

Jade didn't know how to process all the new facts coming at her regarding this man… This boy? This guy? She wasn't sure what to call him.

"Fuck." Ben said with a long sigh, which encapsulated how Jade felt.

"It's why you did it, isn't it?" Penny asked him.

"To get the downpayment for the braces."

She knew that. "Wait. Are we still paying for them?"

"Making monthly installments."

He was making orthodontic payments for his little sister's teeth. That was also why he took food home to her and rarely seemed to buy his own.

Cole reached out and cracked his knuckles. "Penny, sit down and let me finish this." He glanced at her and then at Erin and Jade. "It wasn't noble. I had to start paying for her braces. I also used the money to buy the RV we now live in."

"Why did you go to all that trouble?"

"To escape. I had to get Penny away from Chance. I knew that."

Jade flinched. She so easily dismissed the ugly RV, being disdainful of the stripped flooring and stained countertops. He had such limited resources. That was their plan?

"Why? Why did you have to escape from Chance?" Jade asked.

Erin answered her question. "Because he's particularly mean to little girls."

Cole's gaze flipped up. He and Erin shared a long eye lock. Cole nodded. "Yes, that's why."

"Mean? Like how?" Ben asked.

"Name-calling. Terrifying her. Mocking anything that she might care about. Well, some of what he did to me isn't appropriate for young ears to hear. But he never actually hit me or did anything sexual in nature. He was just sadistic and so fucking mean. The meanest person I've ever known."

Cole nodded. "He still is."

"He's awful." Penny added, shuddering.

Fuck.

This was all too much.

"How did you escape?" Erin asked.

"One of my brothers was in jail and needed bail money. After they paid the bail bondsman, they skipped out because he was guilty and would have stayed in jail. It was my only shot. I convinced Chance to leave Penny in my care so everything appeared normal. He thought he'd come home and find us still there. Meanwhile, I jacked Penny from school by pretending to be Chance. I decided to come here to find out if you were decent, Mrs. Rydell. That was all."

"Where'd you come from?"

"Just about everywhere. The last address we lived at was in northeast Oregon."

"So you basically…"

"Kidnapped Penny," Cole filled in as he stared forward and his tone grew hollow. "If Chance finds us, he'll say I kidnapped Penny and he'd be right, too."

"Why now? Why'd you decide to do it now?"

Cole shrugged. "I'd tried to take her away before, when I was fifteen and seventeen, and both times he got physical with me. He threatened to have me arrested. He meant it. She's legally in his custody. But she had to get out."

"Describe your life with Chance." Erin instructed.

"Tiny rooms in trailers. Unfinished surfaces, infestations of rodents, no food or decent clothes. That was how we lived. Chance is constantly getting into scams and survives by doing petty crimes. He's good enough at it that he doesn't get caught."

"He was always like that. He must have considered what he ripped off from me and Jack a windfall when he left here. He was always a con artist, cunning, but lazy, uninspired and a complete chicken-shit."

"He still is. But Penny needed new clothes, healthy food and some privacy. She was regularly exposed to all the shit we did. She witnessed it. She would have been ruined if we stayed with him. I knew I had to change the course of her life by getting her away from him."

Erin nodded. "So you took her out."

"Yes." He whipped his head up. "I regret what happened to Jade. But none of the rest. I would do it all over again if I thought I could save her from becoming losers like the rest of us."

"And what did you foresee as my role in this scheme of yours?"

"Chance will find me eventually. I knew it would all come out at some point. I hoped… you were much better than Chance."

"And?"

"You definitely are."

Erin's head tilted. "Cole, what do you foresee happening now?"

He swallowed, glanced at Penny and then away. He seemed to brace himself. "When I go to jail, I hope you'll take custody of her."

The statement was so simple, soft… and explosive.

Penny jumped to her feet, screaming, "NO!"

Erin jerked back. Several family members gasped. Cole just shrugged; he looked right at Erin and said, "You know what her life will be with Chance. You understand more than all my words what her life has been like to this point. Even if he doesn't abuse Penny, he wouldn't care if someone else did. There's a reason I sleep on the floor beside her or right next to her, it's so no one else can get to her. Someone tried once, and Chance didn't care. She can't go back to him. There's no one else but you. Can't you forgive her for being related to me? And Chance? Can't you ignore her last name? She needs you. She needs someone good. Someone has to save her and I always knew it can't be me."

CHAPTER 25

COLE KNEW THE EXPLOSION his words would create, which mostly came from his pint-sized sister.

Penny was screaming and swearing at him with hysterical tears. The impact of seeing her so upset brought tears to his own eyes. But he stayed tough, clenching his jaw and not reacting to Penny while watching Erin.

Erin's mouth dropped open as did most of those around her.

Cole pressed the issue. "You know, Erin. You know exactly what it's like for Penny."

Erin's mouth compressed. One short nod let him know he had her sympathy. "Yes."

Jack stiffened. "Erin, we need to talk."

Jack would, no doubt, end this. Jack had no loyalty to a Poletti. Erin had barely a smidgeon. Almost in a panic, Cole added, "Arrest me. Now. Today. Just leave Penny out of it. Keep her here. Let her be young and innocent and… free. Free of all the shit she's had to endure so far."

Penny threw herself at him. Her little arms wrapped

around his neck and she began sobbing against his chest. He relented with a look of sadness as he put his arms around her, kissing the top of her head and pressing his cheek on it. "Shh. Penny. Shh. It's for the best. It'll be okay..." he muttered, doing his best to soothe her.

Penny merely cried harder. "Th-they can't take you, Cole. Please... just leave us alone and we'll go away. I'm sorry Jade got hurt and all that but... just leave us alone!" she screamed before burying her face in his chest again and muffling some of the shrillness.

He petted her smooth, black hair and kissed her head again. She was beside herself. Hiccupping, crying, and sniffling.

"Where do you live now?" Jack asked, straining to be heard over Penny's mournful cries.

"In an RV parked in the middle of nowhere. Off Sidling Road."

"All right. Let's bring it here. We're not doing anything important today. Quit crying, Penny, before you hyperventilate. We've got a lot to figure out and you might wanna save some tears for that." Jack's voice was clear and decisive, as if that were the end of it.

Cole's head jerked up at the unexpected interruption. Jack was already rising to his feet and Erin looked up at him with surprise in her gaze as well. Jack squeezed her hand and gave her a nod. Unspoken communication that they both understood.

Ben leapt to his feet. "Get up, Cole. Dad's right. We'll bring your stuff here. Penny can stay here too."

"No."

The word was singular, soft but firm. Turning, Cole found Jade sitting there. His stomach bottomed out. He was doing his best to ignore her, being unable to validate his own actions and wondering how she now felt about him for making her his victim.

But Jade must have decided enough was enough. The time had come to simply pull the plug on all the niceties they did for Cole and put him in jail. He deserved it.

No wonder she was chosen to succeed Jack Rydell. Jade took command of all of them without standing, looking up, or even explaining herself.

Jade finally lifted her eyes and stared hard at Cole. His nerves rippled through his spine. Then she addressed her dad. "I'll go with him. Penny can come too, if she likes."

Penny's arms tightened around his waist.

"Jade—" Ben started to speak while looking from Cole to her.

Jade rose and almost sounded tired when she replied, "I'm in no danger from Cole. He won't throw me out and hightail it outta here with his RV and kid sister. He won't become a felon on the run. I'll be fine."

Erin pressed her lips together but nodded slowly. "I believe Jade's correct. But Penny, why don't you stay here?" She raised a hand and added, "Not as a ransom to make sure Cole comes back but simply because I'd like to spend time alone with her and perhaps, Jade would like some time alone with Cole."

Cole agreed. Gently tugging Penny back, he said, "Erin's right. Stay here, Penny. Relax until we get back. Okay? Everything's okay."

Penny sniffled and rubbed her eyes with the backs of her hands. Then she rubbed her nose. Lifting a red, splotchy, defeated face, she nodded and turned to Jade. "You promise to bring him back here?"

"I promise," Jade solemnly replied.

Penny nodded and released him.

Everyone rose to their feet. Penny gave Cole a long, hard hug, and he patted her head. "I'll be back soon."

She looked up at him with a storm brewing in her eyes. "This time. You're trying not to."

"Not on purpose." He watched her as she went to Erin with a pronounced stomp of her feet and crossed her arms belligerently over her chest. No one could mistake how Penny felt. It was nice to know the world was not yet ending.

But that moment was coming soon. Cole knew he'd be losing Penny.

With that thought, he turned around, searching for Jade. Finding her, he nodded and she came forward to go with him out the front door.

In the moments before the door shut behind them, a silence descended between them. But Jade didn't stop. Stomping across the yard, she strode over to where her truck was parked. Cole followed behind her a few steps, clearly getting the message. Her anger-fueled walk said it all.

Flopping into the passenger seat, he waited until she pulled out onto the road. Her jaw tight and her fists clenched around the steering wheel, she finally said, "You're twenty years old?"

He turned towards her, blinking. She nearly floored him. After everything that just happened and was said, his age was the only issue that set her off?

"Uh, yeah."

"Two years outta high school?"

"Uh, no. I never went to high school. I dropped out seven years ago."

Her eyes shot up to him and she replied, "Oh. Yeah."

"I'm not like most twenty-year-olds. I never got to be a kid. Not really. I started taking care of Penny when I was thirteen. Totally taking care of her. Her mom died and the state found us. They just dropped her on us like it was a good choice. It wasn't. She'd have been better off anywhere else. But she was this talkative, smiling, sweet, clueless, little girl. A little, tiny lamb left in a pack of male wolves. That's what the court did for her."

Jade glanced his way. Her expression seemed less fierce. "We'll get to Penny later. You use her to deflect from discussing what you did. You lied to me. You were there when I got assaulted and you didn't tell me? You screwed me and decide it's—"

"No, I didn't."

She aimed an angry scowl his way. "How do you figure you didn't?"

"When I met you, I was shocked to learn who you were. But I never once thought I'd end up with you. No way. You were too untouchable. Like a queen to a peasant."

She snorted at his analogy.

He shifted his shoulders and looked at her. "Oh, you laugh. As if that's unbelievable. It's not. It really isn't. I'm not like you, Jade. I know that. It's not just because I come from poverty that makes me different. It's my whole history. I come from the working class, you come from the ruling class. I saw that in everyone I met here. So my intention in staying here was never to have sex with you. Truth be told, I was always too busy or unhappy or stressed to think about sex. Laugh and snort all you want, but believe me. Forget the stereotype, I'm a twenty-year-old guy who's not that into sex. I rarely find the time or the energy for it."

He blinked, watching her. Her shoulders deflated as he spoke.

"You paint a pretty pathetic, but honest picture."

He threw his hands up. "I'm not painting anything. That's how it was. You think I use Penny to deflect the conversation from me? Penny is all there is for me. My future will always be about Penny. She's my only priority. No matter what.

Doing right by Penny will be the only accomplishment in my life. That means, bringing her here. To the only family female who can help her. Show her all the wonderful things that I can't. Teach her, mentor her, just fucking help her in all the ways I failed even when I didn't know I failed."

There. He laid it out. The entire truth. Including his secrets and lies.

Jade drove for many miles without responding. The silence seemed to fester. When they eventually reached the RV, he sighed at the dusty location and the sorry state of the vehicle. Hopping out, Jade waited for him to open it with the key. Why he bothered to lock it, he didn't know. It was his only ticket to freedom. A mobile home that was far nicer than the place they left.

Jade entered first. She stomped towards the bedroom, opening the bathroom door and came back to where Cole stood.

"You give Penny the entire bedroom?"

"Why not? She deserves it. I usually sleep beside her. She's tough as nails in the daytime, but not at night."

"You fixed it up. For her." Jade stated the obvious.

Shrugging, he crossed arms over his chest. "She's never had her own space, let alone a bedroom. I did what little I could. It didn't cost much."

"But you gave her a new mattress and laid down all the rugs so she had decent flooring. Posters and toys too. You decorated it for a little girl."

He threw his hands up. "I don't understand why that matters."

She stared at him. "I don't know either. I'm overwhelmed. I don't know how to feel. I see you with Penny and the closeness you share. You're such a young guy to be putting his little sister at the top of the priority list, including your own care. Like my own parents do with me and my sister. Maybe Penny's even more of a priority, considering all the effort you put into her. I'm sorry to hear about what you two have done to survive. You have an unusual and noble relationship. But you were one of the guys who attacked me. Penny insists it wasn't you. You didn't touch me. You tried to stop them. You called the police to get me help." Her hands flew up in a gesture of helplessness. "But you were *there*."

"I was there. I'm one of them. I've committed other crimes, that wasn't the first. I came here to find Erin. I want my sister to have a better life. What I have to offer will end up putting her in jail or getting pregnant at age sixteen or any number of other miserable outcomes. I'd literally give my left arm not to have that happen. If she hadn't come to us, I'm sure I'd have turned out just as bad as my two older brothers. We had no role model but Chance."

"And at age thirteen, you decided to do the right thing for Penny?"

"No. I wasn't smart enough to think something out like that. I just knew she was... good. Different. Weak and small. Sweet and cute. She was a joy to be around. There was no other joy in my life. There still isn't. Just her. So I kept an eye on her. Pretty soon, we teamed up against all of them."

"Chance is that bad. I saw my grandma's face even after forty years since the last time she saw him. Forty. I can't even contemplate how long that is. And her biggest concern after finding all this out about you was that Chance Poletti is still alive."

"Yes. He's that bad. He's not a typical villain. He didn't beat us every night, but he burrows into your mind like a tick and finds your insecurities and weaknesses. Then he tortures you in ways your brain can't escape. I knew I was dumb and Chance knew it too. Not a day went by when he didn't mock, ridicule, or tease me about it."

"And Penny?" Jade's voice sounded a degree less angry. Softer.

"Her buck teeth. Tells her she's ugly." He shook his head. "She's not. She's got the biggest smile and an even bigger heart."

"Of course she's not ugly. She's adorable." Jade shuttered. "I can't imagine being a little girl that's made fun of. I'd be a wreck. Beauty is revered in this society and we're taught that it's the most important thing about us."

"Chance knew that too."

"And Penny needed braces not just physically but to disarm all the self-talk she must have received, courtesy of the man who delights in torturing you all."

"Yes." He shook his head. "It's not an excuse. That's the only reason I joined them that night. I needed money to get us out. At that point, I hadn't devised a plan yet."

"But you were set on getting her out."

"Yeah."

"And you couldn't just leave because he has custody of her."

"Yes. He still does. I kidnapped her, Jade. In the eyes of society and the law, which are no small things, it doesn't matter. I'm a kidnapper, a robber and a participant in an assault. There's no sugar coating it or my future. I always knew it would come out. I didn't know when."

"And what did you hope for?"

"I hoped Erin would be a decent person who could take my sister in and give her all the things in life that I can't. Not just material things, but good advice, care, guidance, and all the opportunities in life she needs. She must have everything. Including the ability to read. Braces were my first attempt to make her stop feeling ugly."

"You came here with the intention of losing her?"

"I came knowing that someday Chance could find us and

have me arrested for kidnapping. There's no doubt of that. He simply will. He'll have the law on his side for once. And I hoped by then Erin would fight him for Penny's custody, or Penny would be old enough to make her own choice. Once I met you, I fully expected to get caught for the robbery and assault and what I did with Penny."

"Yet you stayed."

He shrugged as he flopped down to sit on the sofa. Leaning forward, his elbows on his knees, he said, "Jade, there's no life for me. I don't know how else to explain it to you. I already committed the crimes. You think I'm so young? I'm not. In many ways I'm an old man, just waiting to die. I've lived a thousand years, it feels like. You wonder about my sex drive? I didn't have the energy to even try it. There was nothing left inside me for anything."

He rubbed his temples.

She stood there, silent again. Then she snorted and flopped down beside him. "You're incredibly bad at playing the villain."

He peeked to the side. "What?"

"You. You're terrible at being a criminal. Shit. Not even one day and I'm ready to comfort *you*."

"You aren't going to comfort me."

She sighed. "You aren't going to fucking tell me what I'm going to think, do or feel about you and Penny."

"It's a sad story. Penny's just the face of it. But I'm an adult who committed two crimes. Not so noble. Don't forget my part."

"So you want me to hate you so I can insist that you go to jail?"

He shrugged. "No. I don't want you to. I nearly piss my pants every time I try to picture it. But the guilt doesn't sit well with me. At least, it'd be over. Done. I could…"

"Feel better? In jail?" Her laugh was hollow. "Damn it, Cole. What am I supposed to say?"

Puzzled, he straightened up and faced her. "Say it. Please. Shit, you deserve to say whatever you want, more than anyone."

Her gaze studied him. "I don't like being five years older than you."

He snorted. "That's the only thing that bothers you?"

"I mean it. Twenty sounds really young now."

"I've never felt young."

She tilted her head. "Or immature?"

"I'm sure I am. How the fuck would I know? Immature in sex? And because I have no idea how to sit down at a fancy meal with polite manners? I don't fit in with the family you come from but I hope my sister can. I'm immature and ignorant, but I'm not young. It's a miracle that you spend any time around me, aside from sex."

"It's more than that."

"What is?"

"It's more than just sex. You've been my boyfriend. You seemed my age and I've talked about endless things with you. But I still can't get over how much it hurts my feelings that you simply knew so much about me and you hid it all."

The simple honesty of her statement hurt more than if she'd yelled, screamed or called him names. The guilt rippled through him. The hurt Cole saw in her eyes fully illustrated to him what his actions did to her. Valid or not, he'd hurt her deeply.

He put his hand out, wanting to touch her, but realizing it was too soon and too forward. "If it's worth anything at all, I'm sorry."

"I hate myself. I used to be tough."

"You? You're tough and strong and clever and—"

"And not anywhere near as wonderful as I truly think you believe I am."

"I know you are," he replied.

"I need some time with this. Let's get the RV back to the ranch. Are you sure it'll make it?"

Cole rose up, eager to have a task to do. "Positive." That was the only confidence he had. He could make anything run. "However, it'll be the biggest eyesore on your ranch."

"It's fine. I'm…" Her gaze darted off.

"What? Just say it. Anything. You can say anything to me."

"No, Cole. That's really not true. But when I first came here, I found it hard to even look at the RV. It felt so icky. But to realize what it represents to you makes me ashamed. I didn't know how much it meant. It's your home and freedom and privacy. I couldn't begin to comprehend that."

"Jade, it's a shit hole I stripped down and had no money to re-do. It's okay to disdain it."

"It's not okay," she suddenly insisted. "It's not. I come from a place of privilege and snobbery, and I failed to understand what I've never had to experience."

"You're just lucky. Don't regret it." He smiled gently when she fully lifted her gaze to him. "I'm the one who's ashamed. I committed crimes. I've lied to you all and not just once. I'm the culprit because I knew better and did it anyway."

"But we're the ones who don't understand how desperate people get when they don't have family to turn to, let alone, any money or choices. It changes everything."

"It might. Yes. I'll concede that. I still made choices though."

Jade rose to her feet and walked to the door. She paused and dramatically turned back, one eyebrow raised. "Did you? Did you have choices? Maybe if you'd been a single guy, you could have simply left, huh? Walked out on Chance and your brothers and gotten a job. But with Penny in Chance's custody. Did you have any real choices?" Her head shook, and her hair fell over her shoulders. "I honestly wonder. I'm struggling to make sense of it. But I see it, Cole. I see it pretty clearly for what it is."

Then she walked out.

He moved into the driver's seat, inserted the key and tried five times before it finally turned over. It roared to life with a horrible screech and the idle was set too high. It was a monstrosity. But Cole could drive it where it needed to go. Slowly but surely.

The old RV lumbered down the road and Jade followed behind. Cole let the traffic pass him on the main highway. Luckily, there were only a few cars on the road. The RV didn't like to exceed thirty-five miles per hour but the rickety old can made it all the way. Cole pulled over at the ranch gate and waved Jade forward so she could show him where to park the thing. She did and he followed her towards the barn where he first met Ben Rydell.

She walked forward. "Pull it right over there."

Cole finally turned off the old bucket of bolts. Home sweet home.

Then he came out to face whatever the Rydells decided to do with him. Walking towards Jade, he shrugged as he asked, "Now what should I do?"

CHAPTER 26

JADE STARED AT THE RV. Sometimes, one of the hires came with their own trailer or motorhome and parked it on the Rydell land. So Cole was wrong saying they didn't have something like that on the ranch before.

The revelations of the last few hours were so confusing. Jade wasn't sure how to react or feel.

At first, she all but panicked when she realized who Cole was. But he was still Cole. When he hung his head in shame, she could have predicted how he'd tilt his chin and slouch his body. She knew how contrite he felt. The Cole she'd come to know was still there.

He wasn't very good at being bad. That part was true. The size of his body and brawniness of his muscles suggested to anyone seeing him that he was tough and cocky. But Cole wasn't. Not for a single moment since Jade met him.

Confused. Contrite. Caring. Hard working. An incredible listener. *A good person.* To be honest, that's what stuck with Jade. Cole was a guy who'd survived hard times without anyone to cut him a break. He wasn't really a criminal.

Now, Jade had no idea what they should do.

"Can I talk to Penny?"

"Of course you can. You're not under arrest." She added, "I doubt anything else is happening today."

"*Yet.* I'm not under arrest *yet.* But you have to consider it."

"What?" She shook her head. "Why would you want that?"

"The guilt is wearing me down. The endless waiting for the other shoe to drop. It might be nice to end the waiting. Just get on with it."

She waved her hand and replied, "Just go see your sister."

He nodded while pocketing his keys and started walking towards Erin's house. Jade followed eventually, but was unsure what to do next. She saw Cole and Penny walking together towards the beach. She jogged up the front stairs and went inside.

Her grandparents and parents, along with Aunt Melanie were already there.

"He's my cousin?" Those were the words Jade walked in on. Melanie was just finding out.

"Yeah. You're a blood cousin," Erin replied. "Last name of Poletti."

Melanie snapped her fingers. "Yeah. He looks like us. So does Penny. I'd eventually thought of that, but I didn't connect it to us. Penny resembles you more than I do."

"Penny does."

"The RV's here," Jade announced as she walked in and made her presence known. She flopped onto a couch.

"How'd it go?"

"You can't miss the monstrosity, but it's all those two have in the world. It's a palace to them. I wrinkled my nose when I entered it the first time. I wouldn't even sit on the couch without putting a clean blanket over it first. That's how shitty I am."

"Well, Cole's actions weren't exactly stellar," Ben said.

"But how much was his fault? I can't decide."

"Yeah. Me neither," Erin said, sounding glum.

"What did he say? That is, if you want to share?" Ben inquired.

"He said he was sorry. He didn't know who I was when he came here. He never considered we'd be dating. Whatever. It was mostly about Penny. The pisser of the whole thing? I believe him. He's lousy at being sneaky or cocky. We also know from Grandma that he and Penny aren't lying about Chance. But I can't stop thinking he was there that night. It's all so confusing."

"It is," Jack agreed. "And Chance is one of the most loathsome people I've ever met in all my life."

"But Cole isn't," Jade said simply.

"Neither is Penny," Erin added.

"What do we do?" Jade inquired, looking around.

Ben replied, "How about this? You're the victim. What do *you* want to do?"

Surprised by his answer, Jade stared at her dad. "I thought it would be cut and dried with you."

"It should be. But I got to know him pretty well and I don't think I was wrong. That episode went down the way he said it did, I really believe that."

She let out a long breath. "Yeah. I believe that too. And he's fully prepared to go to jail if we take Penny."

"He intended to do that… why?"

"He believes he can't give her the good things in life like opportunity, advice, and the guidance she needs. He doesn't want her to grow up and be like him."

Ben shook his head. "What? Hard working? One of the most trustworthy workers we've had since AJ? I hate to say this, but that remains my opinion. Even listening to him explain, I saw the person I've come to know and trust."

There were heads shaking all around. Jade sighed. "I don't know what to feel."

Erin spoke softly, "What they described? Well, Chance was exactly that way. It took me years to overcome all the shit he put me through. He tortured me regularly when I was younger. I see that in both of them. And it's ironic to realize that we share the same blood. It shouldn't matter. It never has before. But suddenly they're here... with my maiden name and..."

"And we do nothing. We figure out where Chance is and find out about his custody. Cole claims he's a kidnapper and he's technically right. But I have to think some more about this," Jack said.

"I cringe; what if this brings him back here?"

"Chance?"

"Yes. Forty years have passed and the idea of seeing him still turns my stomach. Makes me feel instantly helpless even though I've gotten over what he did to me. After seeing what he did to the little girl in his custody, I, probably more than anyone, know why Cole did the things he did. It shows me more about him than what he did to get the money. I think he had to resort to drastic measures at the time."

"He didn't attack me. He was the one who tried to calm everyone else down. And he didn't know. Even that night, he argued about how they were treating me. I told you that back then when it happened."

"So no calls to Roman yet?" Ben clarified. His gaze scanned the group.

Jade nodded. "No. No one else has to know yet. This stays between all of us for now."

WHEN THEY SHUT the door on the Rydell family, Penny suddenly launched herself at Cole and started to cry. Hard. He soothed her but finally gave up and just patted her shoulder. "I thought you might not come back for me," Penny gasped between sobs.

He would always come back for Penny. He wanted to say so. But, for so many reasons, he could not make that promise. Instead he settled for, "When I go to jail, that's the only time I won't be able to see you. Come on, let's go the beach."

She took his hand and fell in step with him, getting quieter now. They sat down on a log, staring at the pretty view of the river before them. They sat there for a long time. "I like it here."

Cole sighed heavily. "I do too. It's a good place. Good people."

"We haven't had too much of either 'til we came here."

He hated that she sounded like such an old lady. She was too wise for her twelve years on earth. Like she'd seen and experienced too much, too soon. Because she had.

"No. But maybe we can now, Pen."

"You mean, *I* can. Because you planned to leave me here with strangers. You might like them, but I don't know them. I don't trust them or love them or need them. Only you."

He knew that. The pressure of so many failures. He wanted so much for Penny, this little person beside him, and she suffered for all the things he didn't do right.

Still, she trusted him.

"Erin is our aunt."

"She's old. Like a grandma."

"She's great and you know it."

She nodded. "But she's still not *my* family. You are. Why are you trying to leave me?"

"He'll find us. One day, Chance will find us and you know

what he'll do. I came here because I think, with their help, when that happens, you'll still have a good place to live."

"We could run again. If Chance shows up, we could get away."

He shook his head only once. Sharply. "No more. No more running. No more crimes. No more days of us against everyone else. Something changed. And that's these people and this place. We have to make it work, Pen. If I do go to jail, it won't be forever. When I get out, we'll build a real life together. But in the meantime, when it happens, you'll have a safe place to live. Here."

"There are so many ifs, Cole. What if they don't call the police? I was there while you went with Jade. They're sad for us. Erin hates Chance. And Chance might not find us. And what if they don't want me?"

"I think they will. If no one else does, Jade would." For some reason, Cole believed that and felt sure enough to call it the truth. Their new truth. Jade cared about him as a boyfriend and she liked Penny. Cole knew Jade wouldn't let Penny suffer.

"Well, if Chance finds us, what does it matter? He'll take me back anyway."

"Maybe they can fight him in court. Prove that he's an unfit parent. I don't know how. Maybe someone here does."

"This is all so stupid," Penny finally huffed.

He wrapped an arm around her. "I know. It always has been."

She leaned her head against his arm. "I'm glad our RV is here."

He snorted. "That shitty piece of crap?"

"At least, it's ours."

Sighing, he simply let her lean on him.

"So you're my nephew?"

Cole nodded, his guilt returning with Erin's words. "Yes. I'm sorry I didn't just say it. I'm sorry I came here the way I did. I'm mostly sorry for my part in what happened to Jade."

"Your reasons make sense to me. You did it because of Chance. I hoped all these years that fucker was dead. He always told me I was dumb. He tormented me for not being able to read."

Cole snorted. "The mother fucker. He knew why too, huh? That it ran in the family? Yeah, every day he reminded me of how inadequate I was. Big and dumb. How could I argue?"

"Right. Even five-year-olds can read sight words, huh?"

Cole nodded his head. "Yeah. Been told that at least a hundred times."

"He's too stupid to come up with any new shit."

"He *is* shit."

"He is, Cole. He truly is. I used to believe I was too. But trust me when I say, we don't think you and Penny are like him. I mean, I'm not like him, so you two don't have to be either."

"Penny isn't. Please believe me, Mrs. Rydell."

"Let's just go with Erin, huh? See where this goes?"

"This?"

"We're related, right?"

"How can you even think I'm not like him? After the way I came here? And what I did to Jade?"

"I'll tell you why. From the time I spent with you, one on one. Remember when I taught you to ride a horse? We spent a lot of time together. You're nothing like Chance. Even if we hadn't known each other well, your relationship with Penny showed me your true colors. You're simply not the villain of Jade's story. The villain was Chance and you aren't him."

"I still think you can't count on that."

She snorted. "I know my brother, Cole. Do you know your two brothers? What they're capable of?"

He nodded. "Like the back of my own hand, unfortunately."

"It doesn't change. How long did it take before you knew about me?"

"Chance never once told me anything about you until last year. He drove me to River Road and showed me the view of the ranch and resort from the road. That was the first time he told me about you. Suddenly, I had a family member. We never had one before. I knew he lied about how he left here. Obviously, he was kicked off the property. I had no idea what you were like though and I couldn't risk another bad home for Penny. I had to see for myself. And I needed to make money. That's why I showed up here."

"I believe it. You must know that."

He gave her a side glance and a grin. "Although many believe Jack Rydell runs this place, I beg to differ. Jade won't be the first female leader of this place."

Erin waved a hand around. "Nah. I just voice my opinions. Sometimes, they're taken seriously."

"No. You're *always* taken seriously. And never once do you even raise your voice."

"Jade will be far louder than I was. I assume you already know that though." She grinned at her own words.

"I do."

"And you don't raise your voice, huh?"

"Penny's high-strung, and her life is so chaotic, I tried to sound calm around her."

"So... we aren't going to prosecute you. No cops. But we have some stipulations."

He turned fully towards his aunt and replied, "Are you sure?"

She smiled. "Yes, I'm sure. We even voted. It was unanimous. You'll stay here and live in your RV here with Penny. She needs to finish her tutoring…. And so do you. It's part of the stipulations. You'll learn to read while you continue to work here. Penny will stay in school and you'll let us help you both. In exchange for that? We'll give you another chance. No cops. No jail time."

"Really? So we just continue on as we are, without the long commute at night?"

Her head nodded.

"That's too good to be true. I can't just… live here."

"Maybe you think that, but Penny needs stability right now. She needs you. Here. Right here. So Cole, you'll have to make your private peace with what happened. And Jade will have to work out what she thinks about your future with her. But as for living here? Yes, you can. And I want more time to get to know Penny and you. I really don't have any family from my side."

"And what about Chance? What if he finds us?"

"He won't give up. I expect we'll run into him at some point."

"You don't want that."

"No. But I want you two to feel safe. Especially Penny. So much goes back to her."

He snorted. "Now you know my real motivation in life."

His kind, decent, warm, caring aunt set her hand on his forearm. "That makes you someone I want to know."

His heart lifted. No one ever noticed that about him before. Not until the Rydell family. Being here was humbling and wonderful.

"Are you sure?"

"We're all sure."

"What do I do then? Just live there?" He pointed towards the RV.

"Yes. For now."

"I—I'm speechless."

"And come back tonight for your tutoring class. Right?" She put her hand out.

He shook it and nodded. "Okay. We'll be here... Erin."

She grinned. "Can't wait, nephew." Then she walked away and Cole wondered how he'd managed to be so lucky. He had more opportunities now than he'd ever had before.

Despite the personal drama swirling around Jade, life went on. She had to get up each day and do the chores and make sure all the horses were tended to. She had a mini-empire she was still learning how to manage. Meanwhile, Ben finished the replica house.

The entire family decided to celebrate before the final inspection was passed. It was a big group now staring up at the new house from the front yard.

"What do you think?" Ben asked as the Rydell clan stood before the house that Ben and his sister rebuilt. The footprint of the original homestead was back. They'd all watched it being built, from the summer months and fall to its completion. Everyone had been inside and toured it multiple times during all stages of construction.

Jade gazed at the small crowd surrounding her dad, who was staring at *his* dad. Jack Rydell looked at the house as if he'd never seen it before. The elegant, lovely exterior that was two stories high, with a central double door entry and windows all over the front. The gables over the second story provided a grand flourish to the design. The green roof matched all the other roofs on the ranch. The board on batten siding was stained a natural cedar color and river rock went halfway up the walls. That was the theme of the entire ranch. A long, covered porch ran the length of it.

The river-rock chimney ventilated the interior wood burning stove. All the rock came from the Rydell River. That represented a tedious labor of love when Ben personally hauled up the rocks he selected using the bucket of one of the tractors.

The front had a small green lawn, with a cement walkway that led to the front porch steps. It was large but not unreasonable. It couldn't be called a mansion but it was larger than most of the private homes at the south end of the ranch, including Jack and Erin's home.

"It's a dead ringer for the old homestead." Jack finally remarked, and his voice sounded emotional. Jade smiled at the tender expression on her grandfather's weathered face. Grandma squeezed his hand.

"It looks so much like the old pictures." Jade commented as everyone gazed with reverence at the new house. What memories did they recall? She knew some of them through the stories frequently told to her.

When the fire that swept through the valley burnt up the first homestead, it only took fifteen minutes. Most of the original Rydell River Ranch was also lost.

Her uncle Charlie, Ben's younger brother, looked up at it and told Ben, "I thought you'd lost your damn mind last year. But it looks so right. Really, it was a damn good idea to put it back here."

"Explain it, Mom. Say what you told me." Jade nudged her mother.

Jocelyn grinned at Charlie. Her dad gave both of them a look. "How did my wife describe it?" Ben asked in a playfully offended tone.

"When your dad got sick, you had to bring it full circle. That was pretty much the gist of it. This rebuilding of the original house is a love letter to your parents and childhood."

Jack turned his gaze to Ben and said, "That true?"

Ben shrugged, turning away. All kidding aside, Ben looked truly embarrassed. "Yeah. The cancer really scared all of us…"

Erin turned then and nodded. "It *did*. But not anymore."

Jack laughed. "Well, it hasn't got me yet. And I don't intend it to anytime soon."

"I have to agree with Ben; it traumatized me too," Joey added as he held Hailey's hand.

Shane was grinning and gave a shoulder shove to Jack. "Not me. I never worried about Jack for a moment."

"Bullshit." Ian said from his side with a snort. "One day I found you so drunk, we had to carry you home. If I recall, you cried while remembering all the times you were such a shit to Jack… and to me."

Shane let out a deep sigh. "Ahh, yes… the good old days. Damn. I was kind of epic. Remember the time I set the firework off in the pool in old Brewster?"

"I remember a few times when you weren't so epic," Allison replied with an eye roll and a gentle elbow jab in his chest.

Grinning, Shane took Allison's hand in his. "True. But if I hadn't been not so epic, we'd never have started talking about this and all this greatness wouldn't be yours today." He gave her a flirty wink that made Jade laugh out loud. Shane had long hair and was all tatted up, the only brother who never fit the mold of the traditional western family. Older now, they still interacted in fun and youthful ways.

"So you're really retiring to live here?" Hunter asked.

"Really. Can't wait. I'll sit right there with my feet on that railing, a cold beer in hand, letting Jade stress about the schedules, the feeding, the price of hay or grain or the vet care. Let Lillian handle the logistics of vaccinating all the farm animals in one day. Let my daughters be the new Rydells of the Rydell River Ranch."

"Yeah. And maybe a few others could help us too," Jade said with an eye roll. Lillian let out a laugh.

Ian and Kailynn were the operations managers for decades. But after enduring the trauma of having their grandson, Russell kidnapped by Hunter's ex-wife's stalker, they decided they were ready to step back.

Joey and Hailey slowly whittled down their management duties for the Rydell River Resort long ago. Now Silas helped them as much as Jade took care of the ranch. Or he was about to. Jade's stomach pitched as she glanced around.

It didn't take long before the conversation turned into a volley back and forth of fond memories. Jack, Ian, Shane and Joey stood in a line, all staring at the latest version of the original house. Reminiscing together. The brothers acted as though they were young again. Jack spoke animatedly and flung his hands all around. Gray haired now with sloping shoulders and deep wrinkles, yet the four brothers still stood tall together.

Jade tried to imagine the scene forty years ago when her grandma first arrived here. Young and beautiful. Lost and broken. And illiterate.

Startled, she felt a hand on her arm and turned to see her grandma, as if she read her mind. "Grandma, I was just thinking what it was like the first time you pulled in here."

"It all started right there. Right at that spot. Seeing the house all finished and standing here is like blinking and being young again. I was your age, actually. They were so intimidating and handsome. Jack distrusted me. The others were just indifferent." Jade smiled and Erin smiled back.

She didn't need to hear the full details of the story.

She smiled and realized how things had changed. Everyone aged, grew, and matured. Now, the next generation was here and everything started all over again.

Nothing was original or new. The cycle of humanity and tradition lived on.

"Jade?"

"Yeah, Grandma?"

"It's okay to love him, you know. To accept his mistakes and forgive him."

Jade glanced down, towering over her petite grandma.

"You know, I'm replacing Jack in the next phase of the ranch."

"Of course I know. It was my idea."

Jade grinned. Sure it was. That's why they all agreed on it. Jade sometimes wondered if Erin weren't the *real* figurehead of the operations.

"So?"

"So… Cole Poletti. If I stay with him, someday, I could be Jade Poletti."

Erin nodded. "I thought of that. How strange life is. For four decades that name was never spoken here and I was glad of it. But now? I hear it daily. Life *is* a circle."

Jade waved at the house. "I was just thinking that too. The full circle thing."

Erin shook her head. "I was resentful when your dad first told me he wanted to rebuild it. Now? I see it had to be done. So many beautiful memories, a whole lifetime of them, returned to us. From the day I arrived here, until this day. I had no friends and then I met Allison and Kailynn and Hailey. The love I found here is on so many levels and I feel it in so many different ways. From Ben, to Charlie to Melanie. The horses and the land are so sacred to me. The legacy belongs to you now. You grandkids will become what we once were. Adults finding our own ways. And now we're right back where it began, and it feels so right. I'm so happy to see the new house there. Slightly different but virtually the same. And having a Poletti at the helm of the Rydell

River Ranch? That's the oddest, but most interesting thing I could have ever imagined coming from my side of the family."

"I do love Cole. Still. Even now. After all he did."

"Then tell him that. Forgive him. Don't make him suffer, put him out of his misery." Erin waved towards the barns and Cole looked their way. He was always on the outskirts, watching the family, but never belonging to it.

"You think I should?"

"I think he committed crimes just to survive and never meant to hurt anyone. He did it for Penny. And I think he's already punished himself more than enough. The boy isn't tough inside. Outside? Hell yes. But inside? No. He's kind, sensitive, insecure and hardworking. He's funny and shy and polite. He's humble but knows how to be cocky. And he loves Penny. His devotion, care, commitment and loyalty tell me everything. I couldn't have dreamt up a better catch for anyone I love. And I love you very much. So yes, I think you should tell him."

"He's your nephew too."

"Yeah. Never thought I'd have one from my side."

"It's kind of odd. I'm your granddaughter."

Erin shrugged. "Life has all kinds of surprises. So what? If that's on the list of things that bother you, you might want to rethink it."

"What if Chance shows up?"

"It's not *what if*, but *when*. I know him. Chance will find them and do his best to torture Cole and destroy him."

"What do we do?"

"I don't know yet. But we'll figure something out. We have to for Penny."

"Yeah. She can't be separated from Cole. She's everything in his eyes."

"Can you accept that? A little girl being included in the

package? She'll always be part of your relationship, no matter what."

"If it's Penny? Yeah. I can handle her."

"Then tell him that."

She nodded. "I just might." She squeezed her grandma and said, "Thank you. I needed… I don't know, permission somehow. A year ago, I'd laugh at anyone who said I'd be in love with the guy who robbed me at gunpoint… and yet, all I can think about is that."

"Well, when you put it that way, it does sound somewhat deranged."

"I know. But it's not."

"No, it's not."

CHAPTER 27

JADE GLANCED AROUND THE room at all the people she invited to join her.

Andi Sullivan, now twenty, came with her stepmom, Violet who was only thirty-one and they sat on the sofa together. Eliana Hayes, her closest friend, age twenty-three, the niece of Kailynn and Ian, came with her twenty-five-year-old brother, Dominic. Silas sat on a stool. And Emory Alexander, Finn and Brianna's daughter sat on the stool beside him.

Meanwhile, Kyomi Rydell was standing near Jade while drinking a glass of water.

Big eyes and astonishment seemed to be the collective reaction after Jade just finished outlining her future with the ranch.

"Are they like designating you as the next in line for the royal Rydell throne?" Andi asked.

Jade nodded, cringing. "That cringy?"

"It is." Eliana snorted.

"Why bring us here?" Daisy asked.

"I want to know if anyone else is willing to help me

undertake this; I need to know who's on board now before the transition starts."

"Like underlings? Are you saying we'd work for you?" Silas asked.

"No. You'd be working *with* me. But... fuck, I don't know. I've never been a boss. Dad's retiring, along with a whole bunch of them. Grandpa Jack's bout with cancer really put the whole generational thing under the microscope."

"Boss? You need to own it, girl. Pretty damn impressive," Kyomi said, with a bright expression and a wink.

Jade turned to her and said, "Funny you should say that, Kyomi, the woman who ran her own ranch. Now that you're back in the Rydell River Valley, I want you to be my foreman."

Kyomi had just gulped some more water and she started choking. "What?"

"Pedro's ready to retire. You know, all the stuff he does here. I want you to be my new Pedro."

"Oh, fuck. She's right. You'd be perfect." Violet exclaimed as she nodded vigorously.

"See? That's why they chose you as the next leader," Andi added.

"Is it fair?" Jade asked, "Why should they decide who succeeds them when they're all retiring anyway? We're the future, our generation is. Shouldn't we be the ones to choose?" Jade still felt like an impostor.

"It's a shitty presumption, I agree, but I have to say, they were right," Iris interjected.

Jade glanced around at the mostly female faces. All were nodding their heads.

Iris, Daisy and Violet, the three sisters, Shane's daughters. Now they were all in their thirties. The only one missing was the eldest sister, Rose, who lived on the East Coast. Landon was currently living in LA and he had no interest either.

Charlie's boys could have been in contention, but one already worked for AJ and Asher, and the other one didn't want anything to do with ranches... Period.

Lillian sat on a couch, her eyes bright and fastened on her little sister. "Jade, quit doubting this. There's no one else but you. You were born for this."

Eliana snorted. "Fuck, yeah. We'd tell you if we objected to it. There're no shrinking violets here, are there?"

Eliana was Landon and Hunter's cousin. The daughter of Caleb and Josephine. Caleb was Kailynn's older brother.

"So what of it, Kyomi? You gonna work here as the next forewoman?"

Kyomi's gaze scanned the crowd, landing on Jade. "You sure you want me?"

Jade's grin split her face. "More than anyone. You're at the top of the list. I mean... yeah, I'm sure. We're *all* sure."

Kyomi let out a long breath. "It had occurred to me before that I'd like to work here. I was deciding if it were appropriate. I'm a Rydell now, sure, but I had to go through a lot of shit to get here."

Melanie snorted. She was Jack and Erin's daughter. "You're a Rydell, Kyomi. And now, you're the new foreman, er, the *forewoman* of Rydell River Ranch." Melanie was living with Kyomi's brother, Kyle. They shared a deep, long look before Kyomi blinked and looked back at Jade.

"I'd be thrilled to work for you. I have some great ideas. I've missed ranch work. And I've never had so many great resources to work with as you have here."

"You do now. I can't wait to hear your ideas." Jade glanced around at the others. "That's the thing. I want to hear everyone's ideas regarding any facet of our business. I'm just gonna be a suggestion box. Not the dictator. You know? You bring me your advice and suggestions, as well as your wish lists and needs and we'll decide together what we need and don't need. No one is an underling, it's a group effort."

"But when a decision has to be made, you'll be the one to do it." Lillian said with a warm grin at Jade. "You're the authority for things like that."

Jade bit her lip. It felt like such a heavy burden. "When AJ started Reed Ranches, he hired the most experienced guys: Mack Baker, Justin Krantz and Tyrone Nystrome. Our new forewoman is Kyomi, who's easily another Mack, but we need more. The Rydell oldies will soon be gone. Even my dad. Which leaves some gaping holes in the management. There are plenty of jobs to fill with real responsibilities, titles and thankfully, decent wages. But I want everyone in this room to tell me what kind of jobs they want. So that's why I called you all here. I want to make sure everyone has a chance to do something they want to do."

Violet nodded. "The rescue could use more hands. Jack's slowing down. He comes out less often and only treats a specific number of horses. Finn and I have more than enough work between us. Our horse care requires a lot of time, though and can be much more involved. It's hard, and sometimes heartbreaking, but it's also very fulfilling."

Jade nodded. "I have a list. The rescue is already on it."

"Well, boss, let's hear it," Silas said. His gaze was set on her. Mocking aside, she stared at her friend. The word *boss* sounded too awkward for him to use. He grinned and waited for her reply. She rolled her eyes.

"Okay, Silas. Your parents will leave us the resort. How about it? You willing to come home and take it on? Or do you intend to play and hike and fish forever?"

"What about Blake? Or Emory? Don't they have any interest in doing this?" They were Silas's cousins technically, but the birth order was more complicated. Being the son of Jacob Starr, Silas was raised by Jacob's mother, Hailey and their stepdad, Joey. Jacob's sister, Brianna Starr married Finn Alexander, who worked the Horse Rescue with Jack. A boy, Blake and a girl, Emory were their children. Jacob had two more kids with his wife, Luna.

Silas stretched his legs. "I was weaned on the fucking resort. I got your back, Jade."

She rolled her eyes. "What the hell does that mean?"

"It means yeah, I'll return to be the new boss of it."

"No one said you'd be the boss."

"You did. You said *boss*."

"What about the outfitters?"

He nodded. "I'm still gonna do that. Success comes on many levels here, Jade," he said with a wink. His long legs stretched out and his blond, wavy hair curled over his forehead, and on the glasses he wore. He had a long, lean physique and wore the kind of clothes that made him look like a walking advertisement for a high-end, preppy, sports store. Jade often enjoyed making fun of him for his clothes horse persona.

"We need to hire more permanent ranch workers too. The show will need a crew of fresh riders trained in the next few years."

"Haven't you got a bull for a boyfriend who could do that?" Silas snickered.

Jade shrugged. "We haven't fully figured out his role yet."

Iris leaned forward. "I've been wondering about that too. Heard about the scuttle with the Poletti business. And that tired, old RV of his. How'd he get that down here?"

Tilting her head, Jade shrugged, finding the subject uninteresting. "He drove it."

Iris shook her head. "I don't think you get it. I checked that monstrosity out. Cole had to wire and configure that thing to run or it absolutely wouldn't. He's kinda like a magician or a maestro in the field of mechanics. Really. Considering the missing materials and parts, he's got a real talent if he could get that running."

Iris had Jade's interest now. "What are you hinting at?"

"He's a mechanic, not a ranch hand. His true brilliance is being wasted on scooping horse shit, when he should be elbow deep in oil with me."

Jade's heart accelerated. Iris wanted Cole to work for her? No one called him brilliant. He was good at so many things, but to hear Iris wanted him to work for her? Well, hell. Jade was filled with pride. The joy of Iris's endorsement elated her.

Jade licked her lips. "Have you asked him?"

"Nah. Wanted to see where you stood with him first. Can't have a dickhead staying on just because he's good at something I like."

"He's not a dickhead," Jade answered simply.

Iris held her gaze, and a little smirk appeared on her lips. "Okay then. I'll have a chat with him about Rydell Rides."

"Thank you." Jade's appreciation was tempered, and someday soon, she hoped Cole would be her boyfriend. If he'd have her. Only time would tell.

"Onward. We need more ranch hands. We also need more workers for the orchards and the resort. We should have another meeting to determine how much of a staff we require."

"The younger ones need to do those grunt jobs. Like I had to. Nobody handed me anything," Silas complained.

Eliana nodded. "Yeah, I agree. I had to work the cash register at the resort and clean the rooms for summer pay."

They all grumbled that most of them had to do all the grunt jobs.

"And muck the stalls." Iris grimaced. "I hated that chore."

"You haven't mucked a stall in the last twenty years." Melanie snorted. "You're so full of shit."

"Right. That. Shit. This place makes enough of it for the cavalry."

"Considering that… isn't there something more functional we can do with it?" Andi asked.

Jade turned, startled at her suggestion. "We already sell it for fertilizer. But we've got too much for even that. You think there's something more that could be done?" That was so far out of her wheelhouse.

Andi shrugged. "I just read some interesting stuff about other uses for it and I wondered what more could be done with ours."

"That sounds like some shit Hunter should research. Why don't you talk to him?"

Kyomi snorted. "Oh, yeah. He'd totally nerd out over that with you." But her eyes gleamed with pride at hearing his name. "Come to think of it, he needs a new job."

After the shooting that almost took his young son, Hunter quit his high-paying job. They'd only recently moved back to the valley and Hunter intended to do something entirely new for a living.

"Why can't he help us with the finances and accounting?" Jade leveled a look at Kyomi.

Kyomi snickered. "He can. I'll have him get in touch with you. That's the main reason why he didn't come to the meeting. Figured he'd be hit up for his accounting skills."

"And he doesn't want to do that?"

"Oh, no. He wants to. And he expects to. He just has to pretend like he doesn't."

"What a prima donna." Jade grumbled.

Kyomi nodded, still grinning. "Full on."

"What else?"

Jade ran down the endless list she'd been compiling over the last six months. Being shuffled from one facet of the Rydell operations to the next, she did her best to stay on top of all the various tangents. It took an hour for her to read her lists and hear all the suggestions being bounced around. Towards the end, she finally stretched her arms up and sighed.

"You know something?" Andi asked.

"What?"

"The new staff? Pretty chick heavy. The leadership roles of this place are mostly female, rather than male, like they were in the past."

"Gender's not really important nowadays. Anyone can be a leader." Melanie pointed out. She'd been working in the construction industry that was still mostly male dominated.

"Maybe it's becoming that way," Iris answered. "But my experience says the opposite. We've got a long way to go. And it's something real and important that we can't stop opening up to women. So yeah, it's fucking epic, *ladies.*"

Silas lumbered to his feet, stretching his hands up. "Yeah. All true. So I'm out. Ladies, enjoy planning the great Rydell River Ranch and Resort takeover."

Jade threw a pillow at his back and he simply gave her a little grin of appreciation. He also had pride in his eyes when he looked at her. When their gazes met, he gave her a smile. Then he turned to leave.

However, Jade noticed his gaze lingered on Andi, who didn't seem to notice. Jade shrugged. She had enough romantic crap to keep her tied in knots, let alone, worrying over others. Even Silas. Or Andi. She adored both of them. But it wasn't any of her business.

For now at least.

Turning back, she let the strange new feelings percolate through her. Boss. Leader. It should have made her feel empowered. In many ways it was overwhelming and anxiety-inducing. But she was glad everyone took it with general acceptance. No one contested the outcome.

Jade Rydell would be the new leader of the Rydell Family Operations.

After listening to several other plans and ideas, Jade said goodbye when some got up to leave. Others lingered to gossip. Finally, it was just Kyomi and Jade.

Jade gave Kyomi a long, searching look and then grinned. "Some help over here? I'm so far over my fucking head." Kyomi laughed out loud, walking forward and slinging an arm around her shoulders.

"Happily. I'm your forewoman, after all… it's my job." Then they shared a long look, and Jade began to feel giddy. She wondered if Kyomi felt like that too. "I'm really glad to be doing this with you."

"Yeah, Kyomi. Me too. Give me your advice. Tell me everything."

"That, I can do, my friend."

"Cole Poletti."

Cole closed his eyes as he heard his name from a familiar voice. It wasn't Jade. He hadn't heard from her in days and didn't know where they stood anymore. Not since he brought the RV to the ranch.

The deep aching need he felt for her wasn't normal. He didn't know how to relieve it. It hurt a lot. Each time he heard a boot scuffling behind him, he hoped and prayed, as his stomach filled with butterflies, that it was Jade.

But so far, it wasn't Jade.

This time? The voice belonged to Iris Rydell.

He spun around. "Yeah? Getting pretty famous around here. Never gotten so much attention 'til I came here."

"Yeah, lying really does that to some people."

He smirked. "Right. Yeah. It really does."

He didn't need to defend himself. Not to the tough-assed Iris. He thought she was mocking him by daring him to react. Arms crossed over her chest, she tilted her head towards the side of the ranch where his ugly RV was parked. "That piece of junk should have been long abandoned at the dump."

"Right." This woman didn't sugar coat anything.

"Years ago, I had a partner who was the smartest person I ever met. He still is. He married my sister. Left me to become a fucking scientist. Now he's researching brain cancer. Yep, for fucking real. But he had a real talent with engines. He could make anything move. Even that bucket of rust that you managed to rig up and drive here."

His heart pumped hard. She noticed that? No one else noticed. A glimmer of pride swelled in his chest. Saying nothing, Cole simply nodded.

"If you can get that thing running, you're wasting your time shoveling horse shit and mending fences. Put the shovel and the hammer down and come with me."

"Where?" he asked, nearly floored by the sudden turn of the conversation.

"I want you to work for me."

Iris simply spun around without another look back. Cole stood there, stunned. The words she said failed to sink in. Until they did. Galvanized, he eagerly ran after her.

Iris was a short woman. She lifted her gaze when he strode beside her. "You're not fucking with me?"

She laughed out loud. Cole could tell she enjoyed having fun. "No. I'm not messing with you. I don't fuck around about the people I hire for my shop. I love it too much for that."

"You want me to work there? What do you want me to do?"

"Be a mechanic, genius. I want you to start working in my shop and I mean it."

"But why? Why would you do that for me?"

"Because Jade trusts you. That's a good enough recommendation. And after I checked out the inner workings of that ancient RV, you gave me the best mechanics resume I ever saw. I noticed it when we fixed your truck too. I was still on maternity leave and slightly off my game but I'm back now. Get your ass down there if you wanna have some fun with me."

Anyone else might have sounded suggestive or flirty but coming from Iris's gravelly voice, it was merely a challenge from one gear-head to another. "But what about Ben and Jade and all the ranch work? I just learned how to stay on a horse."

Iris stopped dead and put her hands on her hips. "And did you feel it? That sudden realization that you'd been missing something all your life? The majestic wonder and beauty that Jack, Erin, Ian, Ben, Violet, Andi, and Jade all tout and insist on believing? Or was it just another chore?"

A small smile appeared on his face. "The latter."

"Yeah. I thought as much. You're better than me. I found them smelly, stinky and freaking annoying to take care of. So much poop all the time. But that RV? Now that interests me. I might ask you to explain the logic you used on some of the fixes."

If he were a dog, his ears would have pricked straight up. Iris was clearly interested in something he'd done? "I can show you exactly what I was thinking."

"I know you can. That's why you're done with the days of shoveling horse shit." Then her expression softened. "You're really hung up on my cousin and Jade knows I wanted to hire you. She agreed to let me have you. You were supposed to go and join the Rydell operations, now that the oldies are retiring. They need to get a whole crew of young horse lovers. You gotta get outta the way of that. Annoying people, those horse junkies."

He pressed his lips together. She'd be fun to work with.

It seemed like a dream. But for once, this one came true.

"You trust me then? I'm allowed to stay? Despite what I did?"

"You robbed my cousin's business at gunpoint."

"It wasn't loaded. None of the guns were."

Iris gave him a scathing look. "Yeah? Then that makes everything all right."

"No, it doesn't."

"I know. And I know Jade. Since you're still here, she obviously believes your story and must be working through it."

"I won't rob you, Iris."

Iris's teeth flashed. "Well, I appreciate that. Now, let me show you around." They entered the gates of heaven: her illuminated mechanic shop. It had car lifts, tool boxes, and tons of big machinery. It was pure heaven for Cole. He looked around and saw tools and state-of-the-art technology he'd only dreamed of.

"You ready?" Iris nodded at the SUV she had up on the lift.

"I have zero training in mechanics."

"You got it figured out though, huh? Take a look. Tell me what's wrong with it."

He took the flashlight she held out and she nodded her head at him. As if it were the holy grail, Cole accepted her trust and faith in him, turning towards the vehicle to inspect it.

The first thing he noticed was a leak of some type of fluid. He checked out a few more areas and turned off the flashlight.

"It's the transmission. It looks like an oil leak but this model is an older engine that was only made during one particular year, and they recalled most of them for problems with the transmission."

Iris's eyes gleamed with approval. "Yep." That's all she said. The word was enough to stoke his pride. "Now, fix it. The time clock started when you stepped in here. Now earn your pay."

Gruff. Harsh. Direct. Iris was all those things.

Cole was simply grateful. That's what rushed through his mind. She trusted him. Now he could finally prove himself by doing something he knew how to do. He could earn his pay like anyone else.

He never knew how to address the people at the ranch, although they were not entirely Rydells. It seemed fitting to use Mr. and Ms. and Mrs. but none spoke as formally as that. All were on a first name basis. Cole didn't consider himself an equal, however.

"Thank you, Mrs. Larkin."

"Fuck. Call me Iris. Just Iris, Poletti."

He grinned, quickly picking up on the way Iris interacted and liking it. "Okay, Iris. Then, I prefer you just call me Cole. Drop the fucking Poletti."

She nodded, smiling. "No fucking Poletti. Now fix it, Cole."

She spun around and headed towards another vehicle, flipping the button on an ancient stereo that looked like another relic she restored. In an instant, headbanging metal rock filled the air and Cole knew he died and went to heaven.

CHAPTER 28

COLE POLETTI WAS TRULY in his element and it was something to witness. Jade stood in the doorway of Iris's shop, a huge, cavernous building with several garage doors to access it. An RV as tall as Cole's could easily pass through them. There were lifts and all kinds of gadgets and a cool, concrete floor with metal walls and open rafters above.

Jade had watched Cole working in earnest for months. Lifting. Moving. Countless tasks that required mostly his strength and endurance. He finished any work he did exactly as instructed with special care and confidence. He did more than his share of overtime hours. He rarely stopped in fact.

But watching him now, doing what he loved, Cole seemed to grow several inches; and a sense of pride Jade never noticed before became part of his personality.

Iris was right. This was exactly where he belonged.

The ranch was where *she* belonged.

At least, they both belonged here.

An odd sensation filled her chest. Watching him tinker in his favorite element simply magnified Jade's feelings of attraction towards him. She found every single detail about him both interesting and hot. Watching his brain work was fascinating. He still ran everywhere too, as if his habit of picking up Penny would never leave him. The anxiety he lived with all his life still rippled off him though. Jade didn't realize it before.

Now she saw it for what it was. Anxiety. Hurrying for Penny. Not leaving until he finished his work. Never taking breaks or relaxing. Always needing money for food and buying everything that Penny wanted.

And a robbery that happened a long time ago.

It was all true. They were all pieces that comprised him. Jade still loved him.

It was twilight and no one else was in the shop. The only sounds came from the clicks of the ratchet Cole used.

"It's customary to give notice to the boss when you decide to quit for a better job opportunity."

Jade's voice rang out and echoed in the shop.

Cole froze solid. Leaning over the hood of an SUV on the shop floor, he set the ratchet in his hand down gently and straightened up. He looked around to face her.

His eyes started at the top of her head before trailing down over her body. All the way to her toes. She could feel his eyes everywhere they landed. He was bold. And hot.

Surprised at seeing the gleam of sexual interest on her after such a long hiatus, she felt her belly tighten.

"I quit that job." Cole's voice was deep and authoritative. Not that of a twenty-year-old boy, but a mature, self-controlled man. Jade stared big-eyed at him. She entered the shop fully in control and holding the reins of power, but that somehow shifted with one look from him. Where did that come from? "As of now, Jade Rydell, you are no longer my boss."

While she mentally struggled to understand where he was

coming from, he suddenly lunged forward, directly at her. His big body dwarfed hers as he stared down at her closely. The look in his eyes had her blushing in no time. She felt the blast of heat climbing up her neck and filling her cheeks, while her damn toes curled.

"I'm going to kiss you, Jade. Unless you tell me not to."

It was a dare. A fucking dare. Why was he challenging her?

She simply nodded, too tongue-tied and confused to attempt to speak coherent thoughts.

He stepped forward, his leg coming between hers and pushed right into her personal space. She retreated until her back gently collided with the wall behind her, staring at him with shock.

Who was this guy?

"I'm sorry, Jade. For all the bad things I did to get here. I'm sorry I robbed you. I'm sorry for being a Poletti and sharing a family relative with you. But I'm not fucking sorry to be here now. Because I want to be here with you more than anything else in my life."

His mouth tilted downwards before he took hers with a wild, sensuous, roughness that jolted through her. No finesse. Just raw emotion. Cole snatched something from her that he wanted. Something that she usually did to him. He used his leg to push up hers and she could feel his body heat right through his jeans. His arms constricted hers like strong, hard bands around them. His mouth was searing hot, opening over hers in a wet, delicious invitation. She moaned into his mouth when his tongue found hers.

He kissed her for what seemed like hours.

She whimpered and allowed her aching needs to consume her. She ripped her mouth free, breathing heavily as if she'd been sprinting, and said "I had no idea being a mechanic could turn you into a caveman."

He grinned at her joke. She blinked when he held her face in his hands, cradling her jaw. His thumb rubbed across her lips. "It's not being a mechanic, it's you. Just you, Jade."

She felt his words, loud and clear all the way to her toes. They filled her heart with joy.

She put her hands over his. "It's you, Cole. For me, it's you."

His gaze studied hers, his eyes gleaming. "You forgive me." He stated it. No more wondering. No more apologies.

"I forgave you a long time ago. Yes."

He nodded. "I won't hurt you again. I won't lie to you. I won't fuck this up. If you'll just give me another chance." His thumb swiped over her lip and a bolt of energy shot down her spine.

"*I* will though. I know I'll mess up. Somehow. I'll be bossy and too full of myself. I'll forget to lower my voice when I address people. I'll be careless and sorry for it later. I'll try not to, but I know I will because I know me."

His gaze scoured over her and he said, "Any life lesson there?"

She nodded. "We'll both mess up. We have to 'cause we're human. But I think we'll also try to do the right thing."

"Is that what you see in me?"

She squeezed his hands in hers. "That's what I know in you."

His eyes sparked and his mouth curved into a tender smile. "I like it when you're bossy. It turns me on."

"Thank God for that, otherwise you'd be miserable. I can't seem to restrain it."

"I still worry my dad will find me eventually. He'll put me in jail for sure."

Jade shook her head. "I saw who attacked me that night. If he goes after you, I'll go after him."

Cole got very still. "Jade…"

"No. I've thought about this. He ordered your brother to hit me and knock me out. I'll have him arrested. And the other one who was there. Don't you see? I have as much on him as he has on you. So no. Chance can't put you in jail."

"What about Penny?"

"She's first priority. Always. I know that. She's the reason I knew I was in love with you. I'll love her too. She's not a problem to me, she's an asset."

His entire body tensed. That anxiety fully engulfed him. "You're in love?"

Gulping, she held his gaze and replied, "Yes, Cole. I love you."

His eyes closed and his body shuddered. It was that strong that he had a visceral reaction.

"I love you, Cole." She said the words again. She felt like she could say them to him for a lifetime. He was owed that. She didn't hesitate to reveal her true feelings or thoughts. Why start now? He needed to know and she wanted him to know every day.

For the rest of her life.

"There are..."

"Don't say anything. Don't try to convince me why I shouldn't love you. Or why you don't deserve it. I can't help it. I love you." She said it again. Easily. Smiling. With no sign of joking or jest.

"Jade?"

That was all he could manage to say. He was so touched and content.

"A bed."

He blinked. Confused and unclear in an instant. Her words stunned him. "Huh?"

"I want to make love to you on a bed. The usual way that couples do. I still want to do it in the barn again on the sly, or under the trees with only the blue sky above us. I always loved those times. I just want to have it all with you, you know?"

"Have it all? With me?"

"You know what I mean and I'm always right when I make a decision."

His lips finally relaxed and he twitched. "You think you're always right."

"Oh, cowboy, no. I fully know I'm always right."

"Whatever you say, boss-lady." His tone was kidding and flirty, and his eyes sparkled with lust and love. Tender, deep love for her.

She smiled up at him. "Boss-lady. Damn, I love it when you sweet talk me."

CHAPTER 29

"HELLO, SON. HOW'S MY daughter doing?"

Cole froze at the same instant his heart slammed into his chest. Anxiety flooded him the second he heard the familiar voice. Chance Poletti was right behind him. He came to the Rydell River Ranch.

Why now? Why was he there? All the talk of *someday* had truly convinced Cole he wouldn't show up. Yet here he was. Just days after everything came to a head, his damn father shows up now?

Cole whipped around, flexing his hands at his sides. The fluttering in his heart increased as his breath came in short spurts. *Don't let him do it.* He ordered his racing pulse and thoughts to calm down. He always obeyed Chance and gave him all the power while usually overreacting to his presence. Not now.

He'd been working at his new job, feeling glad he was so good at it. It was so much easier on his brain. He could look at a damn engine and map out all the problems and quirks in his head without any effort. Mixing that talent with the right tools, materials and diagnostics made Cole feel an incredible high. Being good at something was an entirely new experience for him.

Outside the main building was a shed for shelving the spare car parts and he was putting some of the inventory away when Chance's voice slithered like a snake up his spine.

"You need to let her go. No one here wants to see you, least of all, us."

There was no one else around. Chance had a knack for showing up during quiet times like the vermin he hung out with.

Chance's eyes widened. "Did you finally grow a pair, Cole?"

In the past, Cole allowed this old fucker to shame him. Chance knew how to intimidate and get to him. Not anymore. "Yeah, I finally did."

"You kidnapped my daughter."

"You put Jade Rydell in the hospital. Pawn for rook. Checkmate. It's over. Leave." He didn't know how to play chess, but he liked the comparison. He also liked being taller, crossing his arms over his massive chest and staring down at his father. He should have done this years ago.

"You won't get away with it."

"I did and I am. I'd kill you before I'd let you take her back to that insanity you call a life."

Where did that come from? Of course, he wouldn't really kill him. Right? He sounded threatening and tough. Like Chance always sounded to them.

Cole never threatened Chance before nor stood up to him. Usually, he cowered and stayed quiet. His way to stand up was by defying him, doing things behind his back, never to his face.

Surprise showed in Chance's eyes. And an odd gleam of something Cole could only compare to pride. For the first time in Cole's life, he saw it in his father's eyes.

"Son. You kidnapped her. I already filed a missing person's report. There's only one place for you now: jail."

"We fucking robbed this ranch, asshole. You think Jack and Ben Rydell don't care about that? Or Erin Poletti?" He sneered hard at his dad.

"You've been playing house with my little sister. Wait 'til she and that old bastard, Jack discover you were there that day too. Right with us. Aiming your gun at their precious granddaughter. You were—"

Suddenly, a warm hand slipped into his. Startled, Cole physically jumped and glanced to his left to see Jade Rydell right beside him. Her eyes were on Chance, but her hand was in Cole's. "They already know. Everyone knows he was there. They know he saw me get hit on the head with the butt-end of a gun. They also know you ordered it. They know Cole called the cops. They know everything already."

Blinking in shock to find Jade beside him, Cole's brain spun. How on earth? How did she know to come here now? And that Chance was here? Then he looked up higher.

There stood Jack and Erin, holding hands. But Penny was holding Erin's other hand. When they stopped near him, all of them were facing Chance, and Erin brought Penny's body closer to hers and wrapped her arms around the little girl. Then Cole saw Ben rushing across the road from the new homestead.

He blinked again.

What in the hell were they doing?

"Jade. Erin. Someone help."

Jade jumped and flipped around when Penny's screaming reached her ears. Penny rushed through the front door, slamming it behind her. Jade was sitting with her grandparents having dinner.

Penny looked like a scared rabbit. Trembling, wide-eyed, with a horrified expression.

All of them got to their feet and rushed towards her. "What is it?" Jade asked, being the first to get to her.

"Chance. He's here. Down at the new place where Cole works. I saw him go in there. Hurry. We have to hurry. Or… or I don't know what. Maybe I should hide. Maybe…" Tears filled her eyes and she suddenly flung herself at Jade. It was exactly as Jade often witnessed her doing with Cole. "Don't let him take me back. Please, Jade. Please."

It was so heartfelt. Uttered in a desperate whisper. Jade soothed Penny by rubbing her shoulders and the top of her head. But the fear that throttled this little body wasn't a joke. The man created wracking shudders in this little girl who was usually a bubbling dynamo.

"We'll find a way to keep you." The words were spoken by Jack as he rose up, ever sure and in control. His back was straight and tall even though his shoulders stooped nowadays. Jade's heart was brimming with love and pride as well as strength and faith. She believed her grandpa would make it all okay. Not only for Erin and Jade, but most of all, for Penny. "We won't let anything happen to you, Penny."

She sniffled as her big tears rolled down her cheeks. "And what about Cole? Can you help him too?"

Jack smiled easily. "Honey, look at my granddaughter over there. She's as crazy about your brother as you are. Of course, we'll do something for him too."

"But Cole said there's nothing we can do."

Erin was gazing at Jack's profile. He didn't turn or say any words to comfort her. Instead, he put his hand behind him, palm up. He was waiting. A moment later, Erin grabbed his hand. Clinging to each other with just their hands, they seemed to have an entire conversation. For the first time, Jade's heart contracted painfully. She never really thought much about her grandparents' relationship. Sure, they got along well. And had been married forever. But seeing them now? She saw passion. Understanding. And unconditional support.

And Jack was just as involved as the rest of them were now.

Carefully, Jack answered Penny, "Cole did lots of stuff, huh? Chance is a fucking idiot, excuse my language, honey, but I've dealt with him once too often in my life. Last time, I watched him torture my wife. I never properly confronted him about that. I think… now maybe it's time that issue got addressed."

Jade realized at that moment, he was still Jack Rydell and this was still his land. His family's legacy. His namesake. At seventy-eight, in that moment, Jack was forty years younger.

"Maybe we shouldn't let him see Penny. You can see her fear. It's heartbreaking. Whatever happens, he can't have any access to her," Jade said.

Erin snorted. "We're not letting him near her."

"But…" Jade's head was muddled. "He does have the law on his side."

"He's never spent a day in his life with the law on his side." Erin's bitterness said everything that nobody knew about her childhood. No one but Penny.

"What are you saying?" Jade needed more clarification.

"She isn't going anywhere with him. Legally or not." Jack announced with finality.

Relief washed over Jade. Thank goodness. Penny ran forward when she opened her arms to her. Hugging her tightly, Penny buried her face against Jade's stomach. "And what about Cole?" Penny whispered, looking up at her.

Always. Cole was always Penny's first concern. She

glanced at her grandparents. They nodded. Jade finally understood how they communicated without words. Gripping Penny's little biceps in her hands, she gently but firmly said, "And Cole can stay too."

"He gets different around Chance."

"Cole does?"

She nodded against Jade. "He gets nervous. Like a little kid, he's unsure what to do."

The anxiety in Cole was something she'd witnessed often.

"So did Erin. Let's go," Jack said tersely.

"We can't leave her alone, she's too afraid. And I need…" *To be there for Cole,* but Jade didn't say that.

"Please don't leave me. I wanna go too. I see lots of things like that all the time. It's not new."

Sighing, Erin relented. "I'm sure she knows the truth. Come on, Penny. Take my hand. Let's go."

Jack nodded. "I texted Ben. He'll meet us at Rydell Rides."

That swiftly, they all trooped out of the front door.

IT WAS easy to find them. Cole stood face to face with Chance Poletti in the back lean-to. It was just one of the giant metal buildings that comprised Rydell Rides.

Approaching them from the side of the building, they remained undetected until the moment they popped out from behind the building. Jade strode forward to grab Cole's hand just as Chance was ranting at him.

She stared at the old man, amazed at how old he looked. He was as old as her grandfather. Stooped, with no hair, the mottled skin of a poorly aging drunk and a half foot shorter than Cole. He was frail and feeble, but still capable of hurling mean insults at Cole.

That's all he was though.

Jade's imagination ran wild. She pictured a villainous fiend called Chance Poletti. In her mental image, he was seven feet tall, three hundred pounds of angry muscle and gristle that could effortlessly take all of them out.

Now, she saw an old, ugly, decrepit man who looked like he'd keel over any moment. She realized then his power was entirely all in Erin and Cole's heads. Whatever Chance might have been in the past, he no longer was.

Chance's beady eyes missed nothing as they darted to the joined hands of Jade and Cole. Then he looked up at her face, then at Cole's.

His eyebrows jutted upwards. "Growing up finally, huh, son? And now you're fuckin' Jack Rydell's granddaughter. Nice. Couldn't have planned it better myself." His sneer revealed his crooked, yellow teeth.

Jade was appalled at this man's sheer nastiness.

She felt Cole's entire body tensing. He didn't like Chance talking about her. She squeezed his hand, thinking of her grandparents.

"Are you jealous 'cause you can't get it up anymore?" Jade snarled. She was angry at this shit hole who so cunningly controlled all those around him. Except for her. He was no more than an ugly, old man to her.

Nothing to fear.

The tension kept rising in the man she loved. He was breathing harshly and she knew how much he wanted to run. Not to fight. Cole always ran. That was his physical response to distress. It must have originally come from this man and all the terrible things he'd done to them.

"You owe me a lot of money, asshole. And this time, I intend to collect it."

The cavalry suddenly arrived. Jade didn't turn around but her heart sang with joy when her grandfather's voice came from behind them. Then she saw her dad jogging towards them.

Chance snorted. But his gaze was riveted on Erin, not on Jack who'd just spoken. It wasn't even on Penny. Chance stared at his sister.

Jade didn't fully understand what was happening but she felt it. A cold shiver of revulsion traveled down her spine. She couldn't describe or give voice to the sense of dread that Chance incited. Her grandmother literally changed and became a victim right in front of her. There was something timeless about her reaction. As if not a day had passed instead of forty years. Erin seemed to collapse, hunching her shoulders and her usually bright, energetic, indomitable spirit seemed to shrivel up and die. Right before Jade's eyes.

Damn. This man was evil. Pure and simple.

And the people he targeted were his damn relatives. Erin was gripping Penny and holding her. Penny wouldn't even look at the man who fathered her.

And Jade watched the giant, strong man she loved, crumple into an anxiety-riddled mess and all but run away scared.

But this time, they had a whole bunch of backup.

"He's a mean, nasty, old man. He'll die soon judging by his red, alcoholic nose. Ignore his shit." Jade said out loud. For Cole and Penny. And her grandmother.

Jack snorted and grabbed Erin's shoulder in his hand. But his gaze remained on Chance. "You robbed me forty years ago. You robbed me last spring. You'll be on trial and Jade will testify against you. You'll lose, mother fucker. Jade is right about you. You need to crawl off and die somewhere. But you'd better leave my wife alone, and Cole, but most of all, Penny."

"Come on, sis. Just a word. Did you ever learn how to

read? You probably already know your stupidity showed up in my offspring. Dumb as rocks. Both of them."

Jade blinked. That fast, he was cutting and harsh.

She grabbed Cole's arm with her other hand as he snarled and started moving forward. "He does it for your reaction. All of it. Stop giving him what he wants." Jade's tone was low. For Cole's ears only.

"Shut the fuck up." Ben's voice said from behind them.

Chance turned. "Ben Rydell. Well, just look at you. All grown up. Remember me?"

"Thought you'd be lying in a ditch, having your bones picked by buzzards. Shame, life didn't go that way for you."

"You all have *my daughter*. Soon as I report that, she's coming with me. No matter what you try to spin. Penny's mine," Chance snapped like a cornered animal.

Penny whimpered and Cole's entire body shook. "I have to go to her," he muttered, releasing Jade's hand as he crossed the space to Penny. He lifted her up from Erin's embrace and she pressed her face into her favorite spot against his neck and shoulder. Her little legs wrapped around his trunk. He kept her face away from Chance. His gaze was dark and fierce as he looked at his father. This was not a twenty-year-old, mild-mannered, anxiety-ridden boy. Jade was proud. In that moment, Cole was a fierce, protective, father-figure saving Penny. She was his daughter in every sense of the word.

Her heart swelled with love and pride but her nerves finally got to her. Chance was overflowing in his evil. Jade finally understood their fear. His ability to use his mind to control people was paralyzing.

Jack simply laughed out loud. "You think anyone around here will believe you? Fuck you, Poletti. You never realized who I am. Jack Rydell means more than anything else around here. Even now. I say you robbed me forty years ago. And again last year. And you assaulted my granddaughter. And you know what that means? It means *it happened*. Cole told us about your plan to move Penny in with her Auntie Erin. They were just visiting us. With your permission. We don't know what lies you're spreading about a kidnapping since you gave Cole permission to take Penny here to visit us. You had to run off with your bail-jumping son, remember? Cole was just keeping Penny safe like any good father would have wanted. So fuck off, Poletti, you got nothing here."

Jade's heart pumped fast and her breath felt tight. Wow. Her grandpa was... heroic. She'd never seen him like this. So calm, cold, and stern. Jack was looking for real justice. She was glad to be a Rydell and overflowing with respect and love for her grandpa.

"You can't prove anything," Chance retorted.

"I can prove all they need to know, after the bail-jumping incident. You were his accomplice. Cole identified you as an accomplice when Jade was attacked. Try me, fucker. Really. My wife hoped I'd never see you again for she feared I'd end up in jail for murdering you. I understand her concerns. I do. Because I honestly had them myself." Jack's tone was smooth as silk. But his gaze was stone hard.

"Dad?" Ben warned.

Jack held up a hand, silencing his son. His eyes never left Chance's. Old man to old man. The standoff was long overdue.

Jack's other hand gripped Erin's. She didn't intercede, Jade realized, and it worried Jade.

"Chance Fucking Poletti, I'm a very old man. I don't have much life left. So I might decide to plant your ugly face in the ground just so I never have to see it again."

Erin whimpered. Jade tensed. Cole stared with obvious wonder at Jack.

"Get off my land, Poletti. This time, I'm letting you go. Be grateful for my temporary mercy. If I ever see you here on *my* land, for any reason, I won't ask questions. I'll fucking shoot you in the face so no one has to ever see you again, you villainous, evil, lecherous, ugly, dumb, piece of shit." Jack didn't once raise his voice. He almost said his threat in a soothing tone. At the end, he raised his hand and swiped it through the air, yelling, "Get out. Go. Now. Before I change my mind and get my gun."

Chance stared big-eyed at Jack and then scanned the group around them.

Jade almost burst out laughing. Chance thought he had all the power and his kidnapping accusation at Cole would keep Cole under his thumb as usual. Then he thought he could take Penny and keep using her as his favorite weapon of choice. Nothing could touch him as long as he had access to Penny. He didn't know Jack Rydell though.

Chance started to turn but Erin suddenly let go of Jack's grip and walked towards Chance. "Wait."

Startled, all eyes landed on her. What in the hell?

"You'll withdraw your accusation of kidnapping against Cole. You'll admit to filing a false report. Then you'll sign custody of Penny over to us."

"Why the fuck would I do that?" Chance snarled.

"Because I said so." Erin shrugged. "And I'll send Jack after you if you don't do it. You heard him. He's an old man with little to lose. You'll end up dead or in jail for the rest of your miserable life. You're just a petty, scared, little man who can't handle anything tough. Now you're an old bully, kicking little girls and young men, but you've lost your nerve."

Jade realized her grandmother must have had a profound realization. Erin's head shook. "I was scared of you all my life. I realize now what a nothing you are."

And just like that, Chance Poletti's power seemed to evaporate into thin air.

Penny's head popped up over Cole's shoulder. She twisted around to finally look at her father. Her tears were still streaming but she was calm. Cole was stunned at his own reaction. Erin's words encapsulated his own experience.

"You terrorized me. But I'll be fucking damned if you do anything to Penny ever again."

Chance sneered at her. Erin merely stepped *closer* to him. "Just disappear and never come back."

"I—"

"You've got nothing. Now go." Erin pushed him hard and he stumbled backward.

Hearing her words, Chance turned and fled.

They all stared, looking stunned as Chance limped down the road like an old dog. He went back to the vehicle he came in and was soon gone.

No one spoke as Chance drove away.

Finally, like a balloon releasing all its air, everyone seemed to exhale a collective breath.

"Did that just happen?" Cole whispered as if he dared not voice his life's wish. He squeezed Penny close to him. Penny wiggled and suddenly grinned with a smile as bright as the sun in the sky.

"He ran away like a little bitch!" Penny squealed with glee, squirming so much, Cole placed her gently on the ground. "Did you see that? Aunt Erin sent him running away from here like a bitch."

No. Little girls probably shouldn't use such language, but considering how she'd been raised, if that were Penny's greatest sin, well, Jade thought it was pretty small compared to what it could be.

Penny rushed towards Erin and Jack, eagerly hugging them both.

Tears filled Jade's eyes as she watched it. But she was mostly looking at Cole and seeing all the emotions as they passed over his handsome face. Love. Joy. Relief. Wonder. His gratitude that for once, Penny had someone more than him to embrace. More than him to fight for her.

Jade rushed towards him, not caring that her dad and grandparents were still there. She threw herself into Cole's arms and started to cry as he held her tightly.

"I didn't know. I didn't know how horrible he was. I didn't know…" Jade mumbled over and over.

Cole rubbed her back and kissed her scalp several times. "I didn't either."

She stopped crying to add, "I was so scared he would get Penny." She shuddered. "No wonder you did all the things you did for her. All these years, you couldn't bear the idea of losing Penny to a monster."

"That's what guides my entire life."

She nodded, lifting her head to pepper soft kisses on his neck, chin and cheek. She stretched up on her tiptoes to hug him as tightly as she could. "I love you. So much."

Cole sagged into her embrace. "Jade…"

He never said he loved her back. But he didn't have to. She felt it. "Penny's safe. You're safe. From now on."

His body started to shake in her arms. The stress and relief overwhelmed him and she was sure the adrenaline high was starting to wane.

"Jade…" he repeated. She heard the emotional relief and gratitude in his tone. Not only for Penny but for himself. She felt his love in the way he grasped and clung to her.

When Jade finally released him, he smiled a shy, sheepish grin that reminded her of the first day she met him when he scurried off to take food to his little sister.

Penny watched them together. Her eyes were bright with joy and devotion. "Does this mean we can stay here forever?"

Jade looked at Cole who glanced around. They all nodded and Jack answered. "Well, yes."

"Does that mean Cole and I can stay together?"

Cole's gaze seemed unsure and puzzled. He looked at Erin for guidance. She smiled with gentleness and Jade realized the man she loved was also in need of maternal love. Thank God he wasn't getting that from Jade but from his own aunt.

"What it means, honey, is that Cole is your guardian and we're also your family."

"Me?" Cole stared big-eyed at Erin, then at Jack and Ben, and finally at Jade.

"Of course you. You've always been her guardian, huh?" Erin said softly.

Cole nodded and Penny grinned. They made eye contact and she let out a huge squeal as she rushed over to him. "Do you hear that Cole? We're free now."

He laughed as he spun her around and Jade feared her heart might burst in her chest from all the joy and love filling it.

All those big, deep, grand moments aside, Cole was overcome by a sense of weariness that left him exhausted.

Now they were inside Jade's parents' house. Her mom was preparing dinner and they were rehashing the crazy, unpredictable, amazing events the day. Cole sat there too, now part of their family.

So did Penny.

But distrust still churned his gut. Chance had never relented in the past. Or walked away without plotting some kind of revenge.

"My guardianship won't stand up in court 'cause it's not legal. I can't… get custody, and he could still…"

"We'll make it legal then. We'll hire a lawyer and draw up

the paperwork. You know how to find him, huh? We'll hunt him down and make him sign it. He only wanted Penny to manipulate and torture in his sick hobby of bullying. That's his life. I know that. Kids are devices to Chance."

Cole nodded his agreement, his gut twisting at the depravity of the man. He couldn't deny the truth in Erin's words. "You knew Chance well."

"As well as you two."

Having no money or resources to fight Chance in court, Cole said, "I've never gone against him. Not in spirit or in the courts."

"No, because that shit takes money and we have it. I know what it's like because a long time ago, I couldn't fight him either. But you still did, Cole, you really did. You still managed to get Penny out and come here."

He glanced around the room. "I think we should stay in the RV for a while. Let Penny grow used to all this and maybe then she'll believe it."

Erin smiled gently. "And you too. You both have to believe in us."

Jack gazed at Erin with a tenderness that melted fifty years off his face. "Erin had her version of your RV. She lived in a trailer."

Cole tilted his head, unsure of what Jack's cryptic statement meant. Jade was beside him, so she squeezed his hand and explained. "Grandma lived in an old trailer that Chance was living in when she arrived. When he stranded her here, she cleaned it all up and lived there for a long time, at least a few years. She needed her own space to believe in her new life."

Erin continued, "It didn't seem like much to anyone else. But it was the first place that I could call mine. *All mine*. It allowed me to think just maybe something inside me was worth having a special little space on this earth. I had to let that sink in before I could handle Jack, the boys and being around a family."

Cole blinked. "It's like we lived the same life except it was forty years apart."

Erin nodded. "I've already thought about that."

"So you and Penny can stay in the RV as long as you both need. When you're ready for something bigger, please let us know. We offer housing for the ranch hands and there's most definitely a place for my niece and nephew." Erin stiffened her back and lifted her chin. "After all, I'm Erin Rydell. And this place is fucking half mine."

She exhaled a long breath and laughed. "Took me more than forty years to be able to completely accept that and embrace it. Don't wait too long, Cole."

Then she tilted her head. "We'll be glad to watch Penny if you two would like a moment." Jade was all but jumping up and down near him. He finally turned and noticed her thumping leg.

Cole nodded. "Right. Thank you." Rising up, Jade grabbed his hand and took him down the hallway into what turned out to be her bedroom. She firmly shut the door, pushing his chest until he stepped back and fell on the bed where she joined him.

Her lips pressed his with force. Her tongue seemed hungry and raw. He finally had to roll her to the side to pull back a little. "Kissing me like that you'd think you were new to this. Should I teach you how to kiss me nicer?"

Her hand cupped his chin. "I wanted to do it that way for hours. This day has been… incredible and unbelievable."

"Does anyone mind us being in here?"

"No one wants to think about it. And we're adults, Cole. You gotta go with that."

Her gaze dimmed. "Besides, I just needed a moment with you." She suddenly shivered and curved her body into his. "I want you to know you have my complete respect. The things you've done for Penny…"

"Were not a sacrifice."

"You saved her life. Her whole damn life, I know that's the truth."

He rubbed her shoulder. "She saved mine too."

"For as tough talking as she can be, she's one bundle of rattled nerves and abstract fears."

"Yeah. We both are."

"She needs you," Jade stated simply.

"Yes. She still can't sleep alone. Not yet. I swear it's the first thing I'll work on with her. To give her some confidence and space. But right now…"

"I saw it too. The anxiety. She's had to endure what grandma said it was like for her. I can live with that, Cole. Besides," she smiled up at him, "I want another go at that barn sex."

Only Jade could make him laugh out loud this day. He rubbed her back. "We're not doing that. It was terrible. Did you ever find out who was in there with us?"

Her head tilted up. Her eyes gleamed. "No. But I'm not sorry we did it. I love you, Cole. I really do."

The words were so easy for her to say. Sliding off her tongue like her own name. But they stuck in his throat. Even though his chest was bursting. Life was too unpredictable. Overwhelming. Taking a shuddering breath he said, "I think I… I mean, I want… to think—"

Two of her fingers touched his lips. "You love me. You don't have to say it. I know it. Whenever you're ready, you'll know it. We have so much time ahead of us now, Cole. A whole lifetime."

His breath released in relief. "I want to say it. I just… can't yet."

"Tell me the day you can."

"Jade... you're..."

She let out a husky laugh. "Bossy. I am. Yes."

He clutched her tightly. "If I didn't have you, this would be so hard to believe."

"Believe me then. You know I don't lie or waffle or retreat. Just believe me."

"I—"

A knock interrupted him. "Cole?"

Penny's voice rang out. He glanced down at Jade in his arms. It was so wonderful to hold this tough, fierce, beautiful, nice girl in his arms. But his mouth tightened and he said, "She needs me."

Jade released him, rising upright. "Of course she does. Remember... we still have the barns."

Her smile was deep, sweet, flirty, and heartbreaking. She really loved him. Jade looked at Cole with all the love he'd always longed for but was denied.

He nodded back. Smiling. "Right. The barns."

But she was promising him much more than that. An entire lifetime.

He opened the bedroom door and Penny ran in and glanced around. Seeing a childhood collection of plastic horses on Jade's shelf, she asked, "You collect Bayner horse statues? You have so many."

Jade rose to her feet, taking one off the shelf and handing it to his little sister. "Yes. I used to. But you know what? I'd love it if I could give them to you to keep safe for me. I'm too damn old now, huh?"

Penny grinned as she started rattling off all the facts she knew about them. Cole had no idea why she even knew about them. Penny and Jade started bonding over a plastic horse as Cole leaned forward, gripping Jade's hand tightly.

She squeezed his back with a little smile, and her eyes never left his sister's.

CHAPTER 30

~ne year later~

"COLE? WHAT IS IT?"

Jade's frantic tone stopped him and he held up an envelope. He couldn't read that well yet but he knew enough to realize what it was. Penny, well ahead of him in her tutoring as Erin claimed she'd be, took it and read the back of the envelope. "Chance?"

"What the hell?"

"Open it." Jade said simply. She discovered him sitting at the RV table, staring at it like it was a coiled snake about to strike.

He slit the envelope. Out came some official looking documents. His eyes blurred. "What is it?" he asked Jade. She knew he couldn't read it. There was no criticism or judgment as she took it and scanned it over. Then she read it out loud.

After she finished, she and Cole stared at each other and then looked at Penny.

"He relinquished custody?"

"How'd they get him to do that?"

"I don't think my grandpa was kidding when he said he didn't always follow the law. Obviously, neither did Chance."

Cole fingered the paper. "I never believed we'd actually get legal custody."

Penny's mouth curved up. "You're my guardian now? For real? And always?"

His heart beat harder. "For real. And always."

She flung herself at Cole before she started dancing around. "Can we… can we move into that house now? The one Aunt Erin said we could live in?"

He blinked in surprise that Penny asked him that. "Do you want to?"

It was considered a small cabin by the ranch hands. But it had three bedrooms. He glanced at Jade and her eyes shone with excitement too.

"Yes, I want to." Penny exclaimed. "I could put my horse collection in it."

Jade's former collection of horse statues now decorated Penny's room in the RV. Hearing that she wanted her own house to live in was new for Cole.

Safety. Permanence. *Home*. Cole blinked when his eyes stung with salty tears. Not now. This was a moment of joy and happiness, not a tragedy.

"Chance will curl up and die someday and we won't know or care." Cole's morose statement was connected to nothing, but he had to say it anyway.

Penny and Jade remarked on his thoughts. Penny nodded. "Good. I'm glad we won't know."

"You'll never have to see him again. It's truly over, Cole."

Cole released the breath he was holding. He and Jade shared a long, piercing eye lock. He swallowed and replied, "I love you."

Her smile came easily. "I know you do. It's nice to hear you say it though, especially without putting 'I think' before it."

He grabbed her waist and pulled her closer, standing up to kiss her lips. No tongue kissing. It was a kiss that showed he loved her and looked forward to a future with her. Penny giggled before she grabbed the notice and exclaimed, "I'm gonna go tell Auntie Erin and Uncle Jack. Bye."

Penny was well-acquainted with most adult signals. "We'll be over soon," Cole shouted to her before she ran off. He stared at Jade long and hard and she licked her lips as he said, "Maybe we won't have to visit the barn so often now."

"You do realize you're home now, Cole."

Home.

With Jade and Penny.

Finally.

Forever.

EPILOGUE

~SEVEN YEARS LATER: YEAR FIFTY-ONE
FROM THE START OF THE SERIES~

~*Jack*~

"ANOTHER FUCKING POLETTI ON my land." Jack whispered into Erin's ear. She lay next to him with her head on his chest. His old, arthritic hips allowed him to cradle her between them.

She laughed, a deep, sexy laugh that he knew his comment would educe. Along with the shared memories that went back years. Decades. So long now, it was almost hard to believe. "It's nice to have a pretty face to put to that Poletti name," Erin played along.

"Jade is pretty, I agree, but you were the prettiest of them all. And you still are." He tickled her side and she let out a sound that was half grunt, half laugh. *Yeah. Right. Sure.*

They had just returned from the marriage of their granddaughter to Cole Poletti.

"I can't believe I'm handing over the reins of this place to a Poletti." Jack's tone reflected the warmth and joy he felt in doing that. His beautiful granddaughter, Jade Rydell Poletti, the bright, tough, courageous, smart leader of all the Rydell operations had proven herself to be the right choice. But in

Jack's heart, the land was the true legacy. The ranch. The horses. His name.

Erin sighed and said, "So many weddings, births and daily lives going on, huh? Lucky we lived this long to see it and how they all ended up, but it's hard too, since everything is moving forward as it should. Life never stops. All the work and strife go on for decades and then age catches up with us all. Everything slows down. If you're lucky to still be alive to see it. I know that part too, but the alternative is worse."

"Jade will run the ranch like I did. That's always been my main dream. The resort and all the other endeavors were just avenues to support the ranch that's always been right here, existing beside this river as it has for more than a century."

"Jade will take her last breath on these grounds. Honestly? I think they all will."

Jack tightened his arms around her. "Do you remember another evening when we sat on this very river edge? At this very beach? Oh, I don't know, I think it was forty years ago or more? Do you remember that night, Ms. Poletti?"

"Oh, yes, I remember a night of quick sex and someone falling sound asleep right afterwards."

"Quick sex. That was fantastic sex. As always. And I'd been traveling too."

"You were an old man even then."

He growled into her ear. "I'll show you who's old."

She laughed, taking his hand. "You'll do no such thing. It'd make our old, brittle hips and backs snap in two, not to mention our necks."

"Over the years, when our kids were playing in the sand, and my brothers were swimming in the river, and their girlfriends and wives were talking to you, my mind always returned to that night. This spot. It never fails."

"Jack Rydell. You twist those perfectly innocent memories into something dirty."

"Dirty, old man, that's me."

"I remember someone's young son catching us in the act."

"Yep, and confronting him while my towel flapped in the breeze. It's a miracle the kid ever listened to another word I said again."

"He did. And now he's retired and we just attended the marriage of his younger daughter. Time is *not* our friend. It goes so slowly when you're young, finding yourself, which, for me, was an unhappy period. And when you find what you want and discover who you are and you start to live it? It's like riding a comet across the sky. Brilliant. Flashing. But you can't hang onto it. You can't hold it forever or keep it. Poof. And it's gone."

Jack felt the shudder as it traveled through her body and didn't miss the morose sadness in her tone. Tightening his arms around her, he knew why she was saying those things. The cancer. It returned last year. Jack beat that shit down again, but it took a lot more out of him this time. And he was still here. Right now. Today. Listening to Erin discuss the subject of *time*.

"We still have the tail of that comet, Erin." He kissed the top of her head. "I'm not riding off into the sunset yet."

She slapped his hand, then gripped it tightly. "I hate it when you make light of something so serious."

"I'm not making light of anything, I'm just stating a fact. Here's another fact: I'm imagining my wife lying naked underneath me. Right here. Forty years ago. And now. All good memories."

Erin choked on a laugh. "You know what I mean."

"You're referring to cancer and death. I know what you mean. But Erin, I'm nine years older than you. It's only logical that I'll go that way." Deep inside him, he believed whatever higher power ruled the heavens, it would not make him suffer the loss of a wife twice in a lifetime. He lost his first wife in his thirties. Now, in his eighties, he had no doubt he'd leave this world before Erin.

He gripped her hand hard and said, "I'd never leave you, Erin. Not willingly. You know that. I'll continue to slay this dragon until I take my last breath. But tonight? I'm right here, Erin. You can't write me off yet."

She turned her head and pressed it against his chest. Like she always did. They could be forty years younger. In that moment, he was Jack Rydell holding his beautiful, wonderful wife. She was so small and petite, fitting him like a perfect glove.

"Never."

"You know, if it happens... you should remarry like AJ did."

"NO. There's nothing to discuss. You know me, Jack Rydell. You *know*."

He did know her. They were ever united as one. Forever.

"Why are you sounding so morose, my darling wife?"

"Just thinking about all the time that's passed and how fast it went. Having you sick last year, well, that was terrifying." She wiped her face as her tears filled her eyes and rolled down her cheeks. She cried more often lately too. Jack's two bouts with cancer nearly eviscerated her.

"How many evenings did you and I sit here? Right here? Discussing the boys when they were young, and the brothers all marrying, and how things grew and changed around here. Then, our decision to have Mel. Remember those days? How old I thought I was at the time. Funny how your perspective changes depending on where you're standing. Thank God for that, huh? Or we wouldn't have had Melanie."

"Yes. Thank God for all the kids, and the grandkids, Benny, Molly, and Amelia." Amelia was Melanie's daughter. Jack was grateful and thrilled he got to see Melanie get married, while thriving in a career that she loved. She was always a unique and special daughter but getting to see her maternal side was a gift Jack would always treasure.

"Think of all the kisses I stole here. We were always looking for some damn privacy."

Erin's laugh was husky. "And a few times, so much more."

"So much more. Never sleeping. Never sneaking around. Just enjoying us. Thank God for our family and this place. But without you, Erin, it wouldn't matter like it does to me."

"I have so many images in my brain of all the kids swimming, playing together, bonfires, picnics, drinking and fun. How much fun we've had over the years. Ben and Jocelyn, Cami and Charlie, Mel and Kyle and all the kids. Not to mention, Ian and Kailynn, Shane and Allison, Joey and Hailey and AJ and Kate of the old generation."

He kissed her again and his arms tightened around her. "Ah, hell, I sure miss Kate." Jack didn't know he had a half-sister until he was damn near forty. When she died, he was seventy-five, and by then, he and his sister were almost inseparable. They missed her often.

"I can't believe she's gone. After all these years. So young. But not really young. I'm now older than she was… so now it seems she died too young."

His gaze drifted upwards to the twilight sky and the view he'd stared at for most of his life. Eighty years ago was the first time he remembered seeing it. The river was streaming down in noisy swooshes. Mountains slashing the sky, as deep and as solid as his marriage to Erin. The rocks, sand, sticks, grass, and trees that comprised the riverbank, and offered secret places to explore and frequent. True, it was all those things. But it always seemed so much more to Jack. His heart beat faster when he was here. His bones felt stronger. His lungs seemed to take deeper breaths, and Jack smiled, remembering it fondly.

The winter mountains stayed a dull brown until the onset

of spring, switching to brilliant swaths of yellow and purple as the native wildflowers raced to replant their seeds. The long, sweltering days of each summer. Beige and platinum replaced the verdant hues of the bleached grasses and driftwood. Then the rich palette of gold, red, wine, and purple of each autumn.

Finally, the winter. The snows blanketing the whole world in pristine, white powder, concealing all the blemishes and debris. Cold. Stark. Silent. Another year, gone.

Jack was getting ready for his own final sleep.

Mortality was beckoning to him.

When he was young, Jack thought if he reached his eighties, he'd have the whole world all figured out. He expected to know most of the answers to the questions he wondered about. He didn't. Not at all. Everything remained a mystery to him and he was no closer to it now in his eighties than he was when he was eight.

The happiest times for Jack were spent on the back of a horse, and holding his wife at the edge of the beach near the river he'd loved and known all his life. But his love for Erin exceeded even that for his horses.

Erin was staring at Jack as he stared at the river. It was darkening into deep shadows. "No one will ever forget Jack Rydell. You know that, right?"

He was quiet for a long time and then he shook his head. "No one will forget Jack and Erin Rydell, the greatest love story ever told."

She snorted. "Right. It's about an illiterate girl from the wrong side of the tracks and the rancher who—"

Jack silenced her with a kiss. "Yeah, I think I read that one."

Her eyes were shut and she kept her lips dramatically puckered until they slid into a grin. She opened one eye to look at him. "Still the charmer, aren't you, Mr. Rydell?"

"Indeed I am, Ms. Poletti."

She sighed happily. "I'm glad my brother was good for something. If I hadn't followed him here, none of this would have happened."

"Yeah. I guess I owe the fucking Polettis a debt of gratitude."

They shared a smile, needing no conversation.

He touched her cheek. "It'll be okay."

She closed her eyes. Fresh tears forming. "Back to that again, huh? The comet talk?"

"Erin, we lived and loved better than most."

"Why doesn't it seem like enough? I want more still. So much more."

"Today. Now. We have that."

She lifted her hand to the back of his neck and tugged his head down. She whispered, "Never leave me."

"I won't leave you willingly."

"No. *Never* leave me."

He smiled and stared into her eyes. "Okay, I'll never leave you."

They both knew it was a lie. Jack had to leave her. He would die first. The likelihood of that was high. His health was deteriorating. He wasn't as strong as he was before the cancer. If it returned? Well, it might just turn out to be the final round.

But even then, Jack promised to be with Erin. Forever. He wasn't given to fanciful thoughts or waxing poetic but he had faith.

"Jack…?" Erin whispered after several moments.

"Yeah?"

"Screw our brittle hips and backs and necks."

He laughed as she flipped over and started to crawl up his torso. Falling back on the lumpy towel they spread over the sand, Jack momentarily feared they might have to call

Ben or Jade to help them get up off the sand. But who cared?

Her lips touched his and they made love to each other as they had for more than forty years. Doing it outside on the beach was no less of a thrill than it was forty years ago either.

Right there on the river's edge, in front of God and the mountains.

The moment was precious. They were still together. Life hadn't beaten them yet.

∼

~Jade~

~Six months later~

Jade glanced up when her husband entered their bedroom. It still thrilled her to call Cole "her husband." She never imagined she'd find domestic life so satisfying or that she'd be so fully content. But with Cole? Everything felt new and exciting, even mundane things like running an errand to the hardware store on a Saturday morning. Jade felt happier than anyone had the right to be.

But this particular morning, Cole's usual pleasant grin was absent. His mouth was set in a frown and his eyes reminded her of times past whenever Chance's name was brought up. Fear gripped her. *Penny?* No. That trouble was all over now and behind them.

"Cole?"

He didn't answer as he walked over to her. The way he approached her told her it was bad and Jade bolted onto her feet. "What happened?"

"Jack died last night."

Jade felt like someone just punched her in the gut... He had to be wrong. Jade couldn't breathe, like he knocked the wind out of her. She crumpled into a heap and began gulping air as she burst into tears. Cole caught her and brought her close to him. He didn't try to shush her but let her cry, and with great sobs and gallons of tears, the pain of Cole's words ripped Jade in half.

Cole's head turned and he lay it on top of hers. She heard him sniffle and knew he was crying too.

"What happened?" Penny asked. Oh, no, the terrible news would crush the budding twenty-year-old. She was doing so well now, successful in school, well-adjusted, and light years away from the mixed-up, anxiety-driven twelve-year-old girl who couldn't read when she first came there.

Jade sucked in a breath and released Cole, turning to Penny as she tried to restrain her grief. Poor Penny. Cole was her only family until she came there. Now she'd lost her dear Uncle Jack and her life would never be the same.

Jade thought of her grandma. And her dad. And Melanie. Charlie. Lillian. Jade could not comfort all of them in their grief while she was still struggling to bear her own. She wasn't strong enough for that. She could not console anyone when she needed so much consolation.

Cole kept his arm around her as he said to his sister, "Come here, Pen."

He always knew how to handle her. She rushed forward and shared his embrace. "It's Jack, honey." His tone was soft and caring, unlike his usual way of being blunt and direct to her. Jade loved him for doing that. He adapted to her. And to Penny. "Jack died last night. We're all so sorry and we'll all miss him very much."

Nothing could change how much it hurt everyone.

Penny cried. Jade cried. Cole cried. They all kept embracing while their muffled sighs and sobs persisted.

"We need to see Aunt Erin."

"Yes. We will. But Melanie's with her now."

"I'm special to her, she'll need me too." Penny's tone was

so matter of fact. Direct. Confident. Penny was a young woman now. She grew up to become soft and strong, graceful and clever, smart and caring.

Jade wiped her eyes. "Yes. You're right."

Nothing felt right. She needed... what? Was there anything to staunch the all-consuming blackness that she felt inside her?

"What, babe? What do you need?" Cole's words interrupted her frantic thoughts. He seemed to read her mind before she could coherently form her thoughts.

"I wanna go... to the barn."

Cole didn't ask which one, or why, or when. He simply nodded, then he turned and tugged her hand. "I'll drop you on the way. Penny and I are going to your grandparents' house..." Cringing when he heard his own words, he shook his head. "Sorry, it'll take a while before I get used to it. Penny and I will meet you at Erin's."

Erin's house. Singular. Jade instantly hated how it sounded.

Jade wanted to go down to her grandfather's favorite barn. It used to be the only barn on the property. It didn't burn in the fire that consumed the original homestead. Now it sat closest to the new homestead Ben and Jocelyn lived in.

They were quiet on the short ride from their small house. Their undersized lot wasn't far from the ranch, but enough to give them privacy and a small yard of their own. The day they'd moved in as the new owners of the small three-bedroom, thirty-year-old rambler, Cole's chest nearly burst with pride. Penny's too. They'd never lived anywhere so nice, let alone, held the deed to it.

Jade's mind was miles away.

She almost moaned when the spread came into view from the road. A sloping, graceful sweep of land that hugged the river surrounded by towering mountains.

Cole stopped the vehicle in front of the barn. Jade shuddered as she gazed at it.

"They met here."

"What? Who did, honey?" Cole's tone was extra kind and soft. She didn't usually respond when people used that tone on her. She disliked sentimentalism. She thought it was sappy. But today, she appreciated it.

"My grandparents did. Jack was right there at the entry to the barn and she stopped her car right about here. He came out to see who it was. And it was Grandma." A small smile brightened her tear-streaked face. "Then the story takes a not-so-traditionally-romantic-turn, but it's their story. So it all matters."

Cole smiled. He knew the story well. She bit her lip. "I should have told him, about our surprise."

Cole followed her disjointed thoughts and conversations. He didn't ask what, he simply nodded. "I told him."

Startled, she glanced at him and said, "When? How?"

"A few days ago. Aunt Erin told me things were not going to last long. I figured you'd want him to know. He was pleased. I think it gave him one last thing in life to smile about. He wasn't going to tell Erin. Gonna let her be surprised. Save it for later. For now. For this."

She shut her eyes as Cole's words registered. Suddenly, she crossed over the console and grabbed his face and kissed him. Penny smiled in the back. When Jade released him, she said simply, "Thank you."

"He also…"

"What? Tell me anything."

The ghost of a smile slipped over his face. "He also mentioned something about having another fucking Poletti on his land…"

Only Jack Rydell's dry sense of humor could make her smile today. "He always liked to rub that in to me."

"I'm glad there are so many damn Polettis on his land now," Cole said softly.

Then he asked, "What about telling the rest of them?"

"Today? It's not the time."

"Jack would and did disagree with that. It's symbiotic. Life and death. Beginning and end. It's about love. Only love, Jade."

She cried at his words and the way he held her face in his hands. He leaned over and kissed the side of her head when she cuddled against him. "Why don't you just come with us?"

"I need… no. I will. I just need a few moments. Here. By myself." *With him.* But she couldn't say that.

"Okay. Text or call if you need anything from me."

"I need you and I'll continue to."

He grinned. "Ditto that, baby." Then he gave her a quick kiss.

Jade exited the vehicle. Watching it leave, she turned towards the barn.

Walking on trembling legs, her tears streamed. Why did it seem so empty and so different now?

She stopped dead and let the tears just fall while loud sobs came from her mouth without a censor. The land seemed barren. Gone of its soul. Devoid of all energy.

No more life force from Jack Rydell.

He literally seemed to change the land when he was standing on it.

She shut her aching eyes. The sun rose like every other morning of her life. It was soft and golden, and the horses neighed, stomped their hooves and huffed. The air was cold. This was the backdrop of her entire life, she thought.

Especially today.

She entered the barn, stopping dead when she heard a boot scuffling.

Her dad.

Ben Rydell turned when he heard her come in. Tears stained his face. He didn't even try to hide them or stop crying.

"For one second… I thought he was walking in. Just like usual."

"How do we…do this? How do we handle this?"

"I don't know."

They stood separated by a few footsteps, both crying. Finally, Jade wiped her tears and said, "I had to come down here. I don't… know why."

"I did too. I don't know why either."

"Were you there?"

"No. Erin was the only one. We… Charlie, Mel and I saw him yesterday… Erin called us and said she sensed something. Even though Dad was having an unusually good day. She said sometimes that happens right before…"

"Why didn't you call me?"

"I didn't actually think he'd die, honey. And if I called you, I'd have to call everyone else. He meant so much to so many. Where do you stop? But I called Cole first thing today."

"I know. He was good with me."

"He always is."

Silence fell and the morning sunlight highlighted the dust particles in the air. The horses shifted and called to each other as usual. Everything was normal. Almost. She shut her eyes, savoring the familiar sounds and how content they made her feel inside. "It seems like he's still here."

"I know."

She shuddered and trembled as another loud sob escaped her throat.

"This is the worst day of my life, Jade."

"I know that, Dad," she whispered. She rarely witnessed her dad in tears or being vulnerable or in need. But he was now. He looked ready to collapse. He choked on his own tears. She rushed forward and hugged him. He held her against him tightly.

"He wouldn't want it to be the worst day of my life. He'd want us to take care of his horses and retell a story of when he acted like a jerk or a hero," Ben said softly.

"He would. But he'd also let us grieve." Her head shook. "We can never find the words to adequately describe what Jack Rydell meant to us. And the land? No epitaph can capture all of the things he did and was to so many people. How, Dad? How do we find the words?"

He sighed, leaning against her. "We can't. That's how it was with Dad. He was the last of a rare breed. Maybe that's what marks his life more than anything else."

"It feels like it all ends with him, the breed goes extinct," Jade sadly concluded.

"Today it does. It feels that way today. Yes. Like the heartbeat of the land under our feet has stopped."

"I literally thought that same idea when I was standing outside the barn."

"The thing to remember is this: Jack Rydell started everything. He was the first keeper of this ranch, and the creator of all we have now. He left us this legacy so there could be no end to it."

Jack's legacy. Jack's voice. Jack's footprint. Jade's mind swirled with the magnitude of his endowments. She said, "He's a legend even now."

"Yes," Ben agreed simply.

They hugged each other for more long minutes. Warm and tight, their arms unwilling to let go.

"Dad? I'm... I'm pregnant. Maybe now isn't the best time to say it but Cole thought maybe..."

Ben leaned back and took Jade's arms in his. He blinked before more tears seemed to form in his eyelids. "Cole was right. That's wonderful news."

"Today? Nothing seems wonderful. Like it can't be ever again."

"Time heals all. I hate platitudes, but they're true. It will heal. Did Dad know?"

"Cole told him a few days ago. I didn't know he told him though—"

"What did Dad say?" Ben asked, eager to hear his own father's reply. She almost collapsed realizing that Ben would cling to his father's last words forever. For his dad would say no more.

"He said it's wonderful news. That we should share it *this* day. Life and death. Something new starts when something old ends. But… I don't know."

Ben sniffled. "Yes, that's absolutely true. Did he also say…"

"What?" Jade asked, crying softly again.

"Another fucking Poletti on my land?"

She couldn't believe hearing that from her dad's mouth while they stood embracing.

"*Dad*," she groaned, smiling.

"You know the story. Right?"

She sighed. "Yes. Grandma told me a few years ago when she was talking about Chance Poletti. Chance Poletti poisoned his opinion of her so when she showed up as Chance's sister, Jack's only comment was: *What? Another fucking Poletti on my land?*"

"You realize what's happening now, don't you?"

She couldn't see his point. "What?"

"It's going full circle now."

"What is?"

"You having a Rydell baby with a Poletti, Erin's nephew."

Ben took her into his arms once more and she clung to her dad like she used to when she was a little girl.

"Dad?"

"What?"

"If it's a boy, do you think Grandpa would like us to name my baby after him?"

Ben leaned back. His eyebrows rose upwards. "Jack Poletti?" Then he laughed for real. "Damn. I'd love to see the look on Dad's face when you told him that name."

"Dad!" She chided with half anger and half laughing. He was right. Jack Rydell would have roared at hearing his name attached to that last name. "You're right. It really is full circle now."

"It really is."

They stood there hugging and crying until Ben leaned back and said, "Well, should we start?"

Start? Start what? Grieving? Learning how to live without the guidance of the greatest man she ever knew? Jack was a force all his own. How did one start living without that huge presence? Without him?

Ben swept a hand towards the stalls.

Right. The horses. Jack's horses. His biggest concern outside of his family.

The huge lump in Jade's throat from crying made talking hurt. Her eyes throbbed too. But she nodded as she stepped forward, looking for the other horse scoop so she could start mucking the stalls. Doing the same job that Jack Rydell spent a whole lifetime doing. Never too proud to muck the stalls.

Side by side, Jade and Ben, father and daughter, started their daily chores. All the routine jobs that came to define their lifetimes continued as usual on this first morning when Jack Rydell was no longer in the barn.

SEVEN MONTHS, two weeks and five days later, Jade gave birth to a healthy baby boy. The story did indeed come full circle when the baby was christened Jackson Poletti, after his great-grandfather, and with their grandma's maiden name.

So fitting and perfect.

For everyone knew there was and could only be one *Jack Rydell.*

ABOUT THE AUTHOR

Leanne Davis has earned a business degree from Western Washington University. She worked for several years in the construction management field before turning full time to writing. She lives in the Seattle area with her husband and two children. When she isn't writing, she and her family enjoy camping trips to destinations all across Washington State, many of which become the settings for her novels.